PRAISE FOR *DISORIENTAL*

"Djavadi here offers an account of an Iranian family, through revolutions, relationships, and diaspora, and she does so with a voice remarkably open to humor, warmth, and love. The prose is at once chaotic and precise, charismatic and familiar . . . *Disoriental* is a wonder and a pleasure to read."
—Rivka Galchen, author of *Atmospheric Disturbances*

"Phenomenal! Insightful and compelling."
—Stephanie Crowe, Page & Palette

"If the history of Iran had to be contained in a book, set in motion and shaken by its revolutions, it would give you *Disoriental* . . . Astonishing, disorderly, extraordinary, and enjoyable."—*Le Devoir*

"*Disoriental* is a rich, irreverent, kaleidoscopic novel of real originality and power. I've never read anything quite like it."
—Alexander Maksik, author of *You Deserve Nothing*

"Woven into the gripping depictions of political unrest, family crises, national upheaval, and personal secrets is an excellent primer on the history of modern Iran."—*Kirkus Reviews*

"Already the recipient of multiple prizes in France, this enchanting novel, well translated and with surprises and delights on every page, perfectly blends historical fact with contemporary themes."—*Library Journal*

"Kimiâ unthreads the narratives of her family history, and the shaping of her own identity, with the insight and verve of a master storyteller."—*Booklist* (Starred Review)

DISORIENTAL

Négar Djavadi

DISORIENTAL

*Translated from the French
by Tina Kover*

Europa
editions

Europa Editions
214 West 29th Street
New York, N.Y. 10001
www.europaeditions.com
info@europaeditions.com

Copyright © Éditions Liana Levi, 2016
First Publication 2018 by Europa Editions

Translation by Tina Kover
Original title: *Désorientale*
Translation copyright © 2018 by Europa Editions

Library of Congress Cataloging in Publication Data is available
ISBN 978-1-60945-451-7

Djavadi, Négar
Disoriental

Book design and cover illustration by Emanuele Ragnisco
www.mekkanografici.com

Prepress by Grafica Punto Print – Rome

Printed in the USA

One day there'll be a place for us
A place called home
—PJ HARVEY

DISORIENTAL

An index of the main characters can be found at the end of the book.

THE ESCALATOR

In Paris, my father, Darius Sadr, never took the escalator. The first time I went down into a metro station with him, on April 21, 1981, I asked him why. His answer was, "Escalators are for them." By "them," he meant you, obviously. You, the ones who were going to work on that Tuesday morning in April. You, the citizens of this country, with your income taxes and compulsory deductions and council taxes—but also your education, your intransigence, your critical minds and your spirit of solidarity and pride and culture and patriotism, your devotion to the Republic and democracy, you who toiled for centuries to achieve these mechanical staircases installed meters underground.

At the age of ten I wasn't conscious of all these ideas, but that helpless look on my father's face—acquired during the months he'd spent alone in this city, and which I had never seen on him before—shook me so much that even today, every time I see an escalator, I think of him. I hear the thumps of his feet on the hard treads of the staircase. I see his body hunched slightly forward from the effort, obstinate and resolute, unshakeable in his refusal to take advantage of the momentary comfort of a mechanical ascent. According to Darius Sadr's logic, that kind of luxury was a sort of abuse, if not outright theft. His destiny was henceforth joined to the staircases of the world, to the passage of time without surprises, and the indifferent gazes of passers-by.

To really understand the complexity of that thought, you've

got to go inside my father's head—my father as he was at that time, I mean. Stormy. Disillusioned. You have to understand the tortuous, magnificently absurd reasoning at work here. To see, beneath the layer of suffering, made more severe by failure, the threads of delicacy and elegance, of respect and admiration. To appreciate the firmness of his decision (not to take an escalator, ever), and the skill with which he summed up in just a few words—he, who had spent most of his life bent over a ream of writing paper—everything that he had become, and everything you represented.

But you know as well as I do that, to claim to get inside a man's head, first you have to really know him—to absorb all of the lives he has lived, and all of his struggles, and all of his ghosts. And believe me, if I start there—if I play the "dad" card already—I'll never get around to telling you what I'm about to tell you.

Let's think some more about the impact of that sentence: "Escalators are for them." That was part of what made me decide to tell this story, even without knowing where to begin. All I know is that these pages won't be linear. Talking about the present means I have to go deep into the past, to cross borders and scale mountains and go back to that lake so enormous they call it a sea. I have to let myself be guided by the flow of images and free associations, the natural fits and starts, the hollows and bumps carved into my memories by time. But the truth of memory is strange, isn't it? Our memories select, eliminate, exaggerate, minimize, glorify, denigrate. They create their own versions of events and serve up their own reality. Disparate, but cohesive. Imperfect yet sincere. In any case, my memory is so crammed with stories and lies and languages and illusions, and lives marked by exile and death, death and exile, that I don't even really know how to untangle the threads anymore.

Some of you might already be aware of me—you might

remember the bloody incident that happened in Paris, in the 13th arrondissement, on March 11, 1994. It was the lead story on the eight o'clock news on France 2. All the next day's newspapers were full of it—of articles stuffed with falsehoods and plastered with pictures of us, with black rectangles blocking out our eyes. You might have seen me in one of those pictures. Maybe you followed the case.

I mean, I could have led with that, you know. Instead of talking about escalators, I could have opened with the story of what we call THE EVENT in our family. But I can't. Not yet. For now, all you need to know is that it's January 19 at ten past ten in the morning, and I'm waiting.

SIDE A

1
THE MAZANDARAN WIND

The wing of Cochin Hospital dedicated to medically-assisted procreation has been a construction site for several months. From what I understand, the building's going to be torn down, and the department moved into the main building on Boulevard Port-Royal. This second-floor waiting room has been reduced to the bare bones. No posters or pamphlets on the walls; just twenty or so gray chairs lined up in three rows, dimly lit by the dull winter light filtering through the scaffolding outside. When I came in this morning, there was one chair placed well apart from the others, against the wall. I've been sitting on it for almost forty-five minutes now, waiting.

We had our first consultation with Doctor Françoise Gautier eleven months ago. On the warm and pleasant spring day of the appointment I'd painted my toenails red, in the slightly naïve hope of matching the image I wanted to give of Pierre and me. I'd decided to wear high-heeled sandals and, despite the army of clouds that invaded the sky while I was getting dressed, wasn't about to change my mind. While looking through our file, sent over by Professor Stein, Dr. Gautier had asked us: "So, are you going to get married?" Her tone was neutral, but the question still came as a shock; I really hadn't thought that, after Professor Stein, Dr. Gautier would care about our marital situation, too. Weren't we there to finally start the procedure? Shouldn't the questions be about medical things now—childhood diseases, heredity, operations we'd had? Were we never going to be done with this marriage business?

"Yes, of course—in a few months," I'd said, in a voice so phony that every time I think about it I want to run far away and die.

The couple sitting across from me was already here when I arrived, as was another one at the far end of the room. Three more couples have arrived since then, each one being careful to leave a few empty seats between themselves and their neighbors. Nobody speaks. The atmosphere is permeated by a silence heavy with resignation and the noises filtering in from the hallway outside. All the faces have a tense look, a mixture of anxiety and vulnerability, that makes them look like kids lost in a supermarket.

Do I look like that too?

I don't think I do, because I don't feel anything, except maybe growing impatience.

The women across from me, whose bodies—like mine—have been turned into a battlefield, have undoubtedly already started storing up a whole range of emotions to talk about later. Long conversations filled with explanations, indignation, stifled tears and liberating laughter. "Do you realize" and "if you knew" and "no, but really," until everything comes out and dissipates into the air and is forgotten. From time to time, when she comes back from her academic travels, Mina acts like that with me (and with Leïli too, of course). She calls me, and pretty soon the details come out, and the stuff between the parentheses, and she laughs incomprehensibly, and coos, and repeats the same story in different tones. She doesn't find it unusual that I listen, hanging on the telephone for hours, because I'm her sister. Leïli listens to her too, but she doesn't have that ball of annoyance lodged in her throat, getting bigger with every sentence. Because Leïli understands her. They share that easy ability to "spill their guts," as our mother, Sara, used to say.

Sometimes I wonder if it's really possible to be this emotionless. Even though it happens to me less than it used to now, the sensation is always there, just within arm's reach. When I was a teenager, I felt like the place inside me where emotions were supposed to be had dried up at some point without me noticing. The world seemed to me then—it still does now—to be behind glass, intangible and distant, like a silent spectacle in which I was incapable of taking part. Even then, I'd already made the connection between that feeling and the images of American GIs back from Vietnam that I'd seen in the movies and on TV. I knew in my bones how they felt, sitting on the family couch, staring at nothing, while people fussed and flapped around them. Their absence, their inability to join in the action, to build a future. Like me, they seemed submerged in silence, like drowning victims floating to the surface.

It won't have escaped anyone's notice that I'm alone.

No hand to hold. No familiar body pressed against mine, brought closer by hardship. Just this long cardboard tube labeled with our first and last names—mine and Pierre's—sitting on my knees. A long tube filled with Pierre's defrosted, washed sperm (that's how Dr. Gautier described it to me).

I can never imagine how, by what process, sperm could be washed. Every time I try, I get a picture in my head of a big sieve, like the one my maternal grandmother Emma used whenishe baked cakes. I could have looked it up on the Internet, but to tell the truth I'm just not curious enough to do that kind of research.

From the minute I set foot in this room, I've sensed that my solitude interested the other couples. A woman coming here alone couldn't be divorced or separated, or they would stop the procedure. So, the fact that she's alone has to mean one of three things (in increasing order of domestic catastrophe):

1) An argument this morning, before leaving to come here;
2) Lack of interest on the part of the husband, who couldn't even be bothered to take the day off or postpone a meeting or business trip;
3) The rarest case: the husband is dead. In which case special authorization from a judge would be required to conceive a child post-mortem.

In any case, a woman alone in the fertility clinic of any hospital whatsoever on the entire planet is a creature to be pitied, even though her solitude makes the bad luck of the other people whom life has brought to this room seem easier to bear. *Thank God, there's someone even worse off than us!* Because this place is the exclusive territory of The Couple. The no man's land where its future, its *raison d'être*, and its ultimate purpose are at stake. The purgatory where the God of Fertility, awoken by follitropin beta injections, decides whether or not he will alter The Couple's destiny. My case doesn't correspond to any of the three possibilities. It's much more complex, more deceitful than that. It's a matter of strategy and manipulation. A plan conceived by gangsters. You have no idea yet, reader, of the risk I'm taking by writing this. Just know that of the thirteen couples I'm looking at right now, the ones feeling sorry for the woman sitting by herself, some would slam me up against the wall if they knew. They'd spit in my face. They'd throw me out in the street. None of them would take the trouble to understand or ask questions, or stop to consider that I, too, am the result of an incongruous combination of circumstances, and fate, and heritage, and bad luck, and tragedies.

That's the reason I'm writing this.

My father, Darius Sadr, the Master of the blank page, the Audacious, the Revolutionary, used to say, in his pensive and visionary voice: "The eyes are better listeners than the ears. Ears are deep wells, made for chatter. If you have something to say, write it." But there have been moments in my life, more or less important sequences of events, when I would have done anything to be something other than what I am. I've changed countries and languages; I've invented other pasts and other identities for myself. I've fought—oh yes, I've fought—against that impetuous wind that rose a long time ago, in a far-flung Persian province called Mazandaran,[1] laden with deaths and births, recessive and dominant genes, coups d'état and revolutions, and every time I have tried to escape it, it has grasped me by the scruff of the neck and pulled me back in. For you to understand what I'm telling you, I have to rewind and start again from the beginning; I have to make you hear—like I can hear it myself, right now, as a nurse glances at me indifferently and moves away again—the voice of my uncle Saddeq Sadr, nicknamed Uncle Number Two. It's a voice in a minor key, smooth as a clarinet, telling what we used to refer to amongst ourselves as *Uncle Number Two's Famous Story*.

"Since early that afternoon, the wind had been blowing so hard that it might just as well have been announcing the end of the world. There hadn't been such a tempest in Mazandarani memory since the invasion of the Mongols! And even back then, what the Mazandaran-dwellers had taken for a storm was actually the devastating blast of air preceding Genghis Khan's

[1] To make things easier for you and save you the trouble of looking it up on Wikipedia, here are a few facts: Mazandaran is a province in northern Iran, 9,151 square miles in area. Bounded by the Caspian Sea and surrounded by the Alborz mountain range, it is the only Persian region to have resisted Arab-Muslim hegemony and was, in fact, the last to become Muslim. To imagine it, you have to picture the lush landscapes of Annecy, Switzerland, or Ireland—green, misty, rainy. Legend has it that when they first arrived in Mazandaran, the Muslims cried, "Oh! We have reached Paradise!"

bloody horde. At any rate, this biting wind blowing in from the frozen plains of Russia could portend nothing good.

"Now, picture the marvelous estate that belonged to your great-grandfather, Montazemolmolk. Two imposing buildings, each with sixty rooms, outbuildings, armories, kitchens, reception rooms, horse-filled stables . . . all nestled deep in the very heart of the forest, at the foot of the Alborz mountains. No fewer than two hundred and sixty-eight souls lived there, all under the care of Montazemolmolk. On that February day in 1896—a Saturday, I believe it was—he had given the order to draught proof the doors and windows and to stay inside until the world calmed down a bit. How long would that cursed storm last? What state would his lands be in when it was over? For hours, these questions and many others nagged at Montazemolmolk, whose mood was as dark as the sky. He lived in the main building, the *birouni*, with one hundred twenty-three armed men whose job it was to protect his lands, and a dozen young male servants.

"Though it was only across the inner courtyard from the *birouni*, the other building, the *andarouni*, seemed as remote and impenetrable as the Promised Land itself. This was where Montazemolmolk's fifty-two wives lived, women who had come from all four corners of the country, with his twenty-eight children, and twenty or so female servants. He was the only man who had the right to enter that building, the only one who knew the heavy scent of perfumes and the quarrels that hung stagnant in the icy air. The shadowy labyrinthine corridors, half-open doors, the rustle of silks, the heady sense of being longed for, desired, the languor of bodies that . . . ahem, well, you know very well what I mean!

"Yet all those nights spent in that place which he had, as it were, peopled himself, hadn't relieved your great-grandfather of the bitter sense that his world was slipping away from him. The *andarouni* remained a mysterious and crazy place, an enigma. On that day, when the land of Mazandaran seemed to have been reduced to nothing but a pebble in God's hand, Montazemolmolk feared, above all, that the women were taking advantage of the darkness and chaos to plot against him. After all, how can you know what's brewing in the heart of a neglected woman? How can you be sure of her loyalty, her sincerity, her love? As time passed and the number of his wives increased, he would feel the sharp blade of jealousy twisting deeper and deeper in his gut each time he set foot on the first step of the spiral staircase leading to their quarters.

"It's not as if this humiliating tragedy, undoubtedly incited by Targol Khanoum, hadn't taken place! Targol Khanoum, who had once been his favorite wife, was the source of an outbreak of itching that had spread among the women's private parts and eventually found its treacherous way to Montazemolmolk's groin. Doctors had come out from the city and a lot of doors had been slammed; objects had been hurled into the courtyard and bunches of hair had been torn out; cries had echoed through the mountains. Dishonor had invaded the estate. At that moment, Montazemolmolk would have *liked* for that evil wind to blow—blow those cursed women off the face of the earth and take all this misery with them. Well, but that's another story. Anyway, after hours spent fiddling with his beard, which was as full and blond as a handful of tobacco, and pacing the room with its six doors that served as his private study, your great-grandfather made the surprising decision to turn the *andarouni*'s emergency key over to one of his youngest servant-boys. The ugliest one. The clumsiest. The one no woman would want to cuddle up to, even as a challenge. So then, Montazemolmolk . . . "

Pause. I can never remember how Montazemolmolk summoned the servant boy. Did he yell his name? Did he open one of those six doors and ask him to come in? Did he send someone to look for him? Sitting in my chair against the wall in Cochin Hospital, I ransack my memory in the hope of finding the forgotten fragments. No use.

I often try to remember that part of the story. Like when I'm at work, standing behind the mixing deck, smoothing out the rough sound of some unlikely rock group. Or at home, lying on the couch, Tindersticks playing in the background. Like a grade-schooler stumbling over a poem he's memorized, I keep starting over, telling myself the whole thing from the beginning, hoping the words will flow out automatically. But I always stop short at the edge of the same black hole.

I could call Leïli or Mina, but I don't. I know, thanks to the sharp intuition that comes from long years growing up beside them, that neither of them remembers the details of the story. My sisters remember other times that I've completely forgotten. Summer nights sleeping on the roof of Grandma Emma's house under a patched-up muslin mosquito net; the books Sara bought us before long vacations; trips to the hammam with my aunts and cousins in the villages of Mazandaran. On the rare occasions when the three of us are all together, without their husbands or children, having dinner in a restaurant chosen by Mina (who has been a vegetarian since THE EVENT), they always end up talking about those times. It's usually toward the end of the meal, when the wine's begun to take effect, softening the edges of our differences and easing the weight of the present. Then they warm up, and laugh, and cut off each other's sentences, and repeat the same sentences as if no others could possibly be used to describe those moments. Sometimes I wonder if the actual purpose of these get-togethers is to get to that point. To those neglected memories at the end of a path that's become otherwise inaccessible. To the little girls that we were back then, lost now in the meanderings of our fragmentary and fiction-generating memories. The adults that we have become need those dinners to access the children we were, to believe they ever really existed.

Well, back to the waiting room. Despite my annoyance, I decide to skip over the missing fragment. I have to face facts; that part of the story has been worn away by time. It's not important, I tell myself, as long as the rest stays intact.

Play: So the ugly, clumsy young servant is there with Montazemolmolk . . .

" . . . who said to him, in his harsh and commanding voice, 'Go and see if they are obeying my orders, and report back to me. Be discreet, do you hear?' But the words were barely out of his mouth before he regretted them. No stranger, even a prepubescent one, would be able to enter that hive discreetly! Montazemolmolk averted his eyes from the boy's face, which was red with shame and excitement, and shooed him out. He was angry with himself for speaking such nonsense, revealing his fears, even though this virginal boy, stupefied at having the key to paradise in the palm of his hand, surely hadn't guessed anything. And yet after the youth left, he was even more nervous than he had been. Half an hour went by; the wind intensified, and the boy didn't come back. Impatience turned into fury, and that fury spread like wildfire through Montazemolmolk's huge body. He seized his coat and his astrakhan hat, deciding to go and see for himself what was happening on the other side of the courtyard. Because now he was certain of it—another scandal was brewing in the halls of the *andarouni*.

"No one who crossed paths with your great-grandfather in the vast, humid corridors of the *birouni* dared to stop him. He was the master of the place, the Khan,[2] with a six-syllable name

---

[2] Title commonly given to one who holds political or feudal power. It may be preceded by "Agha," which means "Sir." The "kh" should be pronounced in the back of the throat, like the Spanish "jota."

that proclaimed his rank and half of Mazandaran as his heritage. But more than all that, he was extremely stubborn. Everyone knew that to try to make him deviate from his chosen path was pure suicide. It was said that even the animals understood that once Montazemolmolk hitched them up, there would be no escaping him. This character trait was often commented on and lamented, in both the *andarouni* and the *birouni*. Everyone was afraid that his obstinacy would lead one day to his death. And if he died, who would take care of them? The truth is that, in those days, when Nasseredin Shah-e-Qâdjar was king, feudalism was still alive and well in the North. The great families, bound by multiple alliances, governed the land and the people. And in return for their labor and loyalty, the lords protected them, took care of them, and arranged marriages for their children. But that's another story . . .

"Your great-grandfather pushed with all his strength against the heavy iron door. But soon the wind got the better of him, and shook him like a father shakes his arrogant son. The door was ripped out of his hands. His astrakhan hat flew off. His coat caught on the branches and tore. But Montazemolmolk didn't give up. He fought with rage that equaled that of the storm, his wild hair blowing into his eyes. Inch by inch, he arrived, exhausted but valiant, at the door of the *andarouni*.

"When he finally managed to get inside the building, he was struck by the silence. It's true that when he went there, it was always quiet. But that was the familiar and delicious stillness of unknown promises, of women with kohl-rimmed eyes and pink lips holding their breath in the hope of being chosen. He was the subject of that silence, the creator of it. The quiet that surrounded him now was dense, and as disturbing as the silence of the tunnels dug beneath the mountains. He took the spiral staircase two steps at a time. Worried, he was proceeding toward the second floor—where the servants and the children lived—when a voice stopped him in his tracks: "And just where do you think you're going?" Relieved to hear the voice of Amira, he turned around and opened the door of her chamber.

"Lounging on multi-colored woolen cushions and enveloped in a turban of smoke, Amira gazed at him through half-closed eyes. Her sarcastic smile was heavy with a whole life lived in this place, with more than half those years—since Montazemolmolk's abandonment of her—spent in this room, drinking tea, eating dates, and smoking opium. Amira had passed so many nights waiting up for your great-grandfather that she could have picked out the sound of his footsteps from among a thousand other people's. Even though Montazemolmolk had discarded her in favor of other, younger women, he respected her more than any other—because she was his first wife, and the mother of his oldest son (and three daughters, all as ugly as boiled heads of cauliflower). For her part, Amira, who was as tall and strong as a fortress, no longer respected him in the least. She didn't call him Khan anymore, but rather 'Sir,' and used the informal 'tu' when she spoke to him.

"'If Sir wants to know what's happening,' she said, 'he should go into the sitting room behind the kitchen. Go on, you scoundrel, before I gobble you up raw!' And Amira's crazy, rasping laugh followed Montazemolmolk's hurried steps as he fled from her once again.

"Montazemolmolk pushed open the door of the sitting room and stopped. They were all there! Normally, so many women together chatter as if they were in a hammam, but tonight, none of them was making a sound. Some of them were gathered around the young servant boy, who had fainted while peeping through the keyhole. He had seen things that no man ever saw—a young, half-naked girl, her legs spread, racked with pain, emptying her insides into a basin. Now, the women drew back to let Montazemolmolk pass. The blood had been cleaned up and the basin was gone. The girl's legs were no longer spread. She was dead.

"Your great-grandmother couldn't have been more than fifteen years old. I can't describe her face to you, because from the moment she was wrapped in the shroud, no one ever spoke of her again. Where did she come from? Who was she? What was her first name? Neither you nor I will ever know. Frozen with shock, Montazemolmolk stared at the inert body, vaguely remembering that he had once spent a few minutes grasping her to him behind a shrub. Suddenly, a tiny bundle swaddled in a white cloth was shoved into his arms. 'It's a girl, Agha Khan!' were the first words that banished the silence and death. For the first time in his life, Montazemolmolk held a newborn in his arms.

"In order to avoid disappointing or disgusting him, his twenty-eight other children had been solemnly presented to him a full week after birth, their faces smooth and their cheeks rubbed with orange-flower water. Their mothers had all given them first names (which Montazemolmolk promptly forgot) by that point. It must be admitted here that, driven by competitiveness and the desire to enchant their husband, as time went by the mothers invented more and more complex names, which they often ended up forgetting themselves.

"Staring at the wrinkled face of the baby, he was horrified by its drab color. But suddenly, the bundle was wrenched from his arms and another put in its place. 'The second! The second one!' Knowing nothing about matters of reproduction, Montazemolmolk couldn't figure out at first what kind of game they were playing. Startled, he turned to the old midwife, whose face was tanned like leather. 'Twins, Agha Khan! Other than Almighty God, no one knew that the poor girl had two buns in the oven. One life for two: that is how He desired it to be.' Suppressing his shock, Montazemolmolk nodded his head in acknowledgment of the aptness of the thought. Even though, since he had spent some time in Russia—and for reasons taken to the grave—he seriously doubted the existence of God, he continued to let everyone else believe in his faith; it was easier that way.

"In any event, Montazemolmolk looked down at his thirtieth child: your grandmother. Unlike her twin, who was as dark as a prune, she had white skin, and the fluff on her head was blond. But above all—Montazemolmolk bent over her face, looking closer just to be sure—she had his blue eyes. The astonishing blue of the Caspian Sea, not a hint of which had yet surfaced in any of his other children. At forty-eight years old, Montazemolmolk finally held in his arms the child he had secretly dreamed of, the one whose eyes would forever be a reminder of his own.

"A feeling greater than posterity flooded through him; an unexpected joy to which the women, eaten up with bitterness, were witness. This emotion didn't simply soften his features and bring a proud smile to his lips; it welled up into his throat and became a syllable, which became words, and those words burst out into the air like a slap. 'She will be called Nour,' exclaimed Montazemolmolk, his eyes never leaving the baby's face. *Nour. Light.* Ill at ease, the old midwife tried to ease the disastrous impact of this announcement on the other wives. 'And what will you call the other one, Agha Khan?' she asked, hoping he would get the message. 'Call her whatever you like.' A terse response that forever ruined . . . "

At this point in the story, Uncle Number Two would pause. The tears that would flow later, after numerous digressions and dramatic tangents, were already choking him. He'd jump up and open one of the packs of cigarettes that sat on every table in his house, take a cigarette out, light it, and draw on it deeply, puffing out his cheeks. Then, after a few restless paces, he'd sit down again, sighing heavily and looking at us with sadness and compassion, as if he were getting ready to tell us some awful news that would turn our lives upside-down:

" . . . forever ruined Mother's childhood."

Mother.

That was what her sons called Nour, emphasis on the "M" to draw out the name, to stretch it, to bestow on our paternal grandmother the status of an icon.

Uncle Number Two's tears would really start flowing when Mother reached her fifth year. At that point, all the mistreatment meted out by the stepmothers, their hearts poisoned by jealousy and resentment, would flow out of his mouth in one long, heartbroken wail. Having to go to the well for water; having to wait on the women at table alongside the servants; being forced to sleep outside; not being given warm clothes in winter, going without food; being shut up for whole days in the latrines and in the cellar; dragging carpets outside by herself and beating the dust out of them; being sent into the forest alone to look for roots to macerate . . . it was a long list. He cried and talked, talked and cried. And finally, made effusive by grief and love, he gathered us into his arms so that we could console each other mutually, while outside, curfew fell in Tehran.

On the other side of Uncle Number Two's living room window, the Revolution was in full swing. Soon, taking advantage of the power blackout and the cover of night, the Tehranis, like a united army of angry ghosts, wove their way up the staircases to the roofs and shouted out forbidden slogans. North to south, east to west, cries of "Death to the Shah!" and "Allah Akbar!," insolent, despairing vespers thrown in the world's face, rang out and echoed. It took a few minutes, maybe a quarter of an hour at most, for the sound of machine guns to follow, and repression to take hold of the city again.

And at those times, while I dreamed of escaping that room to join the night and the rooftops, of adding my voice to that revolutionary and melancholic chant, Saddeq clutched us against the beige sweater he'd bought at Galeries Lafayette (pronounced *Gahloree Lahfahyehd*) in Paris (*Pahrees*) and wept over a grandmother I'd never even known. I was seven years old, and only the blind, unquestioning respect all Eastern children feel for adults kept me from shoving him away and making a run for it.

2

UNCLE NUMBER TWO IS DEAD

Yesterday afternoon I was standing on my front doorstep, about to leave for work, when Leïli called me.

"Uncle Saddeq," she began, in the same flat tone she'd used to announce the deaths of all our uncles, and our dad. I should have known something was up, for her to call me so late. Leïli only calls me really early in the morning, when she's rushing to be somewhere, stressed out and breathless, always apologizing right away for waking me up. Some kind of mental block keeps her from acknowledging that I only get a few hours of sleep a night, and even then, it's with one eye open. She does mention my insomnia when we're around other people—usually as a lead-in to talking about her own desperate need for sleep, which has been stymied for years by her family life and her job. But when she's alone with me, denial sets in. *More* denial, I mean.

"He died this morning. Around eleven o'clock."

At that very moment, I noticed a cockroach running along the baseboards in our foyer, weaving in and out of a crack. My attention was drawn to that gleaming black spot heading toward the bathroom. The apartment's been infested with them for several weeks now; it's the restaurant on the ground floor. Despite the hours I've spent cleaning, spraying every nook and cranny with ever-more toxic products, it seems impossible to "stop the invasion".

As Leïli talked, I managed to step on the roach. I'd pressed down so hard with my foot to keep myself from thinking about

Uncle Number Two that I actually thought I could hear the squishing sound of its guts bursting on the parquet floor. "Are you listening to me?" Leïli had demanded, annoyed. "Yes," I'd lied, wiping up the remains of the roach with an old handkerchief I'd found stuffed in my pocket. I'd wanted nothing more than to hang up. But I could hear that Leïli was crying. That was Leïli, I'd thought at the time. Swimming in her white coat, undoubtedly standing at one of the tall windows in her ophthalmology practice in the 4th arrondissement, her collarbones jutting out, the tip of her nose ice-cold; demanding, as always, to be consoled. Leïli, my older sister, delicate and fragile as old lace. I'd searched my mind for something to say, trying without much hope to comfort her, but before I could find the magical phrase that would have reminded us of Uncle Number Two and allowed us to smile, I blurted out: "Are you going to tell Mom?"

Since she got sick, I've started calling her Mom. I don't know how it happened, or the exact moment I stopped using her first name. I don't know if my sisters have noticed, if they've talked to each other about it. If so, they've never said anything to me. They still call her Sara.

"I don't know. I don't know if Sara—" Leïli stopped. Like a tune you recognize immediately from just the first few notes, I knew that dry silence that came just before the weeping. That silence that sums up, all in itself, everything that Sara was, and everything she no longer is. And then Leïli sobbed.

Sara was tall (five foot eight) and thin (126 pounds)—a *SophiaLoreni* build, as they say in Tehran. Her hair and eyes were black. Her eyebrows were carefully plucked. Her nose had a slight hump at its base. Her mouth, which had the same shape as that of her mother, Emma Aslanian, would have tipped you off—if you were an ethnomorphologist—that she had Armenian ancestry.

Sara was funny. She knew how to speak *tchalémeïdouni*, the slang of Tehran, and to make us scream with laughter.

Sara was: a mother, a teacher of history and geography, a political activist, president of the homeowners' association, president of the PTA, and editor-in-chief of the newspaper *Djombesh* (Movement), which she'd founded with her husband. Up at five-thirty every day, after having gone to bed between twelve-thirty and one o'clock in the morning.

Sara was: overflowing with love and anxiety for the entire human race. As soon as the sun rose every morning, even before she'd put her feet on the floor, she was thinking of what to cook, buy, and prepare to please her family and friends. When she woke us up (with Mozart) at six forty-five exactly, breakfast was already ready (and sometimes lunch too), the bathrooms cleaned, the plants watered, and the troop of stray cats gathered at the kitchen window, fed. We called her "The General," or "Corporal Sadr." Or sometimes "Associated Press," because of her astonishing memory.

She remembered *everything*. Everything she had ever seen and done, everything anyone ever told her. Her memory was dense and compact, a challenge to time and science, and to people who thought their gossip would be forgotten. She knew every telephone number, every address, every date by heart. Historical dates, with a specialization in events relating to her two heroes, Napoleon Bonaparte and Mohammad Mossadegh.[3]

---

[3] The name of Mohammad Mossadegh (or Dr. Mossadegh, as he is known to Iranians) isn't often ranked alongside those of the great men and women of the 20th century, which only proves the extent to which history has been unfair to him. But in 1951, as the democratically-elected Prime Minister, he pulled off the incredible feat of nationalizing the Iranian oil that had been exploited for decades by the Anglo-Iranian Oil Company. I won't linger over that period yet; suffice it to say that, like spoiled children who have something taken away from them, the British didn't appreciate this show of independence. The power struggle lasted two years and the Americans jumped into the fray, fomenting the famous coup d'état of August 19, 1953 that changed Iran's destiny forever. But we'll come back to that later . . .

Birthdays, including those of her countless nephews and nieces, her colleagues, her friends, our neighbors, their children, and even my dad's brothers, who were hardly aware of the fact that they'd been born in the first place.

And then, suddenly, none of it. Nothing, anymore. Nothingness.

Her brain became like something drowning in the ocean. A cork floating in the immensity of oblivion. It happened a few months after THE EVENT.

For a long time, I was convinced that she needed me, my presence, to heal. That was why I came back to Paris, little by little giving my life a comforting direction, in the absurd hope of making her well. But she didn't need me, any more than she needed the television that stayed on all day in a corner of her room.

Sara was my mother. The other one has become Mom.

I had just hung up, realizing all of a sudden that I was standing out in the street, when I had a vision of Uncle Number Two. He was there in front of me, right in the middle of noisy Belleville. I could see him as clearly as I saw the Chinese prostitutes clustered on the sidewalks.

I'll try to paint that image of my uncle for you, to show him to you, with his faded colors and his surface battered by the vagaries of life, like the Super-8 movies he used to film with his old Beaulieu camera on the beach. Look at his thin, rigid figure coming down the main staircase in his house, lit by the sparkling glow of the big crystal chandelier. Clean-shaven, his salt-and-pepper hair swept back, his torso swathed in a custom-tailored tweed jacket buttoned ostentatiously over the stomach. His pocket handkerchief is orange; his trousers brown corduroy. His black leather shoes shine against the carpet, which is blue silk with the geometric floral medallion typical of Isfahan rugs. With his swaggering walk, Saddeq could be a character in an American comedy from the 1970s, a Peter Sellers movie, where he'd play the role of a rich, gullible big shot. Now he's walking toward Sara, who is sitting at the table in the lounge. It's morning, and Sara is drinking her tea out of a large glass with a handle.

"Don't you look chic!" she exclaims, with a genuine smile, while behind her Leïli and Mina giggle into their quince jelly-stained napkins (as for me, since the moment I heard Uncle Number Two leave his room, I have been waiting by the door that leads to the garden for his permission to go outside and play). Saddeq tilts his head to the right and laughs like a shy teenager who has just been paid a compliment by the prettiest girl in the neighborhood. *Chic* (pronounced Iranian-style as *sheeeek*) is his favorite word. The one he hopes to hear every morning; the one he always deserves, no matter the situation.

That image of Uncle Number Two is from the winter of 1978, a few months before the end of the Revolution, part of which we spent in his house, the house where my parents were married. I don't remember it snowing that winter, though in Tehran the snow usually piles up for months, as high as some low walls. Didn't I hear Sara say it was a Parisian-style winter? Was she talking about that winter, or another one? I'd memorized the expression even though I didn't know what winter in Paris was like. But it seemed wonderful, like everything French, from its politics to the smell of the shampoo. In the years before the Revolution, Sara used to take us to a French supermarket that had opened on one of the posh streets in the northern part of the city. The place was intimidatingly spotless, and filled with every kind of merchandise that we found terribly exotic. Little bits of France, taken from a whole as inaccessible as a dream, which had, through the miracle of oil, found their way to us. Vache qui rit, Nutella, Danon yogurts, Caprice des Dieux Camembert, Zest soap, Gitane cigarettes. These products in their shiny packages were displayed on iron shelves, easy to see and reach, rather than piled in a precarious mountain, like at our grocer, Agha Mohabati's. The prices, given in both tomans and francs, were so exorbitant that we could barely buy half of the things we wanted. We left the shop with a small bundle of purchases and the feeling of leaving behind us a fascinating world that might, like in the cartoons, disappear forever.

One day, when I was home from Brussels, Sara told me that Uncle Number Two and his wife had moved into an apartment near the city center. A few years earlier, during the Iran-Iraq war, the foundation of their ancient house had been seriously weakened by the bombings, and the interminable process of restoring it was more than they could handle. Situated in a narrow street in the center of Tehran, the apartment was enormous. Staircases led to numerous rooms whose walls were loaded with mirrors. Tapestries and objects inherited from the ancestors joined massive pieces of furniture, all wood and gilding, bought from antique dealers at the *marché aux puces* (*Mahrtshay oh Pous*) in *Pahrees*. The result of all this was a collision of eras and styles as disparate as they were inappropriate, with the overall impression being one of horrifyingly bad taste.

I took the news with calculated detachment, determined not to let Sara stir up any feelings of nostalgia in me that were as painful as they were pointless. I knew Uncle Number Two was sick, stuck at home and unable to get out of bed. I knew it the way you know a piece of information whose real scope is difficult to grasp. An earthquake, an explosion, a distant reality that affects and touches you but remains outside of the present. I was incapable of imagining what he must look like, sunk in old age and illness. In which bed was he lying? In which room, which apartment, which neighborhood? And even if I'd known the name of their new neighborhood, I wouldn't have known where it was. Since the Islamic regime had taken over the country, all the names of the streets and quarters had been changed, Ayatollah-ized, confusing and blurring landmarks and memories. I could have called him, but to say what?

"You won't even talk," Sara told me. "You won't need to. Just say hi, and your uncle and aunt will talk for you."

But even that was beyond my capabilities. Hearing their voices, imagining them in a place that had once been my home too, where I had been happier, surely, than I'd ever be again. How was it possible that that place still existed and that I was no longer part of it? How could something so ridiculous possibly be true? Of course, I knew the answers to all those questions, and a whole lot of other ones too, but nothing could explain the crushing sense of cruelty and injustice that overwhelmed me, and still overwhelms me when I think about it. The truth was that Uncle Number Two had disappeared a long time ago, and the announcement of his death only confirmed what I already knew: that I would never see him again. Like I would never see Iran again. I'd known that the second my feet, wearing my mother's boots, stepped past the virtual line of the border between Iran and Turkey at around four-thirty in the morning on March 25, 1981.

For various reasons, out of all my uncles, he was the one I was closest to. We'd stayed with him for the first time in August 1978. The protest movement against the Shah's regime had radicalized over the summer. While in the larger cities the demonstrations grew larger and occasionally erupted into bloody events, the repression intensified as well, leading to the establishment of martial law. Not a day went by without political activists being arrested or killed. At Saddeq's request, our neighbors, the Nasrs, had taken me to his house the day after Sara was taken to the hospital. She had been involved in a violent altercation with a high-ranking army officer, General

Mansour Rahmani, who had been so enraged that he'd tried to kill my father. Wanted by the secret police, Darius was hiding somewhere in the depths of Tehran. He had left our apartment two days prior, at around noon, on a stifling summer day, urged and escorted by friends with worried faces. Following a fire at the Rex cinema in Abadan,[4] the tension had risen to a fever pitch. For the first time, Darius did not resist and agreed to leave—but as he walked out the door, the expression on his face was like that of a goalkeeper after letting a penalty kick slip through—defeat.

From that day forward, he embarked on a series of comings and goings of varying durations, capped off by a long period underground from which he only emerged in February 1979, two weeks after Khomeini returned to Iran.

Leïli and Mina were already at Uncle Number Two's house when I got there. He was alone. Or rather, alone with Bibi, the loyal servant that had followed Nour here from the paternal *andarouni*. Saddeq's wife, the wealthy heiress to another great Mazandaran family and an unrepentant and likeable snob, had withdrawn to her Mazandarani lands, far from the tumult of the Revolution. Their two offspring were grown with lives of their own; the daughter was married with three children and lived a few streets away from the family home, and the son was busily wasting his parents' money in the United States.

Uncle Number Two was determined to keep us with him,

---

[4] The fire, which occurred on August 19th, 1978, in Abadan, the hub of the oil industry, caused 477 deaths, the majority of which were women and children. The regime was accused of deliberately setting fire to the cinema in order to drive out the subversive elements who had taken refuge there. However, years after the Revolution, documents and eyewitness accounts revealed that the fire had been planned at Khomeini's residence while he was in exile in Najaf, Iraq. The goal was to provoke the anger of refinery workers, inciting them to go on strike and reduce oil production, but also to destroy a place of debauchery and a symbol of Western culture. Clearly the seed of what happened later was planted here.

well-sheltered in his double-locked house where everything that might have reminded us of the outside world—television, radio, the keys to the door leading out to the garden—disappeared a few hours after our arrival. During the day he taught us to cook, sew, and knit, to make dolls out of chiffon and table-linens from cushions. He kept us in a state of artificial normality that was outside of time, like orphans in an Andersen fairy tale who, despite everything, had to be prepared for life as respectable wives. In the evenings he told us his stories, in which Mother always ended up martyred, and he in tears.

The keeper of the family legend, Uncle Number Two had, through the years, thanks to a careful proportioning of reality and fiction, consolidated most of his stories into a personal narrative that seemed to suit his brothers, uncles, aunts, and cousins of varying degrees of separation. On summer evenings, on the terrace of his Mazandaran villa, sitting in a chair turned to face the Caspian Sea, he would serve up these tales with the mastery of a gourmand, puffing from time to time on his narghile and adding just the right touch of comic effect. Sometimes he burst into laughter himself, his head cocked to one side, watching his audience out of the corner of his eye. And we laughed too; the adults, who understood the sexual allusions, laughed even harder than the children.

But now, since he had gathered us under his roof, drama had metastasized in his stories. Not only did we not laugh anymore, now we inevitably ended up clutching one another to the accompaniment of Uncle Number Two's weeping. According to Leïli, who was a font of explanation and analysis, our uncle's sadness wasn't due to his excessive love for Mother, but rather to his love for our dad. Anxiety and fear, she said, had taken over his stories, erasing the comic episodes and replacing them with other, terrifying ones. Beatings, abuse, torture, murder. All horrors that our activist parents were in danger of being subjected to at any moment.

One night, my nose glued to the window, I hatched a secret

plan to escape. Leïli took me by the arm and turned me to face her with a jerk.

"You're so selfish you can't even see that he's taking care of us. He acts like everything's fine, but at night he falls apart. That's called *depression!*"

Leïli's vocabulary, spectacularly enriched by all the reading she did, included words whose meanings were totally lost on me. Those words were all in French, the teaching language of choice from nursery school onward at the very posh Lycée Razi, the French school located in a residential area in north Tehran. Despite its exorbitant fees, Sara had been determined to have us educated there. The reasons that had driven her to such a choice, which was totally at odds with our life in a middle-class neighborhood, her political beliefs, and her work as a teacher in a public school, were complicated. Of course, she wanted to give us every possible chance at success, which without question meant conducting our university studies abroad. Of course it was her plan that, after those studies, we would return to Iran in order to contribute to the country's development. But her outward pragmatism concealed an immoderate passion for France, where she had spent a year herself thanks to a university scholarship obtained as part of her thesis on Jean-Jacques Rousseau. Just one year, like a mirage in the middle of the desert. Where some mothers, dreaming of being beauty queens themselves, entered their daughters in Little Miss pageants, Sara had enrolled us at the Lycée Razi.

Unlike my sisters, I didn't like French, a language I found both convoluted and overblown, and which I refused to have anything at all to do with outside of school. I wouldn't touch the Bibliothèque Rose et Verte books inherited from my sisters and which Sara had carefully organized on the shelf above my bed. I read *Astérix* and *Tintin*, but not in French; I read them in Persian, forcing myself to laugh extra-loudly to annoy my sisters, who thought the translations were ridiculous.

Truth be told, it wasn't French that I was rejecting, but rather the unspoken obligation shared by Iranian students at the Lycée Razi, issued by the upper crust, some of whom were outrageously rich, to consider it as superior to Persian. That led to the certainty that, because they spoke this language, they were themselves superior to other Iranians, to the teeming uncultivated masses lost in the depths of the Middle East, eating rice with a spoon as if it were soup. In class, it was all about competing to see who could express themselves best in French, spend the longest holidays in France, dress in Cacharel or wear Moon Boots in winter. Some of the students even spoke French with their brothers and sisters, calling their fathers "Papa" instead of the vulgar and backward "Baba." The students who were actually French were treated like gods who had been magnanimous enough to come down to our level, so that a little of their refinement might rub off on us. Being accepted by them was the main recreational activity. I mocked their self-importance, even though secretly I dreamed of having a pair of Moon Boots, too.

Two weeks later, Sara left the hospital, pale and much thinner. After a week of convalescence at Uncle Number Two's house (where the TV, radio, and garden keys made a miraculous reappearance), she called a taxi and we went home. My happiness made me forget that claustrophobic sojourn during which I had, nevertheless, learned to sew and to make quince jelly and herbed flatbread.

Despite the daily threats from SAVAK, which continued its Antigonesque pursuit of the political activist's wife, Sara insisted that we return to our ground-floor apartment. She knew that soon something else would happen, something necessarily terrible, to drive us away from there—but in the meantime we had to put on a brave front. We, the family of Darius Sadr, who a foreign journalist had recently dubbed "The Sakharov of Iran."

"There's no reason to be afraid of these jackals, my darlings. They're the ones who should be afraid of us!" she declared a few hours later, as she propped the old mattresses from our cribs up to cover the bedroom windows.

Bear in mind that those mattresses, which we had wet copiously over the years, were intended to absorb any bullets that might be fired by said jackals at our windows in the middle of the night!

All four of us were on the balcony, and my sisters were helping Sara. I watched them, disbelieving. How was this old, flimsy bedding supposed to protect us? How could Sara believe that this would discourage the Savaki and send them wandering off to spend the rest of the night somewhere else? If I were a Savaki—I pictured them bulging with muscles and carrying weapons, like the killers in the American films Darius loved—I would climb up onto the balcony, shove the dirty mattresses to one side, and let loose with both barrels. I was about to open my mouth to share these reflections when Mina, who was visibly entertaining the same doubts I was, elbowed me in the stomach. The dark glance she threw at me—*can't you see this is making her feel better, idiot?*—shut me up immediately.

I continued to watch my mother as she completed her ludicrous work, filled with fear. Before she revealed the probability that we might end our lives riddled with bullets, the thought had never crossed my mind. That our apartment would be put under surveillance, yes. That our parents would be arrested and taken to secret government jails, yes. That Darius would go off to one of his political meetings and never come back, yes. But not that we would die. Now, every time I looked at the blocked windows of the bedroom I shared with Mina, anxiety roared in me like a wild animal. I couldn't sleep. I kept my eyes open all night, flinching at the slightest noise and praying to God not for our lives to be spared—the chaos

happening on earth seemed beyond even His reach to me—
but for the bullets to hit all of us at the same time. Please, God,
let my mother, my sisters, and me die together!

Before I tell you about Sara's altercation with General
Rahmani, I have to introduce you to Barthelemy Schumann.

Bart Schumann was born in New York. A journalist and
left-wing militant, he'd been thrown out of the United States in
the 1960s for his active participation in movements protesting
the war in Vietnam. Exiled to London, friends with Bertrand
Russell, Schumann came to Iran during the Revolution. Like
many Western journalists, he made contact with Darius, whom
he interviewed several times. But unlike the others, he con-
trived to live in our neighborhood and came to our apartment
regularly, often staying for lunch and dinner. On some afternoons he took me with him out into the heaving streets of
Tehran, using me as his interpreter. We were an odd couple,
the big, long-haired redhead and the small, short-haired
brunette, and we always made heads turn. When he was told
to leave, people screaming "US Go Home!" in his face, he
asked me to explain to them his dogged fight against American
imperialism. I did my best, and for better or worse the situation would settle down. Because of this, a special relationship
developed between us, all the more so because he'd never had
children and seemed to regret that fact. Later, in November
1979, when the American embassy was stormed by Iranian students and the archives made public, the theory that Schumann
was an American spy became plausible enough that he was
expelled from the country and forbidden from ever returning.

An interview conducted by Bart was broadcast by the BBC
on August 24, 1978. The subject was: "How General Mansour
Rahmani went to Darius Sadr's home and threatened him with
death, seen through the eyes of his seven-year-old daughter, a
witness to the scene." I'm sure you didn't hear it.

It was recorded on a small Dictaphone the very morning the incident happened, while I was having my breakfast at the home of our neighbors, the Nasrs—whose clinking-cutlery noises sometimes drowned out our voices—and sent immediately to the BBC to become part of its broadcast dedicated to the Iranian Revolution.

A few weeks after THE EVENT, Schumann sent me a duplicate copy on a TDK audio cassette, accompanied by a compassionate letter asking me to grant him a new interview (he said he was working for an American alternative radio station based in Toronto).

I never answered the letter, and only listened to the tape years later, just once, while moving. But I'll try to transcribe it for you here.

B. Schumann: Can you explain to me what happened yesterday?

K. Sadr: I was with my mom at home when we heard noises at the end of the street, over there. There were a lot of people yelling, yelling these . . . you know . . .

B. Schumann: Slogans?

K. Sadr: Yeah, slogans.

B. Schumann: Who were these people?

K. Sadr: I don't know. People protesting.

B. Schumann: And why were they at the end of your street?

K. Sadr: Because General Rahmani lives there.

B. Schumann: The people were protesting in front of General Rahmani's house, is that right?

K. Sadr: Yes. At first we didn't know why they were there, but a man knocked on our window and my mother opened it. He was a photographer. He wanted to hide in our house because the police were chasing him. My mom told him to hide his cameras in the washing machine. He's the one who told us what was happening.

B. Schumann: So you and your mother were the only ones at home?

K. Sadr: My sisters are at a friend's house and my dad went away yesterday. My mom had a bad headache. She was lying down in her room when we heard the noises.

B. Schumann: What happened next?

K. Sadr: The photographer came into the living room with us . . . then somebody knocked on the door. My mom asked me to go and open it. I looked out the peephole first, but someone had put his finger over it. I looked at my mom and she said not to be scared and to open the door. I opened it, and General Rahmani was there with a gun in his hand. Behind him, a soldier was holding a boy by the hair. I started crying right away. Rahmani knelt down in front of me and said 'Don't cry, I'm not going to hurt you, it's your bastard of a father I'm going to kill.' Then he stood up and pointed his gun at a picture of my dad. My mom started to argue with him . . . [long pause]

B. Schumann: What did she say to him?

K. Sadr: She grabbed the front of his uniform and yelled, 'No one's going to kill my husband!' Rahmani put his gun against her temple and yelled, 'Then I'll kill you!' He said my dad had sent people to kill him, him and his family. My mom shouted that he was talking nonsense, that my dad is a journalist, not a murderer.

B. Schumann: And what were you doing right then?

K. Sadr: I was scared. I slipped between a soldier's legs and ran to get our neighbor, Mr. Nasr. I told him to come because Rahmani was going to kill my mom. He came and tried to calm Rahmani down. Rahmani was very angry. He wouldn't stop yelling. He pushed my mom away but she wouldn't let go. She held on to him. He ran toward the door and she fell to the floor. He dragged her toward the door. Mrs. Nasr ran to pick her up. I went into the kitchen to get a knife, and ran into the courtyard to keep him from coming back, but Mr. Nasr caught me and took away the knife.

B. Schumann: And what happened after that? Someone told me Rahmani is dead.

K. Sadr: Yeah. The people were waiting for him right in front of the gate, at the end of the courtyard. Mr. Nasr asked him not to leave, but he didn't listen. As soon as he left, they jumped on him and they . . . [silence] I don't know how to say it.

B. Schumann: Lynched . . .

K. Sadr: They dragged him in front of his house, there was blood everywhere in the street. Mr. Nasr put his hand over my eyes so I couldn't see. Then he took me back to our house. My mom was lying on a sofa, and there were a lot of people around her. A neighbor lady came and yelled, "It's over; he's dead, he's dead!" My mom started crying and said that he had children, that he shouldn't have died. Then a lady came and showed her that her hand was covered with blood, and that's when she went . . . crazy . . .

B. Schumann: She went to the hospital?

K. Sadr: Yeah. An ambulance came and took her away . . .

3

The Many Escapes of Darius Sadr (Episode 1)

The typical brouhaha indicating the arrival of a doctor has started out in the corridor. Maybe Dr. Gautier . . . In a single movement, we all turn our heads toward the door, on alert, like caged animals sensing a presence. No one. A few seconds pass. There are sighs, some of them ostentatiously loud. Then the noises of people shifting in their chairs, and exchanges of irritated looks. I take my mobile phone out of my pocket again to check the time, and then stuff it into my purse, which is overflowing with scraps of paper and useless objects. Strangely, the thought of cleaning out my bag is more unappealing than the reality of having to rummage through all this crap to find whatever I'm looking for. As always, I tell myself I should have taken the time to put the phone into the inner pocket, which is also crammed with stuff. As always, it's too late.

You've probably noticed that since mobile phones became ubiquitous, there's an imaginary line separating people of childbearing age. On one side are the people who have pictures of their kids set as their backgrounds, and are always waiting for the first possible opportunity to turn their phones so you can see them, followed by a tender smile and a "Have you seen this?" that they think sounds spontaneous. On the other side, you have the people whose phone screens are blank, or have a picture of their pet or of some postcardy landscape they photographed on vacation. In other words, something trivial, something banal. Nothing that gives an impression of movement, or participation in the workings of the world (of course, there are also those few brave and trailblazing souls who use photos of their nieces or nephews). Everyone in this room, stuck here waiting, their hands folded in their laps and their faces anxious, belongs to the second category, and is hoping desperately to become part of the first.

It's a strange and disturbing feeling, every time I come here, to be so aware of the deepest and most desperate desires of a roomful of people who are otherwise strangers to me. I know their pain; I know their kitchen-table discussions that last into the wee hours of the morning; the bursts of hope, the discouragement, the sudden feelings of loneliness in the middle of a busy street. I know that all of these women, and maybe even the men, would sell their kidneys—and maybe their souls—to the devil, to have a child. Myself included. I say "even the men" because—well maybe just because of the apprehensive way they always step into this room—it seems like the women are suffering more. Not only because their reproductive systems are being destroyed little by little by the passage of time, but because of the way society looks down on them.

At our first meeting with her, Dr. Gautier explained to us that the pressure on childless women was terrible. "We still have trouble accepting the fact that a woman might not have children. We don't really give her that right." She had three children herself, "but I would have liked to feel I was free to have them later in life." The unspoken purpose of these musings was to prepare me for the fact that medically-assisted reproduction could be a long and painful process. It was absolutely crucial for me to shrug off that outside pressure in order to increase my chances—knowing that the chance of becoming pregnant via artificial insemination was only around fifty percent, with a ten percent increase in the case of *in vitro* fertilization (which would only be attempted if the six attempts at insemination permitted by law were to fail).

Contrary to what Dr. Gautier thought, I didn't feel any pressure—but I agreed anyway. I agreed with everything she said, for fear of betraying myself. Could she really not see? I wondered at every consultation, astonished, while on the other side of the desk, her face greenish in the light of the neon bulbs suspended from the drop ceiling, Françoise Gautier filled out the endless forms that made up our file.

Would I have felt more pressure if my parents were still here? Not from Darius, no. Darius never troubled himself with things like that, which he considered supremely unimportant. Only political events and philosophical questions interested Darius Sadr, caused him to raise his head from the newspaper, which he would fold partially but never put down. We lived alongside him, grew, ate, passed our tests, opened the front door, got sick, earned our diplomas, and closed the front door without him really being aware of it. Our birthdays were irrelevant to him, and so were our troubles. He could be unexpectedly tender, patting our cheeks or scratching our backs vigorously, but then he'd lose interest just as suddenly and go back to his book.

At around the age of six, hearing him talk about historical materialism, the subject of an essay he was writing at the time, I'd begun to take an interest in economics in an attempt to get his attention. I'd first presented my thoughts on a cashless world to Sara as we drove home from the dentist's office one afternoon, certain that she would tell my dad about them that same evening. Starting the next day, and for weeks after that, Darius would summon me to the bathroom every morning while he was shaving and explain to me Marx's and Engels's theories on economics and history. For the first few minutes he would try to simplify his vocabulary, but he'd warm up very quickly, and begin to talk faster and faster, his voice getting louder, and phrases would come out of his mouth that were so complex and abstract that they might as well have been in a foreign language. Since I wasn't really listening to him, I devoted myself to studying the way he handled the shaving brush and razor, trying to memorize his technique so I could duplicate it when I was a grown-up. And that, in a nutshell, is the kind of silently schizophrenic state in which I spent my childhood. Basically, before other developments occurred, I knew I was a girl—but I was sure that, when I grew up, I would become not a woman, but a man.

Later, we came to understand that our father's detachment, classified by Leïli as *autistic behavior*, had nothing to do with a lack of love for us. He simply just didn't care much about everyday life, and kept himself separate from it with disconcerting ease.

Sara, on the other hand, if she had still been . . . (*still been what?*), would have been as fearsome with me—yes, even me—as she had been with my sisters. Before they had even decided to get married, when they'd barely begun dating potential sons-in-law, Sara had started in on them.

"Exactly what are you waiting for to have children? You're not going to spend your life eating out and staring at yourself in the mirror, are you? In fifteen or twenty years you'll regret having wasted all these years!"

I wasn't in Paris to witness these attacks at the time, but my sisters have told me about them so often that I could describe every one of them to you. For Sara, being part of a couple, being married, sexuality—none of that was worth anything in itself. Those were only consensual steps, necessary springboards to reach the higher plane of existence that was motherhood.

Speaking of motherhood, I remember one of the many conversations I had with Bibi, Uncle Number Two's toothless old servant. Despite the fact that I had spent a large part of my childhood with her, I couldn't always understand what she was saying. Bibi was as bony as a bat's skeleton, with a hunched back and oblong breasts that hung down to her stomach. She had invented her own language, a strange, muddled mixture of Persian and the Mazandarani dialect, watered with liters of saliva that built up in her mouth, and which she occasionally swallowed in one gulp like a hard-boiled egg. But we had this particular conversation so often that I'd managed over time to fill in the gaps.

"Do you have your brush, little one?"

"Yes. Here, Bibi."

"Sit down here, in front of me, if you want me to brush your hair. Not on the floor, idiot! On the stool."

"It hurts my butt."

"I don't care! The floor is as filthy as an atheist's mouth! Look at me, pfffffffff . . . no strength to clean it anymore, little one . . . (long, loud sigh). Bibi's looking more and more like a skeleton; time for her to be off . . . "

"Don't say that! I don't want you to die, Bibi!"

"I have to go, to make room for the little ones. That is how the All-Powerful works. He takes one away and puts another in their place. Otherwise even He will lose track of his accounts, like your uncle, Number Five . . . what an airhead that one is!"

"Do you think I'll have lots of babies?"

"Of course you'll have babies! First, you'll have twins. You look so much like your grandmother, you won't be able to avoid it. Twins . . . and then two more, a girl and a boy. Four children! You are blessed!"

Rapturously, I cried: "How do you know all that?"

"I just know it, that's all. Believe me. When you have your babies, you'll come and see me at the cemetery, with cakes and peaches, to congratulate me for being right. And you'll bring your little ones with you, to introduce them to old Bibi. Promise?"

"Promise!"

*

An intern pokes his head through the door, finally. Indifferent to the long delay, he tosses a name into the damp, stuffy air of the waiting room and disappears. The couple seated at the far end of the room shoots to their feet as if they've been jabbed in the side with a pin. They make their way between the rows of chairs with awkward little steps and then rush for the door, probably afraid that the intern will suddenly change his mind and send them back to their seats. Once the couple has disappeared down the hallway, the tension created by the doctor's appearance dissipates into a thick silence, and everyone retreats back into themselves.

As a way to kill time, let me make a comparison here. If we were in Iran, this room, at this time of day, would resemble a caravanserai. Discussions and secrets would be flowing in all directions. Everyone would be up to speed on their neighbors' lives. They would have already discovered several common acquaintances or even family links, and exchanged addresses and mobile telephone numbers. A few of the men, after having talked politics and agreed on the fact that the country had no more future than a septic tank, would have gone out to the restaurant on the corner to get food for everyone. Soon they would come back, sweaty and booming with laughter, carrying pots filled with steaming rice and skewers of meat, paper plates, and plastic cutlery. The women would take over then, serving the food, and everyone would eat so noisily that the next time the intern appeared in the waiting room, he would go completely unnoticed.

Iranians don't like solitude or silence (any noise other than the human voice, even the blaring horns of a traffic jam, is considered silence). If Robinson Crusoe had been Iranian, he would have let himself die the minute he got to the island, and the story would have been over.

This tendency to make endless small talk, to throw sentences like lassoes into the air to meet one another, to tell stories which, like Russian matryoshka dolls, open to reveal other stories, is, I suppose, one way to deal with a fate consisting of nothing but invasions and totalitarianism. Like Scheherazade, who used the power of words to put an end to King Shahryar's bloody crusade against the women of the realm, the average Iranian feels trapped in a daily existential dilemma: speak, or die. Telling and retelling, embellishing, and lying, in a society full of danger and corruption, where the simple fact of going out to buy a stick of butter could end in a nightmare , means staying alive. It's a way of forestalling fear, of taking comfort where you can find it—in meetings and acknowledgments, in the rubbing up of your existence against someone else's. And it's about sweet-talking that fear, and disarming it, and preventing it from doing harm. Silence, on the other hand, means closing your eyes and lying down in your tomb and closing the lid.

Things like democracy and social justice, the ability to rely on a government to take care of your problems, undoubtedly play a part in the fact that the French don't feel the need to get close to each other and communicate and cast their nets beyond the usual patch of sea. The French stay closed in on themselves, protecting their peacefulness and personal space as fiercely as a mother hen with her eggs. I act like that myself. I withdraw at the approach of strangers, sticking to a murmured *hello* when I pass a neighbor. The talkative, sociable child I used to be has turned into a Parisian adult with a face that closes off whenever I leave the house. I have become—as I'm sure everyone does who has left his or her country—someone else. Someone who has translated myself into other cultural codes. Firstly in order to survive, and then to go beyond survival and forge a future for myself. And since it is a generally acknowledged idea that something is lost in translation, it should come as no surprise that we unlearn—at least partially—what we used to be, to make room for what we have become.

Outside, the sky has turned slate-grey. Icy rain is falling on the city now, like a punishment. I close my eyes. As often happens, I am suddenly hit with fatigue, at a random moment when I have no chance of lying down and going to sleep.

I don't know who started using numbers to designate them one to six, but we've always referred to them that way amongst ourselves. When we speak to them directly we say *Amou Djan*, "Dear Uncle," with honey-sweet, very Persian, politeness.

My father became Uncle Number Four only after having the nickname *Amou Farançavi*, French Uncle, for years. That was during the time when he was single, and living in one of Uncle Number Two's guest houses. Back then he was, for the little ones, a mysterious and intriguing character who avoided family reunions and kept himself apart from the confabs orchestrated by Saddeq during which the nieces—with their plucked eyebrows and jeans, their tendency to shorten their skirts and their disagreeable attitudes—were freely commented on and criticized by the Sadr brothers. In fact, his absence from these gatherings, or "witch-hunts," as he called them, would—when he became more sociable—earn him the unswerving approval of those same nieces.

My dad's first nickname was given to him because of a decade he'd spent in Paris after fleeing a marriage arranged by Mother to one of his cousins. But that wasn't his first escape.

The saga of the many escapes of Darius Sadr begins in 1946, in Egypt, where his father, Mirza-Ali Sadr, had sent him to study law even though he was already a first-year economics student at the University of Tehran. He was the only brother to have the privilege of studying abroad—because, even though this taciturn, inscrutable boy, who had always preferred to spend his days reading indoors while his brothers squabbled in the courtyard, was a mystery to his father, he was also the most intelligent of the children. The one who would lift up, and incidentally would need, the Sadr name.

After a few months spent in Cairo in the home of an Iranian lawyer who was a friend of his father's, once the attractions of the city and the initial euphoria of freedom began to wear off, Darius remembered how much he detested his father. He realized that he had made a terrible mistake in agreeing to go where Mirza-Ali wanted him to, to study a subject that had been chosen for him and spend his father's money without counting it. But before I go any further, let me explain to you—with the help of a flashback—where this hate came from.

Picture a May morning in 1944, in Qazvin, the city where Mirza-Ali and his family lived, halfway between Mazandaran and Tehran. While the effects of the Second World War— shortages, inflation, poverty—make themselves felt all over the country, somewhere in the world the Americans and Soviets are discreetly negotiating Iranian oil concessions, like true gangsters. In the central square of Qazvin, a five-year-old boy with torn and dirty clothing advances toward Mirza-Ali, who looks like a movie star, dressed in the *faranghui* (Western) style, with a black fedora angled just so on his balding head. Mirza-Ali has just left an important meeting with the notable and holy men of the city, about the necessity of restoring the damaged dome of one of Qazvin's sacred monuments, the Peyghambariyeh, a mausoleum housing the remains of four Jewish prophets who predicted the coming of the Messiah.

Absorbed in their interminable sequence of goodbyes, the men haven't noticed the little boy, who dodges between their legs. Now he grasps Mirza-Ali's jacket in one of his filthy hands and gives it a strong tug.

"Baba, baba, give me a toman. Baba *Djan*, please . . . "

In the silence that greets the imploring little voice, the word *baba*, which every child in this country uses to designate his father, resonates like an interrogation. Thinking this is a joke, Mirza-Ali seizes the boy's ear and yanks him away. "Go and beg somewhere else, you dirty little pest!" But at that moment, his eyes meet the child's.

Freeze-frame.

The camera zooms in on my grandfather's face, distorted with rage. Look at what's happening in his blue eyes. Something has disturbed them. Something that one word— "astonishment," for example—wouldn't be enough to describe. It's an incongruous emotion, tormented, that requires one of those long multi-word German constructions that enlightened Persians (like Mirza-Ali) discovered at the start of the war when Reza Shah cozied up to Hitler. A hybrid collage that would combine "astonishment" with "violence" and "truth" with "bitterness." To really grasp Mirza-Ali's confusion, let's switch now from this close-up (his blue eyes) to the reverse shot: the little boy's eyes. Huge blue eyes, filled with tears. But not just any shade of blue. The blue of the sky over Najaf. The same bright turquoise that has shone miraculously out of Mirza-Ali's face since his birth. Mirza-Ali, the only one of the eleven children born to Rokneddin Khan and Monavar Banou to have eyes of that color. And the only one to be born in Najaf.[5]

Forty-six years earlier, Rokneddin Khan, appointed head of the grand bazaar of Qazvin, had gone to Najaf to solidify relations with the merchants of Baghdad, who were holding their

---

[5] From Wikipedia: Najaf is a holy city in Iraq, that contains the tomb of Ali, cousin and son-in-law of Mohammed, the founder of Shia Islam. The third-holiest city of the faith after Mecca and Medina, it was here that one Ayatollah (the highest rank in the Shiite clergy) Ruhollah (his first name, meaning Spirit of God) Khomeini sought exile in 1964, after violently opposing the "White Revolution" of the Shah. Khomeini left Najaf in 1978 for Nauphle-le-Château. I'm sure you remember that.

annual meeting in that city. Certain that the presence of his family—his wife Monavar Banou, who was seven months pregnant, and his ten daughters—was an important asset, he had insisted on bringing them with him. And to make an even greater impression on the famous merchants, he made an incredibly generous donation to Najaf's clergy, to be distributed by them (but not by *him*, of course) among the local poor and helpless.

A few days before their return to Qazvin, as Rokneddin Khan was proudly wrapping up his business affairs, Monavar Banou was seized with terrible pains in the small of her back, and barely had time to lie down before her uterus, as well-trained as an assembly line worker, expelled its load. A double miracle! Not only was the baby a boy, *finally*, but (and here, Monavar Banou's heart melted with love) he had blue eyes. But not just *any* blue, remember—and on this point Monavar Banou was intractable to the end of her days; the exact turquoise blue of this little corner of sky that, like a veil of beneficence, protected the mausoleum of Ali (Peace be on Him and His descendants), and behind which, Monavar Banou was sure, lay the gates of Heaven.

Nothing more was needed to convince Monavar Banou that her son, her prince with the eyes of Light, was a personal gift from the All-Powerful to thank her for her loyalty, her patience, her moral rectitude, and a bunch of other qualities with which she suddenly saw herself endowed.

Back in Qazvin, she made an executive decision: there would be no more children. She no longer wanted her body, touched as it had been by eternal grace, to serve as a mundane object into which Rokneddin Khan discharged the same way he would into a urinal. If anyone dared to object on her husband's behalf, she simply retorted: "The man can scratch his own itches now; I have a life to lead!" And that life could be summed up in two words: Mirza-Ali.

From then on, Monavar Banou became her son's publicist, implementing a forceful strategy designed to ensure that Little Ali would be a venerated child. I don't know all the minute details of her plan; all I do know, from Uncle Number Two's stories, boils down to two main parts (those of you who are familiar with the rites of Shia Islam and its intense martyrology will easily understand the reasoning behind her choices).

Part One consisted of only taking the baby out in public on high holy days, when processions and lamentations took over the city. People's religious fervor was at such a fever pitch back then that any event having to do with Ali quickly turned passionate. Standing in the dusty Qazvin sunlight, Monavar Banou watched with jubilation as men rushed to admire her boy, to touch him, and finally to lift him off the ground and raise him toward the sky, like a victorious hero back from some distant war. Like a King.

Part Two took place on Mondays. Why Mondays? Because Monavar Banou had decreed that it would be that way. So, every Monday, Little Ali would receive the sick and handicapped, in a room of the family home that his mother had fitted out. As soon as the sun rose, these unfortunate people, some of them come from the most far-flung villages in the region, lined up at Rokneddin Khan's front door in the hopes of kissing the child's divine eyes and being healed. The most desperate ones, the fathers carrying their dying children in their arms, the ones afflicted with blindness and paralysis, clung to his clothing and begged him for the ultimate gift: his saliva. *Oh, just the tiniest bit, little Ali Khan, with your fingers, just here on my forehead!* Little Ali would glance discreetly at his mother, who was hidden behind a half-open door, waiting for the go-ahead. If Monavar Banou blinked her eyes, the boy would wet two fingers in his mouth and pass them across the forehead of the sufferer. If Monavar Banou opened her eyes wide, he signaled his refusal by looking down.

Later, after Monavar Banou had died half-crazy, when all innocence had gone from Mirza-Ali's body, he put an authoritative stop to these fanatical practices. But he never forgot who he was, or the place he held in Qazvin society. He established a role for himself as something halfway between a Wise Man and an Upholder of the Law. He was the one people called on to settle a conflict between merchants or mediate a quarrel between communities. The one everyone sought out for advice concerning the city's affairs. Truth be told, the Qazvinis continued to regard him with respect and awe that were not of this world. No one questioned his aura, or dared to contradict him, for fear that they might be struck down by the Almighty. Life was already so hard. No one challenged him. Ever. Until that little beggar-boy appeared on the streets of Qazvin.

So now, back on this May morning in 1944, as Mirza-Ali continues to twist the little boy's ear, he feels rising up in him the fear of someone who has been caught red-handed. There's no point in prevaricating; eyes that color could only have sprung from his very own loins. He lets go of the boy's ear and shoves him to the ground. The child cries out in pain and Mirza-Ali makes a dash for his house. The men who have witnessed this scene know exactly what's going on. Even if they weren't positive at first that Mirza-Ali fathered this little boy, even if they haven't noticed the color of the child's eyes, the strange violence of Mirza-Ali's reaction speaks for itself.

Now the little boy runs after him, calling even more loudly: "Baba, baba *Djan!*" His lilting voice, agonizingly sincere, fuses with air molecules and floats down the streets. You can see it gliding along the walls, into the windows, and through half-open doors. Now it's inside the houses. All of them. It even makes its way into the draught-proof room where Nour shuts herself up every morning to luxuriate in a solitary pleasure she's only recently discovered: reading. Despite the difficulty this hobby presents for a woman who's never been taught, Nour passionately devours the novels Darius has finished with.

Soon, there isn't a single person in Qazvin who doesn't know that Mirza-Ali Sadr has had a son with a prostitute, one of those poor girls possessed by djinns and banished to the notorious areas in the southern part of the city. Soon, voices will rise up to confirm that this little boy can't be the only skeleton in his closet; how many others are there who, not having the turquoise-blue eyes as proof, have fallen through the net? For that matter, wasn't Ali (Peace be on Him and His descendants) faithful to Fatima until death? No gallivanting around; no little bastards left to fend for themselves! Mr. Sadr isn't so high-and-mighty, after all—in fact, he's nothing at all; not even as good a man as Mahmoud the grocer, a widower with five children who still hasn't remarried.

And just like that, like a new garment that has been soiled and become suddenly unappealing, Mirza-Ali lost his aura. All the work that the pious Monavar Banou had done was ruined by a street kid whose mother set him at her son's heels every day to beg him for money.

The situation became unbearable for Mirza-Ali. Not only did he have this dirty little runt following him wherever he went, but the men stopped greeting him the way they used to, didn't rise to their feet when he passed, and—worse—started chattering to each other the minute his back was turned. Mirza-Ali was a very devout man, and he had no doubt that it was God Himself, the Mighty and Intractable, who had thrown the child in his way, to punish him. But for what? For having taken his pleasure in the rougher parts of the city? Or for having partaken in idolatry since birth? Wait and see.

Three weeks later, early in the morning, with the child

already waiting for him on the pavement, Mirza-Ali, instead of running away, walked toward the boy. The child opened his mouth to launch into his pleading litany, but Mirza-Ali gestured for him to be quiet. He grabbed his chin and lifted his face to him. He wanted to make sure, absolutely sure, of the color of his eyes before he acted. In the next instant, a familiar and complex emotion washed over him. His six sons had blue eyes—but they were the same blue as Nour's. Not one of them had inherited this specific shade; not one. So of course this little brat, this less-than-nothing, as small as the ant that ran up the elephant's trunk and brought the giant animal to its knees, would be the one . . . Unnerved, he let go of the boy's chin as if it burned his fingers. "I'm going to walk ahead of you, and you follow me without a word, understood?" Incredulous, the boy nodded. Mirza-Ali tilted his hat forward so that he wouldn't have to meet the dumbfounded gazes that would undoubtedly punctuate his walk through the city to his notary's office. Pushing open the gate, he knew that half of Qazvin would shortly have their noses pressed to their windows (curse them!).

He officially acknowledged Abbas—as the boy said he was called—and asked for papers to be drawn up in his name. It was a humiliated man who signed the notary's register, a deposed king obliged to atone for his sins in public. He wiped away the drop of sweat that had beaded on his forehead and replaced his hat. With a burst of pride, he realized that he was still what the British called a *gentleman*. A perfect one! They could drag his name through the mud, scoff at him, insult him, but they could never say that he hadn't acted rightly toward this little boy, who had now formally become—by his decision, and his alone—his seventh son. At the door, Mirza-Ali discreetly slipped the notary an envelope full of cash to cover the boy's needs until he reached his eighteenth birthday.

That afternoon, when Mirza-Ali returned home, another surprise was waiting for him. His fourth son, Darius, who had rushed back double-quick from Tehran, was pacing the courtyard, a revolver in his hand.

As soon as he had learned of the little boy's existence, mad with rage, Darius had stolen a gun from his older brother— Uncle Number One, who was an army sergeant at the time— and made for Qazvin, to kill Mirza-Ali.

Darius never talked about that episode, any more than he talked about his father, so whatever he felt as he waited in the courtyard for the sound of Mirza-Ali's footsteps is as much a mystery to me as the black line he drew through that half of himself. I know I'm being a tad simplistic, but I would say that the desire to eliminate his harsh, inaccessible father had always been there, inside him. As a good student of psychoanalysis, you'll probably say that what I'm talking about is nothing but a poorly-handled Oedipus complex. Now, while Freudian theory may never have made it across the Bosporus Strait to the East, I will admit that that's a perfectly plausible reading in the case of Saddeq, who had arrived the night before to console Mother. But not in the case of Darius.

Darius, I believe, detested his father for who he was. Because he represented blindness and fear, the ruin of the precious thing that is thought. He hated him as much as he hated the religion of which Mirza-Ali had been his first representative. All his life, first through his readings and then through his political involvement and revolutionary awakening, Darius had been fighting men like his father, conservative authority figures whose principal activities consisted of protecting their own power by keeping people trapped in a fossilized social hierarchy and in absolute ignorance of the fact that any other world could be possible. More than once I heard him say that religion, like tyranny, dried up the capacity for analysis, with the sole purpose of imposing a single feeling: fear. "Fear is their only weapon, and the revolution is about turning it back on them," he would say, with conviction.

The discovery of Mirza-Ali's betrayal of Nour, whose sons considered her to have been muzzled, sacrificed, served up on a platter to a family of mystical half-wits, was undoubtedly the moment Darius had been waiting for to carry out his morbid fantasy: ridding them all finally of this liar, this phony wise man, this charlatan who was as deceitful and hypocritical as a mullah.

So, on that day, Mirza-Ali entered the courtyard, and Darius pointed his gun at him.

Since I can't describe Darius's feelings for you, I'll tell you about Mother.

Let's go into the room she used as both sitting room and bedroom. A room with several windows, one of which over-looked the courtyard. Shut up between these four walls, weep-ing in Saddeq's arms, Nour heard raised voices outside and lis-tened carefully. She immediately recognized her husband's sharp, dry voice, but it took her a few seconds to recognize Darius's, so rare was it for one of her sons to shout as loudly as their father. She turned to Saddeq.

"Is that . . . ?"

"Yes," he said, disconcerted. "It's him. God only knows what he's capable of doing."

Mother leapt to her feet and dried her tears. She knew, bet-ter than anyone, what her rebellious son was feeling. It was his face that she watched every time Mirza-Ali summoned his six sons to the courtyard like a colonel conducting an inspection. While his brothers always submitted to the exercise without a grumble, Darius took his place in the line like a beast being led to slaughter. He kept his head lowered until the tip of the pater-nal shoe stepped hard on his toes, forcing him to look up. Pain flickered in his eyes, but his face remained strangely impassive.

Infuriated, Mirza-Ali continued to press down with his foot—and the harder he pressed, the hotter the rage burned in Mother's chest—until the pain became too much, and tears trickled down the defiant boy's cheeks. Along with her anger, a sort of panic seized Mother's heart. If the boy could tolerate this level of pain, if he was able to face it without flinching, who knew what he would be capable of once he grew up? Years later, standing at the kitchen window, Sara would experience that same feeling as she followed Darius with her eyes, an envelope containing his first open letter to the Shah tucked under his arm.

Mother burst into the courtyard and inserted herself between the gun and Mirza-Ali. She would have preferred not to cry, but just the sight of Darius put an end to that resolution.

"Don't do this," she begged. "Please, son. Don't do this. If you pull that trigger, you'll be a criminal. You'll end up in prison, and . . . "

As the words tumbled around in my grandmother's head, seemingly having no effect on her son, she became aware of an unexpected flash of clarity in the back of her mind. All of a sudden, she knew with absolute certainty the origin of the anguish that was eating away at him. She had felt the same thing when she read the book she'd found among Darius's things, its pages battered and filled with scribbled notes. It was Darius she'd seen in that tortured character. Darius who was . . . who might become . . .

"What do you want? To end up like Raskolnikov?" she shouted.

The shock of hearing his mother say that name was so great that Darius's arm fell to his side. Suddenly, reality took on a new dimension. He saw her now. No longer the powerless, docile mother, but the woman who had read Dostoyevsky, had patiently deciphered each sentence, had educated herself in silence. This woman, he did not doubt, had the strength to stand up for herself against her husband. She didn't need her son to defend her anymore. Their eyes locked for long minutes, during which an unspoken exchange took place, a series of revelations, of pride and encouragement; everything that this woman and this young man, this mother and son, had never said to each other, and would never say.

The noise of the footsteps of Mirza-Ali, whom everyone had forgotten, interrupted the scene.

"Where are you going?" asked Nour, dryly.

"I'm going in!" answered Mirza-Ali, raising his bushy eyebrows as if to emphasize the vacuousness of the question.

"Fine. I'm leaving. I'm moving to Tehran with the children. Bibi will come with me."

There. It was said.

In all the thousands and thousands of times she'd imagined this scenario, Nour had pictured the sky darkening and filling with storm clouds, trees being ripped from the ground, the earth cracking and splitting apart. She had imagined the house trembling and falling into ruins like a toy, imagined screams that could be heard for miles. But here, now, nothing happened. The world was calm, rooted in its ancient equilibrium. The dense summer light illuminated everything as brightly as it had a moment before. The breeze rustled the leaves of the apple tree. Mother felt something like a cool burst of oxygen rise up in her and make her head spin. She felt incredibly alive, and the strange sense of being naked. She had stopped paying attention to the three pairs of eyes that watched her. Slowly, she crossed the garden, stepped into her room, and disappeared. Mirza-Ali still stood frozen in the courtyard, watching Nour's silhouette as it melted into the shadows of that unhappy house.

After a year of silence, Mirza-Ali summoned Darius to Qazvin. Mother, who was settled in a house in Tehran a few streets away from the one her sons shared, insisted that her son go to see his father. The time for reconciliation had come, and Darius had to take a step toward his father. Mother enlisted the help of Uncle Number One in convincing his brother, and finally, after a series of discussions, entreaties, and meetings, Darius gave in.

Of course, no one would ever know what happened during the encounter, which lasted all of thirty minutes. The only thing Darius would say on his return was: "I'm going away to study law in Egypt."

"But you're already at the university here!" cried Mother, for whom Egypt was as far away as the moon.

"That's true, but I'm going. I'm leaving the country."

So now we're back in Egypt again, watching Darius—who bitterly regretted his decision. He hated his father—yes, hated him—and had no reason to stay in the country.

One night, while the Iranian lawyer (to whose home Mirza-Ali had sent his son) and his family were sound asleep, Darius packed his things, quietly opened his bedroom window, tossed his bag into the azalea beds, and climbed out. At a cabaret in the city center, he found a taxi driver drunk enough to agree to drive him to Alexandria, where he took the first ship to Italy. Darius stayed for a long time in Europe, which had been devastated by the war, and was still in ruins. He travelled from country to country, working as a laborer in ports and train stations and on construction sites, feeling triumphant at finally being able to put his progressive theories into practice.

Every day, he took pleasure in watching his muscles develop, the skin on his hands toughen, his gaze sharpen. Every day, he rejoiced at feeling in his own flesh and bones what the word "proletariat" meant, yet with the knowledge that he, a son of the bourgeoisie, had the ability to leave this miserable life behind while his companions would undoubtedly die in it. But for now he was with them; he was one of them. In the evenings, immediately after dinner, he would rest his work-numbed body and think about the servants in his father's house—far more than he ever thought about his brothers. Mule-headed Hosseini, Little Ibrahim, Djavad-Ali the Turk . . . he had spent his whole life with them, without ever knowing them. Without knowing how much they were paid, or even if they were paid at all. Without wondering where they slept. So much injustice, carried on from generation to generation. The madness of believing oneself to be superior. Slowly, the feeling grew in him that he owed a debt to them, a duty to accomplish.

4
THE MANY ESCAPES OF DARIUS SADR (EPISODE 2)

The creaking of a chair makes me open my eyes. I must have nodded off, because I have the unpleasant sensation of being suddenly jerked awake. I shift in my chair, careful not to let the tube fall. I sit up straight, trying to gather together the thoughts that drifted while I dozed. What time is it? I can't bring myself to take my phone out to check the time. Often, at night, just as I feel like I'm finally falling asleep (usually at around 4:45 in the morning), I still have the irritating certainty that any noise at all will keep me from sleeping. I know that the faintest sound, no matter how distant, will resonate with the same intensity as a Metallica concert. So, afraid of being startled awake when I've just fallen asleep, I lie there with my eyes open until the sun comes up. I know what you're thinking: get some earplugs, you idiot! But you know what? Earplugs cause other problems, starting with the panicky feeling of being cut off from the world. What if something happens? What if someone dies? Sleep isn't about resting, it's about letting yourself settle, like the sediment at the bottom of a wine-barrel. I'm nowhere near trusting this world that much.

It doesn't take me long to discover the source of the creaking noise. The couple that's been sitting across from me for hours has finally been called. Their haste, and the way the wife pushes the man aside so she can go first, smacks of the nervousness of a first consultation. Now, as I'm sure you can imagine, all the faces that had turned toward them turn away in one synchronized movement and close back off, like houses in a private development whose lights suddenly turn off at the same time.

A new couple, rather oddly matched, soon takes the place of the one that just left. The woman is alarmingly blond, with a UV-fried face and shiny lipstick. The man, who might be Indian, is crammed into a dark business suit and looks like he's going to a funeral. He glances around uncomfortably, sitting on the very edge of his seat as if ready to bolt. Pragmatically, his wife pulls a small bottle of water out of her purse, followed by a sandwich wrapped in plastic wrap, and hands them to him. I think to myself that if she took the time to make him a sandwich before they came here, he's probably the one who's infertile. This deduction has hardly crossed my mind when I'm reminded of one of Sara's musings on the subject of our neighbors, the Hayavis, married for many years but without children. "Of course *he's* the sterile one. If she couldn't have children, he'd have divorced her ages ago!" And there you have the Iranian woman's lot summed up in two sentences.

I remember, when I had the mumps, dutifully staying in bed as the local doctor, who had been called in urgently, had ordered me to.

"You have to stay in bed so that you can give your husband beautiful children, understand? If you move, you might become barren."

"You mean I wouldn't be able to have babies anymore?"

"That's right! And I wouldn't wish that on any woman, you know."

Terrified by this warning, which was a direct echo of Sara's remarks concerning the Hayavis, I refused to get out of bed, even to brush my teeth. Later, I learned that infertility only occurs in men who contract the mumps as adults, due to inflammation of the testicles.

I watch the new couple until the wife suddenly looks up

and meets my eyes. Embarrassed, I quickly shift my gaze to the window, as if the speed of the movement will erase the minutes I just spent staring at them for no reason.

Outside, the world just keeps careering crazily along. Cigarettes are stamped out on the damp sidewalks; windows fog up; baskets of bread are thumped down on tables. Three metro stations south of here, my mother is sleeping in front of the television news, helped along by sedatives. On the other side of the city, Leïli, running terribly behind as usual, is with a patient who has agreed to skip lunch hour in order finally be seen. In a small house in the western suburbs, Mina, sitting at her desk with a cup of green tea on her right and a pack of cigarettes to her left, is preparing her lessons for the history department at the Sorbonne, where she is doing research for an essay on Louis Massignon. None of them know that I'm sitting here, waiting.

I thought that this stage, unlike the other ones—the consultations and tests and analyses and results—would be quick. As if, now that I've finally reached this critical point in the experience, I would be rewarded. Bravo for being conscientious, disciplined, docile. Bravo for hanging in there. You've won the privilege of no longer having to sit in waiting rooms with people who are still in the earlier stages of the process. Now you can just knock on the door, go right in, and spread your legs for the thousands of spermatozoa that have been taken out of hibernation and are ready to make their way upstream and join the fray.

Our societies are good at organizing the waiting process. People wait in line all night for the latest model of a computer, concert tickets, video games, and big sales. We wait on the first day of the month at the public transportation ticket windows. We wait at universities, at supermarket registers, on the telephone, in any and every government office. South of the Mediterranean, the lines for visas start at dawn in front of the Western embassies. In other places, poverty and war do the work. Waiting is a progressive, insidious phenomenon, an activity in itself. And while we wait, whether out of necessity, need, desire, or imitation, we don't revolt. The whole strategy is to drain people of their energy, their ability to reflect and oppose. To reduce them to immediate goals, as fleeting as a single pleasure. Whenever I say things like that, my sisters always give annoyed sighs. "You're exaggerating!" they say, putting extra emphasis on the "x" as if they were pressing on a brake pedal to cut me off in my frenzy. They don't want to talk about society and politics any more than they absolutely have to; they'd rather we focus on family stories, and the kids' school and cultural activities. My parents used up their tolerance for these subjects a long time ago.

October 1948. Darius is twenty-three years old. His shoulders broad and his hands callused, carrying a small suitcase bought in Hamburg in one hand and a packet of unfiltered Lucky Strikes in his pocket, he has come back without warning. A taxi drops him off in front of Uncle Number Two's house. He rings the doorbell. Bibi opens the door and informs him, without preamble, that his father is dead. "A heart attack, they say. It's too bad, but after all, it is not as if he hadn't had a full life!"

Darius has come home just as the fortieth-day ceremony is in full swing; it is the official end of the mourning period, when the whole family gathers one last time before letting the soul of the deceased go wherever the Almighty has determined. He is faced with the whole tribe at once, busily nibbling sweets and drinking bitter tea while they wait for the evening feast. On his mother's side they pass him from hand to hand like a ball, hugging him hard and planting loud kisses on his cheeks. On his father's side, the aunts, with their pale

skin and eyes as black as watermelon seeds, ignore him completely. He, they have decided, was the second main cause of
their brother's death. The first, of course, was Nour, that
bitch who was now presiding silently over the ceremony in
her widow's garb, her hair cut as short as a boy's.

Not long after her wedding, encouraged by some new
acquaintances who were among the most fashionable women
in Qazvin, Nour had allowed Mona the Hairdresser to cut off
her long teenage tresses. Mirza-Ali, who was not at all pleased
with his young wife for taking such a liberty, had forbidden her
ever to do it again. She had not had her hair cut since. But
when the telephone rang and she learned of her husband's
death, she immediately sent Bibi in search of a pair of scissors.
The latter protested.

"I have plucked thousands of chickens, Madam *Djan*, but
hair—"

"I don't care! Now, cut!"

Bibi cut. Right to left. Left to right. Under her shaking
hands, the undulating, craggy landscape of her native
Mazandaran appeared on Mother's head. Faced with this disaster, she was obliged to call Sanam the Hairdresser, who had
no choice but to deploy her clippers. Now, however, Nour was
displaying her short hair without a qualm.

That evening, in the presence of the other brothers,
Uncle Number One presented Darius with his inheritance in
the form of a check for an exorbitant amount. Darius
refused it.

"But what do you want us to do with this money, Darius?"
demanded Uncle Number One, angry at this brother who, for
the sake of pride, was showing such intolerable ingratitude.
Uncle Number One had remained close to his father out of
affection, but also out of an oversized sense of duty, and he considered himself to have been much more deserving of complet-
ing his studies abroad. He would have practiced law with the

ambition of becoming a judge. But their father hadn't chosen him, and now look how Mirza-Ali's decision was being repaid.

"Do whatever you want with it. Give it to Bibi; she'll know very well how to spend it," Darius replied, lighting a Lucky Strike. "Here, I'll give it to her myself."

"You're out of your mind!" exclaimed Uncle Number Two, grabbing the check out of Uncle Number One's hand. "Fine, let's not talk about this money anymore. I'll deal with it."

So Uncle Number Two opened a bank account and deposited the check in it. Twenty-six years later, the day before we left Iran, he withdrew the money, gave part of it to Sara, and sent the rest of it to us in France, in small installments.

If you're wondering whether or not Abbas Sadr received his own inheritance . . . well, I'll let Bibi tell you . . .

"Bibi?"

Bibi is sitting on a low stool, a white copper dish in her lap, sorting grains of rice. "Hmm?"

"What happened to Abbas?"

"What? Abbas who?"

"Ben Abbas. Our . . . " [long hesitation] " . . . uncle."

"Don't ever say that name in this house, little one! If your uncle heard you, he would wash your mouth out with vinegar, and then go to bed for weeks with one of his migraines before dying of sorrow!"

"I know, but . . . he isn't here."

"And where has he gone again?"

"I don't know. To Mother's grave?"

"It isn't Friday."

"Yes, it is!"

"Well, if I can't remember what day of the week it is anymore, how do you expect me to remember what happened to . . . " [throat-clearing noise] "God forbid I should say his name aloud!"

"Have you really forgotten?"

"Of course I haven't forgotten!"

"Then tell me."

Bibi examines me as if determining whether my soul is pure enough to withstand such dangerous confidences. She works at her mouthful of saliva. She lowers the platter to the floor with difficulty and stretches out her leg, which makes a sound like a money-box being shaken.

"If you repeat a single word of what I'm about to tell you— even ONE WORD—I'll put pepper on your tongue and then cut it off."

"I won't tell. I swear; I swear! Not a word."

(Long hesitation, during which Bibi noisily swallows.)

"*Ey baba!* What are you making me do? Go and close the door, little one."

I obey. Bibi motions for me to sit down beside her. She leans her face close to mine, her expression as serious as if she were about to reveal the secrets of the atom bomb. When she speaks, I can feel the long hairs on her chin tickling my cheek.

"When your grandfather—may the Almighty do with his soul what it deserves—died, your uncle, Number One, went to Qazvin to find this . . . " Bibi clears her throat loudly to avoid saying the forbidden name. "He had become a street scammer, living on his own since the death of his poor mother. Your Uncle Number One gave him his portion of the inheritance and said to him—you know how he is, as blunt as a dog's balls—(here she imitates Uncle Number One's overblown way of speaking): 'Certain of my brothers'—he was thinking of Uncles Number Two and Six—'will never accept you, so the best thing for you to do is go away.'"

"Did he really say that?"

"As far as I know. What, do you think I was there?"

"And then what happened?"

"Your uncle bought him a plane ticket and—whoosh, he went off to the other side of the globe."

"Which side?"

"The side they say is called *Amirika!*"

"He went to America?!"

"That's what I just said."

"What does he do over there?"

"What do you think he does? He's a Sadr. He shakes his little pipe and makes babies."

Now that all his brothers were married with children, Darius moved into Mother's house in Tehran, and seasons passed. He became a member of Tudeh, the Iranian communist party; attended its meetings faithfully, organized its debates, and then abandoned it when he realized just how subservient the party leaders were to the USSR. He gathered a few friends around him and established the basis for a new party that had similar beliefs to Mohammad Mossadegh. He started a monthly cultural salon and started writing a massive novel in the vein of Dashiell Hammett's *Red Harvest*, which he'd discovered while he was living in Europe.

Brain firing on all cylinders, impatient to change the world, and desiring most of all to be left alone, Darius agreed to whatever Mother wanted. This was how she got him to agree to be married without realizing it. Then she went to the home of one of her brothers in Mazandaran and asked him for the hand of his youngest daughter, Guila, who was no beauty but was sufficiently docile to do as she was told. And anyway, Nour didn't have time to look outside the family circle for the pearl every mother dreams of for her son. She wanted to marry Darius off quickly, before he got permanently stuck in the quagmire he called *politics*. She was afraid that he would turn into one of those long-haired subversives who hide in forests and foment insurrections and assassinations; that he might be the next to volunteer to kill the Shah.[6]

So as not to scare him off, Mother kept Darius far away from the marriage preparations and didn't tell him the wedding date until only a week before the ceremony, as they sat at breakfast that morning. Darius nodded, lit a cigarette, and went back to his writing. Perplexed, Nour watched him walk away and turned to Bibi.

"Do you think he understood me?"

Bibi made a skeptical face and shrugged her shoulders.

"Who knows? He's as closed-off as a virgin's pussy!"

"Oh, those Sadrs . . . " Mother murmured, and let out a long sigh.

According to Uncle Number Two, on the day of the wedding, Darius stayed calm until midday. His customary silence didn't worry anyone. After lunch, occupied with the preparations for the evening, the family had dispersed, leaving him alone. At four-fifteen sharp, when Uncles Number One, Three, and Six came for him, to accompany him to the room where the marriage vows were to take place, Darius wasn't there. His wardrobe was empty. A letter had been left in plain sight, leaning against a copy of *The Brothers Karamazov*. Uncle Number One opened it and read it aloud. A whole sheet of paper for three measly sentences: *Tell Mother I can't. I'm leaving. I'll be in touch.* No apologies, and no regrets.

Darius had vanished again.

[6] I'll just remind you here that an attempt to assassinate Mohammad Reza Pahlavi took place on February 4, 1949, on his arrival at the tenth-anniversary celebrations for the University of Tehran. The Shah was struck with two bullets, one in the cheek and the other in the back, but no vital organs were hit. His would-be assassin, Nasser Fakhr-Araï, who was said to be both a member of Tudeh and close to the clergy, was killed on the spot. Following this incident, Tudeh was outlawed until 1950 and the Shah changed the Constitution to give himself more power at the expense of Parliament.

*

A few months later, on August 16, 1953, another flight shocked the country. The Shah courageously set off to spend a few days in Rome, leaving the CIA, in a joint operation with Britain's MI6, to carry out Operation Ajax and overturn Mossadegh's nationalist popular government. Today, these kinds of events don't shock us, but in the early 1950s, a coup d'état fomented by an America at the height of its anti-Soviet paranoia, and hoping to cement its strategic position in the region, was almost unbelievable. In just a few days, rioters disguised as communist militants plunged Tehran into terrible chaos. Targeted assassinations, murderous confrontations, violent protests. The streets were filled with fire and blood, and on August 19 a military unit entered the city and took control of it. Mossadegh was arrested and his house pillaged. In the wake of their victory, the Americans tightened their hold on Iranian oil and Nelson Rockefeller assured Eisenhower that: "We have total control of Iranian oil. Now, the Shah can't make a decision without consulting our ambassador." Ha ha! Whoever controls the oil controls the world, right? It's nothing personal, okay? It's just business!

Devastated by the gangster-movie scenario that had just unfolded in his country, Darius, who was now in Paris, was hesitant to go back. If he returned to Iran, sooner or later he would find himself back in Mother's clutches. He sent telegrams asking for news, but kept delaying his return.

Ultimately, he stayed in Paris for eleven years and earned a doctorate in philosophy from the Sorbonne. He published a six-page weekly in Persian and made an agreement with the news vendor on the Champs-Elysées, who sold it to Iranian students in exchange for a percentage. He lived at number 4, rue Huyghens in Montparnasse; made the café Le Gymnase on the corner of the Boulevard Raspail his office; met Sartre, Ionesco, Mauriac, and Beckett; attended a performance of *The Rite of Spring* choreographed by Béjart; watched a lot of American movies; followed Maria Casares down the street one day; played chess on Sunday afternoons in the Luxembourg Gardens; wrote an essay more than eight hundred pages long on communist dictatorship; caught head lice; lost his hair, and, of course, fell in love.

It was a photo that made him return to Tehran. A portrait of herself that Mother sent him and which Leïli still has; a rectangular black-and-white one with scalloped edges. Her hair tied back, two deep lines running from each side of her nose to the corners of her mouth, Nour has her head tilted slightly to the left and looks directly at the camera. Her heavy-lidded eyes are clear and deeply melancholic, like the flame of a candle which, flickering, realizes that it will soon go out. The back of the photo is completely covered with cramped handwriting. Over time, the black ink has faded to dark blue, and the letters have thickened, making little blobs. Only a few words are still legible, fragments of a love attempting to soften the beloved: . . . *for you to look at me . . . the days . . . without meaning to . . . grown older in your absence.*

That return marked the end of Darius's long disappearances from the country—but even so, for the rest of his life he'd hold onto the habit of running away. He vanished from dinner parties, leaving Sara to deal with the guests. He took off in the middle of political meetings and the telephone would ring abruptly in the middle of the night, warning us that he wasn't there. He'd go out to buy a pack of cigarettes and come home hours later. Part of him had always been an exile, alone even in the middle of a crowd. He gathered people around him, but excluded himself from the gathering. He was rational, but threw himself into difficult situations when others chose to tread more cautiously. In his war against routine, Darius was made for the hand-to-hand fights that no one wanted to have. Marriage wasn't part of the picture, and yet . . .

They were introduced in 1963 by Seroge Artavezian, an Armenian from Qazvin who was a longtime friend of Darius and a maths teacher at the high school where Sara Tadjamol taught history and geography.

Seroge had noticed this girl, whose mother was Armenian and whose body, slim and elongated, didn't match her face, which was as Eastern as a Safavid-era miniature. Sara Tadjamol was enthusiastic and playful, laughing heartily in the teacher's lounge and friendly with the school's entire staff. Seroge, a divorcé with a weightlifter's build and a nicotine-yellowed moustache, didn't dare to imagine that a girl like Sara would choose to spend an hour alone with him—but she might appreciate the elegance of his friend Darius, a journalist with the daily newspaper *Keyhan*, and so resolutely single that his friends had laid down several hundred tomans for whoever introduced him to a girl who could conquer his dissolute ways.

Seroge organized a dinner party with two other couples at Souren, a restaurant located in an opulent townhouse and frequented on a daily basis by Darius. Built by a Qajar prince who had fled Iran after the accession to power of Reza Shah, the place had been bought by two Armenian brothers from Isfahan who had turned it into an English-style club with a restaurant on the ground floor, an enormous smoking room, and a gaming room upstairs. Everyone knew Seroge's intentions that night—with the exception of Darius.

"Darius *Djan* [thirty-eight years old, dressed in a dark blue suit, white shirt, and mauve tie, hair slicked back, a large ink spot on the middle finger of his right hand], may I present Sara Tadjamol," said Seroge with enthusiasm. "Sara *Djan* [twenty-five years old, hounds tooth miniskirt and short-sleeved black cotton turtleneck, hair cut like *NathalieWoodi*], this is Darius."

They shook hands, looking one another directly in the eye—since they were exactly the same height (around five foot six).

Years later, when their children—fascinated as all kids are by
that incredible, elusive moment when their parents met—peppered them with questions, Darius said that he'd really liked her
legs (a feature to which he was always susceptible in women)
and the simplicity with which she ordered salad with her entrée.
Sara said that she'd always wanted to marry a bald man with
blue eyes. Darius wasn't yet bald then, but his expanse of forehead suggested that he would be, and fairly soon.

Of course, these brief explanations, marked as they were by
the prudishness of a generation of Persians a thousand leagues
removed from the sexual revolution, didn't really convey how
quickly they began to date: he, the dyed-in-the-wool bachelor,
and she, the young woman who had refused every one of the
suitors sent by the most experienced matchmakers in her family. Why did she agree to see him again? How did he get in
touch with her after that evening? What did they say to each
other? Still, they clearly liked each other, sitting there facing
each other, enveloped in the aroma of chicken *pakievski*, the
specialty of the house.

Thanks to modern science, we now know that attraction
between two people is partly due to a hormonal process that
starts the moment they meet. It's a complex process that owes
as much to molecular chemistry as to dozens of other manifes-
tations and projections that are as unconscious as they are real.
But we know without knowing. Part of the mystery remains,
and we can speculate about that endlessly. Did Darius's spirit
see in this young woman, whose eyes were as black as his were
blue, the one who would finally help him shed his middle-class
intellectual habits to become a revolutionary? A woman who
would stay by his side always and cross borders for him? Did
Sara's soul sense that this man would turn her life into a singular existence that would become the plot of a book—a book
that would be a bestseller in Tehran while its author smoldered
in exile? Maybe . . .

Later, when Sara suggested to Darius that he meet her mother and brothers (her father had died when she was a teenager), Darius heard once again the noise of the handcuffs snapping closed on his wrists, pinning his arms behind his back.

"I don't think there's any hurry. I can always meet them at the wedding."

And that is how, to avoid the horror of being formally introduced to the family, Darius Sadr jumped from the frying pan into the fire and proposed! Luckily, Sara had never been the kind of girl who dreamed of a spectacular proposal, with her lover down on one knee, hand pressed to his heart. Quite the opposite, actually. The fact that one of the most important events of her life, the one people had been preparing her for since childhood, around which so many stories had been spun, took place in a car on Avenue Roosevelt, in front of the home of Seroge Artavezian, as they waited for him to join them for dinner, was in perfect agreement with what she wanted out of life. Behind the surprise she felt was the exhilarating sensation of finding herself suddenly on the crest of modernity. Of being existentialist. SimonedeBeauvoirian. No; she wasn't the type of girl to dream of a romantic proposal—but she wasn't going to pretend like she hadn't heard anything, either.

"Okay, then please send your brothers to see my family (read: send your brothers, who I still haven't met, to ask my mother for my hand in marriage)."

"Sounds like a good idea," agreed Darius.

Six weeks later they were married. Seroge Artavezian, who was just inches from winning the bet of the year, spent the night before the wedding at Darius's. The next day he didn't leave his side for a second, and went with him in the late afternoon to Uncle Number Two's house, where the ceremony was set to take place. Saddeq had taken care of the arrangements so he could sweep Mother out through the garden gate and avoid the possibility that she would be humiliated again if *Monsieur Le Phénomène* (pronounced *Mohsio Loh Fenohman*) decided to pull another disappearing act. After the ceremony, Darius, who had refused dinner or a party, took Sara to dine with him alone at a delicatessen that had recently opened in the city center.

And so, the most modern couple in the family was born.

With my unfailing punctuality—a compulsion inherited from Sara that was obsessive and not always advantageous—I arrived at the secretary's office this morning at nine twenty-five precisely, five minutes before the meeting time. I'd spent the preceding half-hour in the cafeteria near the hospital entrance, drinking a coffee and flipping through the newspaper I bought at the kiosk near the stop for the 91 bus. At nine-twenty I left the paper on the Formica counter and headed for the scaffolding-enclosed building at the far end of a car-filled driveway. Once again, there wasn't a single construction worker in sight. At this rate, the work might never be finished.

After updating my file and ticking a few boxes on the computer, the secretary handed me a piece of paper and told me to go to CECOS (a French acronym meaning Center for the Study and Conservation of Human Eggs and Sperm) to get the vials of sperm. At my confused expression, she guessed that I didn't know how to get there and gave me directions. She undoubtedly—and logically—thought that I'd been there with Pierre when he donated his sperm. The thought that I didn't know where it was hadn't occurred to her.

CECOS is located in the basement of the main hospital building, the entrance of which is located on Boulevard du Port-Royal. It's a huge place, glaring with neon light and furnished like the lobby of an employment office. Except for the posters inviting people to donate reproductive cells, you'd never know that behind these walls, every single day, white-coated specialists collect, triturate, package, refrigerate, index, and warehouse sperm and egg cells destined to be implanted in the warm cavern of a woman's uterus in order to transform, in the best-case scenario, into human life.

While a nurse checks my passport, Pierre's identity card, and the proxy he signed authorizing me to pick up the vials of his sperm, I look at the posters. "Give hope—DONATE EGGS," reads one of them over a background of portraits of several women of various races, laid out like a mosaic. Another one shows a young couple in profile, holding hands: "A baby is the greatest demonstration of love that Patrick could give his Éléonore—SPERM DONATION." And the same couple, this time facing each other: "Want to donate sperm to them? Nothing could be simpler!" Who are these slogans meant to be addressing? I can't imagine there are many curious people coming to tour CECOS in the evening after work, or on a Saturday afternoon to relax. The people brought here every day by sterility or illness would probably prefer movie posters or reproductions of fine art, to help them forget about their own organs for a while.

I say *probably* because, what do I know? I'm not in their shoes.

Pierre sent me a text last night to tell me he wouldn't be here today. He had to go with a colleague to a difficult work site outside Paris. *I'll leave proxy and ID in your mailbox early tomorrow morning. If there were any other way I'd be there, believe me. Good luck. P*

To tell the truth, I was relieved. I had no desire for him to come. I've always preferred to go through life's pivotal moments alone (the word "ordeal" seems really pompous to me all of a sudden, even though it's the right one). Sensing sympathy or compassion bothers me deeply because I feel—maybe wrongly—like I have to pretend to feel emotions that

I'm not feeling. That's one of the reasons why marriage is beyond my capabilities.

I waited for about forty minutes before the same nurse called my name and gave me a tube similar to the one photo labs use for large prints. I'd never thought about the way the sperm, washed and defrosted (let me just say again how incredible the whole thing still seems to me), would be given to me. The tube was discreet; I could have walked around with it for hours and no one would have given it a second look. Those of you who crossed paths with me this morning at around ten forty-five, crossing the Boulevard du Port-Royal and then the Rue Saint-Jacques, would probably have assumed I was a professional photographer. Teenagers attracted to the exciting life of artists might even have envied me, just like I used to envy the guys in black standing behind the mixing desks in the concert venues I've been haunting since I was a kid.

5
LE VAGIN, *AND* OTHER INNOVATIONS

Sometimes, in the middle of Parisian crowds, sitting in a café or on a folding seat on the metro, in a century driven by technology and machines, I catch myself thinking about how my grandmother was born in an *andarouni* and took her first breath while being held over a clay basin. I'm the granddaughter of a woman born in a harem. My life started back there, in the midst of that beehive of wives ready to kill each other for the chance to be the one chosen to spend the night with the Khan. There, at the moment when Death and Life violently collided, propelled by an insane wind blowing from the Russian steppes, amid the screams and the blood and the brutalized innards of a fifteen-year-old girl, and the tiny bodies of two motherless babies wrapped in white cloth and presented to Montazemolmolk, who had chosen so many women what was another, who destroyed this one's childhood with one blow. There, on the prosperous earth of Mazandaran, bordered by an immense lake, a hyphen between two countries, reduced to shreds today but which were once great empires. A lake descended from an ancient ocean, the Paratethys; a lake so large that people call it a sea. The Caspian. Complex and teeming with fish, and of a blue that insinuated itself into the eyes of a generation, and then was distilled into the next (actually, Caspian would be a nice name for a little girl . . .).

After so much time and distance, it's not their world that flows in my veins anymore, or their languages or traditions or beliefs, or even their fears, but their stories. If I'm the one who remembers Uncle Number Two's stories and the conversations with Bibi best, if I'm the one who has brought them across borders like hidden treasures, reciting them to myself at night long after we'd left Iran so I wouldn't forget them, lying on a mattress at the foot of the sofa-bed where Leïli and Mina were sleeping, if I've tried to preserve them and even if I've failed, and let them sink down into the recesses of my memory, and if I'm the one who keeps trying to unearth them again, maybe it's because it was once written somewhere that one day I would be alone in a hospital under construction in *Pahrees*, 2,643 miles from Mazandaran, with a tube of sperm in my lap.

After Leïli was born, Darius decided that he didn't want any more children.

Wait, no. That's not how I should start.

I should start like this: Darius had never wanted children. Only after he'd realized that, for the woman he'd married, marriage had no point other than parturition, did he consent to have one.

Leïli's birth, eleven months after their marriage, showed him that he could feel joy at being a father. Since he wasn't the kind of man to let his wife do all the work, he changed diapers, got up at night with the baby, and cooked homemade apple-sauce. He reveled in watching his daughter get bigger and learn to walk; rejoiced at hearing her say her first words, which became sentences, and then questions. If I had to make a comparison to help describe Darius's attitude toward paternity, I would say that it was like one of those big carnival rides the crowd loves at the *Foire du Trône* (*Luna Park* for Iranians). You have no real desire to ride at first, but your friends drag you along, and you give in, and you come off it afterward pretty enthusiastic, like, *okay, I was wrong, that was worth doing.* That doesn't necessarily mean you want to ride it again.

And besides, if you were Darius Sadr, there were other, more stimulating attractions all around you, calling your name. The Vietnam War and the intensification of bombardments in the North; the re-election of Nasser and the violent crackdowns on the Muslim Brotherhood and, in Iran, nothing less than the assassination of Prime Minister Hassan Ali Mansour in front of Parliament and the accession to power of "the man with the pipe," Amir Abbas Hoveyda.

Sara stood firm. Leïli had just turned fifteen months old, and the desire for another child was becoming an obsession. Her counter-attack intensified in the form of daily monologues.

Every morning when, immediately after appearing at the breakfast table, Darius's face disappeared behind the newspaper, or a copy of *Le Nouvel Observateur*, which he ordered from Paris, Sara launched into one of her emotion-filled tirades. It hardly mattered that Darius didn't respond to them, or—at best—threw her a glance accompanied by a mocking half-smile, relegating her desire for a second child to an endearing whim or a pipe-dream which, of course, women had from time to time, but frankly, if they stopped to think for two minutes together, would never last. It didn't even matter that he ignored her completely. She kept on.

For whole weeks, Sara's arguments battered against Darius's obstinate silence—until the morning of January 20, 1966. Have a good look at the black-and-white photo in that day's edition of *Keyhan*, and imagine it in place of Darius's face: a picture of an authoritative woman, a dark-skinned widow with a tight smile and hair marked by the most famous white streak of the twentieth century.

On that morning, far from snow-covered Tehran, Indira Gandhi began her first day as prime minister of the country that had kicked the English out and sent them back home. A female prime minister leading a country with a population of almost five hundred million! A remarkable event! Unprecedented!

The Historic and the Domestic blurred into one another, and Darius lowered his newspaper with a jerk. He fixed Sara with a dark gaze.

"Why do you want another child? Indira Gandhi is an only child, you know!"

Every time my mother told this story, she would laugh uproariously. Tears streamed down her face, and her words came out in strangled gasps. Her friends would laugh along with her at the thought of the crookedness of men, who would use any expedient to confuse their wives and get their own way. But Sara's laughter was different, marked not by the original fatality that dominates male/female relationships, but by amused tenderness. No one but Sara understood the adorable subtlety of Darius's statement. The layer of hope, hidden beneath bad faith, which said: *is it possible that we've created the next Indira Gandhi?* And if Lëili stopped being an only child, would it ruin her future—and Iran's along with it? And, just beneath that, another layer, tinged with selfishness and a hint of warning: *I'm not Jawaharlal Nehru, the illustrious father of Indira—yet—but I need all my energy to become him, and what I certainly don't need is another child!*

So, while Indira organized her Green Revolution, to free her country from the yoke of foreign powers and guarantee its self-sufficiency in food, Sara decided that she would also have to work for her own independence.

Since, as with every man, nature had only assigned him a jump seat in the back of the reproductive train, and the business was out of his hands, Darius took no interest in the second pregnancy. At about the same time as Sara's belly began to grow bigger, he was made columnist at *Keyhan* and his days at the office got longer. He also began writing an essay on

Palestine and Israel ("that Western enclave in the East," as he called it). It was the outside world that set the tempo for his life.

Sometimes in the middle of the night, when Sara brought him a cup of coffee, dark circles under her eyes and each day more round-bellied than the one before, Darius pretended not to notice. She clung to the advice that her brother-in-law, Uncle Number One, had taken her aside to impart on the day before her wedding. "Darius is a wild stallion. It takes stubbornness and courage to take him, but once he's gentled, you'll see, I hope, that he's wonderfully loyal." Sara had wondered at the time about the *"you'll see, I hope"* part of it. What did that mean? Was her marriage going to end in divorce? When she got to know Uncle Number One better, she realized that his obsessive honesty often resulted in tactlessness. But the advice he had given her still came in handy when she worried about Darius's indifference and disinterest in his child, to whom she often talked about its father—just so the baby would know it had one.

Night after night, month after month, sitting at the living room table with an unfiltered Camel between his fingers, Darius filled countless pages with his pen (a Pentel, which had only recently become available in Iran). At the same time, in their bedroom, Sara, pale and nauseated, struggled in silence with the vagaries of her pregnancy. 1967 was such an eventful year that Darius rarely came to bed before dawn. The bombardment of Hanoi, the Six-Day War, the death of Che Guevara, Nicolai Ceausescu's election to the presidency of the Council of State in Romania, the war in Biafra, the Kurdish revolt in Iran, the death of Mossadegh in exile in Ahmadabad . . .

When she learned the news of Mossadegh's death, Sara spent the day of March fifth in tears, both for the man and for the country that had lost him. Then she went to see her mother, who was the same size as she was without being pregnant, to borrow a black dress. On March sixth, 1967, Sara arrived at the high school in mourning dress. The students clustered around here. "MyGod, MyGod, who is dead, Sara *Djan?*"

"Mossadegh," she answered, as if it were obvious. The Great Man was the subject of her class that day; she discussed the nationalization of oil and the coup d'état organized by the Americans and the British, and the sham trial which Mossadegh attended in pajamas as a sign of protest, and after which he was condemned to spend the rest of his life under house arrest in Ahmadabad, under constant surveillance by SAVAK. At the end of the day Sara went home.

That evening, as she was giving Leïli her dinner, the telephone rang. She picked up. A man's voice said, without preamble: "If you repeat your circus act tomorrow, we're going to have to do something about you."

"I teach history," Sara responded, her heart pounding.

"And if you want to keep doing it, and then going peacefully home and feeding your daughter, be very careful what you teach!"

The man hung up.

The premature birth of Mina on the afternoon of October 25, 1967 rescued Darius from a dilemma that had been tormenting him for weeks: write what he thought about the grotesque and ruinous coronation and get fired from his job at the newspaper, or resign.

The next day, a Thursday, marked the coronation of Mohammad Reza Pahlavi and his wife Farah Diba. Twenty-five years after succeeding his father Reza Shah, the King had figured it was time to shift into high-gear megalomania and become, on the same day as his birthday, *Shahanshah*. King of

Kings. And not only *Shahanshah*, but also *Aryamehr*, Sun of the Aryans. *Shahanshahé Aryamehr*.

For the past month, as the warm autumn sun shone down, Tehran had been preparing for the festivities. Scrubbed clean and dolled up, cleared of its beggars at red lights, its street-peddlers and stray dogs and neuralgic traffic jams, the city resembled a middle-aged woman made up like a whore for a wedding; the ornamentation serving only to reveal the terrifying ugliness that was usually hidden beneath chaos and dirt. Policemen and soldiers stood on every street corner, watching manfully to ensure that order was maintained, twirling their truncheons in the fear-thickened air. In the overloaded class-rooms, students were taught a new song—the Coronation Hymn—before each day's lessons began. Every morning, lined up facing the flag, chins high and arms held stiffly at their sides, countless little Persians recited with passion: *Long live our Emperor, without whom the country has no future. God grant him eternal life!*

If you saw the black-and-white images transmitted from the other side of the world on your TV screens, you couldn't have missed the huge portraits of the Shah, his wife, and their eldest son, the Crown Prince, surrounded by garlands of light and multiplying into infinity along Tehran's main streets. You might have thought to yourself that the studied smiles had more to do with terror than love. Maybe you didn't sense grandeur, but rather the artificial construction of a myth; an overblown attempt to equal Cyrus the Great, the conquering founder of the Persian Empire. You might have laughed, remembering similar portraits of Stalin or Mussolini—the same bulging torso, the same super-humanity. *Ha ha, those ridiculous Iranians, still stuck in the '40s!* You couldn't possibly have missed the giant replica of the imperial crown erected on an enormous platform; the Tehranis as tiny as Lego figures at its base, with their noses pointed skyward, seeming not to understand what was happening to them. And there, at the very bottom of the screen, in the midst of all the cars, you might have been surprised at the sight of a taxi racing toward the north of the city, anxious to unload its bulky cargo as soon as possible. Panicky and nervous, the driver had taken care to close all the windows—but if the camera could have slipped inside and lingered on Sara Sadr, slumped in the back seat, her breath coming in gasps and her chest puffed out as high as Mount Damavand, you would have heard her, as clearly as the poor driver, who was imploring the Almighty to knock this crazy woman unconscious before she brought him any more trouble—you would have heard her unleashing a string of insults in the direction of that grotesque crown. The kind of insults that fly down the narrow and notorious back streets of Tehran's working-class neighborhoods, slippery as spittle, sharp and fiery as the blade slashing her innards.

Half an hour earlier, Sara's water had broken in the middle of the living room. She was just entering her eighth month and, despite her surprise, she had taken her time, calling a taxi and putting Leïli in the care of a neighbor woman—and refusing, despite his insistence that she do so, to alert Darius.

At the same time, Darius was shut up in his office, staring at a blank page and chain-smoking. Article or resignation? Resignation or article? He couldn't make a decision. Neither would save him from permanent surveillance by SAVAK—or the inevitable arrest on some trumped-up charge, followed by torture and certain death. That fate, which had befallen some of his *mossadeghi* friends, could not be his; he had something more important to accomplish first. What? He didn't know yet, but it was like . . . like a gunshot. An uppercut. A grenade poised in the putrid, repressive air. He could feel it in his muscles, in his eyelids, which ached with lack of sleep. If he, the black sheep of two horrendously rich families, raised among people who cared nothing for the future, crammed with book-learning, a doctor of philosophy from the Sorbonne, didn't do it—didn't tear down the Empire's insolent red curtain to reveal the nauseating infection beneath—then who would?

He chewed over these thoughts, which had been brewing in his head for some time. He remembered that morning, when his reflection in the bathroom mirror had looked strangely mature. Of course, he had aged; his forties had set in and left their marks and lines here and there, but this was something else. He exuded a remarkable impression: a solidity, a confidence, a will from within. As if he were finally ready to assume true manhood. Now, sitting at his desk, not knowing what to do—article or resignation?—he wondered if he shouldn't let his beard grow in, alongside the mustache he already sported, to mark this new phase of his life. He was deep in consideration of this new question when the telephone rang.

When Sara arrived at the hospital, she was immediately taken into the delivery room.

She must have been the first woman in all of Tehran to come through the door of the Aban Hospital's obstetrics department alone. All the others arrived in the middle of a frenzied mob that grasped their elbows, mopped their brows, carried overnight bags—to the accompaniment of a cacophony of arguments over the baby's first name, the date of circumcision, and the number of guests. The modern world and the fear of death had replaced the basin of the old days, but the comedy of labor and delivery remained the same. The child was doomed to be born in the middle of its tribe, amid its quarrels, its love and neurosis, so it would know from the very start how things were going to be.

Sara's solitary state intrigued the nurses. Was she a widow? Had she run away? Had she survived some sort of disaster? They found two telephone numbers in her file. Next to one of them, her obstetrician, Dr. Mohadjer, had written "home" in his sinusoidal handwriting. The other one had no designation. The nurses chose the gentlest, most diplomatic one among them to make the call. No one answered at "home," so they tried the other number.

The ringing of the telephone smashed into the smoky silence of Darius's office like an axe. He jumped. All his musings vanished into the air and were sucked in by the infuriating noise. Exhausted and muttering to himself, he picked up the phone.

"Hello?"

"Hello, Sir."

"Hello, Madam."

"Tell me . . . do you know Sara Sadr?"

"Yes, she's my wife. What's going on?"

"She's in labor, Sir. She's all alone. No offence, Sir, but that just isn't done . . . "

Pulled from the turbulent waters of his inner conflict, Darius abandoned the blank sheet of paper, pulled his jacket from the coat-rack, and ran for the door. "My wife's in labor! One of you will have to write tomorrow's editorial!"

Now listen to the galloping of the wild stallion, who, as Uncle Number One had predicted, is starting to slow down. Here's Darius arriving at the maternity ward well after the battle was won, pressing his nose to the window of the nursery reserved for baby girls. Surprised and overwhelmed, he sees his second daughter, Mina, who is wrapped in a white blanket and surrounded by a dozen tiny Farahs who will never have any doubt about the origin of their first name. Darius stares at her and smiles, and thanks her in his head. He didn't want her, and now she's saved his skin. She's his guardian angel. Eleven years later, when Mina saves his life once again, this time by vomiting on a soldier whose gun is pointed at his temple, Darius will think back to this afternoon.

The next day, while Sara, Darius, and Leïli leaned over

Mina's cradle and commented tenderly on the shape of the baby's ears, nose, mouth, and chin, looking for family resemblances, the Shah, with Napoleonic pomp, crowned himself at the palace of Golestan. Then he seized the crown created by Van Cleef & Arpels with jewels from the Persian imperial treasury and placed it on the head of his wife as she knelt at his feet. Once the crowns were on the heads, the newly-imperial posteriors installed themselves next to one another on the Peacock Throne. One hundred and one cannon blasts were fired to herald the start of a new era, and, to remind everyone of God's presence amidst all this decadence, the chants of muezzins rose from every minaret in the city.

The festivities came to an end. The foreign journalists left the city, not to return until four years later, in October 1971, on the occasion of the even more grandiose and ruinous celebrations of Persepolis, with their Hollywood allure. Beggars and dogs took to the streets once more. Life resumed its course. Spring chased away the memories of winter. Seasons passed, and then years. Richard Nixon became the thirty-seventh President of the United States; Neil Armstrong walked on the moon; France mourned General de Gaulle. Darius Sadr's essay, entitled *The Arabs and Israel*, was censored and banned from the market. Sara Sadr was summoned to the National Ministry of Education and reprimanded. The reason: a reading of Miguel Angel Asturias's *Mister President* in her class. The inspector made a note in her file that at the next instance of insubordination, her teaching duties would be taken away and she would be transferred to an administrative role. Which is exactly what happened, a few years later. All of these events, and many others, were recorded in detail in the two diaries that Sara wrote for her daughters; two notebooks that she filled alternately on some evenings, after she finished grading papers.

Leïli is six years old now, and Mina is four. They have light chestnut-brown hair, the color of barely-ripe dates. Leïli's eyes, which were green at birth, have turned hazel, while Mina's are a just a bit darker. They look like their mother: heart-shaped faces, rosebud mouths, little humps on the bridge of their noses. Leïli, who is terrifyingly intelligent, can recite poetry by Khayyam and Rumi and beat her father at chess. Mina, who is much less gifted, admires her silently and envies her in bursts of tears.

Darius has let his beard grow. He trims it like Trotsky's, and its light color is a reminder of his former blondness. Along with his blue eyes, the beard makes him look like a foreigner, a European or American intellectual visiting the East. In the evenings, when he stops to buy fresh almonds from the street vendors, they toss English words at him with the joyous ease of a show-off looking for a tip. *How much, mister? Very fresh!* Darius loves to watch for the expressions of surprise on their faces when he answers them in Persian.

"*Irani?!?*"

"*Irani!*" Darius grins, savoring the moment.

It's as if some impenetrable barrier has been breached. Suddenly, the street vendors stop being social outcasts in an inegalitarian society, who come from the shantytowns in the south of the city and have been on their feet all day, their skin leathery from the sun and the cold, who will grovel for a few pennies, and turn in the span of a few seconds into citizens just like Darius, who speak the same language he does. Darius lingers, and they exchange a few words, interspersed with smiles and amused face-pulling. The groveling inevitably comes, and the spell breaks, when he gestures to them that it's fine; they can keep the change.

Getting into his car, the paper cone of fresh almonds damp in his hand, Darius thinks about social contracts, public housing and family allowances. His mind wanders to France, with its democracy and social welfare services. The Shah has had a laugh at the world's expense with his White Revolution,[7] which consisted of bursts of publicity and self-congratulations while oil money was misappropriated in the millions. What a fraud; what a hoax! Trying to westernize a society forged in misery and oppression is just another bunch of bullshit from the corridors of the palace; just so much fairy dust sprinkled from its balconies to put on a show. Justice and equality, safety and trust are the real modernizers, Darius is certain of it. No need for a White Revolution with all its solemn speeches. Who would go and pray at the mosque when their child gets sick if they have national health and a hospital nearby? Who would clutch the hems of the mullahs' robes if they have a government that listens to them? Who would allow the theft of oil money by the ton if there is universal suffrage? Oh, but no one wants a democracy. For now, what makes the Shah tick is the continuation of his authoritarian policies, the creation of the most powerful army in the Middle East, and getting spoiled by the Americans, who are thrilled to see their munitions factories bouncing back after the post-Vietnam depression and to count the money as it rolls in. To each his own way of groveling.

In October 1970, the Sadr family moved into one of the first functional, modern apartment complexes designed for the upper middle class and built near the city center. The place had been baptized with the incongruous name of *Mehr*, Affection. There were three four-storey buildings, separated by

---

[7] The name given to a series of reforms undertaken by the Shah in 1963 and encouraged by the United States as a way to modernize Iran and turn it into an economic and military power. The positive effects of some of the reforms—literacy and the right to vote for women—were soon counterbalanced by other phenomena: poverty, rural exodus, and inflation, but above all corruption, repression, privileges granted to American military advisors, and the absence of democracy. The White Revolution had numerous opponents, including the Shiite clergy. The leader of this religious opposition, Ruhollah Khomeini, was arrested in 1964 and sent into exile.

two large courtyards. Every apartment had a balcony and its own parking place; the ones on the ground level also had small gardens. At that time, only a few of them had found buyers.

Since they had decided to leave their fifth-floor rental apartment and buy one with an extra room for Mina, Sara had visited *Mehr* several times. She was still torn between the apartments on the top floor (pros: quiet and light-filled; con: stairs) and the ones on the ground floor (pro: garden; cons: noisy, and with a bay window that overlooked the street). Unable to make a decision, she asked Darius to go with her one day.

"Sara, for God's sake, make up your own mind! You're a free and independent woman, fully capable of choosing which apartment you want to live in."

"If I could do that, do you think I'd be asking you to come with me?"

Darius remained obstinately silent for the entire visit, which lasted more than two hours, but there was no escaping Sara's interrogation once they were alone together in the courtyard.

"Are you planning to say something, or not?"

"What do you want me to say?"

"Which one you prefer, Darius *Djan*; isn't that why we're here?"

"I don't know. Let's take the one on the fourth floor," he suggested.

"Which means the girls will end up with downstairs neighbors again, and won't be able to run around without disturbing them."

"Okay, then the one on the ground floor."

"But if someone decides to rob the building we'll be the first apartment they hit; you do realize that, right?"

"We won't be the only ones on the ground floor."

"But it only takes once, you know!"

They would have gone on like that for hours, Darius

impatient and Sara persistent, if a young woman with light brown hair and green eyes, a bag of groceries in one hand, hadn't overheard their conversation.

"We live on the ground floor." Darius and Sara turned to look at her. "I don't know if anyone's told you, but there's a watchman who lives in the third building. He makes the rounds twice a night and locks the main entry gate. Oh—sorry, I haven't introduced myself. I'm Mina. Mina Nasr."

"Mina! Just like our daughter!" exclaimed Sara. "We have two girls, Leïli and Mina."

"I have a daughter too, Marjane. She just turned seven."

"Leïli's seven too! Which number is your flat?"

"Seventeen."

"Then we'll take number eighteen," Sara decided.

If something as powerful and unexplainable as friendship at first sight exists, it had just happened between Sara Sadr and Mina Nasr (who quickly became Big Mina, to differentiate her from Little Mina). I'll leave Sara and Big Mina to carry on their conversation now, under Darius's relieved gaze, and tell you a little bit about the friendship between the Sadrs and the Nasrs.

Big Mina was (and still is) married to Ramin, an electronic engineer wild about technology and gadgets, as scientific as Darius was intellectual. The years went by, more children were born, and the two families became so close that they basically merged into a single unit. They spent most of their evenings together, either with the adults going to dinner and a movie as a foursome, or with the children. Gradually they invited other neighbors into their circle as well, forming a tight-knit, chaotic, noisy little community.[8]

---

[8] To make an analogy that might help you visualise the general atmosphere, let me say that *Mehr* was kind of like Wisteria Lane on *Desperate Housewives*, only with fewer murders—but with the Revolution added into the final season on top of everything else.

Ramin invented a system that made it so the front doors of the two apartments could be opened from both the inside and the outside, so that the children could go in and out without having to ring the bell. The children had the comforting sense of having two mothers and two fathers: one brunette mother, Sara, who worked and knew how to console and to listen; and another, who varied between chestnut, blonde, and sometimes red hair, Big Mina, who didn't work and who organized games and enormous afternoon snacks. The parallel between Darius and Ramin was less obvious, but Darius relied on Ramin to handle most things having to do with everyday life: tying shoelaces, understanding math and physics homework, fixing things, inflating bicycle tires. With his love of films and TV, it was mostly in the evenings that Darius spent time with the children. He sat with them in front of the television, watching old American movies from the 1950s—westerns, *Columbo, Rich Man, Poor Man*—and told them anecdotes about the actors, even the most obscure ones, whose filmographies he always knew. Now, I can imagine your surprised expressions: *wait, Iranians watched Columbo?* Just think about it: from the moment the United States rests one authoritative hand on a country's politics, with the other hand it loads the people with all sorts of military, industrial, cultural, and food products. Imperialism is no joke! Not only did Iranians watch *Columbo*, they also watched *Bewitched, Little House on the Prairie, Peyton Place* (completely unknown to the French), and *Days of our Lives* (ditto). They also picked up CBS on their TV sets, drank Coca-Cola, ate KFC, drove Chevrolets, and fucked on Simmons Beautyrest mattresses.

By the mid-1970s, the bonds of friendship were so tightly knotted between the Nasrs and the Sadrs that they withstood the events that rocked that decade.

One memorable spring, Ramin returned from a conference in London with a strange, intriguing device capable of reading films that were reduced to smooth strips and wound inside big cassette tapes. The VCR. He connected the machine to their TV monitor and then spent the afternoon cobbling together the sophisticated system he'd come up with on the plane: pulling a cord out of the device, running it along the brick wall that separated their apartment from the Sadrs,' and connecting it to the Sadrs' TV so that both families could watch the movie at the same time.

That evening, after dinner at the Nasrs', Ramin asked the Sadrs to go home and turn on the television. Then they gathered the children in the living room and explained that if they went to bed and fell asleep right away, he would let them watch *The Sound of Music* on a loop all the next day.

Thirty minutes later, in a simultaneous movement, Sara and Big Mina turned out the children's bedroom lights and then the lights in the corridor, and went into their respective living rooms. Each of them approached her husband, who was seated comfortably on the sofa, a glass of whisky in his hand. From the TV screen came the sound of soft piano music. The film had started.

Wide shots, images of Paris, a sunny morning. Now the camera pans over the rooftops (Sara's heart clenched with love for the city, and Darius smiled, recognizing Montmartre); glides along a building, and stops at a window. Cut to the same window, seen from the inside. A woman with short hair and immense blue eyes, dressed in a negligee, walks away from the window back into her room. Above her bed is a large black-and-white photograph of a nude woman curled up (both couples flinch slightly). Now a medium shot of the woman, who bounds the stairs and enters a living room bathed in golden light. As she flips through her mail, the title of the film appears in yellow letters, in a rounded and unusual font: *Emmanuelle.*

All the next day, troubled and uncomfortable, as shaken up as if they were hung over, Sara and Big Mina avoided each other. Neither of them had any idea how to address what had happened the previous evening: the film, the continuation of its effects into the bedroom, the certainty that on the other side of the wall, at the very same time . . .

The day after that, they acted as if everything were normal, meeting for a cup of tea after breakfast and chit-chatting about nothing in particular. But their way of speaking and interacting had changed. They were at once closer to and more distant from one another; less familiar and more intimate. Bound together forever by a secret as senseless as a crime.

During the years that followed, the Revolutionary years, the Nasrs continued to serve as the wall against which the Sadrs braced themselves to keep from falling. In late July 1980, one month before the start of the Iran-Iraq War and the bombardment of Mehrabad Airport by the Iraqi army, the Nasrs emigrated to the United States, leaving the Sadrs to face the ravaging storm of the new decade alone.

End of flash-forward. Back to the Sadrs' move to *Mehr*.

Three bedrooms, a small kitchen, a living room-dining room combination with large French doors opening onto a balcony. Across from the balcony, the small garden. And, thank God, a hall bathroom for guests and another for the family. Even under normal circumstances, Sara hated sharing her bathroom with strangers, but for a while now she had been finding the slightest odors unbearable. No one knew it yet, but she was at least four weeks pregnant.

This time—though Indira had just been re-elected to her position with an absolute majority, combining the ministerial portfolios of the Interior, Information, and Energy—Sara hadn't even bothered speaking to Darius about it.

He learned about his wife's third pregnancy at Le Fumoir, a club reserved exclusively for men. He went there on the first Thursday of every month, in the company of doctor friends he'd met during his younger years in Paris.

One of them, Doctor Farzin Mohadjer, who had a French wife, was the best-known gynecologist—and the best-known womanizer—in Tehran. He had pursued Sara, as was common knowledge, as well as Big Mina, the wives of all his friends, and virtually every other upper-middle-class woman in the country. Other than the degrees he'd earned in France, which had guaranteed him a solid reputation once back in Iran, the thing that had made him famous was his use of the French word *vagin* to designate that intimate part of the female anatomy that Persians, prudish and reserved, never mentioned by name. While still preserving its marshy mystery, the distance created by the language had endowed the Secret Organ with a scientific aura that had miraculously eliminated the ancient prohibition. Relieved of the crude and nauseating vulgarity with which it was plagued when spoken of in Persian, it was now free to resurface, and exist.

And that's how the word *vagin*—along with its Persian variants *vâjan*, *vâdjan*, and *vadjin*—made its remarkable entry into the vocabulary of Iranians and became a fashionable word. It quickly spread beyond the boundaries of the upper class to reach the middle class and even below. Saying it gave one the exotic, gratifying feeling of being European—in other words, erudite, elegant, and modern all at once. God knows why, but it gave people the same kind of pleasure as pronouncing the name of Yves Saint-Laurent (or rather *Eev San Lohren*).

With their mouths full of pastry and saffron pistachios, women talked to each other about their *vagin*; first giggling and blushing, and then more naturally and easily. They confided in each other, giving details of size and flexibility, clucking over the damage caused by successive births. Little by little, gaining assurance, they edged toward clandestine waters, revealing the ways in which *le vagin* reacted, what it preferred, expected, hoped for—all with the gravity of intellectuals expressing appreciation of the possibilities of a perfectible material. But for as much as they discussed their *vagins*, keeping the husbands and their equipment out of it for the sake of decorum, they never talked about their *sexuality*, you see. They were careful to stay in the grey area of empirical observation, miles away from their own marriages and the nocturnal sweatiness of their bedrooms, where they could be free without risk of rumors or dishonor. Practicing the Persian art of hypocrisy to perfection, they made sure that not a single breath of this libertarian wind reached the conservative ears of their husbands. Who knows what a man would be capable of, if he were to learn what goes on in the heads (and the libidos) of the women who live under his roof? Better to let them keep living their lives peacefully, in parallel as always, nestled in the comfortable certainty that they are in control of everything.

Let's listen in on a discussion between Darius and Uncle Number Three. It's Friday night, and the weekly meeting of the Sadrs is taking place at Uncle Number Five's house. Before I go any further, let me introduce you to Uncle Number Three.

Uncle Number Three was an anxious, unstable man, always stressed and prone to stomach problems. When he walked, he gave the impression that it was his head, and the dark magma boiling in it, that made his massive body move, rather than his feet. You might have said that he kept himself on a tight leash. He had enormous pale blue eyes, but his gaze always seemed to be turned inward, searching for something that was perpetually missing. At the family meetings he always sat on the very edge of his chair, his coat next to him. All of a sudden, sometimes even before dinner was served, he would stand up, mutter some formulaic niceties, and head for the front door. His wife and five children, helpless in the face of his abrupt change in mood, would follow him out. His odd attitudes were the butt of all kinds of silly jokes, but that was all. No one dared to really try to label of them, for fear of turning the whole thing into something truly serious. Leïli had ventured to use the term *lunatic*, but only in private conversation with Mina.

Darius had a special affection for the brother who preceded him, with whom he had shared more than he had with the others. Uncle Number Three was the only brother he called and socialized with outside of their weekly meetings, undoubtedly in an attempt to soothe the strange unhappiness that had been with him, according to Darius, since childhood.

On that Friday night, Darius joined Uncle Number Three in the garden, where he had been standing alone for some time. Wordlessly, Darius offered him a cigarette.

"You must know what it means—*vâdjan*," Uncle Number Three said, bluntly.

Astonished, Darius wondered if he'd heard his brother correctly. "What?"

"*Vâdjan* . . . or something like that."

"Where did you hear that word?"

"I walked in on a conversation between my daughters. Shirin was saying to her sisters, 'If your *vâdjan* is ready, it doesn't hurt at all.' [Sigh, followed by agitated head movements] I don't know what they were scheming about this time and frankly I don't care, but I'm afraid Saddeq will hear about it . . . "

Uncle Number Three was referring to the time that Uncle Number Two, on his way home after an evening out, had seen Shirin with a group of young people, gathered around some motorcycles. She was in the arms of a young man quite a bit older than her. To Uncle Number Two's overwrought way of thinking, "being in the arms of a young man in the street" was the exact same thing as "sleeping with a boy right there on the asphalt with all of humanity watching." The next day, Saddeq had called his brothers together and launched into a diatribe as lengthy as it was impassioned: the family's tarnished honor . . . the Sadrs humiliated . . . the laughing stock of Tehran . . . our position in society . . . etc. Conclusion: Uncle Number Three was required to put a stop to the affair, punish his daughter severely, and, if possible, find her a husband before it was too late. Too cowardly to contradict his brother, but also too disenchanted to confront his daughter, Uncle Number Three instructed one of his sons not to let his sister out of his sight.

Darius had too much respect for individual personal freedom to get involved in these things. In fact, he was actually quite happy to see Shirin's generation rebelling against their parents' foolishness and embarking on the adventure of life with a devil-may-care attitude—which led him to lie extravagantly to protect his niece:

"Don't worry, *vagin* just means that time of the month. Shirin must have been explaining the . . . you know, the physiological . . . transformation . . . to her sisters."

Uncle Number Three took a deep drag of his cigarette, still troubled. "I thought that time of the month was the *period*! That's what Mariam [his wife] has called it for ages!" *Period* was, of course, the other linguistic singularity introduced into the Persian language by Dr. Mohadjer.

"*Vagin, period*, they're the same thing, man. Same exact thing!" said Darius, laughing heartily.

Driving home, while we slept in the back seat, Darius was still laughing as he recounted the discussion to Sara.

On that first Thursday in November, delayed as usual by a delivery, Dr. Mohadjer, enveloped in his cashmere coat, arrived at Le Fumoir late. The other members of the group, warmed by Scottish whisky, a thick fug of smoke hanging over them, were huddled around the backgammon tables. Darius, confronted with an unlucky opponent, was riding high. He stroked his beard, took his time throwing the dice, joked, called for more drinks, laughed at his own luck. It was right in the middle of one of these prolonged belly-laughs that the doctor's hand clapped him on the back. "Congratulations, old man!" There was no need to say more. When Mohadjer congratulated a man like that, the machine was already in motion. Just like that, Darius's bubbling brain went flat. His laughter died away and he sat open-mouthed.

Silence fell around him. Everyone stared at his face with the strange impression that he had been put on pause. The phenomenon was so fascinating that each of them began channeling his inner doctor. The neurologist made an attempt at diagnosis only to be contradicted by the psychiatrist; the ear, nose, and throat specialist recalled a similar case involving a Jew in Shiraz and the cardiologist laid him prone on the floor. An ambulance was called and he was taken to the hospital.

Half an hour later, a panicked Sara rushed into the lobby of the Aban Hospital, where Mohadjer was waiting for her. Terrified, she had leapt into a taxi bare-footed, fully expecting to be greeted with news of a stroke. Denial was pointless. She would resign from her teaching job and stay with him as long as she had to. Never mind if her daughters were traumatized by seeing him suffer; he would die at home. She was thirty years old, only a year younger than her mother had been when she became a widow. It was just life; you accepted your fate, as her mother had accepted hers—with selflessness and dignity.

But Dr. Mohadjer's face, which was now swimming into focus in front of her, didn't seem too worried. There was no sign of catastrophe marking his attractive features. After two deliveries and dozens of consultations spent scrutinizing that face, trying to figure out what lay behind each of his expressions, each of his silences, the words he left unsaid, Sara knew it by heart. And there, beneath the glaring neon lights of the overcrowded lobby, as surreal as a movie set, she was sure that the slight twist to Mohadjer's mouth had to do more with an inconvenience—like the difficult digestion of an overly sour pickle—than with a serious concern.

"I'm sorry, Sara. I thought he knew you were pregnant."

His dark gaze held a hint of reproach—which he made sure she saw, because this was neither the time nor the place to talk about it aloud.

Darius's room was dark and respectfully silent, like a baby's room. Lying in bed, a Valium drip in his arm, Darius's eyes and mouth were closed.

Mortified, Sara sat down next to him and gently took his hand. When he woke up, she wouldn't avoid the discussion. Maybe even an argument. She deserved it. In eight years of marriage, they hadn't argued once.

Sara detested conflict. Exchanges that blew up. The yelling. Those treacherous noises that filtered through the walls, letting the neighbors know that everything wasn't all right in your household. You might think she was worried about her image, but it was nothing like that. Above all, she was afraid that, once the argument was over, they would never be able to get back to what they had before, that initial closeness. How could they go backward, sit together again on the sofa after the children had gone to bed, chatting and eating oranges sent from Mazandaran? How could they face the relatives when they went to the weekly Sadr family meetings; how would they just take their usual place as if nothing had happened? And, more than anything, how would they avoid another argument? So she always stopped herself before things began to heat up. Not at the edge of the precipice, but miles away from it, while she could still turn around and, if there was a mirror behind her, look at her reflection in it. She reminded herself at those times of a horse with nostrils flaring, sensing an obstacle, lowering its head and backing away. Years later, when Mina became a teenager, she would realize that this character trait, which she had always thought of as inner wisdom, was really a weakness that didn't help anyone.

Darius's fingers, the tips of which were ice-cold, moved

weakly in Sara's hand. She thought, wiping away tears, that if he could, he would jerk his hand away and point his index finger at her and order her to leave the room immediately. But she was surprised to feel his hand press hers slightly, with unexpected tenderness.

6

THE GODS OF GENETICS

The smell of hydrogen peroxide wafts over from a doctor crossing the hallway, and dissipates into the air, reminding me of sixth-grade biology class. The mirror of the microscope that I could never manage to tilt so that it reflected the tiny bulb's light onto the dark particles sandwiched between two slides stuck together with pearly liquid. I should mention that I basically slept through biology class, starting on day one. I was terrified, so I just disappeared inside my own body.

Things like biology classes were completely incomprehensible to me that year, the year we first arrived in France. I was confronted by a world that I could see and touch but didn't know how to talk about. There were so many words and names that I just didn't have. Flowers, trees, birds, reptiles, organs. The words you learn as you grow up in a country, the ones the language reserves for people who are immersed in it and denies to those who just dip their toes in every now and then. The words for Saturday-afternoon strolls and summer camps and weekends in the country. Words from peaceful lives, lives that belong to the people living them. I knew some of them in Persian, but even in my own language I didn't know most of them. Today, my vocabulary, which I ironically call "botanical," is probably at the level of a grade-school student—and a city-dwelling one at that. I haven't advanced very far at all. Out of laziness, undoubtedly. Or maybe to remind myself of that lost, wordless girl whose chalk-skinned teacher leaned over her shoulder to tilt the mirror with a rapidity that was both embarrassing and liberating.

This scar that runs across my vocabulary is my only concession to vanity; the only hint of resistance in my . . . efforts to integrate, let's call them. I use that expression for the sake of convenience, because it means something to you, even though, brought up on a steady diet of French culture since childhood, I don't really care what it conveys. Besides, since we're on the subject, I think it lacks both sincerity and openness. Because to really integrate into a culture, I can tell you that you have to *dis*integrate first, at least partially, from your own. You have to separate, detach, disassociate. No one who demands that immigrants make "an effort at integration" would dare look them in the face and ask them to start by making the necessary "effort at disintegration." They're asking people to stand atop the mountain without climbing up it first.

What's more, the concept takes me back immediately to my teenage years, and the music. To *Disintegration* (1989), The Cure's eighth album, brilliantly dark, whose lyrics—which I spent hours translating—were rescued by Robert Smith when his house burned, and to *Integration* (1990), a box set that included the four singles from that album.

The psychologist appears in the doorway and calls on a couple. She says the name in a kind of respectful murmur, as if she doesn't want to disturb the rest of us. We look up at her and she lets us look, indifferently, hands in the pockets of her wool cardigan, like she's used to it.

While the couple gathers up their things and moves to join her, the psychologist glances around the room and recognizes me. She smiles at me with pleasure, as if I were a star pupil whose presence here, with the tube in my lap, is partly due to her.

So, we've done it.

We've completely fooled everyone.

"Dr. Gautier isn't here yet," she says to me, "but it won't be too much longer."

Her voice is just as reassuring as I remember it. I nod and smile, as if to say "oh, it's not a problem, don't worry . . . " I presume I'd be within my rights to heave a couple of irritated sighs, but I can't control the affable, polite smile that springs to my lips. Anyone familiar with Iranians will know exactly which smile I'm talking about; they're as recognizable as an Isfahan carpet. If there is a God of Lies, Trickery, and Hypocrisy, he must be both Persian and extremely resilient, hiding in a corner of our brain, ready to jump up and remind us who we are and where we come from in case we ever sneakily try to forget. Even if I disintegrated myself one hundred percent and then integrated to the point that I seemed as French as Catherine Deneuve, believe me, it would still be there. I'll never be French enough for that full-face honesty, the demonstrative irritation, a well-placed "This sucks!" That stuff comes out when I'm at home, but as a kind of delayed reaction, dwelt on and amplified.

"Good luck," the psychologist says to me with a knowing smile, before following the couple out into the corridor.

I mouth a silent but sincere *thank you*.

Turning back to the rest of the room, I realize that everyone's looking at me. There it is; they've gotten it. I'm the day's winner, the one who has jumped over all the qualifying hurdles and will soon break through the pink or blue ribbon at the finish line. Now they know exactly what my life will entail over the next hours and days and weeks. Anxiety, waiting, the dangerous game of analyzing even the slightest physical symptom. No need to have experienced it, they'll just have googled it—not once, not just a quick spin on the Web, many, many times. There's no end of forums and discussions, often written in absolutely disastrous French, filled with an occasionally pornographic level of detail, on the post-insemination phase.

I shift uncomfortably in my seat and think of Anna, who must be on the bus bringing them—her and her group—back from Prague. I'm sure she's asleep. Yesterday on the telephone, I asked her not to call me. "I'll call you when it's done." "Okay," she'd replied. And I can count on Anna, who is emotionally the exact opposite of Sara, Leïli, and Mina, to keep her word.

As my companions retreat back into their shells, I get up quietly and head for the cafeteria.

We saw the psychologist in November, two months ago. We were actually supposed to have the meeting in May, but it had been postponed three times because of the construction and then it was summer vacation. In the meantime I'd had all the required medical testing done and we'd seen Doctor Gautier several times for her analysis of the results. Logically, the consultation with the psychologist should have been done before the testing. Her assessment of our solidity as a couple, the legitimacy of our desire to have a child, and our capacity to be parents were mandatory conditions for proceeding with the protocol. But, because of the accumulated delay, Dr. Gautier and the higher-ups had decided to do the process backwards.

In May, on Pierre's initiative, we'd drawn up a list of our tastes, flaws, skills, habits, fears, ambitions, and all the little things that made up our daily lives. Then we'd spent the whole afternoon at a café together, studying it. We were like two offenders-in-training meticulously planning out a heist, the scope of which only we were aware. Or maybe a couple preparing for an appearance on one of those game shows where you have to answer ridiculous, intimate questions to win a weekend in Croatia.

But the further we advanced in our enterprise, the less important the list seemed. What mattered was the complicity it had created. If, as planned, the appointment had happened two days later, we would have been amazing. A perfectly rehearsed routine. Brilliant improvisations. We would have won the weekend in Croatia hands-down. But it was postponed, and the list stayed in my handbag until the November morning when I took it out and stuffed it in my coat pocket, like a cheat-sheet.

Her first-floor office was small and impersonal, lit by the dull sunlight from outside. It was one of those autumn days as opaque as tinplate, when it never really seems to get light. The cold that had seeped in through the walls, mingled with the sharp scent of some kind of soap, made you feel like you were standing next to the freezer cases in the supermarket. As we shook hands, she apologized: "They moved me in here a week ago because of the construction work. I'm sure you've heard about it; it's turned the whole place upside down." Her hand was ice-cold; her smile easy. It was the first time I'd ever visited a psychologist, and in my nervousness I'd naively imagined that she would be dry and authoritarian, but she had a welcoming expression, like someone who doesn't want to cause any harm, but feels that they have an important role to play.

"So you saw Professor Stein about . . . fourteen months ago, and your first appointment with Dr. Gautier was . . . [the sound of pages being turned] six months after that, is that correct?"

The psychologist took off her glasses, which were attached to a chain around her neck, and lifted her eyes from our file. Still looking at us, she let go of the glasses, which bounced off her imposing chest, clad in a chunky loose-knit dark red sweater.

We nodded simultaneously. Our chairs, which were a few feet apart, were on the other side of her bare desk. Before sitting down, I'd wondered if other couples scooted the chairs together in a sort of natural expression of the desire to be closer to one another during this ordeal. Was that kind of thing, with the chairs, something she usually paid attention to? Had she deliberately put them far apart?

In my uncertainty I'd ended up not doing anything, but once I was sitting down I was careful to angle my body toward Pierre's, hoping that position would be enough to suggest positive things about our relationship.

I waited for her to pounce on us about marriage, the way Stein and Gautier had. "When are you getting married?" was the question I'd concentrated my efforts on the most. There was no way we were going to improvise and risk getting tripped up. I'd practiced my response in front of the mirror that morning, and in my head on the way over. If I could get past this first step with the feeling that I'd been convincing, the rest would seem clearer. I had to keep my voice low, speak softly and articulately, control my breathing, and avoid fiddling with my hands too much. (As a teenager, my passion for Lauren Bacall had led me to buy her book, *By Myself*, at the flea market in Saint-Ouen. In the chapter devoted to her arrival in Hollywood and her meeting with Howard Hawks for the role of Slim in *To Have and Have Not*, she explains that Hawks had driven her up into the Hollywood hills and told her to act angry while keeping her voice low. According to Hawks, as soon as women felt strong emotion, their voices automatically turned shrill. I've always remembered that advice and used it often, more or less successfully.)

I should mention that talking to strangers is torturous for me, except when I drink. Sometimes, at the bakery, the fact of having to add "not baked too hard" plunges me into such confusion that I change my mind at the last minute. Even if the words do come out, they're just inaudible muttering, which is even worse because then I'm inevitably asked to repeat myself. Often, when eating out, I confine my order to "same" and just have whatever my dining companion is having. Even though I'm extremely suspicious of anything resembling armchair psychology, I'll admit that I'm sure I know the origin of this fear—which, I want to clarify, I don't feel in Persian. It goes back to when we first came to France, when, every time I opened my mouth, people reminded me that I had an accent.

"Oh, you have an accent; where are you from?"

Shit, here we go again!

"Iran," I would mumble, timid and resigned.

"Ah . . . "

Then a long silence, during which I could see in my interlocutor's eyes that their Iran was located somewhere between Saudi Arabia and the Lebanese Hezbollah, an imaginary country full of Muslim fundamentalists of whom I suddenly became the representative.

Then, once the fact of the accent had been established, the mechanism went into motion. My conjugation mistakes and grammatical errors were pointed out, and of course I suddenly couldn't stop making them. The other person would start to speak more slowly, punctuating references to a book or a politician or an advertisement with: "You may not be aware, but . . . " Believe me, no one misses the foreigners. No one can resist the cheap pleasure of scratching that itch of difference. Language is definitely the easiest way to catch them out and corner them, until the façade of normality they've spent a long, painful time acquiring cracks and hangs in shreds from their embarrassed body. In an attempt to escape from that kind of everyday sadism, I retreated very early into silence, letting music cascade through my brain and rinse it clean. With hindsight, I've realized that the silence transformed my strangeness into mystery, and that mystery into attraction, which isn't such a bad thing. But while my artificial powers of seduction grew, my voice lodged in my throat as if in a tomb. Still, days like that one in November do happen, where you have to be ready to look people straight in the eye and demonstrate that you're not so dense, right? Talk, leave yourself open, say things, tell . . . well, not the truth, but tell it with the ease and facility of an impostor.

The psychologist turned to Pierre, still smiling, and asked him: "How are you?"

I'm still not sure if her friendliness was sincere or just a ruse designed to get us to confide in her. In any case, it was clear that the date of our wedding was of no interest to her. I was simultaneously relieved and disappointed that I wouldn't get to trot out my explanation.

"I'm fine," answered Pierre, shrugging and grinning as if butter wouldn't melt in his mouth. "I've sent my latest results to Doctor Gautier." (I'd had no idea about this, but I decided to let it roll straight off my back. After all, did I really need to know?)

"Yes, I've just seen that. At any rate, you seem to be handling the treatment well."

Pierre nodded, seeming almost flattered.

We'd been supposed to meet in the cafeteria half an hour before our appointment, but Pierre had arrived late as usual. When he'd taken off his woolly hat, I'd been shocked. His hair was cut so short that you could see his scalp. Without his black curls, which were such a distinctive feature that if I'd been drawing him I'd have started with them, his head looked ridiculously small for his muscular body. His eyes, which were even larger than mine, seemed naked, giving him the look of someone lost in the world. I hadn't expected him to spring such an unfamiliar look on me just before an appointment that was intended to assess our credibility and reliability as a couple, two notions that we'd spent a ridiculous amount of time establishing. I should have said something to him about it, but I didn't. It was pointless to create a conflict at the last minute that we wouldn't have known how to resolve.

To distract myself from my dismay I'd thought about my sisters, about what they'd say if they met him. Leïli would undoubtedly display her usual tact: "I don't understand what you see in him; he's so *immature!*" *Immature* was the word she reserved for anyone older than thirty who still wore jeans and tennis shoes for anything other than a hike in the woods. Mina would roll her eyes, meaning: "What do you want me to say; you always do what you want anyway!"

As we'd walked into the building and Pierre, his hat in his hand, had explained why he was late (work, as usual), I'd thought to myself that, with his ears and the nape of his neck bare like that, he looked like a soldier about to go into battle for the motherland—and that was probably his way of showing how honest and responsible he was. A man above suspicion.

I watched him answer the psychologist's questions about the results of his tests. He really was doing well. His perfect white teeth made him look almost like a little boy. He didn't smoke, barely drank, and often disarmed waitresses by ordering strawberry milk. From the beginning, I'd particularly appreciated the elegance of his attitude toward his illness. He never showed anger, never complained.

"And you," said the psychologist, turning to me, "how are you coping with the situation?"

"What situation?" I asked, my expression serious and my voice as low as if I'd just smoked a whole pack of unfiltered Camels.

I knew exactly what she was talking about, but right when she asked me, I figured that a little naïveté would give the impression that we'd gotten beyond those kinds of questions a long time ago.

"Pierre's HIV positivity," she said, with a patient smile.

"I've learned to live with it . . . " (Tender glance at Pierre) "Wouldn't you say?"

"Oh, yeah, we manage really well!" he exclaimed, as enthusiastically as if he were talking about our last kayaking trip.

"It's never affected your desire to have a child?" persisted the psychologist. "You've never thought that having a baby under these conditions might be particularly difficult?"

"Of course we have . . ." (And how!) "But at the same time, we don't want to condemn ourselves to not having a family, just because it's difficult."

I couldn't have been more sincere, though I wasn't thinking of Pierre's HIV positivity.

Two hours later we were still in her office, chatting calmly. I had the pleasant feeling that we'd managed to achieve a kind of serenity. The hardest part was over; the heaviness of questioning and doubt had gradually evaporated into the air, which had been warmed by our breath. The room seemed larger, airier now. We'd taken off our coats and draped them across our laps. We weren't lying anymore. We'd stopped making intense, unblinking eye contact, each seeking the other's approval.

The psychologist accompanied us to the door and shook our hands. The pressure was frank, encouraging. Smiles all around.

"Well, goodbye. Don't hesitate to make an appointment with Dr. Gautier right away to start the insemination process . . . better to plan ahead now, things are moving so fast!"

"We will!" chirped Pierre.

There, that was done. We'd won the day.

The lightness I felt once we'd stepped into the corridor wasn't only about our certainty, or with our relief at having finally finished this first part of the journey, after a year and seven months. What I felt was so stupid that it's almost painful to think about it now. To put it simply, I had the joyous, ephemeral feeling of being just an ordinary girl, which I hadn't felt for so long.

As I write this I can feel Leïli's warm breath; her dry lips pressed to my ear to keep the other girls, cousins of varying degrees slouched on sofas all around us, from overhearing—even though the words were in French, a language none of them could understand. She could just as well have spoken out loud, but no. What she had to say to me had to be doubly hidden. It couldn't even make contact with the air, or mingle with the bright light warming this house nestled in the valley, where I spent my happiest holidays ever, in the summer of 1979. Her words were for me alone. They penetrated into my body, drop by drop. Nothing complicated or extravagant at first. Her tone was heavy with reproach, but that didn't bother me; I was used to it with my sisters. And then, suddenly, that last word, black as night, venomous, that I didn't know, that I was hearing for the first time, and yet that I understood. Could feel. So true and so tragic at the same time. The word that turned my life upside-down.

Speaking of lives turned upside-down, the direction of Darius's changed with Sara's third pregnancy. He'd never wanted a boy—or children at all, but you know that by now. But, for a while now, he'd been imagining a boy with blue eyes like his, the deep, clear blue of the Caspian Sea—it didn't matter that that sea, striated with grey bands, scars left by industrial fishing and uncontrolled tourism, was no longer actually very blue. A boy of ten or twelve, whom he would tell things he could never tell his daughters. Things like . . . he didn't know what, exactly. But the difference was there in his laughter, in his way of lighting a cigarette, of understanding the world. He saw himself resting his hand on the boy's fragile little neck as they crossed the street, paying attention to his physical development and his sorrows, monitoring how he moved the backgammon pieces. He heard himself calling the boy "son," or maybe "little man."

At first, he'd really been annoyed with himself for having such an outdated desire, which was nothing less than an insult to his daughters. And not only to them, but to all the girls who had been and would come into this world amidst a fog of disappointed sighs, in a roomful of adults whose mouths were twisted with indifference and resignation. Because the East, that land of prophets and misery, would always rather have sons; one more pair of hands to work, one less dowry to save for, the carrying-on of a name. Darius cursed himself for falling into the trap. He hadn't spoken of it to Sara, undoubtedly thinking it would pass. With a little willpower, he would get over this silly whim. Except that, one day, he stopped in front of a shop that sold children's clothing and toys and, without thinking, pushed open the door.

It was the first time since he'd become a father that Darius had gone into that kind of store, several of which had recently opened in the city center. They were very fashionable places where perfumed, solicitous saleswomen followed you around patiently and knew what you wanted before you did. Time evaporated like smoke in there.

An hour later, Darius emerged from the boutique carrying shopping bags full of blue clothes that matched the color of his imaginary son's eyes. When the cashier asked him if the clothing was a gift, he'd answered, with new pride, "No, it's for my son, Zartocht." *Zartocht.* Zarathustra. He didn't know why the name Zartocht had popped into his head. He decided to name the baby that, despite the slight hint of pretentiousness he would undoubtedly have to justify.

Months went by. Sara's belly grew rounder, and Darius's hopes rose. Women would take one look at Sara and exclaim "It's a boy!" with glowing faces.

Sonograms didn't yet exist in Iran at that time, and besides, who needed a sonogram? The signs—products of an empirical science refined through the centuries in the shadow of a phallocratic society—never lied. In summary: a woman (Sara, six months pregnant) who was made beautiful by pregnancy was carrying a boy. When a woman was made ugly (Sara, pregnant with Leïli and Mina) it meant she would have a girl. I say "in summary" because nothing was ever said that concisely. There were torrents of comparisons, anecdotes, and comments before the actual diagnosis was made. To these were added a whole series of other elements serving mainly to confirm the prophecy. The shape of the belly (jutting forward: boy; spread out: girl); the smell of the mother's urine (sour: boy; foul-smelling: girl); libido (healthy: boy; flat: girl). And if none of that were enough to convince everyone that Sara was pregnant with a son, her mother Emma, who read coffee grounds, like every Armenian woman, had clearly seen lines that she described as *penisoïdal* in the granular furrows of her daughter's cup.

Just one detail darkened this idyllic pregnancy: Sara didn't want a boy. Because Sara didn't like boys. Sometimes she even let slip a disgusted grimace when her sisters-in-law pressed smacking kisses to their little imps' sweaty heads. How could they look at these strange beings with pride, as if the future of humanity was in their clumsy little hands? How could they hug and squeeze and clasp those ill-formed bodies against their own? For Sara, a boy would mean nothing but trouble as long as he lived. From his skinned knees as a child to his marriage to the first girl who spread her legs in the backseat of a car, along with the inevitable chin-scar. But, as usual, she didn't show these feelings, and consoled herself by trying to imagine Darius with a little blue-eyed son, dressed all in blue, perched on his shoulders. Where was she in that picture? What was she doing? Probably off airing out the kid's blue bedroom so it wouldn't smell so much like goat.

But let's leave Sara to her pregnancy and go back to

Mazandaran. It's time for me to explain why Darius wanted a blue-eyed son so much.

Of all Montazemolmolk's daughters (in addition to the rest, a good dozen more were born after the twins), Nour was one of the few to have gotten married and had children. Her twin sister didn't marry until after their father's death, at the age of thirty-eight—and then she had three disastrous marriages in a row, two ending in divorce, which ruined her for good. For reasons known to him alone, Montazemolmolk refused to marry off his daughters. He received suitors, some of whom had travelled from distant villages; listened to them describe their fortunes and good qualities, nodded his head at regular intervals, and then showed them to the door, instructing them not to return. Exasperated by their daughters' impatience, his wives begged him to relent. They cried and shouted, refused to sleep with him, but Montazemolmolk couldn't be swayed. When my grandfather, Mirza-Ali, heard from a cousin rejected by Montazemolmolk that the old Mazandarani apparently had a blond daughter with blue eyes—eyes even bluer than those of Mirza-Ali himself—he made the journey to Mazandaran to ask for her hand. Montazemolmolk didn't have to turn him away, because he declined even to receive him (people whispered that not only was Nour his favorite daughter, but that he loved her even more than his sons).

Insolent and prideful, Mirza-Ali refused to be dismissed. He came back, and insisted. Came back again. Sent emissaries, fine carpets, gold necklaces, sheep, horses. Soon, the stand-off between Montazemolmolk and this gentleman from Qazvin turned into a saga that made its way over the walls of the compound and found its way into the mountains. From there, it spread even further. Suspense and expectations gave rise to the most far-fetched ideas. One of Montazemolmolk's young servant-boys was bribed to listen at doors. A woman pretended to get lost in the woods and sought refuge in the *andarouni*. People split up into groups to watch the road, made bets, held their breath every time the Qazvini came and went. Only Nour, aged sixteen, the subject of all the commotion, took no interest in the whole business.

She had known since her birth, since the Almighty had chosen her to inherit her father's eyes and deprived her of a mother, that her fate was not hers to determine. So why concern herself with what would happen to her? Besides, no one ever asked her. She and her strange beauty drifted from room to room like some wandering, inoffensive ghost. "As God is my witness," Bibi swore to me, "before she got married, even a fish caught on a hook acted more lively than your grandmother!"

After gathering information about Mirza-Ali's family and investigating the possible interest of an alliance with them, Montazemolmolk agreed to negotiate.[9] He ordered one of the rooms in the *andarouni* to be prepared, with the most beautiful narghiles brought out, and a sumptuous table loaded with aromatic pastries, baskets of fruit, and cardamom tea. Then he summoned Mirza-Ali and introduced him to a dozen of his daughters, the oldest and ugliest ones. When the door opened to admit a gaggle of ungainly virgins, Mirza-Ali felt a mixture of excitement and discomfort start in his belly and rise up into his chest. He'd never been in the same room with so many

---

[9] Since the St. Petersburg accords of 1907, in which the British and Russians divided up Iran without bothering to inform the Iranians, and then the Constitutional Revolution, which lasted almost four years and resulted in the creation of Parliament, Montazemolmolk had been worried about the future. It was a time of insurrection, structural change, and foreign occupation. Shared between two great powers, the Persian state was weak, without resources or a military, and leeched off by a political class that was idle and passively Europhilic. "Who knows?" he said to himself. Becoming friendly with these rich Qazvinis, who were very influential in the market, might prove useful one of these days . . .

women he didn't know. Throughout the country, custom pro-
hibited men from seeing their future wives, just as it forbade
women to be seen with their hair uncovered. But here, in this
land of plenty, mores were freer, and the women acted with the
ease and assurance of the prostitutes which Mirza-Ali, the
Blessed Icon with eyes of Light, frequented as discreetly as if
he were a British spy.

Perfumed, plucked and waxed free of body hair, their skin
whitened with curdled yogurt and their eyes lined with kohl,
the candidates paraded in front of Monsieur Qazvini. They
might just as well have been naked, so strong was their feeling
that their souls, filled with complex emotions, were bared to
him. If Mirza-Ali had been able to hear their inner voices, he
might have been unnerved by the litany of pleading and
prayers, composed of a single word, just one word, infused
with so much desperation: "*Me!*" He might, if only out of
politeness, have showed a flicker of interest, a smile, a pout;
anything, but *something*, something they could have used to
make up a story to tell themselves in their lonely beds, during
the long remainder of their lives.

But Mirza-Ali, who had never been refused anything since
earliest infancy, quickly understood the workings of
Montazemolmolk's household, and remained as icy as a
Russian blizzard. No amount of pastries or tea brewed with
pure mountain water could overcome his pig-headedness. He
wanted the young girl with blue eyes. Period. Where was she?
Why wasn't he being allowed to see her? Vexed by the boy's
nerve, Montazemolmolk looked him slowly up and down and
then, without a word, left the room.

A true son and great-grandson of the *bazari*, what Mirza-Ali
took away from this grotesque and implausible scene was that
the old Mazandarani was clearly losing his marbles. By giving
ground in this way, he would end up letting his best item go
for less than its value. All Mirza-Ali had to do, as his mother

had told him, was be patient. "With patience, my dear boy," Monavar Banou had said, "you can make a beggar into a king."

Six months of negotiations later, Nour, accompanied by Bibi and a dozen servant girls and advisors, was dispatched to Qazvin, to the home of the man who was going to become her husband. On that day, Montazemolmolk, rifle in hand, vanished into the forest at dawn and only reappeared the next day, the bloody carcass of a doe draped across his horse. To everyone's surprise, he didn't hang the doe from a tree so that it could be butchered and sent to the kitchen for the evening meal. Instead, he dug a hole in front of the *birouni* and buried it. When the anecdote was relayed to old Amira in her fortress, lost amid billows of opium smoke, she laughed scornfully: "That doe is the little girl with blue eyes that he didn't have the balls to hold on to. He's burying her now, the same way he buried me!"

The journey through the Alborz Mountains took seven days. Sitting on her tiny stool in the kitchen of Uncle Number Two's house, Bibi told me how, all through the journey, the peasants, who had heard of the marriage as the news echoed through the mountains, ran to meet them. They invited the party into their homes, sang and danced around bonfires, loaded their horses with food and gifts. Children ran barefoot behind their convoy until a wall of dust kept them from going any further.

Shut up in her father's compound since infancy, frightened by so many people staring at her, Nour kept her eyes downcast, murmuring timid words of thanks. I always envision her now as fragile and resigned, like a butterfly in a net, but back then, when I could barely understand half of what came out of Bibi's mouth, I filled in the gaps with the imagination of a child seeking adventure. I'd heard extracts from *One Thousand and One Arabian Nights* declaimed in the powerful voices of the storytellers in the working-class parts of central Tehran, and I superimposed on the willful face of Scheherazade, on her way to the palace of the insatiable King Shahryar, the pale face of my grandmother, whom I knew only through old black and white photographs.

Nour, who had never seen any part of Mirza-Ali except his shadow, had no idea what lay in store for her in Qazvin, a city where, each day, all she had to do was breathe in the air, which was filled with a murky substance called "pollution," to feel herself in exile.

Located at the foot of the Alborz mountains, Qazvin was built by the Sasanian King Shad Shahpur, who reigned over Persia from 240 to 275 C.E.[10] Ravaged by the Arabs and destroyed by the Mongols, it was the capital of the Safavid Empire in the 16th century before falling into decline.

But by 1911, when the convoy transporting Nour entered Qazvin, the city had regained some of its glamour and greeted the modern era with confidence. A photographer had set up shop between two mosques, and the grocer, Djafar Agha, sold a medicine imported from the West, as effective as opium and called "aspirin" (pronounced *ah-speer-eehn*). A cinema was under construction in the main city square, and the sidewalks and streets had begun to be paved with asphalt. But Nour's eyes, which had only known forests, rivers, and mountains, saw only filth and chaos. The distress that swept over her had to do

---

[10] A Qazvini aside: It will probably shock you to learn that every one of the countries of the Middle East has a city where the men are reputed to be homosexual. In Iran, it's Qazvin that holds this dubious, tragicomic distinction. The homosexuality of the Qazvinis is fodder for numerous jokes in which mullahs play a featured role. The reason for Qazvin's reputation remains a mystery, but it's probably not unrelated to the fact that Obeid Zakani, a famous 14th-century satirical poet and confirmed anti-cleric, was born in the city. In any case, 'Qazvin' now automatically means 'homosexuality,' and the over the years the legend seems to have been turned into reality. If Uncle Number Two were alive, his old ears—and not for the first time—would be burning . . .

with the lack of a horizon. Yet it was here that, under the terms of the masculine bargaining of which she had been the object, that she would have to live the rest of her life. Almost thirty years later, a prostitute who had yet to be born would deliver her from that fate. In all that time, Nour had never returned to her native Mazandaran. Instead, Mazandaran—and I can hear the distant drum-roll of impending disaster—would, thanks to a royal heist born out of a coup d'état fomented in Qazvin, come to her.

Let's linger for a minute on that coup d'état, whose shock waves could still be felt in 1979 and beyond. Because everything's connected, right? Because, as the punks used to shriek, History is just an endless loop across time, a permanent going backwards, a *No Future*. By the time you finish reading this chapter, you'll have realized the extent to which Mazandaran and Qazvin, Qazvin and Mazandaran, are important. Not only to my little story, but to the Big Story. So, to yours, too. Unfortunately, when it comes to Iran, the West and its hegemonic outlook are never very far away.

In the early 1920s, Persia, which was ruled by Ahmad Shah Qajar, a young and inadequate monarch, was in a state of decay. The British lusted after its oil and used it as a support base to destabilize its former ally, Russia, which had turned Bolshevik. In the forests of Mazandaran, armed rebellion against foreign occupation was raging. Elsewhere, the Spanish flu and famine had caused tens of thousands of deaths. The army was about as effective as a flat tire; only its Cossack division, formerly led by the Russians but now in the hands of the British, was operational.

In autumn 1920, the British secretly decided to overturn the government and entrust it to the Anglophile Seyyed Ziyâ Tabatabaï, their confidence man. However, they made the non-deposition of the Qajar dynasty, whose hundred-year reign had been a study in decadence, a condition of the putsch. In

October, General Edmund Ironside arrived in Qazvin, where the six-thousand-strong Cossack division was stationed. He picked out a young soldier called Reza, who was charismatic and commanding but virtually uneducated, and put him in charge of operations. Montazemolmolk knew Reza well; the young man had been born into a poor Mazandarani family and would come to him seeking horses when the Cossack division, under Russian command, was billeted in the North.

On February 21, 1921, Reza Khan's men marched out of Qazvin, invaded Tehran, and rapidly seized power. Named *Sarar Sepah* (commander of the armies), Reza Khan became the country's strongman. Four years later, Ahmad Shah made him prime minister before departing for London, supposedly for reasons of health, but really with the intention of never returning. Reza Khan, who feared the press and intellectuals like the plague, forbade all debate and muzzled his detractors. A great admirer of Mustafa Kemal "Ataturk," he wanted to establish a Republic, but the clergy was opposed to it—so, in order to win them over, he abandoned that plan and made another decision: to take the place of Ahmad Shah. During this time, Iran's great families all over the country, refusing to play the game of an unconstitutional succession, joined forces. The patriarchs pushed the bounds of patriotism so far as to gather men and weapons and go to Tehran in order to avoid another takeover. Among them was Montazemolmolk, who would have happily wrung the upstart Reza's neck.

But, fortified by the clergy's support, Reza Khan easily convinced Parliament to depose the Qajars and transfer supreme power to him. He was crowned in 1926 and became Reza Shah, the first king of the Pahlavi dynasty.[11] Once again, intellectuals and nationalists lost ground to the military, the clergy,

---

[11] A name appropriated from another family and going back to the Parthian empire, which served to reinforce Reza's Persianness.

and foreign powers. The wheel of fortune would continue to turn, and history would repeat itself with the 1953 coup d'état and the deposition of Mossadegh, and it would keep turning again until 1979, when the clergy—the most emblematic member of which was living in Neauphle-le-Château—would ally itself with foreign forces, this time directly, and take power.

Reza Pahlavi, the pauper-turned-King, now undertook to modernize Persia, which he rechristened Iran, or Land of the Aryans. He required men to wear Western clothing and used a special militia to tear the veils from women's heads. He made civil registration compulsory as well as the use of last names (Mirza-Ali's descendants became Sadrs in this way, and Montazemolmolk's became Montazemis). He abolished the feudal system and nobiliary titles, and confiscated the great families' land.

And that was how Montazemolmolk, expelled from his compound with his wives and children, came to settle in Qazvin, near his cherished daughter, who was now the mother of six children. Mirza-Ali had no trouble finding him an old residence far from the city center, into which the whole family crammed with some difficulty. With opium no longer within easy reach, Montazemolmolk discovered English whisky, which he poured into his overweight carcass in copious amounts to ease his despair. Like a whirling Sufi dancer, he paced in circles around his room, composing poems about exile and treason and dictating them to whichever of his children happened to be in the vicinity.

Taking advantage of their father's fall from grace, and encouraged by their mothers, the youngest daughters fled to Tehran in search of husbands. According to Uncle Number Two, Montazemolmolk didn't even notice that they were gone. Some years later, learning of the destitution in which the old Mazandarani was living, Reza Shah agreed to restore part of his assets and gave him permission to return home to die. Only old Amira accompanied him; now that she finally had the old bastard all to herself, she wasn't going to let him out of her sight.

Now, while a car sent by Mirza-Ali drives Montazemolmolk and Amira to Qazvin's new train station, let's rewind and go back to Nour and her arrival in the city.

As the sole male descendant, Mirza-Ali Sadr had inherited the family home, an old residence divided into two wings separated by a garden. His ten sisters already inhabited the wing in which he installed his young wife; they were a gang of hatchet-faced bigots with eyes as black as caverns.

Mirza-Ali's sisters detested each other. They argued, backstabbed, cast spells on one another, and chased each other around the garden with a broom. The doors of their multiple bedrooms had slammed so often that on the day he finally inherited the house officially, Mirza-Ali had them all removed. The reputation of the Sadr sisters was so appalling that despite the size of their dowries, no family would send a son to ask for their hand. The arrival of Nour—the Intruder, the Foreigner, the Common Enemy—resulted in a temporary truce. Accustomed to being her stepmothers' whipping boy, Nour now naturally moved into the same role with her sisters-in-law. But while Nour was willing to tolerate mistreatment, Bibi wasn't. The Agha Khan's favorite daughter, treated like a stray dog—this would not stand!

Despite Nour's protests, Bibi alerted Mirza-Ali, who refused to intervene. It was out of the question for him to stoop to settling backstairs disputes. Yet, he couldn't allow his sisters to show disrespect to his wife. After three days of reflection, he came to a decision: if the mountain wouldn't come to Mohammed, Mohammed would go to the mountain. He dispatched a few cousins to visit the city's notables and demand that they supply a husband for each of his sisters. Since no one dared to oppose Mirza-Ali for fear of calling down the wrath of the Almighty, ten claimants showed up at his door before nightfall. They were hardly the cream of the crop, but Mirza-Ali settled for them. He shook the hand of each one of them and congratulated them on joining the family. Among them was Ebrahim Shiravan, the awkward son of a hotelier. Remember that handshake, because it's going to turn out to be crucial for Darius, Sara, Leïli, Mina, and me. I'm not exaggerating when I say that, at that moment, as Qazvin prepared to celebrate the end of 1917, the two of them had just sealed our destiny.

The prospect of marriage distracted the sisters-in-law's attention from Nour, and once again they retreated into jealousy, loathing, and the desire to kill one another.

No one ever mentioned how Mirza-Ali felt when he saw Nour for the first time, when the convoy made its entry into the courtyard of his house. No one knew why he had traveled for miles and spent a fortune to rescue Nour from her father's clutches, or why he had been so determined to have a blue-eyed wife. It's difficult to believe that my grandfather, as Westernized as he was, would have heard of Mendel's laws and the transmission of genetic characteristics. Maybe it was instinct, but he knew that Nour would be the ideal factory in which to deposit his genes and produce a line of descendants in his image—which he took every opportunity to do, from the day Nour was installed in the bedroom next to his own.

No surprise, the gods of genetics did their work. Over the next twelve years, Nour gave birth at regular intervals to six blond-haired, blue-eyed sons, an extraordinary feat of silk-screening that was commented on and admired by all in Qazvin. They were photographed and their portraits were proudly displayed in the photographer's shop window. Women touched them as if they were archangels. Men prayed at the Shahzadeh Hussein mosque to have plentiful sons that resembled them. On the other side of the mountains, Montazemolmolk awaited each birth with impatience. Every pair of blue eyes that emerged from his daughter's belly was revenge against old age and death; the promise that his legend would be propagated throughout the wide world. As far as the old man was concerned, Mirza-Ali had nothing to do with any of it. He, Montazemolmolk, was the sole artificer. Without him there would no Nour, and without Nour there would be no blue-eyed children. Full stop.

The blue eyes became a sort of trademark, a label, a certificate of authenticity. During the 1960s, even after words like *chromosome* and *gene* entered the Iranian vocabulary, the Sadr brothers continued to believe that the color of their eyes was a divine attribute, unrelated to this genetic mumbo-jumbo. Even Darius, who was an atheist and avant-gardist, believed it to an extent. They had married women with brown eyes, but didn't understand why their children had brown eyes. They had procreated as feverishly as if it were a cry for justice, until they finally had a blue-eyed baby, and then they started all over again in the quest to have another one. Nour only loved those of her grandchildren that had blue eyes. They were *hers*, while the others belonged to the other family, the unimportant one of her daughters-in-law.

7
FATE, ACCORDING TO
MY GRANDMOTHER EMMA ASLANIAN

The years of the Russian Revolution were an opportunity for many filmmakers to experiment with, and theorize about, the art of cinematography. Around 1921 two of them, Lev Kuleshov and Vsevolod Pudovkin, carried out an experiment known as the Kuleshov effect, or K-effect, in an attempt to explain the crucial impact of film editing on the human mind. This experiment showed that the perception of an image depends on its context; in other words, on the image that precedes it and the one that follows it. A shot of a face—in this case the neutral one of actor Ivan Mosjoukine, his gaze focused off-camera—followed by a plate of soup, a dead woman in a coffin, or a little girl playing is perceived in three different ways. Taken separately, these images don't tell us much, but their proximity to the face creates clear dramatic intention. A story. When Kuleshov questioned viewers about Mosjoukine's acting, they expressed their appreciation for his realistic expressions of hunger, compassion, and tenderness in turn.

The same thing is true for the events of a life as it is for images in a film. When associated with others, certain apparently trivial events take on new meaning. Links are created. Bridges rise up to connect generations. Connections are formed somewhere in the Universe. Pragmatists call these phenomena Coincidence or Chance, express surprise when they happen, and then go on their way. Skeptics like my maternal grandmother Emma Aslanian, who search the Universe like hunting dogs in search of connections, intuitive leaps, and meaning, who believe in a greater power that governs the world, a God who is not necessarily merciful or protective, call it Fate. And Fate was hovering over Tehran on the morning of July 3, 1971.

At ten forty-five in the morning, as she was having a cup of tea with Big Mina, Sara felt a sharp, shooting pain in her kidneys. Half an hour later, alerted by Big Mina, Darius left his office hurriedly, determined to take his wife to the hospital himself this time. The summer sky was cloudless and blue, with a sun whose contours were as clean and perfect as a fried egg yolk. The air was already sultry with heat. The city was sinking into lethargy, its pulse slowing down, as parched as a dying man's lips. Darius, at the wheel of his white Peugeot 404, felt like he was the only Tehrani rushing toward the future.

Now we're pushing open the door of the birthing room at Aban Hospital, in the full throes of deliverance (as the Armenians call labor). I'll leave you to imagine the soundtrack, bearing in mind that epidurals weren't yet used in Iran. We're arriving right in the middle of the action, at around two o'clock in the afternoon, because up to that point everything had gone routinely. This time, though, the baby's head slipped out of Dr. Mohadjer's hands and retreated back up into Sara's body, while she screamed so hard at the other end of the bed she shook the walls.

As Sara writhed in agony, Mohadjer, his arm elbow-deep inside her, finally grasped the baby and pulled it out with great difficulty, bottom first. At first glance, it looked as if the newborn were dead. The umbilical cord was wrapped tightly around its neck. It was covered with blood and greenish feces. The doctor, paralyzed, wondered who he should save: the mother, or the baby? He closed his eyes. A rush of horror at the thought of announcing the death of either of the two to Darius tightened his chest. Science was no longer of any help to him. Nor was the God he had renounced long ago in a garret, between a Parisian girl's legs. He was alone with Death, who twirled his lasso slowly in air thick with the smell of blood and viscera.

Just then, he felt—or thought he felt—the infant move in his hands. He opened his eyes and saw the tiny, shit-covered ass. "You dragged me into this world; now you'd better prove to me that being born is worth it," he thought he heard. Shaken, Mohadjer pulled himself together and obeyed. He leapt into action. Seized a pair of scissors. Cut the umbilical cord. Did absolutely everything he knew how to do.

At the same time, worn out by anxiety and the tyranny of nature that had taken possession of his wife's uterus, his shirt damp with sweat, Darius left the waiting room and went down to have a cigarette.

He crossed the sun-baked lobby and went out into the courtyard. An unfiltered Camel between his fingers, his mind as crumpled as a piece of paper, he stretched, looking around for a shady spot where he could rest his tired limbs. That was when he saw Uncle Number One getting out of his car. Followed by Uncles Number Three, Five, and Six.

Thinking gratefully that they had come to support him, Darius hurried to meet them. He was too tense, too full of emotion, to remember that none of them had been present at Sara's other deliveries. He'd never been there for the births of any of his twenty-six nieces and nephews. Tradition dictated that it was the wife's family who would be present at the hospital, not the husband's. And when it came to tradition, his brothers were faultless (except for Uncle Number Six, who lied and schemed, always scrambling to save face). Now, as his brothers' eyes, glazed with a strange anxiety and the blinding summer sunlight, came to rest on him, his energy seemed to drain away. A familiar, primitive fear bound him immediately to them, like an umbilical cord.

The last time his brothers looked at him like that had been more than twenty years ago, at the gates of the university of Tehran, where he was a student. They'd waited for him, lined up in a row: Uncle Number One in his army uniform; Uncle Number Three, blinking nervously; Uncle Number Five, biting his fingernails; and Uncle Number Six, his head hunched into his shoulders. They had come to bring him the terrible news reported by a cousin, who had driven hurriedly from Qazvin in the night: the prostitute; the child, aged five, who had been begging in front of the family home; the dishonor.

Uncle Number Two was absent on that July afternoon in 1971, as he had been all those years ago as well, and that fact alone left no room for doubt as to the cause of the misfortune.

"Mother . . . ?" stammered Darius.

"Yes," answered Uncle Number One, once again assuming the role of eldest son, whose duty it always was to deliver bad news.

The Sadr brothers walked through the hospital corridors with the heavy footsteps of the helpless and entered the room where Mother lay; she had fallen into a coma, the way you sink into grief.

Two nurses were bustling around her, preparing her for surgery. On the neighboring bed, Uncle Number Two was recovering with the aid of an IV drip in his arm. What he told them, in a dull voice that contained every possible shade of pain, could be summed up in just a few words. As he did every afternoon, he'd gone to Mother's house. Not finding her in the living room, he had gone into her room and found her lying on the floor, a dribble of saliva on her chin. He had screamed and fainted. Hearing his cry, Bibi had dragged his ungainly carcass into the bedroom; she was the one who had called an ambulance. Saddeq's brothers listened to him in silence, anguish weighing heavily on their minds.

Not once in all the summer nights spent on the terrace of

his house in Mazandaran, recounting the adventures of Montazemolmolk and his descendants, did Uncle Number Two ever refer to that morning, which Leïli dubbed *The Morning of Death*. Whenever the story he was telling came anywhere near it, he would talk his way around it. Why? No one really knew, but all of us, for various reasons, accepted his unwillingness to discuss it—the adults out of respect for his pain, even though some of them considered it extravagant; and the children for fear that their father's authoritative fist would grab them by the scruff of the neck and toss them out of the family circle. The taboo was so great that, even when he wasn't there, no one dared to talk about it (you'll notice that all the family taboos had some connection to Uncle Number Two). But just be patient a little bit longer, dear Reader, and I will reveal to you what no Sadr has ever known. Right now we have a mother and baby to save . . .

In the delivery room, the baby suddenly began to cry. There it was—Life, burning in its lungs. Oxygen flowed into its bloodstream. Its limbs moved. No point in bathing it just yet, decided Dr. Mohadjer, the most important thing was to get it into skin-to-skin contact with the mother's bloodless body. Sara, who was alarmingly pale, didn't move a muscle. His heart pounding (*she has to live she has to live she has to live*), Mohadjer bent close to her ear.

"Hold on now, Sara *Djan* . . . everything's all right. The baby's just fine. Here, touch it, you'll see [he took her hand and placed it on the baby's blood- and shit-covered body]. It's a pretty little girl . . . "

Later, in an amused and triumphant voice, Sara would tell everyone who came to visit her in her hospital room that it was at that exact second, her body flooding with unexpected joy, that she had the idea of naming me Kimiâ. From the Arabic *Al-kimiya*, alchemy, itself derived from the Greek *khêmia*, or black magic, which was in turn derived from the Egyptian *kêm*, black. Hence, Kimiâ. The Art that consists of purifying the Impure, of transforming Metal into Gold, the Ugly into the Beautiful. And, in the semi-darkness of Sara's mind, the Boy into a Girl.

Farewell, Zartocht. Farewell to dirty socks, soccer balls, decapitated lizards, white stains on the sheets, fender-benders. Farewell, ungrateful, perfidious daughter-in-law.

Later on, she would realize that she had been mistaken.

That was my first birth. The second happened ten years later, when we arrived in Paris. Kimiâ became Kimia or Kim or Kimy or "What? Can you repeat that?" To be honest, nothing is more like exile than birth. Being torn, out of survival instinct or necessity, with violence and hope, from your first home, your protective cocoon, only to be propelled into an unknown world where you constantly have to deal with curious stares. Every exile knows that path, like the one from the uterine canal, that dark hyphen between the past and the future which, once crossed, closes again and condemns you to wander.

At ten past four, when Dr. Mohadjer told the man who was now my father that I was a girl, Darius, whose mind was elsewhere, just nodded. His disappointment was dulled by the presence of Death, which, chased from the delivery room, had simply sped down three floors to take possession of Nour's body instead. At the same moment that a nurse with a hook nose swaddled the washed, still-purplish body of Kimiâ Sadr in a white blanket, three floors below, another nurse, this one in a surgical mask, drew a white sheet over the face of Nour Sadr. Depending on which floor of the hospital he was on, Darius found himself receiving both congratulations and condolences.

Once again, Life and Death had rushed to meet each other, just as they had in Montazemolmolk's *andarouni*. Taken separately, there is nothing too extraordinary about either of these events but, when placed side by side, they produce a surprising effect, the meaning of which—if there is a meaning—is beyond us. Seventy-six years had passed between Nour's birth and mine. Seventy-six years during which a new world order had been established, which could be summed up as follows: whoever controls the oil, controls the world. And Iran had become the center of this balance of power.

In October 1925, after reigning for two centuries, the (originally Turcoman) Qajar dynasty had been deposed at the instigation of the British, and replaced by another, which had usurped the name of Pahlavi. In August 1941, Reza Shah was ousted in his turn, this time by an alliance between the British and the Soviets, in favor of his son Mohammad Reza, who, in 1965, in all modesty, declared himself King of Kings. In the meantime the country had been modernized; hospitals had been built, and a generation of doctors trained in Western universities had imported new techniques. Life expectancy had increased and the birth rate declined. Yes, times had changed, but the rituals that welcome life and accept death were the same now as they had in the *andarouni*. A white sheet, a long prayer, and *voilà*, each of us is ready for the journey, on opposite banks of the river, in worlds separated by the cold barrier of the Earth, but eternally connected to each other by the complex and unpredictable chain of genetics.

Grandma Emma learned the news of my birth and of Mother's death at the same time.

She was at home with Leïli and Mina, who had been staying with her since the beginning of the school holidays to give Sara a bit of relief. As soon as Sara told her over the telephone that her water had broken, Emma gathered her granddaughters against her soft-as-brioche body and warned them that it was going to be a long day. Then, to distract herself from her anxiety and entertain the little ones, she took out flour and a sieve and set about making her famous cardamom-seed cookies, her daughter's favorite.

Emma had a whole range of pastry specialties, some of which were set out on the living room coffee table under a protective glass dome. Each of them bore witness to the emotional state that had given rise to their production. Orange blossom-water crepes (easy to make, aromatic, perfect with tea) meant that she had woken up in a good mood. Little tahini rolls (*tahinov hatz*)—very sweet, typically Armenian— gave off the scent of sadness: the death of her parents in a train accident when she was only ten, the sudden responsibility for her brothers and sisters, the struggle to raise them. They were so sweet in order to erase the bitterness of reality. Cardamom-seed cookies had always been associated with Sara. They had marked the rhythm of her life, from her school exams to the births of her children. On that Saturday, July 3, the longer her labor went on, the more impressive the quantities of cookies arranged methodically in metal tins by Leïli and Mina became.

"What are we going to do with all of these, Grandma Emma?" asked Mina, exhausted.

"We'll give them out to the poor, as soon as your little brother gives my Sara some peace!"

Emma had just slid the seventeenth batch into the oven when, finally, the telephone rang. They all ran for the living room, Leïli and Mina crying out joyously: "He's here; little brother Zartocht is here!" Carried away by her enthusiasm, Mina wanted to pick up the phone, but Emma took the receiver from her hands. She had experienced enough unsuccessful deliveries to know that you could never be sure of the news you were about to hear. She was expecting Darius's voice, but instead it was Big Mina, calling from the only public telephone in Aban Hospital.

Gripped by conflicting emotions, her face grave, Emma

hung up the phone. She stood unmoving, her hand still on the receiver.

"Is Zartocht dead?" asked Leïli, anxiously.

Suddenly remembering her granddaughters, Emma shook her head and decided that she certainly wasn't going to be the one to tell them that Mother was dead. Everything in its own time.

"Is it Sara, then?" Leïli persisted.

"No, no, everything's all right, my little chickens. Except that Zartocht is a girl," said Emma, with a weak smile. "You have a little sister."

"Oh, I get it! You look so upset because you made a mistake!" crowed Mina.

Mina wasn't totally wrong. The possessor of ancestral knowledge, Emma was never wrong when it came to deciphering the hidden mysteries of the future. The sole Armenian in the family, she considered herself the only one capable of correctly reading coffee grounds. Whenever anyone other than herself had the temerity to reach for a cup, she always raised her black eyes to the heavens and muttered, scornfully: "If only the Persians would stick to their beloved poetry books and leave the coffee to the Armenians!"[12] It was her grandmother Sévana, born in Izmir, who had transmitted the skill to her mother Anahide, who was born in Istanbul, who had passed it down to Emma, born in Rasht, who had transmitted it to Sara, born in Tehran (though she used it only rarely, and only for other people).

Anahide and her husband, Artavaz Aslanian, had left Turkey shortly before the 1915 genocide and gone to Moscow,

---

[12] An ironic reference to the Iranian custom of opening to a random page of the book *Divan*, a volume by the great 14th-century poet Hafez of Shiraz, in order to receive answers about the future. The divinations of Hafez are taken very seriously by Iranians, who question him at every opportunity.

which they fled at the time of the 1917 revolution in favor of
Rasht, the city in northern Iran where Emma was born. Then
they had left Rasht and settled for good in Tehran, where
Artavaz had found a teaching post in an Armenian school. Even
though she had never seen Armenia, which in 1920 became the
Soviet Republic of Armenia, Emma was deeply attached to the
country. She called it her great-country, the way you'd talk
about your great-grandmother. For her, the art of reading coffee grounds was all the more precious and unique and inim-
itable because its roots lay in the unhappiness of an oppressed
people who had resisted every attempt to annihilate them. It
bore witness to the Armenians' fierce need to know their future
in order to escape a tragic fate, a dreadful feeling that these pretentious Iranians couldn't possibly understand.

So it was with self-assured pride that, one autumn afternoon as the family gathered in her living room, she had seized
the six-months-pregnant Sara's cup and turned it upside-down
in the saucer. She waited for the grounds to settle, put on her
glasses, and picked up the cup, holding it in her hands as if it
were a newborn's face. She tilted it right and then left, turned
it around once and then again, and then held it out to Sara
emotionally.

"Look, there, on the side . . . it's full of penisoidal lines, my
dearest!"

When she found out that I was a girl and Mother was dead,
Emma was struck speechless. What had happened? Was this
lamentable failure the price to be paid for having married a
Persian Muslim and gone so far away from her own people?
But she'd seen what she had seen in those grounds. She knew
how to tell the difference between a line and a slit, by God!
Emma let the girls out to play on the terrace and shut herself
in the kitchen to think.

She made a cup of strong black tea, sat down at the kitchen

table, and attacked the last batch of cookies. One, two, three, four. The sugary warmth soothed her. A gleam of explanation flickered in her mind and developed, growing more complete as her blood sugar rose. She clung to the certainty that had been hers since her parents' deaths: for every being that dies, another is born in its place. Five, six. Slowly the links established themselves, the separate parts fitting together like pieces of a puzzle. Seven, eight, nine. A muddle like this could only happen because . . . because . . . yes, of course! Obviously! The baby had indeed been a boy, right up until the moment when, judging that the time had come to take Nour, the Creator had changed His mind and transformed it into a girl. Emma would have bet her wedding ring that this bit of divine sleight-of-hand had happened *after* the day she had read the coffee grounds in Sara's cup.

My grandmother didn't know that it is sometime between the seventh and eleventh week of gestation when the internal genital organs differentiate themselves as male or female via the atrophying of the Wolffian or Müllerian ducts, determining whether the baby will be a girl or a boy. Nevertheless, she decided that on that autumn day when Sara had told them she was six weeks pregnant, the baby's sex hadn't yet definitively formed—so, God had been able to decide at His leisure how He wanted to fashion it. And she had certainly never claimed that her art could reveal the unpredictable intentions of the Creator! He didn't warn people when the fancy took Him to engage in a little bit of genital tinkering!

Perking up, Emma devoured the final cookie—and put the finishing touch on her explanation. Of *course* that was what had happened; otherwise why would the baby (Kimiâ, what a funny choice of name!) have refused to be born right away, if not because she was waiting for Nour's soul to free itself and come to occupy her tiny body? What can you say to that? For years after my birth, it was with this memorable line of questioning that she silenced anyone who dared to remind of her failure. Still, before she stood up to dress in black and get my sisters ready to go to the hospital, she decided not to read any pregnant women's coffee grounds again before their bellies were good and round.

Emma opened the door of her daughter's hospital room. Sara was as pale as curdled milk and she was sleeping, the (very large) infant clasped in her arms. Just over ten pounds, the nurse had said. Measurements that jolly well confirmed Emma's theory.

She quietly approached the bed and leaned over to get a better look at her granddaughter. The sight of this baby, whose gender had been waylaid by Fate, was troubling. How would she muddle through life, with a body that had been tampered with in such a way? With her fingertips, she eased away the white cloth hiding part of my face. My resemblance to Nour made her jump—a resemblance that, once again, served to prove her right. She was the first to notice it, as clearly as she had seen Leïli and Mina's resemblance to Sara—and thus to her, and to her mother Anahide.

While Emma reflected on the hidden meaning of this birth amidst bereavement, Sara opened eyes reddened with tears (Darius had told her of Mother's death) and murmured:

"Did you see? It's a girl . . . "

"Not quite," Emma corrected her.

"What do you mean, 'not quite'?"

On the day of Nour's funeral, every one of her sons threw himself into her grave and had to be fished back out. Uncle Number Six went so far as to faint down there, six feet underground, on top of the corpse wrapped in its *kafan*, the white shroud in which Muslims are buried.

At the sight of his brother sprawled atop Mother's body,

Uncle Number Two felt his blood run cold with venomous jealousy. He was the one who deserved to stay with her, to protect her from the dampness of the earth, to die symbolically in her arms. Later, realizing that inserting a bit of fiction into the reality helped to heal the wounds, Saddeq would reverse the roles when he told the story of the funeral. Since no one dared to point out his inaccuracies, it was soon firmly established that he was the one who had lost consciousness in his mother's arms.

"And Uncle Number Six, *Amou Djan*, what happened to him?" Mina would often ask, shamelessly.

"How should I know—I had fainted, hadn't I, child? But they told me afterward that he passed out himself, poor thing; he was so shocked by the sight of me, lying unconscious in the bottom of the grave."

When Uncle Number Six—who was a professor of literature at the University of Tehran, the translator of several novels by André Gide, and the owner of one of the largest real estate agencies in the city (and much too much of a snob to come and sit on the floor of the terrace in Mazandaran and listen to Saddeq's stories)—learned of his brother's deception, he made straight for Saddeq's house to clear up the matter. It was a Friday night, and the whole family had gathered there as usual. Uncle Number Six had just returned from Italy where, according to his wife, he was doing business with a marble importer. I found out later that, at the airport, he had run into a cousin who had told him that another cousin had heard Saddeq saying that . . .

In the eyes of his brothers, Uncle Number Six was still a child. The youngest and smallest, the apple of his mother's eye. Even his body had retained the stigmata of childhood. Built like a teddy bear, he had a face as round as a plate, set atop a body that had barely reached five foot two. He loved to drink strong spirits, smoke cigars, tell jokes with salacious undertones, and stare at women. He was sure of himself, unscrupulous, impulsive, and impertinent. Unlike his brothers, he had innate business sense. Even as a child, his blue eyes—small and with no sparkle or charm—had lit up when he talked about how he had taken another boy to the cleaner's. No one knew where he had gotten this passion for wheeling and dealing, scamming and scheming, and real estate. Over time he had built an empire that remained standing only thanks to a horde of attorneys and shifty relations in several government ministries. My mother's older brother, who was also in academia, had told my father about a rumor that Uncle Number Six paid a ghost-writer to do his translations. Darius had burst out laughing at that: "Pirouz is capable of anything!" The same information concerning another professor would have aroused fury in him; he would have launched into a tirade against corruption in education, the opportunism of so-called intellectuals, their charlatanism, et cetera—but when it was about his little brother, Darius just laughed. Sara watched him with resignation when he did this. He would never let anyone or anything get between him and his clan, she thought, with the fatalism of the scientist who knows that part of the Universe's mystery will always be beyond her reach despite all her efforts.

Uncle Number Six's first name, Pirouz, meant Victorious. When she learned—with horror, I imagine—that she was pregnant again, Mother had immediately begun heaving an enormous sack of rice around the courtyard, hoping to provoke a miscarriage. But the baby, who was a strategist even then, clung to his mother's womb. In just a few months he grew so large that she was forced to abandon the bag of rice and take to her bed. He was born by hook or by crook, *victoriously*, and Mother mollycoddled him all his life; it was her way of begging his forgiveness.

Saddeq had spent a large part of his existence in a state of paranoid anxiety about Mother's love for Pirouz, which was so different from her melancholic tenderness for him. He dreaded that one day she might abandon him for good in favor of his youngest brother. The unspoken competition between them had grown steadily over the years but was never mentioned out loud even once. Everyone knew that a black clot of resentment, hidden beneath layers and layers of decorum, family evenings and parties, commemorations and colored plates, had coagulated in the gut of each of them. But no one ever imagined that, one day, it would finally burst.

I remember an unbelievable row. Shouting. Faces scarlet with rage. The other brothers trying to get between them, to separate them physically. "You're nothing but a puppet, Pirouz! You con the whole world and now, what's this? Come to give me lessons, eh?" And later, as my dad and Uncle Number Three hustled Pirouz into the next room: "You can just shut your mouth, Saddeq, knowing the company you keep!" I remember hiding my face against my mother, wondering what company Uncle Number Six was talking about, as he looked at his brother with such fury in his eyes. But because I couldn't ask the question, it stayed tucked into a back corner of my mind for years, until that day in 1981 when I found myself alone in Uncle Number Two's room.

First, some context: January 1981, two years after the end of the Revolution (which by now had, ludicrously and offensively, been rechristened the Islamic Revolution). Actively being hunted by government mullahs, and after months of solitude in a room with drawn curtains, my dad had left Iran in secret. Four months after his departure, Sara took us out of school and installed us in Uncle Number Two's house again. For two months, we'd been waiting for a call from the same smuggler who had helped our father, to follow him out of the country the same way. But, as Saddeq used to say, that's a whole other story . . .

Despite the fact that we've stayed with Uncle Number Two more than once before, this is the first time I've ever resolved to go into his top-floor room with its old painted wallpaper, the door of which—like the entrance to some secret passageway— is always kept closed. I don't want to leave Iran without seeing that room. It is early afternoon, and the adults (various uncles and aunts) and my sisters and cousins are in the living room, caught up in the interminable post-lunch routine. None of them will ever notice my absence, and while it's true that Sara might, she'll probably just think I'm in the kitchen with Bibi as usual.

Saddeq's bedroom has intrigued me for a while now. It represents a complex possibility that has never occurred to me before: that a husband might not share a bed with his wife. When I asked my mother why Uncle Number Two slept alone, she'd said it was because of his migraines—which didn't convince me, especially because Sara got migraines too, but she didn't sleep by herself. To be honest, that explanation only accentuated the perfidious odor of secrecy that I could just smell wafting off Saddeq and his wife. Sometimes I saw my oldest female cousins watching them and elbowing each other, but when I asked why, one of them would always just pinch my cheek and say, "Whatever are you talking about, little darling?" and the others would laugh.

Protected by thick green velvet curtains, the room is so dark that I have to turn on the ceiling light. It is narrow and monastic; the only spot of color comes from a rough woolen coverlet on the bed. These are made by fishermen's wives in Mazandaran. When we travelled there each summer, as we were still unloading our cram-packed cars, they would rush toward us, offering the blankets for sale along with fresh caviar. They knew the "Misters Sadr" would buy everything they had. The caviar always ended up in an omelet for dinner, and the blankets stacked in a corner awaiting our departure.

In late autumn they came out of the mothballed armoires in various Tehran houses and every Sadr, big and small, would fall asleep under them every night until spring came. I creep toward the wall across from the bed. Above the meticulously-arranged top of a small chest of drawers are black-and-white photographs in various formats, yellowed by time. The dominant figure in this intimate and nostalgic exhibition is, of course, Mother. A series of portraits of her constitute its main structure. Around them are clustered photo of the brothers, in groups and alone, as children and teenagers, shy and arrogant, baby-faced or mustachioed. But there are also photos of young Persians here and there, dressed Western-style, posing in front of gleaming automobiles or against the backdrop of the Alborz mountains. There are no pictures of his wife or children, none of his nieces or nephews, and none of his father.

One small photo catches my attention. It is a wide-angle shot, taken in a garden. I recognize Saddeq, around twenty years old. Wavy hair swept back; white shirt and dark trousers; gaze lowered. Next to him, an older man stares straight into the camera. He is similarly coiffed and dressed, half of his face in the shadows cast by the leaves of the trees behind them. I think his arm is around my uncle's shoulders, but I'm not sure. The shadows thrown across their middles, like a veil placed there deliberately to hide a detail, blur the line where one body stops and the other begins. As I gaze at the picture, disturbed, Uncle Number Six's phrase pops into my head.

Just as I am leaning on my elbows across the dresser to get a better look, the door opens. My heart lurches in my chest. I turn around. Uncle Number Two, standing on the threshold, looks as stunned as I must. I stammer, casting around for an excuse and wanting desperately to flee, but he closes the door behind him.

Uncle Number Two adjusts his rimless glasses and, to my great surprise, smiles at me. It is a rictus that mingles sadness and compassion, and he has reserved it exclusively for my sisters and me ever since our father became a revolutionary. I hate that smile. It terrifies me. It implies that I will soon be an orphan, that my father and/or mother will be arrested, lynched, tortured, dismembered, thrown into some dark backstreet in the southern part of the city to be devoured by stray dogs. That smile holds the sincere foolishness of respectable people, of the dusty bourgeoisie who believe that anyone who doesn't live the way they do is inevitably destined for disaster. Out of habit, I force down my anger and lower my eyes. I even make myself return his smile.

He puts his hand on my shoulder and presses gently until I sit down on the bed.

"What were you looking at, Kimiâ?"

His tone is calm but challenging. His breath smells of cigarette smoke and the aromatic herbs of *khormé sabzi*. His small, wide hands with their round fingernails reminds me of my dad's.

"Kimiâ, what were you looking at?" he repeated.

"The pictures of Mother," I reply earnestly.

I know from experience that if I show interest in Mother everything will be fine. I'll become his ally; the niece in whose heart he's successfully planted the seed of his singular love for Nour. He strokes my hair with the palm of his hand, as if smoothing the wrinkles out of a familiar piece of cloth.

"You love Mother, do you?"

I nod vigorously, to give more credence to my little act.

I feel his body tremble with happiness. Then he bursts into tears.

Ten minutes later, when his sobs have finally tapered off, he launches into the story of The Morning of Death.

I listen to him in stupefied silence, weighed down by his

voice, which holds me close, by the heaviness of this sudden intimacy which has been thrown over us like a blanket. Why is he confiding in me as if I were a friend, the kind of friend with whom he would be photographed side by side in a garden, in front of a tree, in a loose white shirt? (While Saddeq weeps, I keep sneaking surreptitious glances at the photo.)

I try to figure out how to balance my alarm with the emotions pouring out of Uncle Number Two, as well as my duty as the little sister obligated to report everything to Leïli and Mina. Guiltily, but diligently, I concentrate on every detail, committing them to memory. After all, surely Uncle Number Two must assume that I will tell them everything, right? He knows how sibling relationships work—the gossiping and telling of juicy secrets while the adults are napping . . . or maybe he thinks I am too young to remember his words. Finishing his introductory remarks now, Saddeq is finally approaching the fatal moment when he finds Nour on the floor. This is where the music shifts into a minor key, heavy on the brass instruments, signaling the dramatic change. The moment when, flooded with a terrible sense of foreboding, he pushes open Mother's door . . . and the brass instruments, and indeed the whole orchestra, falls silent.

Life is such that, even in the darkest depths of the drama, there is always still a little room left for the absurd. For example, this is the sight that greeted Saddeq's eyes when he opened the door: Mother's nightgown pushed up to her waist, and her ass sticking straight up in the air. Two withered globes, spread wide enough to show that unfathomable place, the source of life, as unimaginable as the Forbidden City. In the tiny space between his horror and his panic, a crazy sensation made itself felt: an extraordinary desire to laugh. And it was the effort of keeping this laughter forced down inside him that had caused Uncle Number Two to pass out.

"All my life I'd tried to imagine her death, and the way I'd handle it. Which is idiotic, I admit, because anyone could have been there when it happened—but I knew it would be me. I always knew that. It was my mission in life to be with her; God picked me out for it especially. It was my duty to be by her side. I'd always pictured myself bursting into tears, hurling myself toward her, screaming her name, begging her not to leave me. I'd imagined myself in the ambulance, holding her hand and talking to her and kissing her so she wouldn't be afraid. But no; I laughed! God! I abandoned her, Lord forgive me! I didn't measure up, yet again."

I don't know how to transcribe everything Uncle Number Two said, and anyway I've forgotten most of it. I don't know how to help you envision the whole array of sighs and head movements that went along with the words. All I can tell you is that life's irony and feelings of guilt seemed to overwhelm him completely. And then the words stopped, giving way to just head movements and tears that streamed like rain down his hollow cheeks.

It felt like we sat there together for a long time. Long enough for me to realize—still while staring at the black-and-white picture—how alone Uncle Number Two was, trapped in a lie on which he'd built his whole life. Eaten up for years, ever since realizing who he was, by the fear of never living up to Mother's expectations.

We were a lot alike.

I didn't tell my sisters about the things Uncle Number Two had shared with me until years later, in Paris, a couple of days before Leïli's wedding. Time had softened the impact of the revelation, reducing it to a tragicomic story about a past that seemed unreal now. Anyway, neither of my sisters cried out in astonishment, or asked questions.

With the passage of time, the flesh of events decomposes, leaving only a skeleton of impressions on which to embroider. Undoubtedly there will come a day when even the impressions will only be a memory. And then there won't be anything left to tell.

On the Sadr family tree, a majestic thing with a broad trunk and graceful branches hand-drawn in the style of a Persian miniature (Uncle Number Two used to have a beautiful one of those in his house), only the male heirs are shown.

Which means that, contrary to what you might imagine, given the size of this family and the more or less significant degree of consanguinity, Darius Sadr's branch is very easy to spot. Watch it thrust skyward, full of hope and courage . . . and stop, perplexed, in the void. A bird killed in full flight. A stump.

Me to Bibi, one day: "Why don't they put girls on the family tree? We exist, don't we?"

Bibi: "You *think* you exist, little one, but you don't."

Me: "Yes I do!"

Bibi (resigned grimace): "Wait until you're my age; then you'll understand . . . "

All of a sudden I put down my cup and stand up to leave the cafeteria. What if Dr. Gautier is already there? What if she's already called me? The tube of sperm clutched in my hand, I hurry anxiously down the path that leads to the buildings (still no construction workers on the scaffolding). I run up the stairs to the second floor and ask at the reception desk if the doctor has arrived yet.

"Not yet, Mrs. Favre [Pierre's name]. She's in a meeting with senior management. She just called; it won't be long."

I glance around the waiting room. My chair is occupied by a fortyish woman; a man with pure white hair stands next to her, his body pressed against the fogged-up window. They're holding hands. It's obvious that they're deeply in love; they just met too late in life. There are no other free chairs.

Now I'm waiting in the corridor, one wall of which is adorned with a bulletin board displaying a collage of baby pictures sent by parents who have emerged from this maze victorious. Here and there are little colored paper hearts, undoubtedly drawn by some compassionate nurse wanting to put love at the center of the war that is fought daily within these walls. The whole thing conveys hope, a *"hang in there and keep loving each other and you'll see, your dreams will come true"* kind of message. Next to the bulletin board is the door to Professor Alain Stein's office, otherwise known as the Antechamber of Possibilities.

The first time I came to this department (after a four-month wait for an appointment) Pierre escorted me directly to this door and knocked, and we went in. Professor Stein's role in the chain of protocol was to receive new files, check them, and, if he judged them to be valid, submit them to the committee of experts (of which he was a member) responsible for making the final decision. If a file was accepted, it automatically meant that the case would be one hundred percent covered by Social Security based on six inseminations and four in-vitro fertilizations. I can hear the mechanical rolling noise of the escalator, punctuated by the louder, dull thumps of Darius's feet on the steps of the staircase. And there's your shadow, falling over these pages . . . you, whose taxes are the source of this republican generosity.

"You are planning on getting married, aren't you?" Stein had asked us, in his tenor voice.

It wasn't a question or a confirmation, but a suggestion—one it would be in our best interest to follow.

"Of course we're going to get married!" I'd almost shouted the words, terrified that we were about to be refused. The incredulous look Pierre shot me brought home the absurdity of my response. Thrown off-balance, stammering, I'd added a temporal qualification that was completely random and which, I hoped, wouldn't affect our case.

"Soon. We're, uh, thinking about a date."

Except that three months had gone by (positive reply from the committee). And then nine (first appointment with Dr. Gautier, the physician in charge of our case). And then eleven. Up to today. And we still weren't married.

Access to medically-assisted reproduction is reserved for married couples—but also, though most people are unaware of it, for couples in common-law marriages. So, we'd provided a certificate of common-law marriage to Cochin Hospital.

The day before our interview with Dr. Stein, we'd gone together to the registry office in the 10th arrondissement, where Pierre lived. Pierre had done his research, and he'd assured me that it was only a formality, much easier than getting any other document. I didn't believe him. Born in Tarbes to a middle-class French family and living in Paris since the age of eighteen, Pierre had a radically different experience with bureaucracy than I did. He had never spent whole mornings at police stations, in waiting rooms filled with people of every nationality stacked on top of one another and sweltering in a thick atmosphere of contained anxiety. He'd never been faced with a civil service employee who demanded papers and proof with such irritation that you felt like the dirt on the bottom of someone's shoe. Pierre was confident and rational, because there was no reason for him to be any other way.

I'd met him in front of the registry office, my handbag crammed to bursting with documents proving my existence on this earth. I'd stepped into the elevator to the third floor of the vast building with the icy certainty that at some point I'd be subjected to an interrogation.

But it was amazingly simple. The room was empty, the staff laid-back.

What I felt was beyond relief; I experienced something close to joy as I watched Pierre ask for the form, fill it out for both of us—full name, date of birth, address (his)—and sign it. Then he slid it toward me so I could put my signature next to his own. He'd filled out the form because his handwriting is beautiful, clear and graceful, while mine looks like a car accident. While I was signing I noticed the small print, barely visible clause at the very bottom of the page, warning that any dishonest or misleading information was punishable by five years' imprisonment and a fine of forty-five thousand Euros. *What did you expect?* I asked myself. Of course it was going to be complicated; of course I'd be paralyzed with fear at some point, sooner or later.

Thump went an ink-stamp at the bottom of the form and we were outside, standing on the sidewalk, officially joined—not by a life together, but by the same lie, and the same threat.

Since then, the image of that certificate being slid into our file by the liver-spotted hands of Professor Stein has joined the pile of images I push out of my mind whenever they try to sneak in. I know they're there, waiting, but I won't let them get to me. My technique, which I've been perfecting since childhood, consists of immediately turning my attention to something else. A stranger, an object, a song, a newspaper. That's how I avoid the black despair that threatens to flood through me whenever I think about my parents. I stopped taking tranquilizers a long time ago, because one day I realized that I was, quite simply, alive. Now I've become so stubborn about it that I'll allow myself to be tortured by insomnia even when there's a full bottle of sleeping pills in the medicine cabinet. I listen to music, cool and melancholic rock, until dawn breaks outside my window, bright and soothing. Of course, there are no photos of my parents on display in my house, which is a necessary condition for my technique to work. I imagine this is how people used to deal with life before tranquilizers were invented. We all carry a defense mechanism inside of us, a talent for survival that enables us to take part in daily life despite the horror that surrounds us. You just have to let the mechanism work, and believe in it.

Pierre was sure that no one would check. "It costs too much to do that kind of thing, and I really don't think the hospital has that kind of money in the budget." It was a reasonable conclusion. I rationalize things to myself the same way when I skip out on paying a parking ticket in Brussels. Anna does the same thing when she signs my checks to pay the electricity or telephone bills. Lack of government funding is a blessing sometimes, I swear.

Today, maybe even in just a few hours, this whole nightmare will be over. My body is ready; I'm calm. I have nothing to do this afternoon (I've arranged to go to work at around six p.m. and only be there for the last session, a Canadian trip-hop group I mixed last year).

There's no reason for the insemination not to work.

I mean, of course, there's every reason . . .

. . . and at the same time, absolutely none.

8
The Revolutionary Storm

S o. Not only was I a girl, but I hadn't inherited Darius's
blue eyes, either. If you could flip through the massive
spiral-bound photo albums in which Sara carefully
arranged and dated every photo of us, you would see me as a
baby, dressed in clothes originally intended for Zartocht of a
startlingly bright blue that accentuates my olive skin and
makes me look like an overripe eggplant. Then you would turn
the pages, quickly, the way everyone does with other people's
photos. The blue goes away. My complexion lightens and my
body gets taller and thinner. I meet life head-on in improbable,
DIY costumes—Cleopatra, Cro-Magnon Man, an astronaut,
and Bruce Lee—all concocted by my sisters and Marjane, Big
Mina's daughter. My face reflects the happiness of a child
spoiled with attention and flickers with shifting resemblance—
sometimes to Nour, sometimes to Darius, as if a fundamental
choice hasn't quite been made.

We left our apartment on the morning of February 21,
1981, leaving those photo albums behind on the bookcase in
my parents' bedroom, along with everything else we owned. I
don't have a single photo of myself as a child. Neither do my
sisters. We have no pictures of our parents as young people, or
of their wedding, or of Sara's pregnancies. The entire story I've
been telling you is one without pictures. I have no proof to
show you. None. Not even a birth certificate. You just have to
take my word for it all.

I still think about those albums sometimes, and wonder

what happened to them. Where did our photos end up? Did someone at least rescue them? When I was a teenager spending my Saturday afternoons at the flea market in Saint-Ouen with a bunch of drunken, noisy punks, I used to stop sometimes at the stands run by old bric-a-brac dealers, where hordes of casings and lenses and Super-8 cameras stood beside hundreds of snapshots arranged in rows in old cardboard boxes. Most of them were black and white; full-length portraits, pictures of weddings, family photos, trips to the seaside, all in obsolete formats. As I looked at them I'd sink into a kind of bubble, silent and outside time. The world around me would fade away and I'd feel a kind of uneasy sadness well up in me. We were those people whose lives were turned upside down by wars and deportations, by reversals of fortune, by precipitous departures and death. We were that dressed-up family, smiling and confident and proud, whose picture, proof of their existence on earth, had been catapulted through space and time to land here, between my silver ring-adorned fingers. I told myself that there were no flea markets in Tehran where our photos could have ended up. And even if there were, who would dare to sell or buy them? Because my father's face, with its half-bald head and blue eyes and Trotsky-esque beard, had become the symbol of the Westernized, atheist intellectual. The anti-Islamic-revolutionary. The traitor.

Sara had raised me the same way she raised Leïli and Mina. She dressed me in skirts and put barrettes in my hair. She arranged dolls inherited from my sisters on the shelf above my bed and read me the *Martine* books (in both Persian and French).

Darius did things differently.

As soon as I could walk and talk, Darius stopped paying attention to my gender and treated me the same way as he would have his imaginary son. He took me with him to run errands, carried me on his shoulders, and tossed me into the sea. Later, since I was stronger than my sisters, he would ask me to help him load the suitcases into the trunk, or organize his bookshelves in the library, or wash the car. I was flattered and pleased that he included me in his life and gave me such singular attention, and so I always did exactly what he wanted. I'd even try to anticipate his wishes, preparing a bucket of soapy water and a sponge when I thought he might decide he wanted a clean car. In the face of my enthusiasm he eventually let me take care of things myself, only coming out into the courtyard when I called him, and then only to inspect his Peugeot 504 and praise me.

Because I was the only girl in the neighborhood who behaved this way, the other girls my age started keeping their distance from me. To be honest I wasn't really very interested in them anymore either, preferring to play ball with the boys, walk on ledges and take stupid dares. We, the girls and I, were perfectly synchronized in the immediate realization that we had nothing more in common with each other. When their mothers invited me to their birthday parties I stayed in the corner, waiting for the ordeal to end. Or I helped the mothers put everything away and clean up, which earned me compliments and slices of cake to take home for my sisters.

On sunny days I would watch the group of girls in their light sundresses sitting in a circle on the small front lawn belonging to our neighbors the Pourvakils, talking for hours, and I was glad not to be part of it. They'd throw surreptitious glances at me when I played "who can jump from the highest step." I found them soft and pathetic, and they must have thought I was rough and bad-mannered.

Now, before it's too late, before the storm of the Revolution rises and invades my story, let me go back to my resemblance to Mother.

The older I got, the stronger this resemblance grew. My

flat nose. My wide mouth and small, perfectly straight teeth. The roundness of my chin. My hair, as smooth as a Chinese girl's. When we went to Mazandaran in the summers, Montazemolmolk's descendants—half-crazy great-aunts and fat, wealthy great-uncles—would cry out when they saw me: "It's incredible how much she looks like my sister!" before going back to their incessant rounds of *târofs* (a highly systematic practice that consists of offering guests a permanent stream of nibbles, which are always refused).

One of the great-aunts, Parvindokht, lived in a dilapidated old Baroque-style house built by her father in the central square of the city of Shahsavâr. Its main dome, which gleamed like an emperor's ring, beneath which my great-aunt's bedroom lay, could be seen from the winding road that linked Tehran to Mazandaran. After spending five hours in the car (and vomiting several times), as soon as our car rounded the last curve, we would jostle each other in the race to spot that dome, our faces pressed to the window. The sight of it, which we greeted with cries of joy, meant the end of the journey and the start of summer vacation.

That cold, damp house was our time machine. It fascinated us from a distance, but we went inside without much enthusiasm. Accompanied by uncles and aunts and a large number of their children, we crossed the silent entry hall, which was about as welcoming as a cemetery in winter. Enveloped by the acrid smell of mold, we climbed interminable flights of steps. Here and there, the large double-locked doors made us shiver and giggle.

Once we'd finally reached the top, breathless and sweaty, we waited in front of a small wooden door until Great-Aunt Parvindokht gave us her permission to open it. "Well, what are you waiting for? Come in, children!" I suppose each of us secretly hoped that that voice, as clear and light as a young girl's, would stay silent, freeing us from the chore of this visit— especially me, who knew what lay in store.

The old lady, who was the size of a sea monster, was sitting cross-legged on her bed, which was improbably huge and dangerously high off the ground. It was the only piece of furniture in the little room, the walls of which were craggy like a witch's skin. Sitting on the floor, pressed against one another, we observed her in a low-angle shot. The geographic loftiness of this great-aunt—first the dome, then the bed—was her way of indicating that the end of the feudal system, though it had become reality to the outside world, had nothing to do with her. She was Montazemolmolk's daughter, the heiress of a system that would end only with her death. The second we'd finished with the *salamalaks*, while we waited for the old servant women to arrive with trays of tea, she would start looking for me. Even hidden behind my sisters, praying for someone to distract her attention, I could feel her small, button-like eyes scanning the faces impatiently.

"As God is my witness, the very image of Nour! Come here, little girl!" she suddenly exclaimed.

And then I'd be pushed forward by Sara and end up perched unwillingly on the feudal throne. A few seconds later, feet dangling, crushed against my great-aunt's pillowy bosom, I breathed in the rancid perfume of her nightgown. From year to year, I must have been the only person her rough hands with their gnarled joints touched.

As an aside, just let me point out here that my uncles and my father denied the resemblance. "She looks nothing like Mother. It's her twin sister she looks like!" they'd insist, once we were outside again. This was serious business, and their voices were charged with indignation. This wasn't only about a collective lack of imagination or the inability to see a resemblance beyond eye color; it was about a physical and metaphysical impossibility. No one, no mortal, could look like Mother. On the other hand, anyone—even the corner grocer—could, if they wanted to, look like her twin sister, that poor lady with her dreadfully dark skin and her sad eyes, who'd never had any luck, either in her birth or in her death (killed by her third husband, a Qajar offshoot, under circumstances that remained forever shrouded in mystery). Pleased to have me close to her, Great-Aunt Parvindokht launched into an energetic conversation, swaying back and forth the whole time. From time to time she'd press the mauve line of her mouth to the top of my head and give me a smacking kiss. It was like the heat of my body touched something in her memory. She, whose father had refused her both marriage and children, was awkwardly reproducing the gestures of the mother who had cradled her in the chilly rooms of the *andarouni*.

Down below, seeing my peeved face, my sisters and cousins stifled their mocking laughter. The adults, though, watched the two of us with compassion, secretly cursing Montazemolmolk's tyranny toward his daughters.

Very quickly, Parvindokht's tenderness exhausted itself. "All right, that's enough, go back to your sisters now!" She always said that with a sarcastic smile meant to suggest that I was the one who had insisted on clinging to her. Continuing with the act, she discreetly slid her fingers beneath one of the many layers of her mattress, pulled out a Russian Nicholas II gold coin, and pressed it into my hand. Then she'd pat me on the back so hard that I landed on the floor with a thud.

Now that I've mentioned my great-aunt's Nicholas II coins, I guess I could tell you about THE EVENT; enough of keeping it muffled up in silence, the way Saddeq did with the story of his discovery of Mother's body. Only . . . you'll have to be patient with me, Dear Reader. I *am* going to try, but I already know I won't be able to talk about it. I never can.

Picture London, on a grey, rainy March morning. March eleventh, to be exact. After a sleepless night spent in an abandoned factory listening to a dozen bands ranging from Lords of the New Church to New Order, I go home, to a small furnished room above a charity shop near the Elephant and Castle tube stop. My limbs heavy with fatigue and alcohol, with no intention of going downstairs again for the rest of the day, I open my mailbox in case there's a bill in there. No bill, but an envelope sitting atop a stack of junk mail, an envelope on which I recognize Sara's handwriting.

I open it. It contains a letter and, to my great surprise, one of my great-aunt's gold coins. The sight of it immediately snaps me out of my torpor. In the letter, which I read immediately while standing there, Sara explains that someone (I can't remember who) has come from Iran, bringing her this gold coin and a few other things, little bits and pieces saved by a neighbor years ago, before our apartment was commandeered by the regime. Sure that I will have forgotten about the Nicholas II episodes, she makes sure to refresh my memory: my *poor great-aunt*, her *love* for me, her *generosity*, these coins she used to give me in exchange for just *a few short minutes* spent in her arms . . .

As always, Sara has exaggerated. Her natural tendency to see only the good in other people has hypertrophied since we went into exile. Racked with the pain of separation, she's drawn an impenetrable veil of love around the past, which she watches over like a she-wolf. Paying no attention to our feelings, she has imposed her (more and more fantasy-based) vision of things on us, endlessly obliging us to look back toward *our* homeland, the place where, according to her, we were truly loved. Sara, who used to be so funny and cheerful, isn't anymore. She's abandoned that part of herself that contained joy and enthusiasm and replaced it with depression and anxiety, which have slowly invaded her whole being.

I look up. In front of me, the rows of dented metal mailboxes with more or less unpronounceable names scribbled on them. Mine is right in there amidst the others. Anger rushes up in my throat like a jet of spittle. I've chosen to live here, in this dull gray country where there is nothing—no objects or people or sounds—to remind me of the past. Here, I'm nobody's child. No attachments, no accomplices. Free and alone. And I plan to stay that way. To get away from Sara, I go out. The cold is biting, the kind that freezes you to the core. I run to the corner and stuff the letter and the gold coin into a garbage bin.

When I get back to my apartment, soaked and furious, I notice that the answering-machine light is blinking. I press the button while simultaneously opening the window to let out the sour smell of damp permeating what must have been a carpet once. I think I recognize the halting, dazed voice attempting to speak as Mina's. An icy chill, tinged with dread, runs up my spine. My sisters never call me. In the eighteen months I've lived in London, they've never come to visit me, just like they never came to Brussels, or Berlin.

The broken sounds Mina is producing suddenly stop. After a few seconds of silence, Leïli's voice can be heard, flat and dull. Her words rip through my whole body. Even before the message finishes I have bolted barefoot from my apartment. I run, screaming, to the garbage bin on the corner. The envelope is gone.

Darius resigned from the newspaper *Keyhan* on November 13, 1975. It was on that date that Sara began *Our Life*, the memoir written in her Parisian solitude, describing the Revolution years up to our departure for France. Years later, the book would become a bestseller in Iran—that fact alone perfectly demonstrates the schizophrenia of a country from which the author has been banished, but where her book sells like hotcakes. According to Sara, Darius's resignation marked the day they became part of the political opposition.

So my dad stayed at home that year when I was four, which was also the last year before I started school. The time we spent together only strengthened the bond between us. The more time passed, the more I felt the new and intoxicating sensation of being my father's child rather than my mother's daughter. Instead of identifying myself with Sara, I began identifying myself with Darius.

The reason for Darius's resignation had been the appointment by the Information Minister of an acknowledged SAVAK agent, Homayoun Tahéri, to the position of editor-in-chief. Darius learned of the appointment upon his arrival in the newsroom. Half an hour later he gathered his things, left his letter of resignation on his desk, and left without saying a word to anyone. The newspaper's owner, an old Persian who had graduated from Cambridge and who really liked my father even though he thought his articles were too highbrow for their readers, called him that afternoon and promised to keep paying his salary until he changed his mind. He said, without really saying it—just in case the phones were bugged, which they probably were—that he hadn't been able to do anything to stop the appointment. Anyway, at his age, best to finish out his career without making too much noise.[13]

In January, Darius received a letter from the Information Ministry informing him that not only would his salary no longer be paid, but he would never be hired by another newspaper

---

[13] Let's recap. In 1957, in order to demonstrate his power and control every aspect of political life, the Shah had created SAVAK (a Persian acronym for National Intelligence and Security Agency) with the help of the CIA and Mossad, which had a particular interest in any attempt at control in the troubled Middle East. By means of espionage and informing, SAVAK agents had gradually infiltrated every system in the country, giving the people the impression that they were under permanent surveillance. By the mid-1970s, SAVAK had become famous for its torture techniques—both physical and psychological—and its influence on society was so great that Iranians were afraid of everything, including their own shadow.

unless he agreed to an interview with the Minister. He didn't bother to reply. A few weeks later, a ministry employee called us to make an appointment. "I don't want anything from you, so stop harassing me," shouted Darius, before slamming down the receiver. The next day, Sara decided to begin teaching evening classes at the technical high school in addition to her existing classes. They dismissed the nanny who watched me during the day and Darius took care of me. A man who stayed at home and a woman who worked outside the house: that was how, hand in hand, they entered the arena of political combat. They were already the most modern couple in the family; now they became the most underground, too.

Darius bought me jeans and hiking boots. He cut my hair himself, so short that it dried in minutes after it was washed. At any other time my head would have horrified everyone for miles around, but that year, thanks to the famous pop singer Googoosh's appearance on TV one evening with hair as short as a boy's, the *Googooshi* cut had become super-fashionable. Suddenly freed from the obligation to wear their hair long, girls lined up in front of Tehran's beauty salons to emerge looking like their brothers.

I should mention that at that time, in this Americanized Iran, gender lines had become a bit blurred. Young people, especially from the middle and upper classes, were moving toward a kind of universal unisexuality. I know, in view of what the country has become, how hard it must be for you to imagine *that* Iran. The Iran where girls had short hair and boys had long (*MickJaggeri*) or mid-length (*Beatli*) hairstyles; where teenagers and twentysomethings dressed however they wanted, in loose tunics and bell-bottomed trousers, and met at dusk in the dark corners of the city to smoke Marlboros and swap spit. But you have to try to imagine it, if you want to understand why the majority of Iranians considered the rise to power of the mullahs as "the second Arab invasion" (the first being the devastating seventh-century invasion that imposed Islam as the national religion).

Even though these fads weren't associated with cultural upheaval the way they were in the United States and Europe, they still signified a rejection of traditional values and family strictures. Bizarrely, their allure brought young Persians closer to the pagan roots of Iranian culture, to which they were frequently exposed through holidays and festivals inherited from the time when Zoroastrianism was the official religion of Persia.[14] In any case, the trends caused a lot of arguments, misunderstandings, and tears—but also new ideas, such as "teenage angst" and the "generation gap," which conservative society was forced to come to terms with. For the Sadrs, they meant the redoubling of the famous family meetings chaired by Uncle Number Two in his crusade to save the Honor of the family from being tainted by its daughters.

As a child of this generation, my unusual appearance didn't get a second look. And even if it had, no one, not even Uncle Number Two, would have dared to say anything about the way Darius and Sara pushed their style of living past the boundaries of rationality. Only Grandma Emma asked me one day, as we went to the cinema together to see the latest film in the *Herbie the Love Bug* series:

"How does it feel to have your hair so short, sweetheart?"

"Great!"

"Well, that doesn't surprise me."

"What do you mean?"

[14] I mean, look no further than the Iranian New Year, *Nowrouz* (New Day), a celebration whose roots go back to around 300 BC. It starts on the first day of spring, March 21, and lasts for thirteen days. The new year starts at the exact minute when the Earth finishes its annual trip around the sun. *Nowrouz* is preceded by *Chahar-shambé souri*, the festival of fire. On the last Wednesday of the year, Iranians jump over bonfires to celebrate the return of warm weather and the end of winter.

"Er . . . let's just say that . . . if your father had hacked at your sisters' heads that way, I don't think they would have left the house until it grew back again!"

"Maybe you're right."

"Of course I'm right. Your sisters aren't like you."

"What are they like?"

"They are how they are, don't worry about it, honey."

Of course, since at the time I was unaware of the "genital tinkering" part of her theory concerning my birth, I didn't understand that her question was really only a test to confirm it.

During that year, Darius taught me to: play backgammon, fill his pipe with tobacco, shine shoes, use a dictionary, remember street names, make an omelet, cut articles out of the newspaper, read French, watch a boxing match with Muhammad Ali, open Hafez's *Divan*, recite Persian poetry, take an interest in History, identify the flags of various countries, shovel snow off the balcony, love Harold Lloyd and westerns, tell the violin from the cello, speak as familiarly about Martin Luther King and Malcolm X as if they were my friends, start the car, shift gears, and check the tire pressure before we got on the road to Mazandaran.

And then summer ended.

On the morning of my first day of school, Sara woke me up at the same time as my sisters, crushed me to her in a tight hug, and, with excited little exclamations, brought out the new clothes she'd bought for the occasion and hidden in a drawer. White T-shirt, green plaid pinafore, white socks. I really didn't want her to pick out my clothes or dress me, but she was so happy to be able to perpetuate this ritual with me, so grateful to be alive to see me go to school (for Sara, death was a shadow that lurked in wait for us around every street corner), that I let her do it.

While reminding me of how lucky I was to go to school when there were thousands of other children in this country who didn't have that right, she pulled the T-shirt over my head and then held the pinafore out in front of me so I could step into it. When I turned around so she could adjust my suspenders, I was surprised by my own reflection in the mirror that stood between my bed and Mina's. What I felt then was so strange and unexpected that it paralyzed me: the sense of being dressed up as a girl, and the sudden awareness that I *was* one. A feeling that was quickly joined by panic at the thought of having to go to school dressed like this, and behaving accordingly. How was I going to manage it?

Thinking that my emotions were due to the big-girl image I saw in the mirror, Sara pressed her cheek tenderly to mine. "You really are growing up too fast, my baby! You'll see; everything will be fine."

I didn't dare to say anything, so I just nodded. She hugged me and kissed me.

Thirty minutes later, as I climbed the steps of the school bus after my sisters, Darius, freed from his paternal obligations, went out again to walk the shadowy city streets, in an attempt to bring some kind of order to the obsessive magma that had been seething in his brain for some time now.

Alongside the Dad-Darius that had taken care of me, another Darius emerged. A Protester-Darius who spent his nights reading, taking notes, thinking, cutting articles out of newspapers, and filing the articles. He was gathering material, constructing the skeleton of something that wasn't a new essay, no. But what was it? He wasn't sure yet. All he knew was that from now on he was going to say what needed to be said, and write what deserved to be written. No more wasting his time trying to reconcile his thoughts with the repression swirling around him. Maybe the time had come for him to take the path of dissidence, to turn his back on the fate of Darius Sadr, journalist and son of the wealthy Mirza-Ali Sadr, and assume the identity of the person he would now be for the rest of his life.

To quiet down the exhilaration and questions buzzing in his mind and take the tired pulse of the world, he went out to walk at dawn, when the city was in the hands of the poor workers, the ones whose only wealth was their children. Watching them modestly occupy the streets, spending a little time near them, reminded him of the year he'd spent in Europe working as a laborer, and of the promises they'd made to themselves then. It was these promises that really weighed on his mind, creasing the zigzag line just above the bridge of his nose a little more deeply every day. He said hello to the grocer, Agha Mohabati (who got up at three every morning), as the latter opened the shutters of his shop, which was so tiny that there wasn't enough room even to sit down. Then he went along his way, dispensing greetings right and left. On his way home he stopped by the shop of the Armenian butcher, Vahé Milkhassian, for his first coffee of the day. They chatted about this and that until the delivery truck arrived and it was time for Milkhassian to start his workday.

On the night of Monday, September 27, 1976, after a trip to the cinema with the Nasrs to see Sydney Pollack's *Three Days of the Condor*, Darius sat down at the living-room table in front of a stack of blank sheets of paper. He lit a cigarette, picked up his Pentel pen, and started to write.

In the middle of the night, Sara woke up and came to join him. She was astonished not to find him absorbed in a book or sitting on the floor surrounded by cut-out newspaper articles.

"What are you writing?"

"Come sit down. I have something to tell you."

From the sight of Darius's serious face, Sara knew this was going to be a long discussion.

"Let's go into the kitchen instead. I'll make us some coffee."

"Good idea."

In the kitchen, Sara put the kettle on to boil, and Darius fetched some cups.

"So, are you going to tell me what you're writing?"

"A letter to the Shah. Or, rather, to his chief of staff, who will pass it on to him—I hope," he said, smiling.

"A letter to the Shah?!"

"Are you with me?" Darius held her gaze, like Robert Redford trying to make his ally understand that this thing might be *fucking dangerous*.

"Well, I don't know; I'd have to read it first," teased Sara.

Deep in her heart, she'd been waiting for this moment for a long time. After all, hadn't she married him—at least partly—because she saw in him someone with whom life would be more than just *wake up-go-to-work-have-kids-get-old-die*? Hadn't she dreamed of the day when he would be ranked alongside her heroes, Sartre and Camus?

Right then, as they sat in the narrow kitchen, Sara Sadr, who was about to turn thirty-seven, listening to Darius Sadr, forty-nine, expound on the points he planned to develop in his letter, didn't spare a single thought for her daughters, aged twelve, ten, and five, sleeping in bedrooms down the hall. Yet, throughout her life, Sara refused to acknowledge that political action and its dark side, a life spent focused on oneself, were just as important to her as her family. When Big Mina pointed it out to her she got defensive, insisting that she was fighting precisely for the country she would leave to her children. It wasn't hypocrisy or dishonesty, but something else; at least, that's my interpretation. She felt guilty for desiring something else, just as physical as maternity, and couldn't bear the idea that there was another Sara living within her now, nearing forty and anxious to leave her mark on the world. An independent new being who was detaching, little by little, from the other. A year earlier, following a moving, passionate speech,

Simone Veil had pushed forward the passage of an abortion law, and Sara had followed the matter greedily in the French newspapers. That's what she would have liked, secretly—to be that woman, and to have made that speech. And yet she was in a better position than anyone to know what political involvement meant and implied in a country like her own.

The next night, Darius sat down in the same spot and continued writing. Night after night, sustained by cups of coffee prepared by Sara and unfiltered Camels, he wrote what would soon be published and known under the title *The First Letter* (another would follow in the summer of 1977).

At sunrise, when Darius went to grab a couple hours' sleep, Sara took over. She sat down in the same spot and made a clean copy of the pages Darius had crammed with his frenetic crossings-out and chicken-scratch, until it was time to wake us up and get us ready for school. What she read filled her with admiration for her husband; it exhilarated and inflamed her, even as it made her tremble. But she didn't say anything, never asked him to tone down his approach. She just kept to her role as copyist and accepted the path down which he was leading them both.

Their little undertaking was completed on a Saturday morning in late October at around six-thirty. *I hear the sound of your Palace roof collapsing on your head, and thus on ours. Reigning, and not governing, remains your only option now.* That was the last sentence Sara copied, her eyes filled with tears.

That same evening, the manuscript under his arm, Darius knocked on the door of an editor friend who possessed a photocopier—a rare commodity in Tehran. Without asking any questions, his friend showed him how to use the machine and left. Darius, who was about as gifted with a copy machine as an Eskimo, spent hours copying each one of the 224 pages. When he got home in the middle of the night, he saw that the only light on in the whole of *Mehr* was in their kitchen. Sara was waiting up for him. I always imagine her, a Winston-Salem between her fingers, giving free rein to her love of romantic historical fantasies, dreaming of the French Resistance; the Aubracs and Clavels, those amazing couples who had gone bravely, hand in hand, to meet history head-on.

They spent what was left of the night drinking coffee, smoking and talking. They decided to send a copy of the letter in a few days' time to friends in Paris and London, so as not to remain isolated, and to start a movement.

A few hours later, while we were finishing our breakfast in the kitchen (which had resumed its role as the theatre of the mundane), Sara, in the living room, wrote the address of the Palace on a large brown envelope containing the original of the letter. She affixed several stamps purchased at the grocery store on the corner and handed the package to Darius.

"You do know I'm planting a bomb, right?" he said, with a tender, complicit smile. Sara nodded, her heart thumping in her chest. He leaned down and kissed her. She accompanied him to the front door and watched him descend the few steps that led to the courtyard, which was adorned with the autumn colors she loved so much. Then she came back into the kitchen so she could watch him out the window.

"Where's he going?" asked Mina.

"To mail a letter, sweetheart," answered Sara, as if it were the most harmless act in the world. She watched Darius greet a neighbor who was getting into his car, and then cross the courtyard with quick steps and vanish.

On the corner, Darius slipped the envelope into the mailbox. The postman was scheduled to pick up the mail at eight o'clock sharp. He looked at his watch; still forty-five minutes to go. What did he feel at that moment, the one it seemed his whole life had been leading up to? Did he know that he had just placed *the first stone* of a Revolution that would claim him as one of its first victims?

I borrowed that expression from an article in *Le Monde* dated February 2, 1989 and written to mark the tenth anniversary of the Iranian Revolution: "[. . .] *Sadr was the first intellectual to call out the Shah directly. In the open letter he sent to him in 1976 and which quickly circulated among students, many of whom were arrested for having it in their possession, he openly denounced the inconsistencies of the regime, repression and the absence of freedom of expression, and the economic gap between the wealthy and the rest of the population, which was seeing none of the enormous profits brought in by oil money. This letter could be considered the first stone of the 1979 Iranian Revolution.*"

I read that article in Brussels one Sunday morning. My mind effervescent and my nostrils clogged with nicotine, I had just come from an event dedicated to the Flemish artistic scene in Beursschouwburg, a huge concert hall and alternative performance venue. Passing a newsstand on Anspach boulevard, I decided not to go back to the furnished studio I was renting on the other end of the city, but to buy the paper and settle down in a café for a while. I wasn't used to reading the Belgian daily paper *Le Soir* and had some difficulty with it, so occasionally I indulged myself by buying a French paper, usually *Libération*, and catching up with the news from "home." But on that day I chose *Le Monde*, because there was nothing else to read and I was putting off going home.

First there was the shock of seeing that article, and then the gut-punch of reading my dad's name in it. I reread the paragraph several times. An emotion somewhere between pride and appreciation flooded through me. For the first time, a Western journalist was talking about that letter and the decisive part it had played in the Revolution. For the first time,

Ruhollah Khomeini was no longer considered to be the sole architect of the coup. Even today, if you wade into the thicket of essays and articles dedicated to the 1979 Revolution, you'll see that no Western observer, none of the pundits who claimed to be experts on the Near and Middle East, made the effort to see this Revolution as a protest movement by intellectuals, a spark lit in the universities and carried forward by the enlightened youth, rather than as an insurrection orchestrated by the Old Man in the Turban who was then in exile in Iraq. Preferring historical facility and the Western-style drama of the one-on-one showdown, these observers focused their journalistic efforts mainly on the last months of 1978—which were only the home stretch, when Khomeini, now a messianic figure, had come to symbolically represent the opposition and Islam was portrayed as a rampart against the unequal society promoted by the royal court.

The first time I saw Khomeini's face must have been about a year after *The First Letter*. It was a portrait that had been blown up into a poster, which was brought to our house by Uncle Number Five. An influential bazaar merchant, who was also a boyhood friend of Uncle Number Five, had given him the poster to take to Darius. On the back of it, he had written a few words of respect and friendship. Uncle Number Five, preoccupied as always by his household appliance shop and the constant threat of bankruptcy, and who was about as revolutionary a thinker as the washing machines he sold, had accepted the mission unquestioningly. As soon as Darius saw the portrait, he understood the discreet message being sent to him by the businessmen of Tehran's Grand Bazaar (the true heart and soul of the country's economy).

A highly conservative force deeply rooted at the core of Iranian society, with strong links to the clergy and the young Muslim movement, the *bazaris* had for several months now been conducting a secret, aggressive propaganda campaign in favor of Khomeini. At nightfall they filled the trunks of their cars with sacks of banknotes and distributed them among the poorest denizens of the slums in the southern part of the city, making sure to specify that this generous gesture was "courtesy of the Ayatollah Khomeini," which was as deceitful as it was dangerous.[15]

At that time, my parents already had their feet firmly planted in the opposition. Our telephone was bugged. We received dozens of harassing, insulting calls every day. Darius's clandestinely-published letters and articles were being passed from hand to hand; in fact, he was a figure the *bazaris* would have loved to entice into being part of their organization. Except that for such an alliance to happen, he would have had to renounce his atheism, feminism, libertarian ideas, and criticisms of a clergy with a historical propensity for betrayal. Which he refused to do, despite other, later approaches that were much more direct.

After Uncle Number Five had gone, leaving the poster behind on the living room table, I asked my dad who that bearded mullah with the severe expression was.

"That's Khomeini. He's an ayatollah, not a mullah," was his distracted response, even as he scribbled notes on a scrap of paper.

"Does that mean he never lies?" I asked, suddenly impressed by this man's rank, which indicated a permanent closeness to God.

"I don't know. We'll see," he said, reaching for his newspaper. "Throw it in the garbage if you want."

[15] Remind you of anything? It should, unless you haven't been paying attention to the news reports filmed amid the ruins of Palestine, where Hezbollah representatives go door to door distributing dollars to help families survive and rebuild. Every bill they put on the table screams out: "Who cares about you except for us? WHO? The second you've got this money in your hand, you'll never able to forget us!"

"Are you sure?"

"Yes. It's only a poster, you know."

Very quickly, this same portrait, reproduced on an industrial scale, was in the hands of tens of thousands of demonstrators as they took to the streets of the country's major cities.

On that February morning in Brussels, as I had when I stood in front of boxes of old photos at the flea market, and every time Sara spread her memories out around her, and when Leïli called me to tell me about the deaths of Uncle Number One (heart attack in Tehran), and Uncle Number Three (cancer in Toronto), and Darius, and Uncle Number Five (suicide in Qazvin), and Uncle Number Six (car accident in Los Angeles), and finally Uncle Number Two (old age in Tehran), I felt like I was being pulled backward. Like my body was being dragged over the gravel of a history I was trying desperately to escape. I carry within me the same kind of crazy feeling as the hero of Woody Allen's *The Purple Rose of Cairo*, who breaks out of a black-and-white film into the real, full-color world, where he thinks it's possible to forget the past. I'm always chasing after the present. But the present doesn't exist. It's only an intermission, a temporary respite, which might at any moment be swept away, destroyed, pulverized, by the escaped *djinns* of the past.

Beginning in the early summer of 1978, every Friday morning at around eight o'clock, our apartment was invaded by a mob—friends, family, acquaintances, strangers, foreign journalists, and of course SAVAK spies—looking for information, discussions, and meetings. With nowhere else to meet, they had improvised, turning Darius Sadr's home into their headquarters. Even Michel Foucault stopped by once, and stayed for the whole morning. Apparently, all you had to say to Tehran's taxi drivers was "Sadr's" and they'd drive you there without even asking the address. The stream of visitors was so constant that Sara would leave the front door open.

Robbed of our parents, my sisters and I accepted our lot. Leïli and Mina shut themselves in their bedroom all day to do homework or read, while I went out and played in the courtyard. Sara, exhilarated and exhausted, bustled between the living room and the kitchen with Thermos bottles of hot coffee. Sometimes Big Mina would help her. As for Darius, sitting in his chair at the far end of the living room, only his bald head, above which rose a plume of cigarette smoke, remained partly visible. From time to time he would leave the room, a foreign journalist on his heels, stepping over bodies and greeting anyone who hadn't managed to get access to him, and go into the laundry room, where he could be interviewed in private.

Nine days after a state of siege began in Tehran and eleven other cities,[16] on Friday, September sixteenth, late on a grey, warm morning (I remember that I was wearing my blue T-shirt with white stripes), I was kicking a ball around with some other kids when I saw four military trucks pull up at *Mehr*'s front gate. Almost before I'd realized what was happening, dozens of armed soldiers poured into the courtyard. A war scene, like I'd seen in French films. The sudden descent of Nazi soldiers on Parisian buildings. The terror. The raid. Panicked, I was about to make a run for our apartment when a man standing on the doorstep cried "They're here!," hurled himself inside, and slammed the door.

My heart stopped.

As everything erupted into running and yelling, I stood rooted to the spot, paralyzed, staring at our door, which a soldier was now battering open with the butt of his Kalashnikov.

A hand grabbed my arm roughly and pulled. It was from

---

[16] One week earlier, on Friday, September 8, 1978, known afterward as "Black Friday," the army had opened fire on a crowd gathered in Jaleh Square, in central Tehran.

the lady who lived in number 19. I resisted, struggled. Another neighbor picked me up and ran, heedless of my fists beating at him. We ran into number 19 and the wife locked and bolted the door. I struggled down and hurled myself at the door and clung to the knob and wept.

Later, drained of tears, crumpled and wrung-out like a wet rag, I lay by the door, curled up in a ball. Bibi had told me that God watched over every one of us; surely he would see me, and take pity on me, and finish me off. All I had to do was wait. The woman tried to pick me up. "Can't stay down there . . . , " "Cold," "Eat something." In an attempt to convince me, she set me on my feet and made me look out of the peephole in the front door. "See? You can't go out there." I look into the little circle and see a soldier standing in front of the door. I burst into tears.

What comes next is a clumsy reconstruction put together from everything I heard later about that day. I suppose, logically speaking, that if I wanted to relate to you *exactly* what happened inside our apartment, I could open my mother's book and translate her description of events. Maybe I will do that for other things that happened, but not this one.

The door is closed. Two hundred and eighty-seven people are crammed into the one hundred and thirty-two square meter apartment. Some people, including the oh-so-valiant Uncle Number Six, have managed to flee through the bay window in the living room. Some people are lying face-down with guns pointed at the backs of their necks. Some have their hands braced against the walls and are being searched like criminals. Others, like Sara and Saddeq, are sitting on the floor with their hands behind their backs. Behind them, soldiers are pressing guns against their skulls, forcing them to keep their heads down. A high-ranking army officer is standing over the still-seated Darius, shouting sentences punctuated with insults.

At each one, Sara's chest heaves with anger. Darius doesn't react. Sara knows what is in store for him, and wants desperately to meet his eyes, but the weight of the gun-barrel against the back of her head keeps her from doing it.

Rooms are ransacked and looted. Sitting huddled together on a bed, Leïli and Mina watch the pillaging, stunned and terrified. One soldier holds a garbage bag open while another stuffs it with everything he can get his hands on.

Twenty minutes later, the order is given to evacuate the apartment. The military trucks are now inside the courtyard, which has been plunged into a deathly silence. Pushed by the soldiers, everyone climbs inside the trucks. The horrified neighbors press their faces to their windows, watching the first convoy fill up. The spectacle isn't just overwhelming; it's macabre. Sara is the only one held by two soldiers.

By now her head is in so much pain that she's having trouble breathing. The migraine has taken over; it's familiar, always lying in wait. She should have brought some medicine with her. She should have expected this. She tries to focus on her daughters. Leïli and Mina are in Leïli's room, but where is Kimiâ? She looks around the courtyard for me, but it's deserted. She turns her head painfully in the direction of our neighbors' windows, hoping to catch a glimpse of me behind one of them. On the third floor, a neighbor woman, Sonia Vakili, gives her a tiny wave, weeping. Sara sees catastrophe in those tears. She has the sense of being at her own funeral. She wants to hug Sonia and tell her that everything's going to be all right. "Get in!" shouts a soldier. Sara turns to him and asks him if her daughters are also going to be taken away. "We aren't like you. We don't kill children," is the soldier's retort. Anger and fear rise up in her suddenly, and she spits in his face. The soldier raises his hand to retaliate, but a man comes over and gets between them. He calms the soldier down, saying that his brother is also in the army.

"Well, what are you going to do with these traitors?" the soldier asks.

"We'll see, son," replies the man, mildly.

The evacuation continues. Leïli watches the soldiers come and go for a while and then decides it's time to run. She is thirteen years old; Mina is eleven. She's the big sister. It's her responsibility to get them out of there. She takes Mina's hand, which is as limp as a rag doll's. "Come on, get up, we're leaving!" Mina lets herself be pulled along. They dodge between the bodies and reach the living room. Leïli's goal: to make a run for the front door, which is being guarded by several soldiers; distract their attention, and get out into the courtyard. But what she sees in the living room paralyses her. She didn't think for a second that Darius would still be there. She even thought he had been taken first, and would be in a torture chamber in Evin prison by now. But Darius is still sitting in his chair, impassive, his face as white as a bare light bulb. The high-ranking officer is standing closely over him, a pistol in his hand. Beneath my sisters' terrified gazes, he extends his arm and presses the gun against Darius's temple. The movement is so deliberate, so precise, that there can be no doubt about his intentions.

What happens next takes only a few seconds.

Unable to bear this nightmarish sight, several versions of which will haunt her dreams for years afterward, Mina screams at the top of her lungs. She drops Leïli's hand and flies toward Darius—and then, suddenly, vomits on the high-ranking officer's leg, before collapsing on the floor. Is it the thud of the falling body, or the sensation of the vomit on his leg? Whatever it is, the officer turns abruptly, as if an enemy were attacking his flank . . . and the shot goes off.

As the bullet lodges violently in the wall, like wild animals whose harnesses have just snapped, people crash through the bay window. They push and shove and climb over one another and scratch themselves bloody on broken glass and escape via the balcony. The soldiers yell and go after them. No one pays any attention to Mina's fallen body. Abandoned. Trampled. Crushed. No one sees the whiteness of the bone jutting out of her bloody leg. Not even Darius, who has been handcuffed and taken away in the melee.

Night falls over Tehran, suddenly, like a blanket thrown over a corpse. The streets are already empty even though curfew isn't for another hour. Tanks full of soldiers are stationed on the main thoroughfares. On Élisabeth Boulevard, a few feet from the largest barracks in the city, Sara Sadr—freed ten minutes earlier along with the other women—hails an empty taxi. Anxiety floods through her body, yet again. Did all of that really happen? Where is Darius?

During the five hours she's just spent being interrogated by two colonels, the fear left her, to be replaced by tremendous, intense sharpness. She felt her muscles draw tight, supporting her, holding her upright. An incredible sense of strength emanated from her and filled the room. She faced them, answering their questions in a clear voice. Later, when she recounted the interrogation, she would repeat this exchange endlessly:

"Do you have any weapons?"

"Yes. My husband's pen."

"Don't try to act clever with us, ma'am."

"I'm not acting. If his pen isn't a weapon, then what am I doing here?"

And then she'd laughed, like you laugh in an idiot's face.

The taxi stops at the front gate of *Mehr*. The driver, figuring out who she is and where she's been, won't take any money from her. Sara enters the dark courtyard. The silence is so complete that the very air seems motionless. Here and there lights burn in the windows, but not in the Nasrs' apartment.

Sara's heart lurches. Where are they? She's sure that Big Mina will have taken care of her daughters; there's no doubt about that. She knows that Leïli, Mina, and Kimiâ will be with her. But where? Maybe at the Pourvakils' house? Her steps quicken. The Pourvakil apartment is at the far end of the courtyard, hidden behind some trees. Their living room seems to be in complete darkness. Her legs tremble. She looks for another solution: run to a neighbor's house and call her mother. She is just about to move when she distinctly hears footsteps approaching. Until this morning, *Mehr* was a safe place, a fortress of friendship and trust (even though, of course, there are a few neighbors who are *shahis*, royalists who don't speak to them anymore). But it isn't secure anymore. Any SAVAK agent might be hiding in a corner, waiting to jump on her. A hand touches her on the shoulder.

"Mrs. Sadr." Even as she nearly jumps out of her skin, she recognizes the sepulchral voice of *Mehr's* caretaker, whom the children—out of both fear and affection—call Baba. She turns around. Baba's massive body looms up in front of her like a wall.

"They've gone, ma'am."

"Where?" she demands, struggling not to cry.

"Aban Hospital. For Little Mina."

When Sara burst into the waiting room at Aban Hospital, everyone froze. Haggard and breathless, she looked like a war survivor desperately searching for her family in the labyrinth of a hospital.

The hundred scenarios I'd invented since their arrest included "tortured to death" and "killed by a firing squad." It was only when I saw Leïli run to her, saw Sara wrap her arms around Leïli's shaking body, that I acknowledged the reality— but I didn't dare go to her, and she didn't invite me to. There was still that indescribable sense of misunderstanding between Sara and me; I was always waiting for her to come to me, and she accepted the fact that I was keeping my distance. And in the pit dug by this original misunderstanding, so many failures and miscommunications were born . . .

"Where is Mina?" she asked, anxiously.

"In the operating room," answered Big Mina. "Now, don't worry, it's just her leg. She'll be fine."

"How did it happen?"

"You don't need to know that just yet, my sweetheart," soothed Grandma Emma, who desperately wanted her daughter to sit down, have a cup of tea, eat something, and rest a bit first. But Sara turned to Ramin Nasr, calm and determined.

"Tell me, Ramin."

The doctor finally came in at around ten-thirty that night.

Half asleep in a chair, I had trouble following the conversation, which was peppered with mysterious medical terms. I wanted to be as concerned and alert as Leïli, but as soon as my eyes closed I found myself propelled back to apartment 19. I only managed to figure out that the operation had gone well. Then Sara squatted down next to me and took my face in her hands.

"You're going to go back with Ramin. You've got school tomorrow."

"What about Leïli?" I already knew the answer to that, because Leïli, who was inconsolable at not having been able to save Mina, had been glued to Sara's side since she walked in the door, desperately seeking her mother's love and forgiveness.

"Leïli's going to stay with me. You have to go home; you need to sleep. Don't worry. I'll be there when you wake up."

On the way home, Ramin's car was stopped three times by soldiers who emerged abruptly from the shadows. Each time, he gestured to me, sitting beside him, my face contorted and my eyes squeezed shut.

"My daughter is very sick. It might be appendicitis. I took her to the hospital."

The dull gleam of a flashlight shone on my face as the soldiers inspected me, but despite its searching glare I didn't move. I pretended I was an actress, like Ava Gardner (Sara's favorite) or Susan Hayward (Darius's), even though on the inside I was a hysterical mess.

How does a person acquire a taste for subterfuge and lying? To what extent is character shaped by events? Even as I wonder that, I remember a similar scene in Turkey in 1981, in the car that was taking us from the border town of Van to Ankara. Omid, our people smuggler, had warned us that every time we entered a town, soldiers would ask to see our papers. Since we didn't have any, we would all have to keep quiet and let him handle it. He had asked me to pretend I was ill and in pain, and to writhe around in Sara's arms. I took my role very seriously, convinced that our lives depended on the believability of my portrayal. To keep from staring at the soldiers as they clomped toward us in their heavy boots, Sara buried her face in my dirty, tangled hair. I could feel both our hearts pounding. Leïli and Mina clung to each other, looking miserable and beaten-down. As we concentrated on this performance, Omid showed the soldiers his phony Turkish papers, which he'd forged himself, and explained that he was taking his family to the hospital in Ankara. As soon as they handed back his false passport, he discreetly slipped them a few banknotes and the soldiers left us alone.

Fresh from our successful fleecing of the curfew patrols, Ramin's car pulled into the courtyard of *Mehr*. Now, given what I'm about to tell you, the menacing darkness of a stormy night would have been more appropriate, but it was astonishingly bright out. While I'd been flexing my dramatic muscles in the passenger seat, every cloud had fled from the sky, leaving only the grapefruit-sized moon. *The moon had stripped away the robe of night*, as the mystic poet Hafez of Shiraz put it.

The deserted courtyard looked steel-grey in the moonlight. It was utterly silent. Every window was dark. Tehran was, temporarily, under control. Ramin turned the wheel toward his usual parking spot. The headlights shone on a dark shape leaning against the wall that separated our two apartments. I stifled a scream. Ramin's body tensed beside me. In the yellowish glow we saw a beard, and then hollow cheeks. Our fear was immediately replaced by disbelief. "Good God!" cried Ramin, recognizing Darius.

How had he gotten there? Who had put him there? What had happened between his arrest and his return? We never found out the answers to those questions. Darius never spoke about it.

Did I ask him any questions? No.

Why not? 1) Because I was intimidated by Darius the Invincible, Darius the Heroic, Darius the Survivor of Hell; 2) because I was afraid to hear the truth; and 3) because he was inaccessible, monopolized, surrounded, in demand, distant, gone, hidden. He existed now in a world parallel to the one I— we—lived in.

And later, once we were in Paris? In Paris, we didn't talk to each other anymore, about anything. None of us. Each of us was shut up in a silence made of stupefaction and adjustment. In a state of unconsciousness. The past was just anecdotes now, that could be retold, but were only a vast, white, ruined wasteland.

And then? I left. I ran away, to other places, where I could reinvent myself. Until THE EVENT.

Do I regret not asking him? I don't know. Sometimes I tell myself that his mysteries were an integral part of the confusing character that he always was, from his childhood, when he locked himself away to read, to his solitary walks. To want to understand everything about him would have been to destroy him. I grew up with the certain knowledge that he kept most of his life to himself. Anything that I did know about Darius didn't come from him, but from Uncle Number Two.

There, Dr. Gautier has just walked past me. She doesn't stop, but is unwinding her long scarf, which is as thick as a carpet.

"I'm really sorry; they should have told you. I was in a meeting. I'll be with you in just a minute."

She disappears into her office. She often reminds me of Leïli, and not just because she's a doctor. It's her tallness. Her pale, sun-deprived skin. Her total lack of whimsy or imagination, as if her outward appearance has to reflect the gravity of Science. But also her willingness to juggle family life with a brilliant career—which supposes, again just like Leïli (and *un*like me), that she decided very early what she wanted out of life.

Despite her young age (she's barely forty), Françoise Gautier is considered among the top infertility specialists, particularly involving infertility related to the AIDS virus. She is the one in the Reproductive Medicine department who deals with serodifferent couples—in other words, us.

When we had our first appointment, she explained to us (in language she thought was understandable) that sperm washing consists of separating the seminal liquid and the T4 lymphocytes (in which the HIV is present) from the sperm cells. The isolated sperm are then frozen for later insemination. After this explanation, she turned to me and said, undoubtedly thinking she knew what was on my mind:

"Of course there's no such thing as zero risk, but this technique enables us to get pretty close to it."

In other words, there is an infinitesimal risk that I will be infected, which means I'll have to have regular blood tests for several months after the insemination. But, and Dr. Gautier was positive on this point, there is no danger to the baby, since it's during the birth process that the virus is transmitted from mother to baby through the blood, and they have impeccable techniques to make sure that doesn't happen.

During the meeting that followed the psychologist's affirmative decision, she prescribed me daily injections of Puregon from the fifth day of my cycle through the tenth, in order to cause ovarian hyperstimulation. I asked her if that was necessary, given that I'm not infertile.

"Every woman, infertile or not, who comes into this department has to do it," she said. "I've prescribed you the minimum dose and we'll adjust it if we need to."

This seemed unnecessarily and arbitrarily systematic to me, but I did what I always do: I gave in.

The day before yesterday, I came to the hospital so they could check the size of my follicles (ninety minutes' wait). I was examined by an intern who, after the ultrasound, told me that I should do the injection of Ovitrelle that same evening, to free the follicles. On my way out I stopped at reception to make my appointment for the insemination, which imperatively had to take place within forty-eight hours.

You pretty much know the rest.

Since she's going to call me any minute now, I'd better speed things up a bit—skip over events and whole years: the anxiety-filled nights, Darius's writings spread out on the living-room table, barricades and demonstrators, deaths and political meetings and ransacking and fires. Governments overturned. The arrest of the former prime Minister, Amir Abbas Hoveyda, accused by the Shah of being responsible for the corruption; the visit of the American president, Jimmy Carter, to Tehran; the Americans' withdrawal of their support from the Shah. The last-resort nomination of the Liberal Democrat Shahpour Bakhtiar as Prime Minister. There, now we've come to the last picture in our 1970s slideshow: 1979. The year of explosion.

On January 16, I burst into the kitchen. I find Bibi standing at the sink, carefully scrubbing a large cooking pot.

"Say '*Margue bar Shah*,' Bibi!"[17]

"Are you starting with that again? I've already told you, I don't know!"

"What don't you know?"

"*Ey baba!* Leave me alone!"

"But why don't you ever want to say '*Margue bar Shah*?'"

"You never stop saying it, and where has that gotten you?"

"It got him to leave!"

"Who left?"

"The Shah! He LEFT!"

Bibi finally looked up at me. "Is that what all the yelling's about?"

"Of course! EVERYONE is out in the streets! Come on, come with me, we'll go see!"

"What for?"

"To celebrate! He LEFT, Bibi!"

"You think that's going to change anything? Go on, get out of my kitchen. I have work to do, little girl."

Color images on the TV of a plane's crowded interior. Close-up of Ruhollah Khomeini's face, with its long white beard and eyebrows so bushy that they hide his eyes. The commentator emphasizes the fact that on this first day of February, 1979, he is returning to his country after fifteen years of exile. One of the foreign journalists accompanying him leans closer to him and asks, "What are you feeling right now?"

[17] Death to the King.

An interpreter relays the question in Persian.

"Nothing," he murmurs, with a small, ironic smile.

"Nothing?" repeats the interpreter, surprised.

"Nothing," he insists.

In the Pourvakils' living room, standing in front of the television screen, Sara's face twists into a Harvey Keitel-style grimace. Astounded, she turns to Mrs. Pourvakil, who is watching the images without really seeming to understand them.

"Nothing!!!" Sara exclaims. "What does that mean? He doesn't feel ANYTHING even though he's coming home to his own country?"

"Maybe he feels something, but he just doesn't know how to describe it," suggests Mrs. Pourvakil.

"My God, the monarchy has just been overthrown! People are dead! He doesn't seem to get that!"

"He must be tired . . . "

"Tired? From living peacefully in France? In Neauphle-le-Château?" (Silence.) "Well, I'm going to make some tea." Vexed, Sara turns her back to the TV and disappears.

On the screen, the images continue to flow.

The Air France plane has just landed on the runway at Mehrabad Airport. Now, the Old Man in the Turban is slowly descending the stairs, his eyes fixed on his feet and his hand clutching the arm of the *farançavi* pilot. His arrival, applauded by an ecstatic sea of humanity, is being compared to that of Mahdi, the "Hidden Imam," whose name is a signal to every good Shiite to rise up, ready to fight at his side to bring justice to the world.

This is, without a doubt, the end of the Revolution.

The earth has been shaken from top to bottom. The Old World lies in tatters. Violence and blood have turned every street into a crime scene. Everything has blurred into disturbing, euphoric chaos. Mythology is spilling over into reality, and paganism into religion. Ahura Mazda (God of Light) has

defeated Ahriman (God of Shadows). The Angel has van-
quished the Demon. The people have been freed in a monu-
mental, painful disturbance. They were in Hell and now they
stand at the gates of Paradise, like the pilgrim birds in the
poem by Attar who have finally found the King of Birds, the
mythical Simorgh. For all these months while the Old Man
waited in the wings, first in Najaf and then in Neauphle-le-
Château, to be reborn into the world as, successively, Emam,[18]
Messiah, Supreme Guide, and Undisputed Leader, his portrait
has been painted on every wall in every city in the country. His
face has been seen from Tehran to Tabriz; from Machhad to
Adadan; from Qazvin to Shiraz, and even, one September
evening, in the contours of the moon.

Who could have imagined back then that this Angel was
really just another Demon, and the Light an illusion? Who
could have known that, like the Pied Piper of Hamelin, the
Old Man would soon lead the children of his country into a
cave and trap them inside?

---

[18] To understand the importance of this designation, you have to take a
walk on the fundamental side of Shi'a Islam and its clerical organisation,
which is more or less modelled on Christianity. This "imam" isn't the kind
that leads prayer services at the mosque, as it is for the Sunni Muslims. For
Shiites, the title *Imam*, pronounced *Emam* in Persian, designates the testa-
mentary heirs of Mohammed, who are authorised to continue his prophetic
mission. They are the sole guides, the unique holders of absolute truth. The
first of them was Ali, cousin and son-in-law of Mohammed and founder of
the Shi'a faith. The eleven others were all children and grandchildren of the
line of Ali and Fatima, daughter of Mohammed. The twelfth Emam, Mahdi,
is considered to have vanished. His disappearance heralded the Occultation,
and Shiite Muslims live in hope of his return, which will put an end to
oppression and injustice. Khomeini, who went into exile in Najaf in 1964 and
then sought refuge in Paris in 1978 when Saddam Hussein expelled him—a
sort of occultation of his own—gradually acquired a status similar to that of
Mahdi. He became the one whose coming heralded the end of dictatorship.
I'm telling you all this so you'll understand that going from Ayatollah to
Emam was no small feat! Through his own cowardice and stubbornness, the
Shah ended up making his adversary into nothing less than a saint.

We had been staying with the Pourvakils since early January. Sensing that the end was near, the Secret Service and the army had seriously stepped up their efforts at repression. The anonymous phone calls and threats had doubled, to the point that Sara decided we had to leave our apartment for good.

For three months, no one had known where Darius was. No one knew that his childhood friend Majid had fetched him from a secret political meeting that was being watched by SAVAK and hidden him away. Someone had simply called my mother in the middle of the night and told her that Darius wouldn't be coming home. Before, Sara had always known where her husband was, and even visited him in hiding, changing taxis three or four times to extend and camouflage her path. Sometimes she'd taken us with her, holding our hands firmly in the street. But now the game had changed.

Some time after we moved into the Pourvakils', one evening when we were watching the TV news in a silence as sharp-edged as a razor blade, the solemn voice of the journalist announced the latest communiqué from Bakhtiar's government. By joint decision of the government and the army, Darius Sadr had been declared an enemy of the fatherland. Anyone with information concerning his whereabouts was required to disclose it immediately.

I grasped the magnitude of this news when Sara, furious and icy-calm, stood up and walked stiffly toward the telephone. She picked up the receiver and called police headquarters. "Hello; I'm the wife of Darius Sadr," I heard her say. "Tell your superiors that the real enemies of the fatherland are them and this whole bunch of . . . " I didn't hear any more after that. Terror washed over me. What was she doing? Why had she called the police? I was appalled by the idea that she was drawing attention to us again, like on the evening when she had rolled down her car window to challenge General Rahmani in front of his own house.

She was like that, Sara. Always on the alert. Her long-limbed body draped in passion as if it were a custom-made gown. When it came to my father, even passion became too restrictive and cumbersome. She rose up, away from the Earth with its useless laws and pathetic gods, to become a tornado, a bolt of lightning, an avalanche. Sometimes she scared me. Sometimes my fear mingled with admiration, the same kind of thing I felt for Angela Davis and Leïla Khaled, my revolutionary heroines, whom I imagined to be part-human, part-Bionic Woman.

The next day, plainclothes policemen appeared in the streets around *Mehr*. In cars, on the sidewalks, stationed in front of the grocery store, the Armenian butcher's, the bakery. Sara wouldn't let us leave the house or even part the curtains so we could look outside. Truth be told, these rules were meant mostly for me. Since the schools were closed and the streets were full of fire and blood and everyone was going around with Kalashnikovs strapped to their backs, my sisters spent most of their time reading novels. Occasionally, they went out into the courtyard with some neighborhood girls for a little while in the late afternoon, and sat on the grass and chatted. I was the only one who went any further, playing soccer or hide-and-seek, and following the older kids, who were making Molotov cocktails in the parking lot across the street.

Only Mrs. Pourvakil, who was as small and round and bouncy as a basketball, really went out. Every hour, on the slimmest of pretexts, she put on her coat, picked up a basket or just her handbag, and breezed out the door, coming back full of seemingly trivial details: "The guy in the black Peugeot, license plate number 775 48, the one parked near the pharmacy, went in to buy cigarettes. The asshole must think he's a prince or something; smokes Dunhills!" "A different one—he has a checked jacket like the one we bought for Karim last year—has taken over for the bastard who was sitting in front of the high school with a newspaper. I hope God sends him to hell for wearing the same jacket as my son!" To listen to her, you would have thought that every SAVAK agent in Tehran was stationed near our house.

The outings of Mrs. Pourvakil, who Mina had nicknamed Agatha Christie, became a joke to us. We imitated her; her suspicious glances, her movements, which were as discreet as a tank; the Hercule Poirot-esque phrases she'd rattle off every time she came back home. We laughed until we doubled over, stamping the floor, our heads buried in pillows.

Sara listened to her. She'd taken refuge in the kitchen and, bent over the gas stove, didn't seem to want to come out. From time to time she murmured an "ah," which could have meant anything. A few times she called to us—"Girls!"—in an excited voice that made it seem like she was about to take an enormous chocolate cake out of the oven, but when we hurried in there she'd look at us for a few seconds and then say "No, nothing." Mina lingered, hoping for something more, until Leïli whispered something in her ear and took her hand to pull her away.

That evening after dinner, the three of us were in our bedroom changing into our pajamas when Sara called us. She was sitting on the small sofa in the foyer, half in shadow. She'd changed her clothes to go out: wool skirt, black turtleneck, three-quarter length coat, and boots.

"Where are you going?" demanded Lëili, surprised by her appearance, which was as unexpected as it was elegant.

"Come sit by me," Sara said, holding out her arms.

Gently, Sara explained to us that SAVAK would surely come looking for her, that it was only a matter of hours. We would have to be brave and patient, and promise her that, no matter what happened, we would always be there for each other. "Okay, my sweethearts?" Their eyes frozen like balls of ice, my sisters nodded. I imitated them because they knew better than I did what Sara wanted from us. "You know, I've been very lucky to have three wonderful daughters." More nods, as mechanical as those dogs with disjointed heads they sold in toy stores.

Now Sara was giving us more instructions. I was to keep my ears open for outside noises. If SAVAK came now, we could stay close to her and be taken too. But if Sara left the apartment alone, we would never see her again.

She told us to go to bed, and we filed back to our room in silence, Leïli in the lead. Sara didn't hug us, but I felt her eyes following us. We lay down in our beds without turning off the ceiling light. Its harsh white light made us feel like we were in a present that was still bearable. Switching it off would mean resigning ourselves. Then we heard a dull noise, and an explosion rattled the windows.

The bomb had been thrown into our apartment through the bay window. The front door and the windows had burst into shards. The windows of the other apartments, all the way up to the fourth floor, had been partially or totally blown out. Flying shrapnel had pierced the gas tanks of the cars in the courtyard, and gasoline was pouring out onto the concrete. Voices screamed not to smoke. Terrified neighbors in pajamas and bathrobes streamed into the courtyard like animals in distress. The smell of burning and gasoline was stomach-churning. All the lights in every apartment were on, illuminating the courtyard as if for an evening party.

I milled around amid the chaos, barefoot, virtually levitating off the ground. I was so happy that I instantly forgot what I had seen. I pushed through the crowd, heedless of the shoving and screaming, of the hands that reached out to console me. It was as if I were floating above a spectacle that was both terrible and magical, like a parody of a tragedy, without real consequences. It was finished, over. What was going to happen that night had happened. Our apartment was destroyed, but Sara hadn't been taken! We'd been afraid for nothing. We'd trembled for nothing. Just a piddly little explosion.

*

The next morning, on a day of major demonstrations, the cortege started from Kennedy Avenue, which ran perpendicular to our street. Beginning at dawn, people poured into our courtyard to see "the Sadr house." News had obviously spread all over Tehran that a bomb had exploded here, and everyone was coming to see whether it was rumor or truth. I'd asked permission to go into the courtyard; I wanted to watch them stare at the shattered door, and feel once again the joy of the previous night. I even pointed out our apartment, and then watched them slow their steps and in front of the gaping hole, jubilant at seeing them so taken aback by such a minor thing. I didn't feel the need to go inside and look at the damage. I couldn't have cared less.

A few weeks later I got sick, with a fever so high it kept me in bed. The usual remedies didn't work. I loved that fever; the cottony feeling of floating in the air, of no longer being connected to reality, of fading away. Later, drugs and alcohol made me feel the same way, but without the dreamy pleasure of knowing I hadn't done anything to cause it.

One evening, Darius's friend Majid came to see us at the Pourvakils' and decided to take me to see his older brother, a GP. With Sara's help he carried me out to the car, which was covered with a fine dusting of snow, and put me in the passenger seat. Sara stayed behind.

I vaguely remember a small office with purple walls that wobbled like gelatin. A tall man with long, cold fingers examined my bare belly. I remember Majid, his face hidden behind a veil of cigarette smoke. Then the prick of a needle in my arm. And then, suddenly, icy wind in my hair, and my unlaced shoes getting stuck in the mud on the sidewalk.

Years later, in Paris, when Sara told me that Majid was dead and I remembered that episode, she admitted to me that Darius had been hidden in the basement of that medical office.

So he was there, beneath my burning feet as they dangled off the examining table.

On the afternoon of February 13, 1979, thirteen days after Khomeini's arrival and two days after the definitive fall of the Shah's last government, some of our neighbors had gathered in the Pourvakils' living room. The TV was on and everyone was commenting on the news, even the children.

The atmosphere was strange, as it had been over the past couple of weeks; happy and convalescent at the same time. There would be a burst of talking and then, suddenly, silence. Exaggerated laughter followed by sudden departures to the kitchen, to cry in peace. From time to time, someone would plant a loud kiss on top of our heads. Arms overflowing with love embraced us tightly and then let us go quickly, the way you let go of a top when you're ready to spin it. There were no more borders between where we stopped and other people began, between inside and outside. The television newscaster might just as well have been right there in the living room, which might as well not have had a roof or walls, might as well have been out in the courtyard, with all the other living rooms of all the other apartments in the country. Millions and millions of people, bound together, were just one body, the heart of one beating in the chest of another, guts tangled together, the same words and sentences in everyone's mouths. Democracy. Freedom of expression. The right to vote. Extraordinary words, as fragile as newborn babies, bloody and naked, daunting in their beauty, words on which a destiny could now be built.

The doorbell rang.

I ran to open the door.

For months I'd run to hide under the bed every time the doorbell rang. It frightened me so much that I wasn't even aware that I'd done it until one of my sisters came to find me. Those first days of February were a release for me. Suddenly I wasn't afraid anymore. I was like a baby who learns to walk and then does it again and again, experiencing the same kind of victorious pleasure every time. Whenever the doorbell rang now, I ran to open it, to prove to myself that the terror was really and truly over.

A man in a hat and a dark raincoat stood there. The bright sunlight of the outdoors kept me from seeing his face. Not recognizing him, I got scared and backed away. Suddenly, everyone who had been in the living room a minute before began crying out joyously and weeping. It was only when I saw my mother fling her arms around the man's neck that I understood. His face. The white at his temples spreading into his eyebrows now; his blue eyes crinkled by his smile; his cheeks hollow, but clean-shaven as always. Little by little he came into focus, alive and tangible, emerging from the fog. My father. Back home.

10
LEÏLI'S REVELATION

S ummer, 1979. The five of us were together again, in the safe harbor of Mazandaran, among the trees, in the protective pocket of the valleys, where everything that wasn't us had ceased to exist. The weather was beautiful, absolutely beautiful, which was a delight in itself.

Some summers, it rained so much that we spent whole days inside by the coal stove, playing Five in a Row or Exquisite Corpse. In the afternoons, Darius and his brothers smoked opium in a room arranged especially for this form of Mazandarani laziness, drank black tea, and played backgammon. The door was never closed and the acrid odor of the smoke drifted through the rooms like the smell of sweat. Their wives came and went, occasionally taking a puff on the long pipe the men had prepared. Only my mother, that daughter of Tehran, stamped with infallible morality, kept herself apart. She organized games and entertained the older cousins, some of whom were her students. She detested opium, just as she detested alcohol. Anything that altered a civilized man's state of consciousness, his awareness of others and of the world around him was insufferable to her. And even more than the opium, she hated seeing her husband turn into that archaic, boorish individual sprawled out on rough woolen cushions, slipping easily into the rites of his clan. Darius, miles and miles away from their intimacy and their concerns and everything they had built together.

But that summer, the sun had lodged itself firmly in the sky and seemed to have no intention of leaving. Even the evenings, which were usually cool and damp, were as warm as bathwater. After a few weeks spent at Uncle Number Two's villa we had gone with part of the tribe to another house, far from the Caspian Sea and its crowded beach. A wooden house, nestled deep in the forest, that belonged to one of my father's female cousins. We slept on mattresses set out on the bare ground, pressed against one another like cookies in a tin. The bedrooms were on the first floor, in one long row, connected by a huge terrace that made you feel like you were floating among the trees.

As soon as we woke up, the household divided itself into three categories: adults, teenagers, and children. The adults and the teenagers stayed around the house, the former talking politics on the ground-floor terrace and the latter sprawled out in hammocks strung near the barn. The children, pockets crammed with pistachios and skipping-stones, went out to explore the forest and climb trees. Even though they were still young, my sisters stayed in the teenage group—by inclination, but also because of Mina's leg (she refused to give up her crutch, which had become an excuse not to be rowdy).

I went with the other kids—all boys. I was tall and thin, short-haired and flat-chested with big hands and feet, and I looked just like them. Not only because of my hybrid body, which was still resisting all of nature's assaults, but also in my insatiable desire for the outdoors, the forbidden, which most Iranian girls, held in check by mental boundaries set down while they were still in the cradle, considered coarse and vulgar. Girls were brought up to be the cement of the family, the glue that held together generations, homes, and traditions. They were programmed to stay close to aging parents and to adapt to life as if it were a bridge to be crossed. If you need proof, consider the fact that not a single one of the teenage male cousins was present that summer. They'd all been sent to *Amerika*, far from the demonstrations and arrests, to pursue their studies and carve out their destinies. One after another, they had left their sisters behind and disappeared from our lives, never to reappear. They hadn't had any choice in the matter either, but at least they were able to have adventures, and marry whomever they wanted to.

At lunchtime we all met up again—the mothers and the teenage girls and me—in the open-plan lounge/kitchen, a huge space where we engaged in an energetic ballet whose choreography was dictated by our duty to feed the famished hordes. Kept away from domestic activity since birth, the boys stayed outside, martyring insects and birds. No one insisted that I come in and help, but I liked the noisy atmosphere and I loved having my place in it, my legitimacy, even if I couldn't identify with the teenage girls who were always either chattering like magpies or surly because of their periods, or with the young women with their eyebrows plucked by the older ones, or with the wives forever preoccupied with their husbands' well-being.

By some strange psychic mishmash, whenever I imagined myself as an adult, I pictured myself bare-chested, smoking my cigarette on the balcony during the first warm days of spring, like our fourth-floor neighbor in Tehran, on the other side of the courtyard. I had watched him through the slats of the blind on my bedroom window in the early afternoons, while the rest of the city settled down for its afternoon nap. His chest was hairy, and he rubbed a hand over his chubby belly and then stuffed it into the pocket of his jeans, blowing smoke nonchalantly, gazing off into the distance. I told myself that one day I would do exactly the same thing. I'd also have the right to take off my T-shirt casually, and enjoy the sun on my skin. I was so certain of it—it just seemed so obvious—that there was no need to even talk about it (as if anyone would have been interested in my predictions of the future anyway).

As the lunch preparations began to shape up, someone turned on the TV, to a Russian channel that was showing the Olympic Games from Moscow. Withdrawn into itself like a newborn, Iran had better things to do than broadcast these controversial games. Truth be told, the boycotting of them by the Americans as well as dozens of other countries on the heels of the Soviet invasion of Afghanistan meant that these Olympics weren't very interesting, but the proximity of the USSR to this part of Mazandaran, and the ability to get their channels on TV, was entertaining. It accentuated the isolation of this house, making us feel like we were living in a secret, special place. A no man's land, forgotten by the gods.

Everything made me happy.

I was living in a sunshine-drenched Western, and the pure joy of childhood was flowing brightly through me again, soaking into every cell of my body. I jumped on the couches, in the gaps between the languid arms and entangled legs of the teenagers, making fun of their goofy faces and protestations. I clowned around. I laughed loudly. I climbed up the walls and touched the ceiling. I hung from the treetops and stretched my hands toward the sky. Until one day I landed next to Leïli. Look, now, at her face, framed by the masses of her curly hair, and her dry lips, which have just pressed themselves to my ear and murmured in French so that no one else will understand: "*That's enough now. Really, you have to stop. Everyone will think you're a lesbian.*"

I spent the next few hours by myself upstairs, in the unfurnished room where we slept. Suddenly, what I felt could no longer be expressed using simple words. If I'd been able to open my mouth instead of bolting up the stairs to be alone, I would have screamed: "That isn't true, Leïli, you're lying!" But at the same time, on the flip-side of this legitimate confusion, there was the sudden violence of truth. Maybe that was what

I'd been avoiding, by keeping myself separate from the rest of the girls.

I stayed for a long time staring out the window at the peeling bark on the branches of the chestnut tree until it became clear and recognizable. Outside, nothing had changed. Flocks of birds soared in the immense blue sky. The cold water of the river flowed joyously over a bed of stones toward the Caspian Sea. Only this morning that whole quiet world had still belonged to me, included me, but now it was going its own way, leaving me behind, alone.

I didn't know what the word lesbian meant; yet, by some strange alchemy, the second it dropped onto me, as dark as a drop of black ink into a glass of water, I felt it. It had something to do with how I acted, with who I was, and with shame. It must have described that new sensation—heady energy? impish playfulness?—that flooded through me when I was among girls, and of which I was vaguely aware because it disappeared as soon as I shifted to a group of boys. I didn't yet have a large enough vocabulary to define it. It wasn't present enough for me to wonder if it was good or bad, or to question it, or try to control it. Most of the time, it stayed buried in some dark, muddled part of my being. A seed in mud. An air bubble trapped in a glass.

I don't know how long I stayed in that upstairs room, but suddenly Mina was there, a few steps away.

"Come downstairs, it's lunchtime."

I shook my head, my face burning, my lips clamped together so I wouldn't cry in front of her. The room went out of focus again.

"What's the matter?"

"Nothing."

What could I say? Even I didn't know exactly what the matter was. I hadn't done anything wrong. Leïli hadn't insulted me or scolded me. So what had she done, then? Why did I have this sudden desire to vanish from the face of the Earth?

"Come on, quit it. It's not like you to pout like some stuck-up princess."

I looked down without answering. She was right; I wasn't the kind of kid who sulked, so what was I doing there, all alone? I could feel Mina's eyes on me; she was getting tired of waiting. I thought she would grab my arm and pull me along behind her, like she always did when I refused to answer her calls and kept playing in the courtyard. Then I'd be able to stop these absurd dramatics and go down into the living room, with her fragile body in front of mine like a screen. I would be welcomed with exclamations, and after a few seconds I'd smile and everything would go back to normal.

But Mina didn't do anything. "Whatever," she grumbled, and left the room.

It was the first time she'd ever just left like that, without insisting that I come too.

I remember the sound of her footsteps on the metal staircase. Her limp surprised me, as if I were hearing it for the first time, as if now a part of her, caught in that leg, was slipping away from me.

I imagined her coming into the living room, aiming a grimace at Sara, who was keeping an eye out for her. Sara was the one who had sent her to come and talk to me, I was sure. Mina would never have climbed up those stairs otherwise. Why had she agreed to do it? She didn't have the desire or the energy to worry about anyone but herself anymore. Now Mina was sitting in her seat at the big table, where my absence was being drowned by eggplant sauce and herbed yogurt. I could just see her, holding out her plate. She was hungry, and she loved eggplants.

Sara came up early in the afternoon to say pretty much the same things to me that Mina had. Not getting any response, she left, too. Then the sun lost its color and transformed into a violet thread, ready to unravel into the sky.

The more time passed, the less capable I felt of facing their gazes. I could hear their ceaseless racket rising up toward me, like a wall that had become insurmountable. Everything that was familiar had become hostile. I couldn't stop myself from thinking that whatever Leïli had seen in me, others—older and more mature—must have seen too. How could the same light that shone on them ever shine on me again; how could I go back to my role as the baby of the family, everyone's little sweetheart, if I had visibly become something monstrous? For a brief instant I tried to console myself with the thought that no one else had Leïli's diabolical intelligence, or her sophistication. No one else had read Sartre's *The Words* at the age of twelve. But then why had no one else come up to look for me? Why had they gotten used to my absence so quickly? In all likelihood, the fact that neither Mina nor Sara knew what Leïli had whispered to me meant that she had let them speculate about my disappearance without intervening. She had protected them from her prediction while simultaneously giving me a chance to correct my behavior. To change.

Night fell in the blink of an eye. Before pulling out a mattress and lying down in the darkness, I took off my blue T-shirt with the white stripes (you remember, the same one I was wearing when my parents were arrested) and stuffed it into the plastic bag hanging on the doorknob that served as a wastebasket. I felt as if I were showing the same courage as I had in the pediatrician's office, when I watched the hypodermic needle sink into my arm and empty its contents. I loved that T-shirt, worn and too-tight as it was. It smelled like summer. When I wore it, I felt both invincible and protected, like Superman with his cape. But now I was sure that it was mainly responsible for what had happened. Without it on, I would be less sure of myself, less confident. I had to get rid of it so that I could stop being something misshapen and dangerous; so that my breasts would grow and I would turn into a girl like the other girls. I had to give my physical self permission to change into a new form, molded from the remains of my arrogant child's body.

For the next three days, slumped on the couch in one of Mina's T-shirts, I pretended to be sick so everyone would leave me alone in front of the Russian television. I watched the women's gymnastics competition, thinking with regret of the time when I had taken classes in a gym near the high school where Sara taught. Because I had smooth hair and showed particular talent for the balance beam, they called me Nadia Comaneci, a nickname that made me dream of the Olympic Games. Kimiâ Sadr, the first Iranian gymnast to score a perfect 10.

On the fourth day, Darius loaded up the Peugeot's trunk and the hours of goodbyes began. Eventually the car pulled away and drove through the mountain roads toward home. We would never see Mazandaran again.

Six weeks later, during one of his famously interminable speeches, Khomeini told the people, "The pens must be broken!" (Translation: freedom of expression must be muzzled). In response, Darius sent him a letter in the form of an article entitled "Pens Don't Break." That article marked Darius Sadr's official entry into the opposition, and resulted in our first stay of the Khomeini era at Uncle Number Two's house.

On that bright morning in August 1979, as the white Peugeot 504 drove away from the holiday house, the shadow of things unsaid detached itself from the upstairs room and followed us back to Tehran. Then, when it was decided that we had to leave Iran, it went with us from Tehran to Tabriz, travelled through the snowy mountains of Kurdistan and the Turkish villages and the Bosporus Strait and Istanbul, and came to rest in Paris, where it got bigger and bigger, and pushed me further and further away from my family.

I know what you're thinking: the girl whose father wanted a son acts like a boy and ends up as a lesbian, what a cliché. It's true.

But it's only true when you have access to books, and movie theatres where they show *Sylvia Scarlett* or *The Bitter Tears of Petra von Kant*. When you've absorbed May '68 and the Sexual Revolution, and the feminist movement and Simone de Beauvoir. When you've listened to The Runaways and Bowie and Patti Smith, smoking and drinking until dawn in dark places that thump with dance music until you can't tell one mouth from another anymore, one hand from another, a man from a woman. And again, if it were really so common, certain realities would have become commonplace. At the park, mothers would watch their short-haired daughters play with the remote-control cars they got for Christmas and say "Oh, well, you never know, she might grow up to be a lesbian!" And their friends would laugh, or be touched, because children come from us, but they aren't obligated to resemble us, right?

But, seen from Tehran, that kind of cliché simply doesn't exist, in any form. The term "tomboy" doesn't exist; nor does any other term or word that recognizes that difference. You're a boy or a girl, and that's that.

Down through the generations, codes have been put in place. Certain codes for raising boys, and others for raising girls. It's not only about clothes and toys, or "boys don't cry" and "girls help Mommy." It's about the future. About becoming a husband and father, and earning money, and making sure people know it. Or becoming a wife and mother, raising polite, accomplished children, and excelling in the art of housekeeping. No one knows how to raise the in-betweens, or deal with the not-quites. It shocks Westerners that sex changes are legal in the Islamic Republic of Iran. "Oh, there are transsexuals in Iran?" they exclaim, in the same disconcerted tone as if they'd just learned that a nude beach was being established in the Vatican. Because they don't get that, in our culture, the important thing is to be *something*; to fall into one category or another, and follow its rules. Transsexuality exists because there is something worse than being transsexual, and that's being homosexual. That's not shameful. Shameful is losing your virginity before marriage, or having an abortion, or staying an old maid and living with your parents until they die. Shameful is being a drug addict or having an affair or raising children who then turn their backs on you. No, being gay isn't shameful. It's impossible. A non-reality.

I remember one morning when I was about fourteen or fifteen, coming upon an issue of *Le Monde*, which Darius, also an incurable insomniac, often sat up for most of the night reading in the kitchen. One long article was dedicated to American research into whether or not homosexuality was genetic. I remember that as soon as I read the title, I felt a kind of joyous relief, almost hope, at the thought that one day the world might discover that, in fact, what I was (but was still keeping secret) had been woven into me from the first instant that Darius's sperm, purloined covertly by Sara, had made contact with her welcoming egg.

It was a sperm cell that carried a lot of information—including a funny gene that would have travelled down through centuries, through bodies, across Mazandaran and the Alborz Mountains, through the dusty streets of Qazvin with its proud, authoritarian allure, to end up in the moist cavern of Mother's womb. Slower and more capricious than its comrade, the "blue eyes" gene, it would only manifest itself at random.

No, not the first son, it would have decided, *but the second.*

That son would, like me, struggle with it all his life. It was a battle he lost before it even began, and it made of him into a tormented being. Misunderstood. Overprotected by his mother, abandoned by his father. Saddeq would marry a woman and have children. Meddle in the lives of everyone around him. Draw lines of morality. Tell stories and fibs. Make jam. Sew. Cry. Hang on the wall across from his bed, as consolation, an old photo of himself standing with a man next to a tree. He would look at it every day, every night, and wonder bitterly why—*why* he had to spend his whole life hiding.

Now that we've settled the matter of the second son, let's keep going.

No, not the third. But the fourth. That one would carry the gene as well, and pass it on to . . . well, look here. A girl (we've already got a boy with it in the family; it's nice to have some variety). And just to make things fun, let's make it so that everyone thinks from the first sign of pregnancy that this girl is a boy. Only her maternal grandmother, Emma Aslanian, will have an opinion on that point—but it's so bizarre that no one will believe her.

The fifth and sixth sons will be spared.

As I read that article, I felt a thrill of excitement. Soon it would be proven that it wasn't my fault, but theirs—all of them who had preceded me on this earth and had been determined to reproduce. When I finally did tell my parents, they couldn't be angry with me. At worst, they'd frown a bit and heave a long sigh of disappointment, kind of like the one Darius must have heaved when he realized, once he'd gotten over the initial shock of Mother's death, that not only was I not Zartocht, but I didn't even have blue eyes.

The last part of the article, though, put quite a damper on my enthusiasm. It said that such a discovery, if proven, could result in the spread of eugenics—that people would try to get rid of an embryo if it carried the undesirable gene, or would put pressure on doctors and demand prenatal diagnostics. This alarmist view of what I considered liberating progress unnerved me. Why would anyone do something like that? Why such hatred for a person whose homosexuality would only be a tiny part of everything he or she might become? It took me a while to understand that, in every country in the world, the dual feeling of guilt and revulsion caused by homosexuality was harder for parents to bear than any illness. I came to that realization thanks in large part to TV news reports in which teenagers stricken with incurable diseases were always accompanied by their tender, invested parents, who were ready to fight to the end—while adolescent homosexuals, in the rare event that any sort of coverage was given to them, were alone and filmed outdoors, shoulders hunched, numb with cold.

So it was death or exile, with or without the Revolution. Or I could waste my life in the pursuit of pretense. Just like Uncle Number Two. Repressed, ashamed, frustrated, miserable. I could become a wife and mother for the sake of peace, blend in with the masses, avoid devastating whispers and rumors. But even exile wasn't enough. It is said that the American comedian Jack Benny once asked Sammy Davis Jr., when they ran into each other on a golf course, what his handicap was. And the reply was, "Handicap? Talk about handicap. I'm a one-eyed Negro Jew." Exile brought me a lot closer to Sammy Davis Jr.

Now I know that there is a thread linking that little girl who shut herself up for a whole day in an upstairs bedroom in the house in Mazandaran to the woman who is waiting, half-naked, with her feet in stirrups. At eight years old, I couldn't possibly have imagined where Leïli's words would lead me one day. How could anyone believe, when your life stretches out in front of you as vast and endless as the world itself, that one simple word could sum up the whole thing?

I came out of that upstairs bedroom eventually, but I never really left it. Every room I have lived in was that room in Mazandaran. I realized some time ago, when the lines developing around my mouth made me look even more like Nour, that what we call the future is really just a variation of the past.

Right. It's one forty-five, and here I am.

My legs are bare and I have goosebumps even though it isn't cold. Oh—I forgot to mention that I painstakingly shaved my legs last night. You should know that the number one obsession shared by all Iranian women is hair. I'm sure Western readers think that this obsession is found all over the East, but that isn't true. The map of the world's hairy areas is far from being as logical and precise as, say, the map of its extremely rainy ones. While the average Iranian woman is surrounded by countless instruments of depilatory torture from the moment she hits puberty, her Uzbek counterpart can happily go through life with just a pair of tweezers. And the many rituals that precede a Persian marriage include the removal of all the bride's body hair. From head to toe. It's not uncommon that on her wedding day, the day on which she should be at her most beautiful, a bride's white veil is concealing a face puffy and inflamed by merciless threading.

This is the first time I've been in this room, which, with its high-tech machines hooked up to wide screens, makes me feel like I'm part of a scientific experiment. The door is closed but I can hear Dr. Gautier having a discussion in the corridor. Obviously she still has one or two informal meetings to hold before she gets around to my case. To keep myself from getting irritated, I mentally review the text I got from Mina a few minutes before the doctor stuck her head out of her office and gestured for me to follow her. *Just called S, the funeral is this afternoon.*

"S" is our cousin Sima, Uncle Number Two's daughter, who lives in Austria with her family. She must be back in Tehran for her father's burial in the family crypt in Behchté

Zahra cemetery. Who could be at his funeral, considering none of us live in Iran? Why did Mina send me that text? What am I supposed to do? I'm sure you'd prefer for the doctor to come in right now so we can wrap this up. I would too. But since it looks like we have to wait a little longer, I'm sure you won't mind if, despite my unusual position and spread legs, I tell you a bit about the funerary precautions of Uncle Number Two.

One Friday afternoon, Saddeq took us with him to Behchté Zahra, on the outskirts of Tehran, to "visit Mother," as he put it. He wanted to show us where she "was resting." It was definitely during the Revolution, because I remember that as we walked through the immense cemetery we came across many grieving families in black, carrying aloft portraits of young "martyrs" (a very fashionable word back then, and still). Those families were like little black islands, on their knees next to freshly dug graves, screaming and sobbing, beating their faces and chests and crying out for vengeance to the God of infinite solitude. I remember what a relief it was to walk inside the family crypt and get away from those deafening displays of grief and sorrow.

We took off our shoes and lined them up carefully against the wall. It was a big room, dim and carpeted and silent. The walls gave off a smell of damp earth. A large black-and-white portrait of Nour stood on a pedestal near the only high window. Below the portrait, a white marble stele adorned with graceful writing marked the grave. I remember feeling like I was in a huge stomach, like Pinocchio in the belly of the whale. It was a muggy, strange place, but it felt familiar somehow. This was the closest I'd ever been to Mother, whom a part of me—encouraged by the deft maneuvering of Uncle Number Two—dreamed of knowing. I'd come to feel that it wasn't fair that I was the only one of her granddaughters who'd never met her. At the same time, because her death had happened simultaneously with my birth, and because, as Grandma Emma had explained to me, her soul had glided into my body, I felt uniquely connected to her. Children are very susceptible to those kinds of sweeping statements about existence. Yet, the previous night, as we were brushing our teeth before bed, Leïli had informed me that, contrary to what Uncle Number Two wanted people to believe, Mother wasn't sleeping under the ground the way you sleep in a bed.

"Her flesh melted down like butter in a hot frying pan, you know."

"What? Why?" I demanded, terrified.

"Because, underground, the body no longer needs to fight against *earthly gravity*!"

"How can you be stupid enough to believe everything Number Two says?" put in Mina, appalled by my credulity. (Gradually, spurred on largely by Mina and her passion for detective novels, my sisters had started dispensing with the "Uncle" part and referring to our dad's brothers just by their numbers.)

"Then what's in Mother's grave?"

"Her skeleton," said Leïli, shrugging.

"And worms!" added Mina, with a burst of laughter.

After spending a few long moments weeping, sitting cross-legged near the stele, Uncle Number Two explained to us that we would all end up here, near Mother, because he had recently bought multi-level tombs for his brothers and their families. Undaunted by our dubious expressions, he showed us the placement of his own tomb, to Mother's right, and then Uncle Number One's, to her left. At Mother's feet was the tomb allotted to Uncle Number Three. My dad's tomb was at the feet of Number Three, and at his feet was that of Number Five. And finally, at the very back, the furthest away from Mother, was the tomb of Uncle Number Six—with whom Saddeq had finally made peace, after months of mediation orchestrated by Uncle Number One.

We laughed about those multi-level tombs for ages and ages after that visit, imagining our ghosts using an elevator when they wanted to hang out together.

In the end, Saddeq would be the only Sadr to be buried in the family crypt. Other than him, only Uncles Number One and Five died in Iran—and Number One had specified in his will that he wanted to be buried in Qazvin. Qazvin, where Number Five, completely ruined, committed suicide by driving his car off a cliff.

So, in just a few more hours Uncle Number Two will finally have Mother all to himself.

Since my sisters have had families of their own, and thanks to Facebook, which they immediately joined, they've gotten back in touch with most of the cousins we have scattered all over the world. A few years ago, the fact that Mina had Sima's telephone number and called her would have been a significant piece of information in itself; now it seems trivial. They've even made cyber-contact with Abbas Sadr, our (sort of) Uncle Number Seven. Abbas was sent to the United States by Uncle Number One in the early 1960s and now lives in Taylorsville, Utah. He's been married to Georgia, a blond, blue-eyed Mormon woman, for thirty years, and—as Bibi predicted—they've got ten blue-eyed kids.

I never allow myself to wonder if I miss the Sadrs, spread out to the four corners of the globe, as much as my sisters seem to miss them. I keep them tucked away in a dark corner of my mind—but on the surface, like objects drifting on a distant sea. Occasionally one of them comes to Paris, and then Leïli or Mina will organize a dinner party, which always goes off half-heartedly and in the shadow of a past that seems more and more surreal. Chased out of paradise, we've turned partly into foreigners, beings molded by other cultures and other languages, thrown into a life that shouldn't have been ours.

Sometimes I have to force myself to go to those dinners. I really have no desire to dredge up buried feelings, if they still exist. I dread facing close relations about whom, paradoxically, I know nothing. And above all, I hate lying about my life (and yet I do it), the same lie on which Saddeq built his existence. The fact of having assigned himself the role of keeper of the family memories seems to me now like a clever ruse, an easy way to avoid talking about himself, about the inner tumult that drove him to wander the pitch-dark streets of Qazvin at night when he was sixteen or seventeen years old.

My dad told me that story one Sunday afternoon in Paris, as I accompanied him on one of his long walks. I'd thought walking together would help us to regain—even temporarily—something of our old, special bond. I'd thought my presence would soothe him; that the walk would turn into a stroll, and maybe he would finally take me to Montparnasse, to show me the building he used to live in. But instead, I could tell right away that I was bothering him. He stayed silent and walked quickly, as if trying to get rid of an intruder. When we reached the intersection at the Avenue des Gobelins, instead of taking the Boulevard Arago toward Montparnasse, he went toward the Boulevard de l'Hôpital. Despite my disappointment, I followed him quietly. We kept walking, a good few feet between us; me, the tall, gawky preteen, and him, the stranger in the cap.

I don't remember how we ended up on the subject of Saddeq—except that, in my awkward attempt at closeness, I got the risky idea of asking him about his youth. He'd never liked talking about the past—but this time, to my astonishment, he answered. In a strange reversal of balance, just when I was trying desperately to forget my own childhood, Darius agreed to talk about his own.

That was when he told me about the solitary nocturnal wanderings of Uncle Number Two through the streets of Qazvin.

Mother was worried about her son's bizarre behavior, and feared for his life. "Any lowlife could attack him, cut his throat, and throw his body somewhere we'd never find it. If only you were there, you might be able to reason with him," she had written to her eldest son, who was doing military service in Tehran. Finally, she asked one of her servants, a former wrestler called Mulehead Hosseini, to arm himself with a knife and follow Saddeq discreetly. After a few weeks spent roaming the streets behind his mistress's crazy son, Mulehead Hosseini complained to Nour. His feet were covered with blisters; his wife suspected him of cheating; and—*ey baba!*—the lack of sleep was giving him vertigo! God knew he'd give his life to save Mister Saddeq's, but this situation was absolutely ridiculous! It was all well and good for Mister Saddeq, who could sleep during the day, but frankly, Madame *Djan*, this was no way for poor Hosseini to live . . .

That same day, abandoned by Mulehead Hosseini, Mother decided to enroll Saddeq in one of the sewing courses offered by the American company Singer, which had recently opened a shop in the city center. To promote its merchandise, Singer was giving discounts on sewing machines to people who took the sewing courses. One of Mother's older sisters had heard that the price was quite reasonable, and the sewing machines really ingenious. So the next day, accompanied by Mother, who left him in front of the shop, Saddeq went to his first class. He was the only male among a dozen young women. The teacher, a French woman who had settled in Qazvin and was married to a local man, made no distinction between him and the other students and called him *Mademoiselle*.

"After that, Saddeq was so tired from one day to the next that, I promise you, there were no more nocturnal outings!" And Darius capped off the story with a deep laugh, which I hadn't heard from him in so long. I laughed too, more out of happiness at seeing him laugh than at the story itself.

Never once did Darius use the word "homosexual" in reference to his brother. Not that day, or any other. Surely he had made the connection between Saddeq's restless nights and the sewing classes. What was the meaning of this story? After waiting a while for an explanation that never came, I asked my dad if Uncle Number Two had interpreted Mother's decision as acceptance of who he was. Darius knitted his brow, slowed down, turned to me.

"What do you mean?"

Suddenly, I hesitated. "I don't know . . . I mean, Uncle Saddeq was . . . " (Difficult to say the word in Persian, it was so rude, but Darius understood.)

"He was what he was. No one really knows what goes on in people's lives."

"Yeah . . . but even I know—"

"You do, maybe," Darius cut me off. "But I don't know it."

I didn't push it. Having made him talk about the past and even laugh about it was enough of an accomplishment to stop right there.

Even as I go back through all these memories, stretched out uncomfortably on the examining table, I think of the things we didn't share. People die, and time does its work. But the regret remains, sometimes howling in your gut—regret at having left opportunities hanging, like threads on an article of old clothing, but on which you should never, ever pull.

Doctor Gautier opens the door.

I jump, suddenly bothered by my own nudity.

"Sorry," she says mechanically. "Are you all right?"

"Yeah. Yeah, I'm fine."

"Great!"

Energetically, as if wanting to get this mischievous morning over with, she seizes my file from the desk. But I can tell that she's preoccupied, that she's not really there. Her face looks like a crumpled washcloth.

I watch her leaf through my file and try to think of something to say, something light and trivial, hoping to quiet the anxious voice running through my mind, like a cockroach emerging out of nowhere and running across a baseboard. *Dr. Gautier's mood is going to cause the insemination to fail*, whispers the voice. *All those months spent hoping for this moment will have been for nothing. You might as well get dressed now and leave and try again next month.*

I try to calm down. I breathe.

I don't know why, but all of a sudden I need this moment to be simultaneously solemn and celebratory. I need Dr. Gautier to look up at me and smile. The kind of reassuring smile I always looked out for on the teacher's face on the first day of school, that warmed me from the inside when she turned it on me.

Without looking up, Dr. Gautier closes my file and puts it down, balancing it on the edge of a piece of medical equipment.

Maybe I'm expecting too much from her. Does an electrician have to smile at you when he comes to fix your broken circuit-breaker? Do you expect a kind word from the mechanic as he sweats over your car's tires? So why count on it from a doctor?

She puts on a pair of opaque rubber gloves and picks up the tube of sperm. Opening it, she extracts a huge syringe which, instead of a needle, is fitted with a transparent, flexible tube as long and thin as a strand of spaghetti. So that's what I've been holding in my lap all this time!

She sits down on a stool and rolls herself between my legs. She positions the lamp just above her head, so that its bright light turns her face into a black silhouette—which is fine with me, because I don't want to look at her crumpled features.

"Try to relax as much as possible," she instructs me.

God, I'm so relaxed that I think I must look like a cat stretched out in the sun! If she'd look at me even for a second, if she'd take the trouble to speak to me, she'd see how relaxed I am. Unlike her.

I turn my head toward the fogged-up window. I can feel her inserting the tube into my vagina.

Pause. Speaking of vaginas, I should tell you that Doctor Mohadjer was shot a few weeks after the Revolution ended. At that time, anyone with any type of connection, distant or close, to the Pahlavi family, was executed after a sham trial. Dr. Mohadjer's French wife, who went to France with their daughter in the autumn of 1978, had an affair with one of the Shah's half-brothers. Their name, as well as some photos, had been found among this half-brother's papers after he fled the country. Told of the arrest, Darius made a series of phone calls—but in vain. Farzin Mohadjer was executed by firing squad one morning at dawn, along with several other unfortunates. A few weeks later his body was released to his sister, who gave it an unceremonious burial.

While she's inserting the tube, Dr. Gautier explains to me that she's depositing the sperm cells directly into my fallopian tubes, sparing them a large part of the journey. I'm concentrating on my breathing, and register the information only as a scientific fact of which I was previously unaware. "Directly into the fallopian tubes," like those passengers who they let straight onto the airplane without going through all the formalities.

"There, all done!" she announces a minute later.

I turn my head.

She's already standing up, taking off her gloves. I don't know why, but I'm reminded of Julianne Moore's character in the Coen brothers' film *The Big Lebowski*, keeping her legs in the air after intercourse, to keep the sperm inside and maximize her chances of getting pregnant. I'm wondering if I should do the same thing when Dr. Gautier, noticing that I haven't moved, suggests that I put my clothes back on.

SIDE B[19]

[19] Those of you old enough to remember 45 rpm vinyl records know that the B-side is usually less interesting than the A-side. Side B is the failed side, the weak side. The one that was put out into the world but didn't find its place. The ugly little sister who gets shoved along behind the popular older one but without much hope. There have been exceptions, spectacular takeovers and incredible displacements: for example, one of Sara's favourite songs, *I Will Survive* by Gloria Gaynor, was the B-side of a 45 whose A-side, *Substitute*, has faded into the mists of disco history. Or Madonna's *Into the Groove*, which was also a B-side. I remember loving *Johnny Verso*, the B-side of The Communards' hit *Disenchanted*. All of which is just to say that there HAVE been some successful B-sides . . .

1

DISORIENTAL

I t's already six A.M.

We have to be in Vanak Square in forty-five minutes. The
first rays of the sun are warming the kitchen, a sign that,
after the rain we've had over the past few days, today will be
hot and bright. Green, damp patches are scattered across the
lawn. Spring is in the air. I'm standing at the window. Behind
me, my mother and the girls are finishing their breakfast. The
apartment is spotless; the beds are made, the plants watered,
the cupboards filled with clothes and shoes and clean linens
and plates and food—everything I've accumulated over the
ten years we've lived in this flat. Our bags are in the entryway. I learned that we were leaving the day before yesterday,
at around eight P.M. I wasn't expecting it. But I've been hoping for this day, especially since Darius's last letter, which
arrived at the Pourvakils' address three weeks ago. It was
hopeless. I read it in the bathroom, like I do all his letters,
with the door double-locked, well away from the children. I
felt sucked into a whirlpool of emotions. I immediately called
Majid, Darius's childhood friend, who had arranged his departure. I told him we absolutely had to join Darius as soon as
possible; that, this time, it had to work. I couldn't afford to
wait in my brother-in-law Saddeq's home again. He told me
he'd do what needed to be done, without asking any more
questions. And he did.

I never thought this moment would actually come; that to
all the ordeals of the past four years would be added this one,
the most terrifying of them all. Taking my children and leaving.

The man who called me the night before last is named
Omid. He has a young voice, with a strong Turkish accent.

He's the one who smuggled Darius out. It was the first time we'd ever spoken but, aware that our telephone was bugged, he used a friendly, familiar tone. He talked about a trip to visit family, let the kids enjoy some sunshine and fresh mountain air. No need to pack much, he said; a small bag each would be enough. When I hung up I was dazed, crushed by a pain that radiated from my head and invaded the whole world. I forced myself to get up and walk down the hall leading to the bedrooms. All three of the girls were in Leïli's room, excited for the upcoming Nowrouz vacation. I needed to go in and tell them we were leaving, but I couldn't do it. I went into our bedroom and laid down on the bed, which I'd bought in a store in Tajrish, this bed that Mina had always considered her territory. Would we have another bed, other sheets, other nights?

That was the beginning of the end of our ten years in this apartment. Years of joyful, thrilling confusion. Years of excitement and sorrow, of going off to school and political meetings and arrests. The living room table where Darius wrote; the wall with the girls' heights marked on it; the vine planted beneath the balcony that now reached as high as the second floor. Ten years! And in less than forty-eight hours it would all be nothing but a memory. My body would leave this place, in a long, irreversible wrenching that my soul would never accept.

I talked to the girls yesterday. When they'd left for school I packed the bags: some clothes, toiletries, medications. Then I went to see my mother and my brothers, and my brother-in-law Saddeq, with whom I'd left my passport and Leïli's. I went to say goodbye to a few neighbors, including the Pourvakils; the Nasrs left Mehr a year ago for the United States, when the war with Iraq had only just started. Big Mina's brother lives in their apartment now. I miss her every day. I took money out of the bank but left enough in our account to pay the water and electricity bills. Soon it will be the end of the year.

I look at my watch again. It's five minutes past six. I spend another few seconds gazing out at the courtyard and the dark windows behind which people are still asleep, people with whom I've shared so many things. By the time they wake up, opening the windows wide to let in the fresh morning air, beginning this day loaded with the promise of festivities to come, we'll be gone. This day will go by and Saturday will come, then Sunday, and thousands of Saturdays and Sundays will sweep though Mehr. Summer will follow spring, and then autumn will come; these neighbors will grow old and go away, and people who aren't even born yet will take their place. The ordinary rhythm of life and death will continue to flow through this place, which I will recreate in my mind every day somewhere far away from here. Where will we be when the jasmine flowers fall? Will we still be alive in a week, or ten days? I'm forty-three years old, and I'm leaving a whole life behind.

I turn around, my heart in my mouth. I can't look at the girls, or Mama, who has come to give us some advice. I go into the entryway and pick up the telephone and call a taxi. It will be here in ten minutes.

I'm leaving. It's possible that something so terrible is actually happening, just like it's possible to die when you were laughing the second before; it's as simple as that, and as inconceivable. I go back into the kitchen, the little kitchen we've planned out down to the millimeter; the chair where Darius used to sit. I see Emma's face, which is full of sadness she knows will last forever. I walk toward her and take her in my arms and hold her tightly, racked by indescribable grief. "I'm sorry, madaram. I'm sorry."

The taxi drops us in Vanak Square. Two cars are waiting at the curb. A man who looks barely twenty-five, his cheeks still round and his eyes mischievous, is leaning against one of them. Omid, I think to myself immediately. He gestures a casual hello at me, as if we've known each other for years.

We get into the first car, and Omid into the second. Both cars take the road to Tabriz, more than three hundred miles from Tehran. The man I'm sitting next to is a stranger to me. He tells me to call him Reza and shakes my hand with a smile. He has salt-and-pepper hair, a thick neck, a moustache that hides his upper lip, and a wedding ring. As he drives, he chats to me about this and that; his voice is calm and soothing. He doesn't ask me any questions. We look like a family going on holiday: father, mother, and their three daughters.

We travel at a brisk pace and pass through cities and villages buzzing with busy crowds. People hurrying into shops, rifling through merchandise, running red lights. I know that particular atmosphere, the frenzied haste that overtakes everyone when the New Year is just a few hours away—and yet I feel like a hovering observer, watching some distant, terrifying world go by.

The dilapidated walls are covered with obscene propaganda. Endless, expensive frescoes. The accusing faces of ayatollahs, American flags dotted with death's heads, young girls in chadors brandishing Kalashnikov rifles, boys marching atop enemy corpses. In these streets, women have been stoned to death, men hanged in public squares, children lured into the backs of mysterious cars with the so-called Keys to Paradise around their necks, and sent south to be blown up in minefields. In a basement somewhere, someone is being tortured to death. A woman is receiving fifty lashes of a horsewhip for having let a lock of hair escape from underneath her headscarf. Spring temporarily masks the fear, but once again we're in a time of informing and humiliation and being hunted by the wolf-pack. Nothing has changed. How has so much hope been smashed to nothing?

To my right, Qazvin disappears behind the mountains. I repeat to myself that we can't stay here anymore, living half in hiding in our own apartment; the girls can't go on lying about their identity in school, insisting that Darius isn't their father, but a distant cousin. And yet, I am filled with rage. Our country has been stolen from us: the dark forests and rice-fields of Mazandaran, the high cliffs with their raw, terrible beauty, the turquoise domes, the autumn sun shining on Tehran. I remember the spring after the Revolution ended, that first morning without fear, when I woke up next to Darius, intensely free despite the uncertainties, ready to seize the future by the horns. At that moment I believed that we had accomplished what every human being born under a dictatorship longs to do, but rarely achieves. That moment vanished, along with so many others, like mirages swallowed up by the desert. Will I ever come back here again?

We stop for lunch in a shabby little roadside restaurant. We barely eat anything. My head aches. I swallow two aspirin with the dregs of a flat Coca-Cola. I can't figure out how to interpret Omid's anxious expression. He doesn't eat, steps outside twice, throws some money on the table and hurries us out of there, quickly. I watch the girls put on their coats. They look like young soldiers fighting in a war they don't understand, but who have nonetheless accepted their fate.

We get back on the road. At around four in the afternoon, when we're just a few miles from Tabriz, the car pulls over by the side of the road. Omid and the driver get out. Reza gets out of our car, too. The girls, who haven't slept a wink throughout the whole journey so far, go into a panic. Incredulous, I watch the men confer. A few seconds later, the accident happens.

A dark blue car going in the same direction as us is suddenly hit by a white truck that comes out of nowhere. The impact is so great that the car is dragged along for several feet until it is strewn in pieces all over the asphalt. The truck vanishes as abruptly as it appeared. Now the road is black with people running, yelling, covering their children's eyes. The ones nearest to the wreck make catastrophic gestures and wave the crowd back. Omid runs toward his car. Reza climbs into ours. Seeing the distress on our faces, he tries to reassure us.

"Thank God, it's over. Everything will be fine now."

"What's over?" I demand.

"That car had been following us since this morning. Now we can keep going in peace."

I've never found out where that truck came from, or who was driving it. I've never known whether chance played any part in that collision. What still surprises me is that I felt nothing in that instant except surprise. The accident held no more weight than a cloud that drifts in front of the sun, casting a shadow, and then moves away in the predetermined, irrevocable order of things. Sunlight and shadow coexist; a bit more of one means a bit less of the other. Now we can keep on in peace. This reality is all that counts. Simple. Obvious. Our fate was to survive. To back up, take a cross-street, and disappear. That road is still here with me. It's become part of me, just like the two-story house that belonged to the uncle of a friend of Omid's, where we spent the night, and the couple who welcomed us in. And the chicken and rice and potato pancakes they gave us for dinner, and the tea and chickpea sweets, and the little bedroom with mattresses in a row on the carpet. And the other house, the one we stayed in the next day, on the edge of a crumbling village, a house without water or electricity, a few miles from the border. A young man with a shaved head lived there with his wife and his sister-in-law. There was no trace of a Nowrouz celebration; no decorations. The Iran where I grew up ended somewhere between those two houses.

Omid isn't here (where is he?). I'm alone with the kids, sitting in the back seat of the young man's car. He looks at me in the rearview mirror and warns me that at eight-fifteen he's going to pull over on the side of the road. "Two minutes, understand? You get out, take your bags out of the trunk, and go off to the right. Run as fast as you can. Stay calm, and above all don't talk." I'm paralyzed with tension and fear. I can feel the warmth of the girls' bodies as they press against me.

When the car stops, we do exactly as he instructed us. Leïli and Kimiâ hurtle down a slope and plunge into darkness. Mina does her best, slowed down by her leg. I take her hand. Rough tree-bark scrapes our faces. The rotating searchlights of watchtowers surround us. The ground is damp, and there is a sharp scent of mold in the frigid air. Suddenly, two men in military uniforms emerge from behind the trees and rise up in front of us. "Do you have any cigarettes?" I hear Omid's voice in the darkness, answering "Yes, two." How has he managed to join us? With surprising clarity, I can see his chubby young body moving toward the men. I'm relieved; now that he's here, everything will be all right. Kimiâ takes advantage of the pause to tell me that she couldn't find her bag in the trunk. She stares at me, disoriented. I know what this means to her; that bag contained a part, however tiny, of the universe we are leaving behind. And now, even that miniscule, fundamental part is gone. I'm trying to think of something to say that will comfort her when I hear a voice with a heavy Kurdish accent say: "Crouch down and move forward. Quickly!"

"It doesn't matter, my darling; let's go," I say to Kimiâ, who obeys.

The sky is low, and vast as an ocean. The impressive glittering of the stars lights our way. There are no cities menacingly close anymore; there are no more trees. No more watchtowers. Wild rats scurry across the ground. The horses that are supposed to carry us are late. In my exhaustion I see villages rise up on the tops of the hills and then, as we advance, their contours blur and fade, pushing back the edges of the world. The cold burns bone-deep. We can't run anymore; we walk almost in slow motion. Our guides have relaxed somewhat; they allow us to stop from time to time, just for a few minutes. During these short breaks I want to stretch out on the moist earth, take my daughters in my arms, and relax. The way we used to lie on the beach when we vacationed at the Caspian Sea. I want to smile at them and comfort them, and tell them it's two thirty-five in the morning, and today is the New Year, and we're together. Don't be afraid. But fatigue numbs me, and my right knee throbs with pain, threatening to immobilize my whole being. I force myself to keep moving. My lungs fill with icy particles and the strong scent of the earth. I know my mother is awake, alone in my dark apartment. Her parents fled Russia for Iran and now her daughter has gone. In the end, she's become the only one of her family never to have lived in exile. All around her, in Tehran's dim and sorrowful streets, some people are sleeping, while others are waking up as a family. What is Darius doing? Does he even know it's Nowrouz?

The hours fall like stones into a well and disappear into nothingness. It's so dark that I can't see anything at all anymore. I can hear the quick, shallow breathing of Leïli and Mina, and I know Kimiâ is walking ahead of us. She always has to keep herself separate from the general movement, obstinate and incomprehensible, like a snail in its shell. Sometimes

I want to sit her forcefully down and explain to her how fragile life is. I hear Omid's distant voice. Disembodied murmurs, disparate sounds, anger. I manage to make out the word "horses," and then "when" and "day." I know the danger will increase as the sun rises.

The horses finally arrive. The men riding them are carrying weapons. Leïli has stumbled and fallen onto a rock; her forehead is bleeding. The men lift her onto a horse and tell her to cling to the rider. Then they do the same with Mina and Kimiâ. Finally my turn comes. In the time it takes them to get me settled, the girls have disappeared ahead of me. Terrified, I wonder if I will see them again.

Now the grey, cold light of dawn is rising in the black sky. A dog barks in the distance, signaling the possibility of life. "We're almost at the village," says the Kurdish man whose hips I'm clutching.

We're at the bottom of a snowy valley. The house we're staying in is run-down, cramped, and dirty. Darkness presses in on the glow of the small oil lamp hung from a nail that dimly illuminates the faces of the ageless men and women in their traditional clothing. Their eyes hold the mixture of fear and curiosity characteristic of an isolated, rejected, overlooked people. No one speaks. We're near the *korsi* (a sort of traditional heater). Our feet touch the quivering bodies of the lambs lying in the warmth of the hut's floor. One of the men serves tea; the steaming glasses are handed around in air thick with water vapor and expelled breath.

Time passes, and little by little the children regain their strength. The oldest of the men turns to me: "We're going to take you to a stable. You'll stay there all day. No one must see you." I help the girls to stand up. My feet are so swollen that I can't force them back into my boots. City boots, with flat heels. Kimiâ swaps her old Kickers with me. Omid didn't tell me it would be minus thirteen degrees, or I would have bought warmer clothing, socks, hiking boots. I thought, stupidly, that it would be spring here, too.

We crossed the border between Iran and Turkey five nights later. Five nights spent crossing through the steep, snowy mountains of Kurdistan, on foot or on horseback, clinging to an armed rider, buffeted by the wind and numb with cold, exhausted from fear and lack of sleep, completely lost. Five nights listening to the distant howling of wolves.

At three-thirty in the morning on Wednesday, March 25, 1981, somewhere in that icy white vastness, we crossed an imaginary line. "That's it. We're in Turkey," said Omid, who was walking next to me. We stopped a few meters further on. Omid wanted to leave us the . . .

Leïli found this unfinished text, handwritten in French on graph paper, among Sara's things. With her innate sense of fairness, she kept the original and made photocopies for Mina and me. As I told you, I've never felt strong enough to read Sara's book from start to finish, but Mina says this text is an accurate translation of the passage concerning our departure.

Without ever saying it outright, Sara would have loved for one of us to translate her book into French, especially once it became a bestseller in Tehran. She never asked us for anything on principle, so she always brought up the subject indirectly, letting her desire hang in the air, accompanied by sighs that were exaggerated but certainly explicit enough.

"Ah, if only someone wanted to translate my book! Someone who knows me, of course, someone I could work with. It would help the French to understand who we are . . . "

"You think the French are interested in understanding who we are?" Leïli, who still had a lot to learn when it came to tact, would respond.

"Of course they're interested! They need to know that Iran isn't the backward country they see on their TV screens. They should know that we once had someone like Mossadegh!"

"So what? I don't think you quite realize that they couldn't care less."

"Have I asked you for anything, Leïli my love?"

"I don't really have the time, Sara," put in Mina. "And anyway, translation is a craft. You can't just do it casually."

Out of the three of us, Mina was the preferred target for Sara's attacks. She was deep in the midst of a university combined honors program in history and linguistics; designated the "literary" one since childhood, she devoured books as greedily as Grandma Emma gobbled cookies, and she was the logical choice to escort Sara's book across its language barrier. But what Sara didn't—maybe didn't want to—understand was that Mina, just like Leïli and me, had no desire to relive the past, even through our mother's words. Besides, there was something unsettling, disturbing, about those words: they unflinchingly revealed to us her emotions and sufferings, even though she had been careful to protect us from them all these years. Each for our own reasons, we simply couldn't face those images anymore, those events and anecdotes that time had made as terrifying as a decomposing corpse. When Mina finished reading the memoir, she said to us: "Frankly, you should spare yourself the ordeal." She'd taken the book with her on a weekend getaway organized by her university and cried until she turned the last page at dawn. I think my inability to finish the thing was due in large part to her reaction—though, out of guilt at having lied to Sara that I'd read all of it, I did make several attempts. I know Leïli did read it in the end, probably for her own peace of mind, but she never spoke about it.

Mina's thoughts concerning translation, accurate though they were, were really just an excuse—but Sara took them literally, adding them to her laundry list of cultural differences that had sprung up like crab-grass between her and her daughters since we arrived in France.

"Translation, a craft? Believe me, if Iranians had worried about things like that, no book would have ever been translated into Persian," she retorted, with a mixture of bitterness and exasperation. Which was undoubtedly true, at least if you thought about Uncle Number Six and his translations of André Gide (or rather, the ones done by the poor ghost-writer he'd paid to stay silent).

None of us wanted to admit the truth to her, and finally she stopped talking about it. Maybe that was when she decided to do it alone, starting with this passage.

What still bothers me is that we let her think, out of laziness, that we weren't interested, not only in what she had written, but in what she had accomplished. For four years, for a couple of hours every dreary, depressing day, she had tried to create some order out of the chaos of her experiences and feelings, the fiery tide of the past that was consuming her from the inside. This wasn't only an account for posterity, it was an urgent need. No matter what it cost her, she had to record in black and white what had really happened in apartment 18, in order to show those vultures, as she called them, who Darius was. She was the memory of that place, the guardian of their history, and above all, the only one capable of standing up for Darius, who was now being attacked from every direction. The Shah's supporters, now living in Paris and Los Angeles, blamed him for turning the country over to the mullahs and killing General Rahmani; the mullahs, in power in Iran, considered him a Western agent and intellectual scum. The conservatives, who were close associates of the *bazaris*, criticized his obsessive atheism and his radical position against the Islamisation of the country, and the communists, scattered across Europe, declared him a traitorous bourgeois agent of the CIA. All of these groups insulted him in their newspapers and on the radio; all of them sent him threatening letters. Sara wanted the whole world to know the truth, to protect her husband from those thugs, those liars, those killers. But did the whole world—you, in this case—just want to make something out of Darius Sadr?

To be honest, at this stage in the story, I'm not sure how to continue on from Sara's account—or, rather, how to reconcile my distorted child's view with her realistic one, and pick up at the exact point where she left off, in the middle of the mountains in Kurdistan, on the other side of the imaginary line separating Iran and Turkey. Which, as you've probably guessed, is fine with me, because I have no desire to relive the next part of the journey. Since we can, let's jump on a literary magic carpet and zip through time and space, past the night-trains and cars, and land at around nine o'clock P.M. on a well-lit city street.

April 3, 1981. The Asian side of Istanbul. We look like the haggard survivors of some disaster, wandering along the dusty roads. We're thin, dirty, and dazed.

The moment we step into the bright, overheated lobby of the Hotel Sultaniah, every head turns to look at us. Shame makes us lower our gazes to the floor. We move toward the reception desk, which is presided over by a young Turkish man swathed in a red and black uniform, like criminals in a court of law. We wait a few paces behind Omid, letting him do all the talking.

Now that our journey—at least the part that involves him—is complete, Omid has insisted on celebrating our success by setting us up in a "luxury three-star" hotel, as he'd said playfully. "A hotel worthy of a woman like you, Madam Sara." I can still see him watching for her reaction out of the corner of his eye, his young face blushing pink. He wanted to impress her; to show her that he wasn't just an oafish, rough-and-ready people smuggler, but a surprising young man familiar with the Westernized places she would appreciate. I'm sure he'd never rubbed shoulders so closely with a woman like her, the kind who gives her opinion and meets men's eyes. He'd been floored when he heard her retort to an armed Kurd who had made fun of the fact that she didn't know how to mount a horse: "I may not know how to mount a horse, but I know how to drive, and in Tehran, no less. If I were to dump you in the city center with a car, believe me, you wouldn't last ten minutes." Omid still laughed when he thought of the Kurd's face.

The receptionist looked at us, spoke with Omid, glanced down at the money on the counter, and looked at us again. His reluctance evaporated when Omid discreetly laid down a few additional bills. Watching Omid give out money right and left to ease a situation or buy someone's silence, I'd begun to understand what the word "corruption," which Darius so frequently used, really meant. Later, thanks to Leïli, I found out that the French used the Persian word *bakhshesh* (gift) to mean "bribe."

We were assigned two street-level rooms; one for Leïli and Sara, and the other for Mina and me. We locked ourselves into them without bothering to eat dinner.

Though it was modest, the comfort of that hotel seemed extraordinary to us. After so many days spent in stables or ice-cold rooms without water or electricity, sleeping on straw, peeing in front of cows and sheep or squatting in the snow, we were enthralled. We threw ourselves down on the beds and stood, mouths hanging open, watching the water flow from the shower-head. Because I'd lost my bag, unlike Sara, Leïli, and Mina I couldn't bathe right away. Each one of them spent more than an hour in the bathroom and emerged with faces as red and scrubbed as a peeled beet. I would have to wait until the next day, when Sara and Leïli ventured out to a shop a few streets away and bought me some underpants, a pair of jeans, a checked blouse, and a (horrifyingly ugly) mauve sweater, before I could also take a shower and discard my ragged clothes. My long hair was so tangled that the attempt to brush it quickly turned from comedy to tragedy.

That day, late in the morning, we left the hotel transformed. We hadn't yet regained our previous appearance, but at least it wouldn't frighten people to look at us. We went on foot to the port, which was swarming with street vendors, and boarded a *vapur*, the boat that would take us across the Bosporus Strait to the western side of Istanbul. Our destination: the French embassy.

A few weeks after Darius's arrival in Paris, the French Socialist party, some members of which had come to our house during the Revolution, had contacted him to offer assistance: help with obtaining a residence permit, or housing. Darius had refused. As always, he didn't want to owe anything to anyone. But he swallowed his pride for us. Of the four of us, only Sara and Leïli had passports, but they had expired long ago. Sara hadn't been able to renew them, or to apply for passports for Mina and me, because we had been forbidden to leave the country by the government. And anyway, to avoid drawing attention to ourselves, Omid had advised her not to carry papers. So, we had left without any documentation proving our identity. Darius approached the socialist party, then two months away from winning the elections, and managed to obtain for us permits that were usually reserved for French nationals who had lost their passport abroad. This didn't give us French nationality, of course; just the right to enter French territory, and once there, to take the necessary steps to sort out our situation. According to Sara, once we had these magical door-openers, all we would need to do was buy plane tickets in a travel agency, take a taxi to the airport, and board the Air France plane scheduled to take off at 4:38 P.M. So, in nine days, we would have utilized every possible means of transport, from the most ancient to the most modern, to travel the three thousand two hundred seventy-eight miles separating Tehran from Paris.

The fog was so thick that the *vapur* seemed to be sailing in the sky. Frost covered the gunwales, and glasses of steaming tea on handled platters were passed around. Huddled together on a wooden bench, we listened to Sara tell the story of how her grandparents, Anahide and Artavaz Aslanian, had fled Turkey a few months before the genocide of 1915 and the mass deportation of Armenians to the camp of Deir ez-Sor in the deserts of Mesopotamia and Syria. It was usually Emma who told us this story, punctuated with rosaries of insults, first aimed at those "son of a bitch Turk murderers" and then at all the other nationalities—Kurds, Chechens, Azerbaijanis—her poor parents had encountered along the way. Sara's version, a much less emotional one, was that of a historian using a personal story to tell a much broader one; anecdote as a cruel reflection of the world in general. When Anahide and Artavaz were just a few miles away from reaching Moscow, Sara digressed to inform us that imperial Germany, an ally of the Ottoman Empire and present in Turkey throughout World War One, had been aware of the deportations. It seemed even that certain German officers had participated in the massacres—including Rudolf Höss, subsequently head of the concentration camp at Auschwitz. A little later, as Anahide and Artavaz were settling in lodgings near the Moscow train station just in case they had to flee again (which did indeed happen two years later), the *vapur* docked.

Our ancestors, who had been born on this side of the strait, had fled this country to escape death—and now, sixty-seven years later, we were back here for the same reason. Things had come full circle. We were starting our lives over in the exact same spot where they had abandoned theirs. Of course, out of a sort of genetic solidarity distilled in our blood by Emma, we detested Turkey and the Turks. Yet, as our feet touched the soil of Istanbul's European side, the sense of freedom that flooded through us reconciled us with the past in a single stroke.

"That's it! We're in France!" exclaimed Leïli as we stepped into the courtyard of the embassy.

"What do you mean?" I asked, incredulous.

"Well, the soil of an embassy is considered to be the soil of that country."

"Are you sure?"

"Of course I'm sure."

"Did you know that?" I asked Mina.

"Of course, everyone knows that, stupid."

Just imagine! The garden we were walking through was France; the door we pushed open, the room we went into, and the woman who greeted us . . . all of it was France. We had made it. We were on the threshold of the promised land, our finger on the doorbell, just waiting to be let in.

Since earliest childhood, our trust in that country had been so great that, as we followed the woman into a tiny, impersonal office, we had no doubt about the welcome that would be extended to us as stateless Francophiles. *"Every man has two countries; his own and France."* That quote from Thomas Jefferson, which Sara had made sure was part of our education alongside Napoleon Bonaparte, Victor Hugo, Frederic Chopin (another stateless person), and the Declaration of the Rights of Man, was the only thing we were certain of now.

"Forget it; they don't have any *pognon*," a man with a shaved head who was sitting behind the rectangular desk said to his colleague beside him, a cigarette dangling from his fingers.

He used slang on purpose, sure that Sara wouldn't understand it. And he was right. Sitting straight-backed across from them (my sisters and I were standing), Sara looked from one of them to the other, her face troubled. But these men didn't know Leïli. They didn't know that the idiot who thought he could trap her with the subtleties of the French language hadn't yet been born.

"He says we don't have any money," she clarified slowly,

staring at the man so contemptuously that he got up to open the window, visibly uncomfortable.

"Yep, she's right," the other man snickered, leaning forward to stub out his cigarette.

Panic washed over me then, and I can't remember what happened after that.

An image is forming in my head. The four of us sitting near a dented electric heater. The windows are fogged up so I can't see outside. A smell of frying and orange-flower water floats in the air. We're in a tearoom. Sara is explaining to us that everything will be okay. She's going to call Omid; she's going to call Darius. "It's all going to be fine, my darlings. There's no reason for it all not to turn out fine." I don't understand everything she's saying, but one thing I'm sure of is that I do not want to go to France anymore at all. Sara has ordered cream puffs. She cuts off a piece and puts it on a plate in front of me. "Come on, you need to eat. You look like a little bird that's fallen out of the nest." To make her happy, I take a mouthful, but I don't swallow it.

That night, lying in bed in a little hotel Sara found near the historic Karakoy quarter, unable to sleep, I think about Iran: the courtyard of *Mehr* in darkness, the intoxicating scent of flowering jasmine, Baba making his rounds with the powerful flashlight he stole from the army. In four days, the Nowrouz holidays would end. When the pupils of the public girls' school Sara had enrolled me in after the mullahs took power and closed the Lycée Razi came back to class, they'd wonder what had happened to Kimiâ Sadr, and no one would know the answer. Who would ever think that Kimiâ Sadr was in Istanbul, holed up in a hotel, without any *pognon*? I think of my seat next to Azadeh Behechti, who I hated because she was *hezbollahie* and had called my dad a "traitorous bastard." My chair would definitely be empty for a while. "Maybe Kimiâ will come back, children, you never know," our teacher,

Mrs. Ashrafi, would say. Then after a while it would be assigned to another student, who would have become friends with Azadeh Behechti in the meantime. By then it would be almost the end of the school year, and no one would expect me to come back anymore.

While these thoughts ran through my head, I had the suffocating sense of being trapped in a narrow hallway with a door at either end, condemned to be there forever. Behind one of the doors was the Iran of my childhood, and behind the other the France of my dreams. Back then, I didn't know what it meant to have a *traumatic experience*, but I already knew that those minutes spent in the gloomy office at the French embassy in Istanbul had had a devastating effect on me. Everything I'd been through up to that point, as terrifying as it was, corresponded to identifiable codes. There were no traps. The story arc was the same as every plot I knew, abiding by a universal dramatic logic that had been in place since time immemorial. In summary: on one side there were the Bad Guys (the SAVAK agents) who wanted to kill the Good Guys (us). After a bunch of wandering and hardship, the Good Guys triumphed before being pursued by other Bad Guys (the Islamic regime). What had happened in that office, though, was unexpected and terrible. It was night falling in the middle of the day; it was the earth crumbling beneath our feet. When you've grown up with the certain knowledge that France is the steadfast ally, always by your side to protect you, it's hard to accept that it has deliberately planted a knife in your back and is watching you bleed out on the concrete. All those beautiful quotes, all those wonderful characters, Hugo and Voltaire and Rousseau and Sartre, around whom our lives had gravitated, were nothing but a Middle Eastern fiction, a naïve fable for people with romantic souls, like Sara. We had no allies, no friends, no refuge. We had nowhere to go. That was the truth.

We had to wait a week before Darius called and instructed Sara to return to the embassy. This time she left us in the garden and went into the office by herself. When she came out her eyes were filled with tears, and she had a large envelope in her hands.

"It's all right, girls, we can finally go!"

"Really?" cried Mina. "You promise?"

"I promise," Sara said, waving the envelope.

Unlike me, they were happy. I have to admit that my aversion to France was now joined by disappointment at leaving Istanbul. I'd begun to love the city, caught between two continents just like we were. But it was a guilty affection to which I didn't dare admit, knowing how angry Grandma Emma would be if she ever found out.

During the week we spent awaiting the good will of the *farançavis*, we had explored Istanbul—but only the western side. We didn't want to cross back into Asia, as though doing that would have meant one more failure somehow. For the first time, all four of us were in a foreign country together, acting like tourists, which was both unexpected and pleasant. We started eating normally again, and laughing, and wanting things. Sara tried hard to pretend we were on vacation. Every morning she planned out an itinerary that would keep us busy until the evening. She took us to the old Armenian quarter (twice), the hammam (three times), and the bazaar (every day), where she made friends with an old Armenian icon-seller who invited us to dinner at his house. We visited the Hagia Sophia, the Blue Mosque, Topkapi, and Sara described to us the decadence and grandeur of the Ottoman Empire and the birth of the Turkish Republic.

There was something familiar about Istanbul that was reminiscent of Iran before the Revolution. Before women were swallowed up by the Islamic veil, and propagandist murals invaded the walls. Before ration books, and the omnipresence of the revolutionary militia, and the war with Iraq, and the disappearance of products like alcohol, deodorant, and perfume. The city's architecture, the habits of the *Istanbulis*, the rhythm of the days—they were all very similar to what we knew. The sunsets, when the chant of the muezzins rose into the air, had the same melancholy colors as those in Tehran. Our advantage over the Turks was that we could read the inscriptions inlaid on the pediments of the mosques, on the arcades of the bazaar, encircling ancient miniatures and above the immense palace doors. Perso-Arabic script featured prominently on every monument dating from the Ottoman era, and the language, a blend of Persian, Arabic, and Turkish, was still mostly understandable. By opting for a Turkish-Latin alphabet, Ataturk deliberately cut his people off from their Ottoman and Islamic roots, which he thought were the main cause of their underdevelopment. Sara loathed him. In her mind, no modernist thinking could justify depriving a people of its history, forcing it to regard its own cultural richness with the disorientated eyes of a tourist. Her diatribes on the loss of Turkish identity were a roundabout way of warning us to guard against losing our own.

A few hours after we'd left the embassy and bought plane tickets in a travel agency on Isteklal Caddeçi, a taxi dropped us off at the airport. Look at us, walking confidently toward the stocky border guard with a moustache that would make Stalin jealous, standing in a sentry box as green as his uniform. Omid, who insisted on accompanying us, is few paces behind us. Sara hands our travel permits to the guard, who looks at them for a long time, his thick black eyebrows knitting and relaxing. His theatrics don't worry us. Really, what can a little Turkish border guard do against papers provided by the French embassy? Now he looks up at Sara and asks her a question. She smiles and shrugs to indicate that she doesn't understand. Omid approaches and a discussion starts. The border guard stabs his index finger at our documents and then points at us.

"What is he saying?" demands Sara, impatiently.

Omid clears his throat, as if he's having trouble getting the words out.

"He says, 'I know they're leaving, but I want to know how they got into Turkey.'"

Sara looks down for a few seconds. We stare at her, petrified.

"That's fine. I'll tell him."

Now Sara, surrounded by four soldiers, is getting into a black car with tinted windows that is parked in front of the airport's main entrance. Her departure affects me like a shot of pure heroin. I don't feel any anxiety or even fear, because I've stopped existing. Later, I have flashes of lucidity. The hotel room in Karakoy. I'm lying on the bed, or hunched over the toilet bowl. Leïli and Mina are there, inert, listless, silent. I don't know how or why, but whenever I think about Sara the pause button in my brain gets pressed, and my body leaves this world.

During this time, somewhere in the bowels of the city, Sara is being interrogated by soldiers. She's already been through this situation. The same questions. The same dark room. The only difference is that last time, the questions were in Persian.

The hours drag by and new faces replace the earlier ones. The questioning starts over again every time. Family name. First name. Age. Then everything else: her grandparents, her parents, her childhood, her marriage, her political activities, her husband, her children, their departure. And Sara answers, trying not to show any signs of fatigue or exasperation. She asks for some aspirin and they give it to her, but with no water. She eats the lentil soup and the piece of bread they give her, to show that she isn't afraid.

Thirty-seven hours later, her body trembling with fatigue

and her brain in shreds, they shove some papers beneath her nose and a pen into her hand.

"Sign," the translator instructs her.

"What am I signing?"

"A sworn statement. You agree never to come back to Turkey. Neither you nor your children."

"No need to sign; I'm never coming back," she retorts.

"Sign anyway."

The next day we drive to the airport again. This time, I'm glad to be leaving. In the past two days, Turkey has become for me what it was for Anahide and Artavaz—a country whose welcoming exterior conceals a dark labyrinth of terror.

It's a quarter to five on Friday, April 17, 1981. The plane, as imposing and determined as Montazemolmolk opening the door of the *birouni* to face the storm, is heading into the wind at full throttle. Suddenly its engines roar and it hurtles down the runway, picking up speed, tilts its nose up, and takes off. As the East, the Orient, shrinks below us into an anecdote and then nothingness, Kimiâ Sadr as you have known her, sitting near a window, does the same. Soon, I will be born for the second time. Accustomed to coming into the world amidst blood and confusion, to awakening Death and inviting it to the party, this rebirth—from the crossing of the wild, violent land of Kurdistan to the hotel room in Karakoy—is undeniably worthy of the first. Soon my first name won't be pronounced in the same way anymore; the final *â* will become *a* in Western mouths, falling silent forever. Soon, I will be "disoriental."

As the plane soars into the clouds, the present floods through us, full of violent joy.

February 3. This is it! I'm standing in front of the door of the clinical laboratory, unable to breathe.

"Hey! Coming through!"

I turn. A man in a wheelchair is glaring at me as if he's been waiting there for ten years. That's Paris, too—that look. It reflects what this city does to people, whether they're natives or from anywhere on the planet. It makes you impatient, pushy, sullen, rude. It whispers endlessly in your ear that other people irritate and get in the way and invade your personal space. If you don't want to be shoved, bumped into, and jostled, you'd better keep up and keep going. At all costs. No hesitating, no dillydallying. Firmly ensconced in your body as if it were the deft and protective cockpit of an airplane. And obviously if, knowing all of this, you still insist on pausing on the sidewalk—well, you're the one asking for trouble.

"Come on, move!" I take two steps to the side, the bare minimum needed for the guy in the wheelchair to get by.

As he bashes open the laboratory door, I reread the results of my blood work. The effect is immediate. I feel a wave of pure happiness wash over me. Every one of my organs, every one of my nerves thrills to the extent that, once again, I can't move.

My cell phone rings. It takes me a few seconds to realize that it's in my coat. Before leaving the apartment, Anna asked me to keep it in my pocket so I wouldn't have to dump the contents of my purse out on the hood of a car every time she called me. She wanted to come with me, but I refused. I wanted to be alone to face this moment, and the disappointment likely in store. Anna didn't insist. She never insists. Her Flemish culture, as different from my Eastern culture as Bob Dylan is from Motorhead, keeps her in a perpetual attitude of what, depending on the situation, might be interpreted as respect, understanding, polite non-interference, or even—in extreme cases—indifference.

"So?"

"I'm pregnant . . . "

My voice, as flat as if I've just received a shock, is at total odds with the exaltation burning in my throat. I never thought the day would come when I, too, would get to say those words—would be the "I" in that sentence. I've often wondered how it must feel to say it, to announce that the miraculous alchemy has taken place inside you. For the last few days I've been imagining myself barreling out of the lab like a bat out of hell, calling Anna and screaming in her ear that *it worked, I'm pregnant.* But, as Doctor Gautier warned me, the probability of something like that happening was so slight that as soon as the image formed in my mind, it would sink out of sight into the marshy blackness of theoretical reality.

"Wait. You're pregnant?! Oh, *Kimy!!!*"

"Yeah . . . I'm pregnant," I say again, my eyes still wide with surprise.

"Go and wait for me at the bar at La Cantine; I'm on my way!"

She hangs up.

It's exactly what I needed to hear. A direction to take. Somewhere to go.

After a week of intense cold, it started to warm up yesterday. The weather suddenly got milder and a chilly sun is beaming down on the city. Just like when I came in, I decide to avoid the boulevard de Belleville, which is clogged for miles with the folksy chaos of the Friday market. I have no desire to elbow my way through crowds or dodge between trucks and pedestrians. This is one of those strange markets where the products seem to have spent the whole week being passed from one stall to another before plunking down somewhere to be sold. When you live in a working-class quarter with a large immigrant population, you're confronted every day by the cruel reality that your standard of living is proportional to what you deserve in terms of quality and cleanliness. You can sell anything you want here, however you want, to poor people, and people with no job security, and the unemployed, and illegal immigrants, and first-generation immigrants, and mothers of large families, as long as the prices are cheap and you make them think they're getting a bargain.

I walk uphill, up narrow streets that are often deserted and paved with poorly maintained cobblestones. This path is longer, but I can go at my own speed. Phrases and images are whirling in my head, noisy and disorganized. The past rises to the surface like foam on the sea. I can't help but link the death of Uncle Number Two with this unimaginable news. Looking for logic in the extraordinary, a connection within coincidence. "We have to die so that others can be born in our place, right?" Emma always used to say, wanting to find a plausible explanation for this existential injustice. I think of my sisters, and everything I'm going to have to explain to them. Of my dad's face; my dad, who will never know. Of Sara. I send Pierre a text; I don't want to talk to him at all, not right now. I type *POSITIVE!* and then turn off my phone.

I've always wanted kids. Even when I was one myself, I wanted them.

I loved my childhood so much. Even while I was living through it. I was already aware that it was the happiest time of my life; so much so that I didn't like celebrating my birthdays, knowing that every year that went by took me one step closer to adulthood. I had the same difficulty giving up clothes that I'd outgrown for new ones that fit me. I was proud of being a child, of skateboarding when the adults didn't know how, of catching insects they were afraid of, of running and falling and getting up (not even hurt!), of hiding and playing in the rain and jumping into the pool beneath the envious gazes of Leïli and Mina, who would be sitting on the edge of the pool in shorts dangling their feet in the water, unable to swim because of their *periods*. I could see in their faces and bodies what growing up meant, and it seemed like nasty business to me. Pimply foreheads, sprouting breasts, bumps on their noses and new pains and spots of blood in the crotch of your pants. Every day seemed like an ordeal for Leïli, which she struggled through in oversize sweaters stolen from Darius to hide the shameful body she could no longer control. Mina would lie on the couch with her head buried in French books, raising it now and then only to remind us that she hated the whole world for existing. And during all of this I was cannonballing into the swimming pool, a hundred times, a thousand times, screaming with joy to make sure they—and I—knew how lucky I was. I was certain that becoming an adult would involve more sacrifice than privilege, and prevent me from doing more things than it would allow me to. The idea that one day my turn would come, that life would pin me down and strip me of my very self, was unbearable—even though, as I've mentioned, I pictured myself becoming an adult man, standing on the balcony on a spring day and smoking a cigarette. In other words, and to simplify things, I spared myself the *periods* and the long waxing sessions that preceded the arrival of summer, as well as a whole series of other obligations from which men are exempt in the East.

I thought that having a bunch of kids would allow me to counteract this injustice. Surrounded by children, I wouldn't have to grow up completely; I could keep that playful part of my self deep down, that physical freedom in which I reveled every day. I had no empirical proof of this belief, though, because our parents never played with us. No Iranian parent of that generation played with their children. Their job was to raise us, not to entertain us; that was what the older children were for, or the younger, single aunts and uncles. That being said, compared to the other mothers, Sara was much more available to us, and a much better listener. Watching her as she gathered my female cousins around her on rainy days in Mazandaran, or admiring her as she played ping-pong with her nephews (and not bothering to conceal her glee when she beat them), was a great comfort in my reflections.

As I grew up, even long before I became aware of my sexuality, I put the desire for children to bed and took other paths. Dark, twisted ones soaked with music and alcohol and illegal substances, in accordance with the wishes of that other Kimiâ, the one who was born on the evening of April 17, 1981 when our Air France flight landed at Orly airport.

I've tried to remember exactly how I felt when I saw Darius

waiting for us in the passenger pickup area in the airport, behind the barrier separating new arrivals from the people waiting for them, but I can't. I've turned my memory upside down and shaken it like a snow globe, but I can't find even a particle of emotion. Not the tiniest dust grain of feeling that I can follow with my eyes and describe. But I can see myself walking toward him, like in a slow-motion tracking shot.

I think it was somewhere in the air between Istanbul and Paris that I contracted the illness I call "G.I. syndrome." It's as if, all of a sudden, for no objective or tangible reason, the door between me and my emotions slammed shut, cutting off my access to myself. Sometimes, like at that moment, as Darius's silhouette came into focus, I feel as if I've turned into a fixed object around which meaningless shapes are moving. I can't tell people from sidewalks, or sidewalks from buildings, or buildings from cars. This state can last a few minutes, or whole days. Then, abruptly, via the same unpredictable mechanism, the door opens. Things start to move again and colors come back, and I'm back in the world, in full possession of my senses.

The word that best describes my state in that airport is still *whiteness*. And not just my state, but the first image stamped on my retina: the final close-up, my dad's face, white from top to bottom. From his eyebrows to his beard. Infinite whiteness.

My nose is pressed to the window of the car being driven by the man—Mr. Djavan, Majid's brother-in-law—who came with Darius to Orly. It's night-time, and I'm watching Paris rise up in front of my tired, awe-stricken eyes.

I'm having a hard time believing this city really exists. I can't believe the cars parked along the wide, empty streets have owners; that these buildings, lined up in rows like good students in a dormitory, are made of stone and not cardboard; that behind those lighted windows are decorated rooms, living rooms, bedrooms, kitchens, where people are living. Men and women and children, living uninterrupted lives, with clothes hanging in closets, and toothbrushes, and everyday household belongings, and memories. Men and women and children. Old ones and young ones. People who have always existed, who were here yesterday and a month ago and a year ago. A thousand years ago. Does that man crossing the street at a red light know that he's in Paris? And the couple getting out of that car? And that woman on a bicycle? Do they have a past? Will they still be here tomorrow? Will there *be* a tomorrow?

Everywhere I look, I see the word *coiffeur* written above closed shops. I don't know what it means, but this city—if it really exists—is crammed with them. I could ask Leïli, who is sitting next to me, but I don't want to. I don't want to be the only person in this whole city on this Friday night in April who doesn't know what *coiffeur* means. And anyway, whatever it means, it can't be worse than *pognon*, or *lesbienne*.

When we first arrived in Paris, Darius was living in a studio belonging to one of his cousins—the son of one of Montazemolmolk's sons—who had lived in Paris for years. The studio was in Boulogne, on the fourth floor of a modern building on an immense boulevard. The area wasn't very welcoming, and Sara decided that we had to move to the 13th arrondissement, where the Djavans lived. Three days later, we went to lunch at their house, and Sara asked Mrs. Djavan a lot of questions about the schools.

I took the metro for the first time that day. Intimidated and not knowing what to do, I watched Darius and imitated his actions. It was then that I noticed his systematic avoidance of escalators, and asked him why he never took them.

For months, our parents—especially Sara—remained convinced, with that strange optimism felt only by the desperate, that the situation would get better in Iran and we would be able to go back. In fact, so that she wouldn't have to buy anything new except bed linens, Sara rented an old, furnished one-bedroom flat in a grey building on the avenue de Choisy. Our parents took the bedroom, which was just off the living room and taken up almost entirely by a large bed. Leïli and Mina slept on the sagging beige velvet sofa-bed, which they pulled out every night, and I slept on the floor, in a sleeping bag borrowed from Mr. Djavan.

In the middle of the summer, when the owner wanted his apartment back so that one of his children could stay in it, Sara decided that she'd had enough of living with other people's furniture and rented a two-bedroom apartment in a newly-constructed building on the other side of the Place d'Italie. The place already had a washing machine and a rectangular table in the kitchen, left by previous renters. Sara furnished it as austerely as possible: five plates, five forks, and five knives. Two casserole dishes and a frying pan. Mattresses in both bedrooms and boards on trestles. A few weeks later, a TV and a percolator joined our Spartan household.

Summer ended, and autumn began. The apartment began to reflect the grieving process that Sara had begun despite herself. The more unlikely a return to Iran became, the more she entered into resigned acceptance of the situation—and the fuller our drawers and closets became. Nothing extraordinary, nothing fancy, but the sketch of our lives gradually became a drawing, with clear edges. The temporary became permanent. She dropped anchor.

Life itself went through the same basic process as the apartment, but with extreme caution and frugality. Our parents never went to the theatre, or the movies, or to a museum, or out to eat. They never took us anywhere. Lack of money, though it was real, didn't fully explain their behavior. It also had to do with the daze into which exile had plunged them; the solitude, the stagnant grayness of the Parisian days, the heaviness of the silence in a country where no one looks at each other or talks to each other, where feelings are held in like bad farts. But there was also compassion, pushed far beyond excess, when it came to Iran, as if allowing themselves even a tiny amount of well-being in their daily lives meant indifference, or forgetfulness. How could they have fun when their family and friends—and the whole population of Iran—were being strangled by repression and massacred by Saddam Hussein's bombs?[20]

We spent the school holidays milling about, reading and killing brain cells by watching American TV shows. The paradox, even the irony, of it all was that in Iran, our parents had bored us to tears with their endless talk about France—well, me, at least, since my sisters had always enjoyed it—and now that we were here, and the countless hours spent learning the language, geography, history, and literature could be put into practice, they no longer had the energy even to take us to a library, or the confidence to let us go out alone. We had all hoped that a day would come when the five of us could live together again, free and without fear. But freedom is an illusion. The only thing that changes is the size of your prison.

[20] It's difficult to avoid mentioning the longest war of the twentieth century! Eight years that changed the face of the Middle East forever, the official starting point of which was a border dispute: Saddam Hussein's desire to take possession of the oil-rich province of Khuzestan. There are various perspectives that can be taken of this terrible war. The historical one of the Arabs against the Persians. That of a secular Sunni faction against an Islamic Shiite faction which regularly incited Iraqi Shiites, the majority of the country's population, to revolt. That of two dictators wishing to impose their power in the region. After having given sanctuary to Khomeini, France now took up Saddam's side without a qualm, providing him with an astonishing war arsenal. The same went for the Soviets. The ostensibly pro-Iraqi United States sold arms to Iran on the sly (an affair known as Iran-Contra, or Irangate). Everyone turned a blind eye to Saddam Hussein's use of chemical weapons against the Iraqi Kurds and the Iranian army. Isolated and radicalized, Iran drew closer to Syria—and it is undoubtedly at the end of that war, as bloody and ruinous as it was pointless, that the mullahs began to consider seeking access to nuclear weapons themselves.

Despite their love for one another, Darius and Sara were living parallel lives. Sara was consumed with anxiety and sadness, while Darius was at loose ends, like a commander who had lost the war. During the seven months he had spent alone in Paris, he had picked up the habit of walking. Four, five, six hours at a time. Our presence did nothing to sway him from his ritual. Every day in the early afternoon, without saying a word, he would leave the apartment to roam the streets and boulevards, a baseball cap pulled low on his forehead and his hands clasped behind his back, never pausing to sit on a bench or stop in a café. All he wanted was to be alone. Alone with the enormity of his solitude, with the stream of his thoughts, with everything that should have been, and wasn't. He kept up this regimen until his death, lost eighteen kilos, and stopped smoking cold-turkey.

One winter afternoon, coming back from one of his long rambles, I heard him say to Sara, who was sitting and writing at the kitchen table:

"I saw Pirouz . . . " He was as white as the tiles behind him. His voice quivered slightly. He poured himself a large glass of water and drank it down in one long swallow, as if to drown the emotion he felt.

"Pirouz? Your brother Pirouz?" Sara gasped. The news was even more astonishing because, at that time, the countries of the West were refusing to grant entry visas to Iranians. "Where did you see him?"

"On the corner of Boulevard Montparnasse and Boulevard Raspail. He was waiting for a taxi."

"Did he see you?"

"Of course he saw me! I was coming straight toward him; we were practically nose to nose."

"How is he?" asked Sara, thrilled that finally someone was there to break Darius's solitude, even temporarily. "I hope you invited him to dinner."

"We didn't speak. He crossed the street and disappeared down an alley."

"Oh, Darius . . . "

I probably don't need to tell you that at that moment I hated Uncle Number Six with a hatred more intense than I'd ever felt before. I could have strangled him with my bare hands and watched him die, his eyes bulging and pleading, like a movie murderer. Even later that night, lying on my mattress and watching the street lights pool and ripple on the ceiling, I was still picturing myself doing it.

I knew that Uncle Number Six had become incredibly rich since the mullahs came to power, to the extent that he had built a small palace above Tehran and set his four children up in houses in Los Angeles for which he had paid cash, but I didn't know exactly where the money had come from. Real estate alone couldn't explain the enormous influx of wealth. The most probable scenario—especially given his avoidance of Darius—was, according to Sara, that he was serving as an intermediary between the West and the Iranian government. Because, despite France's official position in favor of Iraq and its opposition to the Iranian theocracy, the government had begun selling arms to the Iranians via indirect channels. Not to mention the works of art, pillaged by representatives of the regime and their scions, which regularly turned up on this side of the world. French- and English-speaking, influential, arrogant, unscrupulous, a man of many connections and an unmatched businessman, Uncle Number Six, the runt-turned-businessman, was perfectly suited for the role.

Like a statue crumbling from the inside, Darius never mentioned the encounter, or Pirouz, again. As usual, he kept his thoughts to himself.

For the first two years, Sara didn't go beyond the boundaries of our neighborhood. She'd leave our apartment to go to the supermarket, the bakery, and the laundromat to dry our clothes. She only went out to fulfill our basic needs. If I were to attempt some kind of psychological explanation, I would say that to do any more would have suffocated her like too much oxygen at the top of a mountain. Her body, which she had always considered as belonging equally to her and us, was here, playing the role of wife and mother, but her heart and soul were somewhere else. Her mother was growing old alone; her younger brother Aram was rotting in Tehran's Evin Prison for having sympathized with a small Marxist faction; and one of her nephews had fled Iran via Pakistan and hadn't been heard from since. The largest part of her being was with them; she was their guardian angel, bound by the irrational certainty that if she went away, they would disappear forever. She telephoned Iran at least twice every week for news, even though the connection was always bad for various reasons, and even when the calls went through, the voices sounded like they were coming from the depths of some prehistoric cave. Wherever I happened to be in the apartment, I knew when Tehran was on the other end of the line, because Sara's voice would suddenly get louder by several decibels—not just to make up for the mediocre sound quality, but out of a fierce desire to abolish the distance between them.

When she wasn't thinking about them, she retreated into the past, which had become a parallel universe as well as a field of research, where she could revisit every place, every event, every night spent waiting, praying, hoping. Where she could remember who she was and what had happened, and why they hadn't succeeded. Her memory, her incredible memory, was like an engine in overdrive. Sometimes she would stop right in the middle of the street, lost, her brain teeming with disturbing questions. Was she really in Paris? Why didn't she go home? Where was her home?

At night, both Sara and Darius took tranquilizers so they

would be able to sleep. But neither of them slept. Darius would spend most of the night in the kitchen reading *Le Monde*, while Sara wrote letters to family and friends—letters that took months to arrive, if they arrived at all. The tranquilizers didn't help her chronic anxiety; they only shifted it, allowing her to open the sluice gate of her emotions and, if she couldn't share them with us, at least write them down for others.

A week after THE EVENT, when Sara left the apartment for good and moved in with Leïli, we cleaned out the place and found a dozen boxes in the closet, filled with letters she had received over all those years. They were arranged in order of arrival date, inventoried, numbered, categorized. And among them were hundreds of passionate or admiring letters from strangers who had read her book.

As my parents battled with the djinns of *depression* (a word whose meaning I finally understood in Paris), my sisters suffered in silence and studied, convinced that the only way to do well in a foreign country was to earn diplomas. Leïli had resigned herself to this reality from the moment of our arrival, applying herself without enthusiasm, but with discipline. Brilliant and hard-working, unwavering in her desire to become a doctor, she attached herself to her studies like a train car to a locomotive, trailing from classroom to lecture theatre, from exam to exam, without so much as raising her head to glance at the world around her. Mina, on the other hand, went through a long period of oblivion (diagnosed by Leïli as "post-traumatic stress.")

While she had once been curious about everything, full of mischief and a sharp sense of humor inherited from Emma, Mina had become a completely different person. She was a withdrawn, silent girl, living in a dark, self-contained universe of her own. It was as if time had slowed down in her body. She slept a lot, often fully dressed, she moved slowly, and lived on

French fries and avocados, the pits of which she set to sprout on the windowsill. She rarely bathed and stopped combing her hair, which was always a wild tangle around her face. In the afternoons she would come home from school and, without a word, place her homework in front of Leïli, who, equally silently, did it for her with a minimum of effort.

Yet, out of the three of us, Mina was the one who had been most anxious to leave Iran. When Darius left, she had begged Sara to follow him. "We have to go; we *have* to! There's no point in staying! We're always lying or hiding. It's going to drive us all insane in the end!" she had insisted. She'd been sick of politics, sick of living with the Pourvakils or Uncle Number Two. She'd felt that she deserved a normal life, all the more so because of her leg, which was a constant reminder that she'd paid her debt to the country. Deep down, she thought she'd suffered more than we had, and that her opinion should be worth more in consequence.

But, once we were in Paris, Mina realized that the French had a disastrous image of Iran. During the four hundred and forty-four days of the occupation of the embassy of the United States, nicknamed "the great Satan" by Khomeini, Iran had acquired an unshakeable reputation as a fanatical backwater at war with the West. In the early 1980s, the French didn't really differentiate between us and the *hezbollahis*. Teachers and students would ask us ridiculous and sometimes offensive questions that demonstrated their ignorance more than anything else. One girl asked Mina once, right in the middle of class, how she could bear to come to school without a veil. Another one, astonished to see her eating ham in the school cafeteria, had picked the slice off her plate and waved it around to make sure she knew what it was. Mina recounted these disturbing incidents in a slow, exhausted tone that made it very clear to us how much they had hurt her, like having acid poured on that part of her that had idealized France since she was a little girl.

Similar things happened to Leïli and me, but we didn't take them to heart in the same way. Mina suffered like a rejected lover.

To be honest, even now I occasionally have that same reaction, which forces me to give people a crash course on modern Iranian history so they can understand which camp we belong to. After almost thirty-five years of this, one thing still surprises me, and that is the speed with which France erased from its memory the fact of having welcomed and supported Khomeini, burying its share of the responsibility for the events that followed.[21]

One Monday morning, a few weeks before the French baccalaureate exams, Sara put an end to Mina's downward spiral in a brutal and unexpected way, blowing up in the bedroom we shared and tearing off the duvet beneath which Mina had been hiding for days.

"That's enough now! I'm not going to let you throw away your future!" she screamed.

She seized Mina by the arm and pulled her out of bed and shoved her into the shower, yelled at her again, and marched her to school. The shock of seeing Sara in such a state dissolved Mina's resistance. She cried a lot, but came back to herself after that, little by little. She was never really the same, but she used the resources she had left to create a set of goals for herself, which she now began to pursue methodically.

Nothing in Sara's attitude would have made you think that

---

[21] Why did Valéry Giscard d'Estaing lay out France's welcome mat for Khomeini, who had been expelled from Najaf by Saddam Hussein under pressure from the Iranian government? Was it out of fear that Iran would fall into the hands of the communists, as the minister of the Interior, Michel Poniatowski, warned? Was it because, unlike Carter, he doubted that the Shah was going to leave, and wanted to secure France a strategic position with the Iranians? And once Khomeini was in France? What happened? What deals and promises were made?

she blamed herself. She maintained a distance between herself and us, which we chalked up to her depression. With all her energy being poured into her lost homeland and the people she had left behind, she no longer felt that she needed to worry about us—after all, we were safe. But I sometimes think that her apparent detachment was her way of letting us know that she was helpless, that she didn't know how to be a mother anymore. She doubtlessly didn't know who we were anymore, or what she had a right to expect from us, now that our promised land had turned out to be a road to nowhere. Our uprooting had turned us into strangers, not only to other people, but to one another. People always think hard times bring you closer together, but that's not the case with exile. Survival is a very personal matter.

As for me, not only could I not tolerate our home environment, which swung back and forth between resembling a Bergman film and a zombie movie, but I also had trouble with the normality that had suddenly been imposed on my life. Going to school, coming home, having a snack, doing my homework, handing in my workbook. I wasn't used to this kind of daily routine at all anymore, and I struggled with being held accountable. Also, school had stopped being an enlightening place where you learned to understand the world as a structured, orderly, and welcoming place. Luckily, unlike my sisters, who had only just arrived and already had to study for the baccalaureate exams, I was only in sixth grade, and no one was worried about my future yet. Which gave me plenty of time to think of a way to reconnect with the freedom I'd lost when I arrived in this country.

The revelation came to me a bit later, through the TV (an old, poorly-functioning set left by previous renters and installed in our room by Leïli), which I watched until late at night. That evening, a concert in a small venue was being shown on *Les Enfants du Rock*. Because Leïli and Mina were asleep, I'd turned the sound off, so it wasn't the music that struck me—but rather, the dangerous energy emanating from four young guys dressed in black, barely older than my sisters, strutting across the stage like they owned the world. They were feline, powerful, Dionysian. Their clothes were ripped and their fists raised, rage made the veins in their necks stand out. It was dark and luminous. Secretive. Subversive. In front of them, human waves, dense and insatiable, crashed against the edge of the stage before rising up and shouting in unison. They kept their backs turned to the world, to its values and obligations, to the past; they were drunk with the joy of being there, of living in a different way, of living at all.

I wanted to be there with them.

There, where Iran, and France didn't exist.

Alone and insurgent.

I was so enthralled by the images thumping against my retina that I didn't hear Sara come into the room. Her hips blocked the screen. Her finger pressed the power button, and a black veil fell over the picture.

"Good lord, Kimiâ, it's one-thirty in the morning. You need to sleep!"

Don't count on it, I thought, staring at her.

I am fourteen, but I look older because of my height (almost five foot seven), my large hands, and my eyes, which have lost their innocence. I wear jeans and whatever blouses Sara buys me on sale. Despite her efforts she can never find skirts in my size. Maybe in the adult section, but I'm not old enough to wear those yet. I am thin, but strong; a confusing physique.

For the first time ever, I skip afternoon classes and go to the Fnac in Montparnasse, trawling the rock section in search of the group I'd seen on TV. I find it at the very back, under "U." U2. There are two LPs in the bin, *October* and *War*. I can't afford to buy them, and we don't have a record player anyway, but I discover that I can read the lyrics on the sleeve. I understand a few words here and there, but the rest remain a mystery. I copy the lyrics to *Sunday Bloody Sunday* into one of my notebooks. From that day onward, my life changes. Music bridges the gap between the past and the present; childhood and adolescence; what has been and what will be. A new world has opened up for me, where it is better to be clever and resourceful than to have money.

As a result of the hours spent carefully translating song lyrics so I can understand them, I become a whiz at English. My vocabulary is far more advanced than that of the other students, and I can pronounce the "th," sliding my tongue easily between my teeth. I spend my Sundays at the movies, watching dubbed and subtitled American films. I buy one ticket and sneak into another theater for a double-feature. One day I go into the wrong one and stumble across Alain Resnais's *Love Unto Death*. Shaken, I watch it twice in a row. I discover the flea market at Saint-Ouen, where I unearth an old record player, second-hand albums, and previously-worn clothes. Perversely, the outfits I assemble for pennies give me a new style all my own. Velvet jacket, ruffled 1970s blouse, fringed suede trousers, work boots. Horrified by the dirty things I keep lugging home in plastic bags, Sara stuffs it all straight into the washing machine.

I plunge headlong into punk and post-punk. John Lydon, Ari Up, Ian Curtis, Joe Strummer, Peter Murphy, Siouxsie, Martin L. Gore. Their music fills every emotional and intellectual hole in my life. It becomes my daily bread, my life preserver. Because it puts the world back in its right place and tears away the facades. Because it is aware of the rage and the sweat and the strikes, the working-class quarters and the revolts and the gunpowder. Because it denounces the hypocrisy of power, and demolishes the certainties and social and ideological affirmations that claim to explain to us how the world works. Because it is made so that people like you will look at people like me.

I shave my head on the sides with some old clippers and cut it short as a boy's in back. Sara, appalled, doesn't speak to me for weeks, and Leïli rebukes me for adding to her suffering. I promise her I will keep up my good grades; as for the rest, I tell her it's none of her business. Oh, and I begin swimming every day. At noon, instead of going home for lunch, I go to the pool next door to the high school. The official reason: I love sports. The secret reason: I dream of having a body like Peter Murphy, the sexy lead singer of Bauhaus, instead of my hybrid body whose strangeness sometimes makes me ashamed. I think my flat bum and narrow hips are already a good start; the rest—long, slender muscles, straight shoulders, well-defined thighs—depends on my own perseverance. I think of my body as my only country, my only homeland, and I will draw its contours the way I want them.

Now I'm sixteen. My deep knowledge of the underground scene enables me to go out in search of people who listen to the same music as I do. I've reached my adult height of nearly five foot eight, and curiosity propels my lanky, solid body through the city streets. I stamp Paris with my own footprints. It has become my city, a liberating and insidious place.

My route takes me to the Forum des Halles one Saturday afternoon. It's a meeting place for teenagers estranged from their families; social services cases, gutter punks, Goths, young homosexuals rejected by their parents, and marginal members of society just passing through. A motley, aimless group that grows and shrinks with the season and the vagaries of chance. My looks are unusual enough that they elbow each other to make room for me. No one asks me where I'm from. No one cares. No one's waiting for me to let slip a grammatical error. They call me by whatever nickname occurs to them, or just "K," the initial of a first name most of them don't know. They're defensive, unpredictable, disruptive, loudmouthed, brazen. Sometimes in the metro, when they're sprawled out on the bench seats singing at the top of their lungs, they offend the reserved politeness instilled in me during my upbringing— but they're not cruel. Some of the girls react to my presence in a way I find comforting. They make sure to stand close to me, ask me to walk them home, play with my hair. One of them, Barbabeau (a nickname given because of her elaborate witch-clown makeup), always sits in my lap, exclaiming: "You've got knees like a guy!" I love it when she says that, because she's acknowledging my bizarre physique while, at the same time, letting me know that it's no big deal. Every time I see her I wait impatiently for her to come and sit in my lap so I can hear her say those words.

With these people, I learn to exist in an infinite *now*. To drink beer and cheap wine, smoke, drop acid, and spend wild nights in abandoned buildings and crowded dance clubs and tiny bars with battered stools. I learn to talk to the bouncers, guys who let me slip into concert venues without a ticket. I learn what "to hit on" means. And above all, I learn, to my relief, that sexuality has no boundaries except the ones we impose on it. Being homosexual or heterosexual doesn't mean anything. These considerations, so contentious and polemic in the harsh light of day, are too porous to resist the nights of this restless decade as it winds down. After a certain hour and in a certain light, edges blur. The middle-class wives, taking advantage of their husbands' absence on work trips, slum it in lesbian nightclubs. They come early and sit in the corner with a glass of wine, patiently watching the girls dance, looking for the right one. Men in business suits ditch their girlfriends and slip into the bathroom to join the young guy who smiled at them before turning away petulantly. Couples arrive together and then, by mutual agreement, split up to go on the prowl. AIDS is still just a distant rumor, a disease too exotic to find its way into these dark basements, thumping with savage urban sounds.

"Do you know what time it is?"

I've hardly opened the door when Sara is there, right in my face. There are black circles ringing her eyes. Her stare pins me against the door, strangling me. She knows I left the restaurant where I work three nights a week at around midnight, and she wants an explanation.

"I don't know . . . five o'clock?"

I try to speak carefully, to control my alcohol-numbed tongue. I know the horror she's endured waiting up for me all night, along with all the other nights she's spent pressed to the window, watching this city, which she used to love for its beauty, turn cold and hostile. Who can she call to find out where Kimiâ is? Who can she ask for help? Who can she talk to about what she's going through?

I can almost see the panic running in her bloodstream and tensing her limbs. It's the same as it was in Tehran when she waited for Darius. The same as it is on the telephone when she talks to Emma. I know her thoughts always go in the same direction, circling around the nightmare that plagues her and paralyzes her: death. Death, which might pounce on one of us at any moment, and take us away from her. Part of me is sorry for her and wants to reassure her, to comfort her and tell her how irrational and destructive her fear is, but the other part, which is becoming harder, ever more imposing, rejects this moral entrapment and the tyranny of her feelings.

"No, it's five-*twenty!* And when you stay out until five-*twenty* in the morning, do you know what that makes you?" (No, she shouldn't have said it, but she couldn't stop herself . . .)

"A whore!"

Sara looks at me with disgust. The whiteness of my scalp where my hair is shaved. My hollow cheeks, which make my dull, black-shadowed eyes look huge. The leather jacket I found God knows where and never take off. And the acrid smell of me, a mixture of cigarettes, damp carpet, and saliva that envelops me like a funeral shroud.

What I've become exceeds—by far—anything Sara could have imagined. She rejoiced at giving birth to another daughter, a familiar creature whose joys and sorrows would be her own. But I'm not a girl. She doesn't know what I am, but I'm not a girl.

On some of the sleepless nights spent waiting, Sara's thoughts go back seven years, to the journey between Iran and Turkey, and stop painfully on the moment when, petrified with fear, she asked for someone to take down little Kimiâ, who was riding with her on her horse that night. She wants to forget it, to erase it from her memory. She wants to smash her head against the wall and reduce it to shards. She said, with tears of helplessness quivering in her voice: "Take her down. I can't . . . " In a minute, masculine hands had taken hold of Kimy and pulled her down to the snowy ground. Kimy hadn't said anything, didn't resist, didn't try to cling to her. Her body made a faint noise as it slipped down. Then one of the Kurdish men had climbed into the saddle in her place and the horse started going again, slow enough so that Sara had time to turn and see her, her little silhouette lost in the immensity of the night, surrounded by the large figures of the men. Kimiâ was moving forward, even as she was getting further away.

What happened? What did she do? Why couldn't she keep her daughter with her? She's gone over the incident again and again, every second of it, and she still can't understand it.

It was ten past three in the morning when the horses finally arrived. Just two of them, even though they'd been climbing this hellish mountain for hours, their legs buried in snow up to their knees, spurred on by boorish armed men. Worn down by the effort, Sara tried to keep an eye on her daughters, praying that they wouldn't slip or twist an ankle or fall right in front of her eyes. She'd asked Omid to look after them, but Omid had gone ahead. By the time they reached the top of the mountain she was drenched in sweat, despite the bone-searing cold. Her head ached so badly that she'd swallowed her last two aspirin with a handful of snow. Leïli and Kimiâ were there. Mina brought up the rear, slowed down by her leg. The men who were riding them dismounted. They walked for another good thirty minutes, Mina clinging to her. Then the horses arrived. Just two of them. They said that more would come soon. While they waited, they hoisted Mina and Leïli up on one of them. Then Sara and Kimiâ onto the other. The littlest one with her mama, like you do with cattle.

At the first gallop, Sara felt terror cut off her breathing. If Kimiâ stayed there, they would both die, crushed beneath the horse. She pictured their bodies buried in the snow, the animal trampling them. She saw Leïli and Mina lost forever in these mountains. The throbbing in her throat was choking her. Kimiâ's back pressed against her chest was too heavy. She resisted; she tried to bear it. But suddenly the words burst out of her mouth, broken, beseeching. "Take her down, I can't . . . " She turned around to look at her. This was her punishment, this horse moving slowly forward. What she saw in that instant was like a nightmare, a fever dream. No, the little girl back there wasn't Kimiâ. She couldn't be there, still walking, exhausted, vulnerable, like a tiny old woman, while she, Sara, was seated comfortably on a horse.

Sara knew right away, in the deepest part of her gut, or her subconscious, or wherever it is that truths go to nest—she knew, even if she pretended not to for a very long time, that something had broken the moment her daughter's feet hit the snowy ground. That invisible thread that was her pride and joy, the indissoluble connection between a mother's body and her child's, snapped in a single instant. A rift was created, right then, and it has only grown wider since.

Even now, sometimes, under the effect of the sleeping pills, she imagines that she let herself drop down onto the snow, while Kimiâ stayed on the horse. Yes, that's what happened! Kimiâ rode on ahead after her sisters, and Sara walked, waiting for another horse to be brought. The joy that she feels as this scene plays out in her head is like the happiness of hearing good news. She'll get up and tell Kimiâ right away.

But Kimiâ isn't here, and Sara doesn't know where she is.

And why don't you know where Kimiâ is? screams the sharp voice of her guilt inside her. *Because that isn't the truth!*

It's in writing down the events that brought them here, in a notebook borrowed from Darius, that the monstrous reality truly hit her. The image in her mind of Kimiâ walking forward and falling behind at the same time wasn't a hallucination or an optical illusion; it was from *her* that Kimiâ was getting further and further away, even as she moved forward. It's *Sara* who left *her* behind. Kimiâ's childhood ended at that moment, in that solitude, in that silence, in the shock of having been abandoned. And that mistake, that single mistake, weighs more heavily on Kimiâ now than everything good Sara has done for her.

"I am not a whore!"

"Yes, you are—it's the only explanation!"

Darius appears behind her, dressed in pajamas, his face white and cracked like the wall of an old building.

"Since you love being out so much, leave! Go on, get out of here; I don't want to see you again!"

"Sara . . . don't say that . . . " Darius's voice trembles. He's expressing himself, finally.

"Why shouldn't I say it? And if I don't say it, who will? You?!"

Sara is screaming now. Except that she doesn't know how to scream, and her voice coils in the back of her throat like a tornado. She screams with her mouth, which works hard with the effort, and the veins in her neck, which bulge. I don't wait for what she's going to say next. I open the door and go.

I finished out that year in a squat in Pernety, a dilapidated building where punks went to crash after a night of partying. We lived in complete chaos and disorder, sleeping on rotten mattresses in freezing rooms with smashed-out windows, strewn with beer cans and food wrappers and cigarette- and joint-stubs. I swallowed everything anyone gave me, from hard drugs to alcohol to medication, to chase away the images that crowded my head as soon as the sun went down. I wanted to dissolve and disappear. I didn't give a damn that I was killing myself. Most of the regulars were guys; girls only came to spend a night or two, to sleep off a hangover, or for a casual fuck. I kept my distance, determined to avoid any kind of trouble, and didn't let anyone get too close. Some nights, when the music was too loud or a fight broke out, I'd gather up my stuff and leave. Usually at those times I ended up on the quayside between the Bastille and the Gare d'Austerlitz, where the giant sculptures are on display. I'd curl up in one of their smooth, hollow interiors to hide and read until sunrise. I read mostly poetry; I loved Henri Michaux, whose obsessive wonderings about the body and drugs resonated with me. I showered at the swimming pool, washing my underwear at the same time, like Sara had taught me during the Revolution, when we were staying with Uncle Number Two and didn't have many clothes with us.

I didn't go to school every day, but I still managed to keep up with my studies and pass the exams, bent over my books for hours in cafés—often the café on the ground floor of our building, where I could discreetly watch through the windows for Darius or Sara leaving for the day, or Leïli coming home from the university, or Mina from the library.

Against all expectations, I earned my high school diploma. I'd promised myself that, if I managed it, I would go home that same night to tell my family. Not out of pride, but because I wanted to. I wasn't just a teenage runaway. I'd left because I didn't feel like I belonged with them anymore. The distance had enabled me to figure out that: 1) my parents couldn't be *my* parents anymore, like they used to be, and I couldn't be *their* child as they had known me, either; and 2) I didn't want to live with them anymore. I'd decided to share these conclusions with them, but also to promise that I would always keep in touch.

I rang the doorbell. Sara opened the door, her eyes reddened from crying (my fault, I figured immediately). I waited for her to turn her back on me, but she pulled me into her arms and held me tight, the way she had when I was little and came home from playing in the courtyard with scraped knees. I hesitated for a few seconds and then put my arms round her. She stroked my hair. I noticed that she had to lift her arm up to do it, because I was taller than her.

"Kimiâ . . . oh, Kimy . . . Grandma Emma is gone. My mama is dead."

And she burst into tears.

I'm often reminded of Emma when I go to La Cantine, because of the cake sitting prominently beneath its glass dome on the zinc counter. Today, Anna is waiting for me at the back of the room. Usually she sits at the bar leafing through newspapers, but this time she's at a table near the window, a cup of coffee steaming in front of her, watching the outside. As soon as she sees me, a knowing, impish smile curves her lips, the kind of smile gangsters have in 1950s noir films when they've just done a successful break-in somewhere.

Instead of sitting down, I hold out the results of the blood test, hoping to buy a little time before she launches into one of her enthusiastic tirades about the future. Listening to her talk about the future still makes me anxious, even after six years together, and she knows it, but she can't help herself. For Anna, the future is an extension of the present and this is what makes my gut twist—only better. It's a vast, enchanting horizon that extends the sea, and toward which we're strolling, cocktails in hand, with the nonchalance of a couple of amateur yachtsmen. But for me, the future is more like one of those overcrowded, rickety buses wobbling along a road in Africa, which you keep an anxious eye on, wondering if it's going to turn over. If it's true that people's bumps and hollows need to fit together in order for them to complete one another and move forward together, then my hollows of doubt fit perfectly with Anna's bumps of confidence.

While she looks at the blood test results, I take off my coat and try to catch the waiter's eye so I can order. When I turn around, Anna is staring at me with eyes so clear and blue it's as if they've been painted by a watercolorist.

"I can't believe it! One shot!" she exclaims.

I nod, unable to control the goofy smile that spreads across my face. She jumps out of her seat, takes my face in her hands, and kisses me.

3
ANNA I

The first time I saw her was on the number 71 bus to Ixelles. At first I only noticed her hair; it was the kind of hair that had been damaged by lack of care and too much dye; it looked stiff and rebellious, like Blondie's hair, or Chrissie Hynde's. It screamed *rock and roll* and gave the impression that she'd just rolled out of bed after multiple orgasms. Except hers was red.

Since I'd begun matching my look to the music I listened to, I'd dreamed of having hair like that, but despite liters of dye, hairspray, and beer, mine—inherited from Mother—remained dishearteningly lustrous and silky. One look at my hair was enough to understand why rock could never have been born in Asia.

After the awkward growing-out process of the so-called samurai cut (shaved on the sides and mid-length on the top), which had wrung cries of distress from Sara, I'd decided not to bother with my hair anymore. Letting it grow was the only alternative. But at the same time, accepting its length was like choosing a femininity I had still never explored. Without really knowing how to go about it, I wanted to let that submerged, silent, unknown side of me rise back up to the surface. I wasn't a teenager anymore, and I didn't want my hair to make me look like one. Thanks to my wandering life, I had courage now that I hadn't had before.

When I first came to Brussels, I was eighteen years old and my hair fell past my shoulder blades. The greatest advantage of this "big hair," as I often heard people call it, was that it hid me. Hid my timidity. My dull insomniac's complexion. My foreign face. It was the curtain behind which I hid and peeped out at the world, waiting to gain some self-assurance. Imagine me arriving in this unknown country on a dark, rainy Sunday afternoon in October, getting off the bus I'd boarded five hours earlier at the Porte de Pantin metro station, with everything I owned in a backpack and two thousand, five hundred and forty-eight francs I'd saved during a summer spent working days at a supermarket meat counter and nights at the restaurant. I'd chosen this city for two reasons: because it was in the North, an atmosphere that suited me better than the flashy countries of the South; and because they spoke French here. Believe it or not, despite my tendency to fling myself into the void, I was still cautious in some ways.

Unlike France, in Belgium immigration hadn't yet become so commonplace among the population that nationalities and identities blended into one another. Non-Western foreigners still stuck out like a sore thumb, especially because they all gathered in certain areas, not having the right to settle just anywhere in Brussels. My features gave away my origins, but my smooth hair and long legs created visual confusion that acted as a kind of smokescreen. Not quite sure of where to place me on the world map, the Belgians generally opted for Latin America. They figured I was Brazilian or Argentinean: the hot brunette, sexually switched-on, ads for fizzy drinks. If they ventured so far as to engage in conversation with me, though, their fantasies were shredded the moment they heard French coming out of my mouth. "Wait, you're *French?*" they would exclaim, their tone conveying something between wonder and certainty. And I would nod, with a spontaneous smile. The fact that my Parisian accent, which was the source of so much controversy in France, always came to my rescue in Belgium never failed to amuse me. "Where in France are you from?" "Paris."

"Ahhh!"—an exclamation that was always loaded with hidden meaning, speaking volumes about the simultaneous attraction/repulsion that Belgians feel when it comes to Parisians. The fact that I came from Paris weighed so heavily on the scale of cultural appreciation that, even when I told them my first name, they didn't ask where I was *really* from—though it must be said that, straddling three cultures as the *Bruxellois* do, and being accustomed to all kinds of convoluted names, the question hardly occurred to them. So much the better, because I didn't want my new life to be tainted with the same reluctance that had poisoned my old one in France, first by keeping me from feeling at home, and then by removing my desire to feel at all. I let the Belgians think what they wanted. Sometimes I would even tell them a different first name, decking myself out in adventurous ancestors, or relatives who had gone to live on the other side of the world. I reinvented myself according to my mood, or the intensity of the light, or how many glasses of beer I'd had, always marveling at the realization of how one individual could be viewed so differently depending on the story he (or she) made himself part of. I became not only Brazilian and Argentinean, but also Hungarian, Tajik, and Franco-Vietnamese. Just like Uncle Number Two, I was discovering that a dose of fiction helps make the truth more bearable.

Anna's hair is made for her face.

If I noticed it even before seeing the rest of her; if I immediately associated it with the goddesses of rock, it's because it's in total harmony with who she is. The whiteness of her skin, the pale blue of her eyes, her straight Protestant nose; her mouth, which is slightly asymmetrical, like the tilde above the Spanish *n*. Anna has an exotic, disorienting face. A face of autumn and fires in the fireplace and hard cheese, of grainy bread and dark forests and fog, of rain boots and yellow raincoats and cinnamon buns and dinner at six o'clock.

The second time I saw her was at Métamorphose, a bar behind the Place de Brouckère which I ventured into by chance, attracted by the purple velvet curtain protecting the entrance from the stares of passers-by. Pushing open the door, I was almost immediately confronted with the pale moon of her face, haloed by her bright hair and illuminated by the yellow light of the lamps hanging above the bar. Believe it or not, in a sudden flash of clarity I still can't explain, I knew right then that this girl could drastically change my life. The feeling was so strong that I was about to close the door again and run away, but the waiter greeted me with a "Hello!" so enthusiastic that I felt like I didn't have a choice. But I waited for her to leave the bar and walk to the back of the room before I came any further inside.

I had absolutely no doubt about who, what, she was. She was Flemish right down to her clothes, which were deliberately careless-looking. She felt the cold; she was chilled to the bone by the freezing, rain-filled gusts of wind that seem to be blowing through this country at all times. Casting furtive glances at her from the bar—she was slumped on a bench seat in the company of three guys, beneath a giant portrait of Kafka—I thought of the lyrics to a song by Won Ton Ton that was often playing on the radio: *I should be glad I was born in Belgium.* So this was what it meant to be Belgian. This was what it looked like to be young in this country, which seemed to be evolving in a hollow of the world, detached from the movements of History. Elsewhere, hundreds of miles away, the Berlin Wall was coming down amid uproar and astonishment, while these kids—and others like them—hung out in nice bars, and talked, and laughed, and made it seem like what they were was more than enough to fill a whole life. In a strange way, Brussels reminded me of the East, with its simplicity and its naivety, and the nonchalance with which it let time pass.

More than to be *with* this girl, I wanted to *be* this girl. I wanted, even if just for an hour, to slip into her skin as if it were one of those interiors in the Habitat catalogues that make you believe that living in them guarantees you a smooth, comfortable life. I wanted her carefreeness, her casualness, her freedom that wasn't the result of a hard-won battle, but simply a fact of life. I knew perfectly well that, whatever my existence was or would become, I would never be like her. If, just then, coming up to order another round at the bar, she had asked me to follow her, I would have done it without question, just to see where she would take me.

But she didn't come up, and I left Brussels a few months later, in late February 1990, for Berlin. A week before my departure I saw her at the Beursschouwburg, at a cocktail party celebrating the Flemish artistic scene. Two songs in English, sung in a *MarianneFaithfulli* voice with her group Genet (a name that speaks for itself), and the room went crazy. Her bass guitar slung over a shoulder, her mouth pressed to the microphone, she was powerful and violent, possessed by a contagious fury that was in total contradiction to the childlike image she'd presented at Métamorphose.

I came back to Brussels three and a half years later. In the meantime I'd lived in Amsterdam and met Marteen Maes ("Maes like the beer," he'd said with a laugh) in the bar where I worked every night, a few streets away from the Stadsschouwburg, the municipal theatre.

Marteen Maes was fiftyish and well over six feet tall, with hands like baseball mitts and disheveled sandy hair, and blue eyes that were washed-out by alcohol and sleepless nights, but as lively as those of a hundred-meter sprinter. He wore Italian shoes, cashmere turtlenecks, and a long black coat that hid his legs. If Rasputin had decided to be reincarnated, he would definitely have chosen the body of Marteen Maes.

When, at around nine forty-five one night, he strode into Klein Bar and arranged his heavy, elegant body at the bar, he gave the impression that he brought his past along with him like a fellow traveler. No one sat down on the stool next to his, as if people knew instinctively that the place was taken. He gave off the fascinating scent of a bygone era. Years of unbridled sexuality, pallid mornings, damp hotel rooms, train journeys, starry nights, friendships sealed in the chasing and conquering of parallel worlds. He had stopped smoking in the same way I'd let my hair grow, not for any noble reason, but to emphasize the fact that Death had spared him so far, had given him an unexpected—and largely undeserved—reprieve.

He started our first conversation by telling me about his arrangement with alcohol. As a favor, he asked me to serve him beer first, which had the same effect on him as it would have on a concrete wall, and then, at eleven o'clock sharp, even if he hadn't finished his glass, to pour him his first vodka. I adhered scrupulously to this ritual every night for three months, feeling as if he and I were bound by a secret pact. He'd stay until two in the morning, eyes bleary from a dozen shots, as if waiting for someone to arrive. Anyone. A stranger—male or female—who would open the door and change the course of things instantly and forever. He believed in the magic of bars, and in chance. "Two things that were made to go together, Kimy, just like my hand and this glass," he would say in French that was grammatically perfect but chopped to pieces by his northern accent.

Klein Bar was mostly frequented by young people who went out in groups, staying until dawn, smoking and getting drunk. Because it was bar service only, sometimes one of them would linger and talk with Marteen before rejoining their group. Indifferent, with the look of an ageing dandy, Marteen didn't insist, and it was toward me that he directed his loneliness. Kimy, the girl behind the bar, tattooed arms, unfiltered Lucky Strikes, silver rings, dressed in black, hair halfway down her back, exuding free, loveless sexuality. And that was how we started chatting, getting deeper and deeper each night into a strange complicity that took giant leaps forward when I started allowing myself two or three shots of vodka (usually Cheap Blonde so I wouldn't be totally broke by the time my shift ended at dawn).

When he asked me where I was from, after a few attempts at evasion, I doled my past out to him in bite-sized morsels. He wasn't the kind of man who was easy to lie to. And there was something charming about his way of creating intimacy beneath the pink neon of the bar lights that made me want to be honest. In those moments, if Marteen were a place, he would have been a chalet deep in the mountains. Even as I write that sentence, I'm realizing that I talk a lot about mountains—but just know that I hate mountains, just like I hate taking baths and getting massages. There's an excess of well-being in these places that I have absolutely no idea what to do with. And yet, I was born at the foot of the mountains, not just once, but twice . . .

Marteen was the first person I told about our departure from Iran, thanks largely to the vodka and the album *Henry's Dream* by Nick Cave. I wanted him to know that I'd had my share of adventures on this earth, too. He listened to me without interrupting. If he was moved, or intrigued, he didn't show it—or, if he did show it, I didn't notice, so wrapped up was my mind in the tangled threads of my story, as torturous as the journey itself. After that, a new chapter opened up in our exchanges. When he felt like no one would come up and bother us, he would say to me: "Tell me about your little feet in the snow, Kimy." Later, I realized that, thanks to him and his stubborn insistence on making me repeat that story, I had managed, little by little, to find a way of talking about it. Our conversations had acted like water on whisky, diluting the emotion and the heaviness, and undoubtedly the pain too. The nights passed, and Marteen talked to me like no one had ever talked to me before. He taught me who Stanislavsky and Tadeusz Kantor were. He told me about how Malcolm McLaren had stolen everything from Guy Debord and the Situationist International. He brought me a book on Paul Delvaux, a painter I had discovered and loved thanks to the sleeve of the Bauhaus LP *Dark Entries*. He introduced me to electroacoustic music, Steve Reich and Gavin Bryars. I listened with the intoxicating feeling that maybe I'd earned my spurs enough to deserve this, that all of it—all the loneliness I'd struggled with every day—hadn't been in vain.

A week after the premiere of the play he was directing, he told me he was going home to Brussels. Up to that point I had thought he was Dutch, and that Amsterdam was his home. He hadn't thought he needed to clarify anything; his own identity preoccupied him less than Baudelaire's misogyny, or the tragic end of Anton Webern. At around midnight, getting a bit heated, he shot at me:

"How long are you going to stay in this dive, Kim? Come with me; it's time for us to do something with you."

"Like what?" I asked, laughing.

"Whatever you want! What do you want to do? Stop washing those glasses and tell me what you want to do, for God's sake!"

"Mix music."

"You want to be a DJ?"

"No. I want to work in music venues."

"To stay hidden in the dark, eh? The North isn't dark enough for you, is it? You're going to spend your life hiding?"

"I like hiding."

"Okay, this might be possible. I know a guy who might be

able to help you. Ian Bennett. I'll pick you up tomorrow at seven."

"Really?"

"Yeah. Really."

That very night I said goodbye to Ludwig, the owner of Klein Bar, and told him he could keep my salary for that month.

The next morning, as sheets of rain poured down on Amsterdam, washing away the sins and superficial pleasures of the night before, I closed the front door of my building behind me, my baseball cap snugged down on my head. This constant rain, which purifies and restores order and imposes prudence, is probably the best explanation for why this country is the way it is. Perched on his bicycle and swathed in a hideous waterproof poncho, the Dutchman goes his own way without worrying about others, while scrupulously obeying the law to avoid accidents and conflicts. Calvinist culture, the cornerstone of this society based on organized and well-ordered freedom, trust, and indifference, couldn't have found a better field in which to sow itself.

Here's what I'd learned about the Dutch: each person is free to be who they are, to want what they want, to live how they choose, on the condition that it doesn't harm the well-being of anyone else, or the general equilibrium. It's a philosophy of life that's the exact opposite of Persian culture, where erecting barriers, getting involved in other people's lives, and breaking the law is as natural as breathing. But it's also unlike the Judeo-Christian rigidity of French culture, where actions are endlessly hindered by words.

Marteen was already there when I came outside, seated behind the wheel of his black Volkswagen, a paper cup of coffee in his hand. I opened the passenger-side door and climbed inside. "Sorry, I'm soaked."

As I lit a cigarette, he started the car. He looked rough, and his breath still smelled of alcohol. He breathed in the smoke I exhaled as if it were his lover's perfume. Just then, a sigh rose from the back seat, followed by a groan. I turned around and saw a body curled up asleep beneath a white Perfecto jacket. I immediately recognized the hair, which was now platinum blonde.

"She's my niece," whispered Marteen. "She performed in Utrecht with her group last night. She had an argument with her girlfriend and it spread to the rest of the group, and she decided to call a taxi at two in the morning so she could share it all with her old uncle. You see? You might forget your family, Kimy, but by Christ, it'll never forget you!"

"What's her name?" I asked, trying to hide my surprise.

"Anna. Like my mother."

Anna De Grave. The name I'd read on the program someone handed me at the front door of the Beursschouwburg.

Anna De Grave and Marteen Maes still lived in a world where a niece could find refuge with her uncle.

Now that you know how I met up with Anna again, and before I tell you about my London travels, let me transcribe for you one of Grandma Emma's letters to Sara, written on May 19, 1989. This is the only letter I've kept; the rest are in cardboard boxes in the basement of Mina's house. Every time I read it, my grandmother's wide, loopy handwriting makes me think of the way she'd open the windows to "let the cool in," as she always said.

My darling girl,
I received two letters from you yesterday. One from two weeks ago, and the other from four months ago. The envelopes had been opened and sealed again with Scotch tape. I hope the bastard who read them will also read this one and find out what I think of bastards like him. Damn this

country! If I tell the grocer that his dates aren't fresh, he says to me, "If you don't like them, don't buy them!" If I go to the bank to withdraw money, the teller looks me right in the eye and says, "Pay me the same amount and I'll give you your money." I'm glad you aren't here to see it. Can you imagine? My age, my white hair, my face, as wrinkled as a wet rag, nothing stops them. People have become sad and nasty. But at the same time, you can't blame them. You put anyone in a cage and deprive them of everything, eventually they'll try to kill and eat one another. That's what they're doing to control us; they're turning us into animals. Anyway, they don't care if we die. They don't need us in order to exist.

But I've come up with a solution: I haven't gone out in almost a week and a half. That way at least there's no risk of my being arrested, because you know me, I have trouble keeping myself from speaking my mind. Tahéré, the care-taker's daughter, runs my errands for me, and I stay at home and look after your brother. He's only been a shadow of him-self since he got out of prison. I don't know what those bas-tards did to him, exactly how they tortured him. I've asked him, but you know how he is, he keeps everything to himself, as if I'm too stupid to understand, or too fragile to take it. The fact remains that they gave him back to me in pieces! But it doesn't matter. He's alive, and you'll see, he'll get back to him-self. Try not to worry about it too much.

Well, here's the real reason I'm writing: my instinct is telling me that something's wrong with Kimiâ. Your last two letters both end with "Kimiâ is fine too and sends her love," but that's all. First I wondered if something had happened to her, something serious you were afraid to tell me about, but I don't think so. I haven't seen any sickness hovering around you or your family and, believe me, I've drunk plenty of cof-fee since I got your letters. So then I wondered if maybe it wasn't an illness, but something else. Maybe that thing I've kept deep inside me all these years. I'm glad I don't have to tell you in person what I'm about to tell you, even though I'd trade the rest of my life in a second for the chance to hold you in my arms and at least see where you're living now. If you're standing up, my dear, sit down and listen to me.

When Kimiâ was born, you were so happy to have a daughter, even to the point of giving her that crazy first name, that I didn't want to tell you. But what I felt at her birth has been proven over time, and believe me, I've been keeping an eye out for the signs. I've watched her and even asked her questions. I've been careful, you see, because I didn't want you to chalk it all up to what you call my "irrational interpretations," the superstitions of an old Armenian woman whom these sons of bitches have driven half-crazy (by the way, Tahéré told me yesterday that there are whispers going around that the Old Man is very sick, and that he is near death. God knows I've never wished death on my neighbor, but that one, I hope he croaks, even if it won't change anything).

I wish I had gotten it wrong back then, but unfortunately, the older Kimiâ got, the more I saw that I was right. I wanted to talk to you about it a thousand times, when I saw how disturbed you were by her behavior and the way she was. But with the life you had, there was never any time, and I didn't want to add any more worries to all the ones you were already dealing with. Sweet girl, my prediction wasn't wrong, even though you all made fun of me when she was born. Kimiâ is a girl, yes, but only in appearance. Inside, Kimiâ is a boy, the boy she would have been if Nour hadn't taken her last breath just as Kimiâ was trying to take her first. Take the time, please, to think about what I've just written, before you read the rest. Go and make a cup of tea, or drink a glass of water.

Well, I'll keep going. Everything you were afraid of when you thought you were carrying a boy, she will do—as she has always done. Even, and this is the hardest part for me to write, bring you a daughter-in-law. This is what I've been trying to say. Kimiâ is old enough to think about sex now, which I'm sure is complicating both her life and yours. Sara, my love, my little one, if your daughter prefers girls, let her prefer girls. Accept it. After all, she isn't responsible for her birth, or for Nour's death. Who knows what destiny has in store for us?

Who knows why our lives are what they are? Maybe you wouldn't be who you are if you hadn't been the only girl among brothers. Maybe I wouldn't have been the same if my parents hadn't moved to Tehran. In this life, both fate and free will have their parts to play, only the proportion changes, depending on the event.

Promise me you won't be ashamed of Kimiâ now for what she is, because she's always been this way, and you've always loved her. There's no reason for that love to change. You took her to France so she would live and be happy, so let her be. Look at your brother-in-law Saddeq; he hasn't had a single peaceful day on this earth, the poor man. Always covering up who he is, even though it's as plain as the nose on your face.

Okay, enough chatter. I've promised Tahéré an almond cake because her girlfriends are coming over, and even though baking is such a chore for me these days, I have to do it. And you should go and take your pills, because all my babbling must have given you a terrible migraine. I should be angry at myself, but I'm not. Don't you be angry with me, either. Tell the children how much I love them.

Emma

Even before we got to Brussels, Marteen handed me a piece of paper on which he had written down the name and telephone number of his friend Ian Bennett, former mixer at the legendary Marquee Club in London. Instead of rushing to England right away, he advised me to call another of his friends, Rob Neckelbrook, a sound engineer at the Theatre de la Monnaie, so I could pick up some technical basics first.

Anna didn't wake up until we were in Brussels. The three of us spent the weekend holed up in Marteen's enormous, minimally-decorated apartment, drinking and smoking, eating frozen meals, listening to music and talking. We were like survivors of some huge disaster, endlessly postponing the moment when we'd have to venture out and explore the world.

Those two days were enough to confirm what I'd already

suspected: the difference between two individuals of the same gender can be just as significant and unsettling as the difference between a man and a woman. I'd known men who were a lot more like me than Anna was, even physically. Men who had nothing mysterious about them except the way their genitals worked. But Anna was the complete opposite side of the coin from me, like those Russian soldiers you see in some parts of Mazandaran where the sea narrows, whom we were forbidden to watch, and who intrigued us so much. The world had narrowed between Anna and me, too, putting us—the girl from Anvers and me, the Tehrani—face to face. I watched her go from room to room the way you watch a cat move through a house. She had the same ability to make a place her own, the same way of claiming ownership of things and then losing interest in them. She was unpredictable, sometimes talking for hours and then suddenly clamming up. Exhilarated and closed off by turns, she carried within her a rage that, strangely, only made her more fragile. In Belgium, anger seems pointless and anachronistic. Life there is made for living, not for thinking about.

On Sunday, a friend of Anna's called and she left to meet her. The next day it was Marteen's turn; he went off to Athens to spend two weeks with his partner, a Belgian woman of Greek heritage. An hour later, I called Rob Neckelbrook.

Rob Neckelbrook was a barrel-chested tank of a man with a Bastos cigarette dangling from the corner of a mouth hidden by his bristly blond beard. He let me watch the last rehearsals of *Daphné* by Richard Strauss, explaining to me in *brusseleer*-scattered French the "*trucs de base,*" just the basics.

Day after day, sitting next to Rob behind the enormous mixing table, I felt a thrill of excitement unlike any other run through me at the moment when the house lights went down and the stage lights came up. The silence that fell at that moment was unique; it was both an invitation to wonderment and a warning. You had to live up to your own expectations as well as everyone else's, to the hours of work and the hopes and desires and dreams. Even now, even though concerts have become formulaic and predictable, I still hold my breath when the changeover happens, filled with pure pleasure and extreme panic at the same time. Sometimes I think I might shoot up off the ground like a rocket.

When I came back to the apartment on the evening before Marteen's return from Greece, Anna was there. The melancholy sound of Lou Reed's *Berlin* was coming from the speakers. From the way she looked at me, I could tell she had wanted to surprise me; she was like a leprechaun jumping out of a box. But I wasn't as surprised as she would have liked me to be. My "G.I. syndrome," I guess. After a moment's hesitation, she turned down the music and felt compelled to justify herself.

She'd come to tell me goodbye because they'd decided to leave, she and the other members of Genet, and rent a house a few miles outside Anvers to record their next album. As she talked, my head filled with rock and roll fantasy images: the group holing up together, composing songs, lying on soft couches, arguing . . .

But even more than the desire to be part of that secret, exciting universe I'd dreamed about so much as a teenager, I could feel the hunger rising in me to be in a house—and not just any house, but Uncle Number Two's place in Mazandaran. Usually it was summer weather that caused (still causes) that strange feeling inside me, when the desire to be there, and the pain of not being able to go, wage war deep in my gut. (This, I think, is why I hate summer so much.) But back then, when Anna said the word "house," I felt a yearning so violent that I could have sat down and cried. That's the tragedy of exile. Things, as well as people, still exist, but you have to pretend to think of them as dead.[22]

When Anna finished her explanation, her hands stuffed in her pants pockets, we looked at each other for a long time—or maybe it was only for a few seconds that seemed much longer. As *Sad Song* ended to the throbbing of the harmonium, the logical next step, we both knew was for us to fling ourselves at one another and end up on the sofa. We were among the thousands who didn't know how to do anything but that, especially when a little bit drunk or just lonely. Sex to pass the time, or for lack of imagination, or out of fatalism. Sex, for want of anything better to do. But the moment for one of us to make the first move had passed. Then another, and another. And then the song ended.

"Want a drink?" I asked.

"Yeah. What should we listen to?"

"Whatever you want."

We drank and talked until seven the next morning, simultaneously surprised at and proud of ourselves for having taken a steeper, riskier path. She didn't ask me any questions about Iran, and I was grateful to her for that. I'd finally managed to strip myself of everything; I wasn't anything but myself anymore, and I savored that victory as much as I did Anna's presence. When the sun began to glow through the window, she took me for breakfast in a friendly, rustic Flemish café near the Place du Jeu-de-Balle. That night was the beginning of our story; at least, that's how we tell it to anyone who asks, even though it took us six more years to meet again and end up on the sofa.

Here's a short snippet from the conversation we had that night—with hesitations, approximations, and various types of silences edited out.

---

[22] My apologies, reader, if it seems like you've read that sentence before, but I can't keep myself from writing it.

"Do you want to have kids?" Anna asks.

"If I only think about what I want and ignore the rest, yeah, I can't say I don't want them. I'll probably never have them, though. What about you?"

"I'm a lesbian. It's not the kind of thing I think about."

"Why not?"

"I don't know, it's just how I'm wired, I suppose. Anyway, I don't think I'm a family sort of person."

"It doesn't have to be a 'mommy and daddy' thing though, does it?"

"What choice is there? People don't have enough imagination to do it any other way."

"We're not all destined to become one thing or another. Kids have nothing to do with it. Look at Patti Smith or Chrissie Hynde; they've got kids, more than one, in fact, and that hasn't kept them from being who they are. They're even more avant-garde than most lesbians who make fun of women for wanting a family."

"Well, yeah, but you're talking about a time when rock was a lifestyle. It meant something back then. It defined the people who made it and the ones who bought their records. But it doesn't mean much anymore; look at Oasis. Now groups get together and make money and don't piss anyone off. The rest of it is something from another time, like a myth. Musicians only *act* rebellious now, because even that brings in the cash."

And then she went off into a tirade about the death of rock and roll . . .

So, Anna left for Anvers, and I went to London.

I never found the Ian Bennett I was looking for, though I found plenty of others—there were Ian Bennetts who were architects and florists and mime teachers and real estate agents, but none who were sound engineers. The phone number Marteen had given me was for an Indian laundromat near

King's Cross. I tried to contact Marteen; I left messages, but he never called me back.

I started to think that Ian Bennett didn't really exist; that Marteen had made him up to get me out of Klein Bar (and all the other bars where, out of aptitude or laziness, I could have spent my life working to pay the rent and buy food). Marteen was complicated enough, and mischievous enough, to plunk me down right in the middle of things on a pretext as slim as the search for a fictional character, just to see what came out of it. He had taken precautions, though, by advising me to spend time with Rob Neckelbrook first. I imagined him sitting on his leather sofa in his softly-lit apartment, a bottle of Triple Westmalle in his hand, listening to my messages on his answering machine and wondering when, for God's sake, I was going to stop sniveling and start living my life. The future proved him right, as it turns out, and I was actually surprised by how things came together after that.

My roamings through the city looking for Ian Bennett very quickly enabled me to leave the shabby hotel I was staying in and move—thanks to Ian Bennett the real estate agent—into a small furnished room in Elephant and Castle with a shower down the hall and a rent of nine pounds a week. I got a mixing job in a bar in Earl's Court that featured live jazz music five nights a week. When the owner, a former punk who had made a fortune in novelty T-shirts, found out that I was looking for a certain Ian Bennett who had once been a mixer at the Marquee Club, he invited me for a trial run right away.

"If you know a guy who mixed at the Marquee, you can't be too bad."

"I do all right," I lied.

"Two weeks, okay? If it works, you're hired."

"Great!"

That was how, even before I came to the definitive conclusion that "Ian Bennett" was nothing but a setup, I found a place to live and a job.

Now that we've come to this point in the story, as I'm seeing myself sitting in my furnished room in Elephant and Castle, my eyes glued to the beat-up answering machine left by a former tenant, I'm wondering how to proceed. It's two-thirteen in the morning (there's something chillingly clinical about the exactness of the time displayed on the upper right-hand side of my computer screen). I'm going to get up. Open the window. And, maybe, stop there.

4
THE EVENT
(I WOULD HAVE LIKED TO COME UP
WITH SOMETHING MORE ORIGINAL . . .)

4:34 A.M. I'm back. Couldn't sleep at all. Anything I might have written in an attempt to postpone the moment when I would have to confront THE EVENT seems completely pointless and meaningless to me. Life itself doesn't even seem very significant. Since I put the first word down on the first page, March 11, 1994 has been there like a blindingly bright light, drawing me inexorably toward it. All the digressions and small talk in the world won't help avoid it this time, like Uncle Number Two with his Morning of Death. I thought the flow of writing it out might help me to move forward with it smoothly, to pass through those dark, blocked-out places inside me I've created without even realizing it. I was wrong.

I've tried for so long to get those images out of my head. I've pictured them so vividly, so realistically, that even now I sometimes feel like I'm the one who discovered his body in the middle of the living room. Like I'm the one who waded through his blood.

His throat, slit from ear to ear.

His chest, ripped apart by five knife wounds.

Three deep slashes through his stomach.

His eyes, open and terrified, staring at the ceiling.

The smell of his blood.

I would rather have died instead. I would rather have spared Sara from living through it.

I had prepared myself to face his death; I'd trained like an athlete for the big game. I'd even prepared myself to find both of them dead in the living room.

For most of my adolescence, every afternoon when I came home from school, as I put my key in the lock but before I turned it, a voice in my head would freeze me in my tracks: *are you really sure you want to open that door? Will you be able to handle what you find without dying right then and there?* It was only when I thought I was ready, when I thought my heart wouldn't fail me, that I would turn the key and open the door. Sometimes I'd hesitate for long minutes on the landing, the key in my hand, unable to take another step. Sometimes the noise of the elevator, or a neighbor, would make me bolt inside. Once I was in the entryway, as the peace and order of the living room slowly registered on my retina, a new wave of anxiety would wash over me. *What if they were in the bedroom? What if they'd been killed in there instead?* I found out later, on the night of Darius's funeral, as we sat in Leïli's house, lost, empty, unable to sleep despite the pills, that my sisters had acted the same way.

Our fear wasn't exaggerated, nor was it the result of childhood trauma. It had begun when Darius was summoned to the Ministry of the Interior in December 1987. We never found out exactly what happened in that basement room; like everything else that concerned him, he never talked to us about it. To be honest, we hadn't even known about the summons until one evening when, sitting at the kitchen table doing my French homework, I overheard my parents having a conversation. Their voices came to me muffled by the thickness of the wall between us, but I was intrigued by what little I could hear. At one point, I got up to open the door and stood there listening to them.

One of the men present in that basement had informed Darius that French intelligence had just intercepted a list of names, his and those of a dozen other members of the political opposition living abroad whom the Iranian government was planning to eliminate. According to this man, Iranian agents were scattered throughout France, using false identities, laying the groundwork for these murders. The man had offered to put a police guard in front of our house, but Darius turned him down. If you listen hard right now, you will hear the mechanical grinding of the escalator again, and you'll hear Darius say "What right do I have to accept? How pretentious would it be of me to ask the French to go to work every morning just to pay for my protection?"

"You're right," Sara admitted. "Especially for the neighbors' sake. It isn't their fault that we are who we are. Anyway, police or no police, if they want to kill you, they're going to do it. You're out walking four hours a day; that's more than enough for them to follow you and plunge a knife into your back. I'll talk to the children and tell them to be extra careful."

The more I listened to them, the more it seemed to me that the situation excited them. The fact that the Iranian government was finally showing itself, that the enemy was approaching—and in its real guise as a terrorist villain—put meaning back into things. Into exile, and separation, and the endless Parisian days that stretched out emptily, one after the other. They hadn't forgotten about Darius. Despite the silence to which he had been reduced, and which was consuming him, they were still scared to death of him. I knew my parents well enough to picture the expressions on their faces; that way they had of looking at each other with a passion no one else could ever understand. In those moments, they weren't just a politically active intellectual couple; they were also a little bit Bonnie and Clyde. It emanated from them like the smell of gunpowder—the sense that they held the pulse of the world in their hands.

The next day, when Sara gathered us in the kitchen to talk to us, I had the same feeling.

"Don't tell me it's going to start all over again!" Mina wailed.

"It has never stopped, darling. We have to be proud of the fact that these cowards still want to kill your father. It proves that we're . . . "

And Sara launched into the old argument, the one we knew by heart. We looked at her without listening, full of a kind of crepuscular feeling, a mixture of weariness and terror; the exact opposite of how she felt. For six years we had worked every day, out of desire (Leïli), convenience (Mina), or necessity (me), to achieve something close to the normality experienced by other kids our age, even though something always came along to thwart us. In any form—wars, families, depression, letters, information, and now murder—and at any time, the past could always rise up in front of us, tragic and unavoidable. We were like those sticky climbing men you throw at the wall that start moving down as soon as they hit it. Our destiny was the tragedy of loss.

I was in Berlin when I heard that Shahpour Bakhtiar had been assassinated.[23] It was a sunny August afternoon and Berlin, which had become the capital of unified Germany only

---

[23] New Wikipedia entry: A former cabinet member under Mossadegh and opponent of the Shah's regime, Bakhtiar was the last resort of an ill, defeated king who agreed to name him Prime Minister in January 1979; a move that was overdue and proved inadequate to save him and climaxed with his departure, accompanied by his family, on January 16. Bakhtiar's government fell on February 11, 1979, after the officers of the Air Force revolted and the last factions loyal to the Shah were occupied. In April, Bakhtiar, who was married to a French woman, disguised himself as an Air France steward and left Iran for Paris. In 1980 an assassination attempt against him failed, but eleven years later, on August 6, 1991, a commando squad of three highly organized individuals made their way past the four riot police stationed in front of his house in Suresnes. Bakhtiar and his secretary were killed with knives. A year later, on August 30, 1992, the Iranian Minister of Intelligence, a cleric named Ali Fallahian, stated on television: "We will hunt down those who oppose our regime outside the country as well. We have them under surveillance as we speak."

a couple of months earlier, was thrumming day and night with techno music, the irresistible sound of transition. I was staying in a building that had formerly been the headquarters of the electric company but had now been taken over by artists and nihilists of every sort, a few streets away from the famous Tacheles art squat. That day, Jules, a Frenchman who was training to be a circus performer and always dressed in clothing so ragged he looked like a scarecrow, was sprawled out on a deck-chair in the courtyard, his face turned up to the sun, a joint between his fingers and a copy a few days old of the newspaper *Libération* open by his feet. I remember seeing only the two words: "BAKHTIAR ASSASSINATED."

Suddenly I was outside, running like a madwoman toward Kumpel, a café where I could make telephone calls because it had an old coin-operated phone. Sara answered.

"What happened to Bakhtiar?" I gasped, breathless.

"Oh, I see, so poor Bakhtiar has to be killed for you to call home! You're a few days late though, you know."

"I know," I said, irritated. "So, what happened?"

After telling me about the particularly clever way one of the commandos had gotten close to a friend of Bakhtiar's as a way of contacting him, and the sordid details of his murder, she added: "So, you see? Police protection doesn't do any good. Bakhtiar's son even works for French intelligence, and look how it turned out! If they want to do something, they're going to do it."

Other assassinations followed, elsewhere in Europe. A baseball cap was found at some of the crime scenes, like a signature left by the killers. Each of these murders was one more step toward terror. Each of them gave me a brief respite from my anxiety while making me dread the next one even more. Where did Darius's name fall on their list?

During the months that followed Bakhtiar's death I called home regularly, though I never talked about what was worrying me. I would have loved to get Darius on the phone, just once, but he never picked up, always leaving Sara to deal with the outside world. Sometimes I almost asked Sara to put him on the phone, but I always chickened out at the last minute. The complexity of my feelings toward Darius was paralyzing. I couldn't talk to him like a daughter to her father, because he'd stopped being one a long time ago. I couldn't approach him as one adult to another; my life was too different from his, and it might even be received as a haughty reminder that he wasn't what he used to be. Since our arrival in France he had become so distant, so unreachable, that I actually didn't really know who he was anymore. I was sure he knew that I was worried about him, and I left it at that.

Despite my fear, I never thought of going back, not for a single second. The contentment I'd found by distancing myself from my family ruled that out completely. Raised in a culture where the community takes precedence over the individual, I'd never been so tangibly aware of my own existence. I finally felt like I was in control of my own life. I could make decisions that had nothing to do with the past, or with the way an immigrant has to act in order to gain legitimacy in their host country. English had become my language; it was pragmatic, reduced to its primary function: communication. No one around me had the right accent, or a huge vocabulary, or perfect grammar. We spoke to each other from a place where identities didn't matter anymore. If you looked at the whole picture—my room in the squat in Berlin, the beat-up mattress on the floor, my unusual looks, my sleepless nights spent working in a bar or going to concerts—you might have thought I was in some kind of a downward spiral, a human wreck floating with the current. But it was the opposite. I was putting myself back together again, rediscovering happiness, getting back on my own two feet, as if after a long illness.

My sisters were angry at me. They were young mothers with

busy lives, and they would have liked me to be there, to soothe their family dramas, or at least take my part in them. If it was Leïli who told me that one of our uncles had died, it was because she and Mina took turns spending evenings and weekends with Darius and Sara, so they wouldn't be alone. Mina refused to speak to me altogether. She blamed me for having made the egotistical choice to live my life, when we weren't allowed to have luxuries like that. In her eyes, I lacked the kind of humanity that consists of sucking it up and accepting things. "You've always done what you wanted anyway!" she still flings those words at me every chance she gets. That's why, on that March morning in London, as soon as I recognized her voice on the answering machine, I knew what had happened.

Even before Leïli's terrified voice replaced Mina's gasping, I felt as if I were being ripped apart on the inside. That feeling lasted for years. Years when I could easily, if Sara hadn't still been alive, if I hadn't clung to music, if I hadn't abused all kinds of substances, have done the unthinkable, the one thing from which there is no coming back. My fury and pain were so ferocious that I had to stay deep inside myself all the time, so they wouldn't get out and destroy everything.

I don't even know how we survived those first few days and weeks after Darius's murder. To the confusion that goes along with any death, there was added an unbelievable amount of chaos. Leïli's apartment was always crammed with people, just like our apartment at *Mehr* years earlier. The telephone never stopped ringing. At least half the calls were from Saddeq, devastated and sobbing, whom the government had refused permission to leave the country, condemning him to grieve for his brother from afar. We had become a nerve center toward which a stream of people from all over the world now gravitated, people with no connection to one another. Sadrs from Europe and the United States, the Nasrs from Washington, the

Pourvakils from Cincinnati, longtime friends and unknown admirers of Darius, forgotten political opponents, former pupils of Sara's who were now living in Europe. But also investigators and journalists, intelligence agents, and all sorts of undesirable characters.

Like his life, like the blood that had leaked from his savaged body, his death slipped out of our hands. Most of our efforts were focused on minimizing how much of it we lost. We knew how much he hated eulogies and glorifications. He had laughed when he thought about who might come forward to speak at his funeral. In his show of disgust for the mortuary performance, lay the remains of his adolescent nihilism. Part of him had always resisted any kind of preservative demonstration. It was a part of him that I had loved, and that Sara, who was far more traditional when it came to these kinds of things, had deplored.

"But you'll be dead, Darius *Djan*. Why should it matter to you who does what?" she would say to him, reproachfully.

"Unfortunately, you can never be dead enough not to hear the cawing of the crows."

She had begged him hundreds of times to write his memoirs, but he had refused. Sometimes she had even brought us into the argument.

"Tell him what a terrible mistake he's making! What's he going to do; die, and take a whole part of this country's history to the grave with him? Is that your plan, Darius? If you've done all these things just to keep them to yourself, then frankly you shouldn't have bothered! And you really shouldn't have dragged me along with you!"

Darius always answered that future generations, which Sara was so worried out, didn't need him in order to study history, or to understand it.

"Of course they need you!" Sara would argue. "Because the whole world is lying to them, and will keep lying. Because no

history book published in Iran will ever talk about the
Committee for the Liberation of Political Prisoners (founded
by Darius) or the Committee for the Rights of Man (founded
by Darius), or the battles fought by everyone who died in the
Shah's prisons, and then Khomeini's."

But Darius just shook his head at her words. "I'm no historian. It's up to the historians, if they're worthy of the name, to
do their jobs!"

We waited now for Sara to crumble, but she stood firm.
Faithful to Darius's instructions, she forbade anyone from
writing, talking, or communicating on his behalf. She was no
tearful widow; she was a political oppositionist whose husband
had just been assassinated. Once again, she was chased out of
her home, from the rented apartment in the 13th arrondissement, which had now become a crime scene. Once again, she
found herself penniless. But she had things to say, and she had
no intention of letting the "crows," who were so anxious to
hitch their names to Darius's, say them for her.

At the funeral in Montparnasse Cemetery, before a compact, tightly huddled, silent crowd, Sara was the only one who
spoke. Without shedding a tear. Without a quiver. It was a grey
March day, the sky loaded with clouds. She began by explaining why we were in Montparnasse, which Darius had affec-
tionately called "the Quarter." She even managed to smile as
she talked about his young days at the Café Gymnase, his
apartment on Rue Huyghens, his newspaper, sold to Iranian
students. Then, without raising her voice or changing her tone,
she launched into a violent attack on the regime of the mullahs.
She knew, and we knew, that among the hundreds of individuals in black gathered around the grave that day were agents
on a mission. They were there to listen—so, by God, they
would listen!

I was sure that she had imagined this scene thousands of

times, just like she had imagined each of our funerals. She'd spent most of her adult life fighting against Death. It was a war in which she'd won every battle except two: Emma, whom she hadn't been able to bury, and now Darius, whom she had left alone in the apartment just for an hour, while she ran out to do the grocery shopping. Death had come and knocked on the door, and Darius, who was usually so reluctant to open the door, had opened it.

What had they said to him to make him open the door? Who were they?

Standing in front of her husband's coffin, Sara didn't need a police investigation to tell her the answer. Now she looked like a general on the field of battle, taking responsibility for defeat, and for her own lack of clairvoyance. And yet, her war-like stance was only a façade. You only had to look at her face, to see what was really going on inside her. Her voice was clear but her expression was lost, like when you get off the train in a foreign country and look around for some point of reference, to help you get your bearings. It was Darius she was looking for. There, in the crowd. Darius, who she had always looked for, in any crowd, in every crowd. Darius, who was forever escaping her, fleeing, vanishing into the labyrinth of the world. I think it was right then that I realized that, without him, she would never be able to see life as reality again.

I'm glad he died the way he did. By killing him, they raised him up out of the silence into which he had been plunged. Even now I repeat that phrase to myself often, like a mantra, to help me accept it.

His killers have never been arrested.

According to the investigators, they slipped out of the country a few hours after the murder, undoubtedly by way of Germany. Back then, the Iranian secret police were known for carrying out technically impeccable covert operations, but not attaching much importance to the repatriation of their agents. This was the case with Bakhtiar's assassins, who were arrested in Switzerland and extradited to France, where they were tried and sentenced. But the men who murdered Darius managed to get out of France quickly, undoubtedly because the operation had been so simple that they'd had plenty of time to plan their escape.

To explain why I think that, let me take you back in time again, back to Qazvin, many decades ago. Think back and remember Ebrahim Shiravan, the son of a Qazvini hotelier, who was obliged to report to Mirza-Ali as a suitor for one of his sisters. Remember their handshake—Mirza-Ali's phony smile, Ebrahim's sheepish air—as hypocritical as the marriage that followed. One of the two assassins, Kamran Shiravan, was none other than the youngest son of that couple. If Emma were still alive, she would have seen in Darius's murder a retrospective act of vengeance for poor Ebrahim, forced to marry an arrogant, bigoted woman seven years his senior, and to support her for the rest of her life.

Kamran Shiravan arrived in Paris two weeks before THE EVENT, invited by a French company that sold electronic supplies. That's what he told Sara and Darius, and what was confirmed by the investigation. Anxious to see his cousin as soon as possible, he made a beeline for their house the day after his arrival, with bags filled with pastries from Qazvin, and saffron pistachios. Darius welcomed him with open arms. According to Sara, loneliness and advancing age had awakened in him an unprecedented and surprising affection for his family members, even the ones—like Kamran—he hadn't had much to do with in Iran. He was deeply touched that they hadn't forgotten him.

Kamran was younger than Darius, a lanky, jovial, talkative man with a moustache, whom we usually saw at the Nowrouz festivities at my uncles' houses. Married and the father of three children, he was an engineer with a successful business. He wasn't known to be very political.

That evening, Kamran stayed for dinner with Darius and Sara, and entertained them with family stories. Before returning to his hotel near the Opera, he embraced Darius and kissed him on both shoulders as a sign of respect.

Two days later he came back, this time with a friend, Nasser Velayati, who lived in Munich. Velayati claimed to be a long-time admirer of Darius; he said he had fled Iran because he was a communist sympathizer. Germany had cured him of communism, but, since he wasn't permitted to practice law as he was trained to do, he had opened a copy shop. Velayati hadn't seen Kamran since leaving Iran, and counted himself lucky to kill two birds with one stone by meeting Darius too. I'm telling you all this so you'll see that this reunion, cloaked in very Persian warmth, was so well-orchestrated that it didn't arouse the least suspicion in either Darius or Sara. Even Mina, who was usually annoyed by their lack of caution, couldn't find any fault when Sara told her about the evenings they'd spent with Kamran and Velayati. In our minds, anyone who wanted to kill Darius would necessarily be a stranger, one of those Iranians who came out of nowhere every so often and demanded to see him.

On Thursday, March 10, 1994, Kamran came to see them in the morning. He told them that Velayati had gone back to Munich, and that he was leaving for Tehran himself the next day at around noon. But the following day at around 8:30 A.M., as she was crossing Boulevard Vincent-Auriol on her way to the grocery store, Sara thought she caught a glimpse of him in a taxi. She imagined that the taxi was cutting through the 13th arrondissement on its way to the ring road, and from there would take the highway to Orly Airport—but why so early, since Kamran didn't have to be at the airport until ten o'clock? She had probably been mistaken; it mustn't have been Kamran after all. But with his Iranian looks and beaky blade of a nose, Kamran was recognizable from miles away . . .

Sara kept thinking and wondering all the way to the supermarket. There, beneath the fluorescent lights, in the orderly, oppressive aisles, the questions multiplied and grew, and ballooned into Anxiety. Sara carried around a whole array of anxieties, some more intense than others; some more bearable than others; but the Anxiety she felt where Darius was concerned was always number one on the list. The one with a capital A. Finally unable to stand it, she abandoned her shopping cart and hurried home. She rushed through the streets, arriving breathless at the apartment. And she knew, the instant she pushed the door open, as the horror leapt out at her like a wild beast, that it had been them.

It was the bloody kitchen knife lying discarded next to Darius that left no room for doubt. Sara never put that knife in the cutlery drawer anymore, in case Leïli's or Mina's children might find it and hurt themselves. She kept it hidden up high, in the cupboard with the glasses. Kamran had come into the kitchen with her; had helped her set the table. He had even insisted on helping to put the dishes away after dinner. He had seen. Watched. Taken note. The bathroom floor was strewn with damp, bloody towels from the linen closet. They had taken the time to clean themselves up before leaving, because they knew the habits of this household. They knew that Sara went to the supermarket on Friday mornings, and that an hour later Darius always went downstairs to meet her in the café.

The receptionist at the hotel where Kamran Shiravan and Nasser Velayati had been staying confirmed to investigators that Velayati hadn't checked out the previous evening. A taxi had come for both of them just before seven o'clock that Friday morning.

The taxi driver, an Iranian of fifty or so named Hassan Djahanfar, was arrested and interrogated three weeks later as he attempted to leave France for the United States under a false identity. During his trial, Djahanfar explained that he had driven Shiravan and Velayati to the 13th arrondissement separately. Then he had waited for them in front of the *café-tabac* at the corner of the Boulevard de l'Hôpital and the Place d'Italie, and taken them to the Gare de l'Est. The train for Munich had departed ten minutes later, right about the same time Sara was finding Darius's body. Djahanfar was found guilty and sentenced to life in prison, but twelve years later his freedom was exchanged for that of a French engineer arrested in Tehran for espionage. The details weren't revealed until two days after the exchange, when it was too late to do anything.

No one in the family ever saw Kamran again. No one knew what had happened to him, or where his wife and children had gone. One part of the Sadr family, the bigoted and conspiracy-obsessed branch, refused to believe in his guilt and publicly accused Sara of having made the whole story up. They were the descendants of the Sadr sister who, in their day, had accused Nour and Darius of being the main cause of Mirza-Ali's death. After all, Sara was a stranger in the family, right? And an *Armenian* on top of that. Who knew what those people were capable of lying about in order to besmirch the honor of an exemplary citizen and a man as devotedly religious as Kamran?

The Iranian newspapers, mobilized to defend the regime, took up this cry and painted Sara as a hysterical liar on the Western payroll. The propaganda was effective enough that Saddeq actually ended up calling Leïli, asking her in a troubled voice if Sara was sure about "what she was putting out there." "What do you mean, 'what she's putting out there?'" snapped Leïli.

"Well, my dear . . . Sara wasn't even *there*, you know . . . I mean, how can she be so sure?"

"What? This is Paris, *Amou Djan*; we have police and a justice system. My mother's not the one who decides who killed her husband!"

"I know, I know . . . but if she could stop and think for a minute about the damage this whole thing is causing here. It's tearing the family apart, and everyone is blaming her."

"Papa has been assassinated. You think this is the right time to talk about this bullshit?"

Uncle Number Two, miserable and offended, burst into tears. Wild with fury, Leïli hung up on him. Pushed by his children, he called back a few days later to apologize.

As the family crumbled in Tehran, Sara mourned her husband in Paris. She left her daughters to sort out the apartment and turn it back over to the owner, and moved in with Leïli and her family. "Go away," she said, and closed the door of her room on our helpless faces.

She stayed in there, shut away, barely touching the meals we took turns bringing her. We always found her either sitting on the edge of the bed, her back to the door, reading Darius's writings, or standing at the window, watching the crowds teeming in the street outside. We would just put the plates down on the bed and hesitate there a few seconds, not daring to approach her, hoping for some kind of sign from her. As the days passed, her body drooped, the muscles growing thinner and thinner. Defeated, we began whispering in the house, so as not to disturb her. Sometimes we could hear her crying, and we cried with her, the way you cry at a heart-rending song. Her silent grief was as devastating to us as Darius's death.

She would have liked to be there and to have died with him. Death, even violent death, had always frightened her less than the prospect of being without Darius. The years had made them into one person. A single soul with two halves, one half in Darius's body and one in Sara's.

A few months later, one morning at dawn, Leïli found her in the kitchen, warming up a pot of milk. Surprised and pleased to finally see her out of that godforsaken room, Leïli asked her:

"What are you doing up so early?"

"Making breakfast for Darius and me," Sara answered, smiling tenderly. "I'm going to have to straighten up the living room before half of Tehran shows up. Go back to bed, darling. I'll come and wake you up again soon."

No photos.

No images.

Just the scissors.

The little sharp-pointed ones he used to trim his fingernails with.

That's all I wanted of his.

He'd taught me to trim my fingernails with scissors.

Those were different scissors, though. We'd left those in Tehran.

In Paris, he'd looked everywhere and finally found a pair that looked like the ones he'd had in Tehran.

I didn't want anything else.

Just those scissors, which shone in the darkness.

Years of darkness.

5
ANNA II

S he was the one who tracked me down, in Paris.

In 2001, I had been working for almost two years as a sound assistant at the Theatre de la Ville, and was living in the Place Voltaire, in a one-bedroom apartment rented from a colleague of Mina's who had gone to do research abroad. I was with Tom, a thirty-three-year-old Austrian who tended bar at The Bottle Shop, a little American bar on Rue Trousseau, where I often went in the evening after work. He was my first serious relationship since THE EVENT.

Tom had the body of someone who'd been an athlete since childhood, had always been well-nourished and taken care of. He had grey eyes and ash-blond hair that looked darker because of the pomade he applied with surgical precision. He wore impeccably ironed shirts, faded jeans, and black loafers. It was a very '60s look, topped off by a set of teeth as perfect as a row of tiles in the bathroom of a luxury hotel. He looked like the kind of guy bar owners hire to attract female customers; one of those cool types who play at seduction, turning the music up and laying the act on thick after midnight to rekindle the atmosphere, but whose real ambitions lie elsewhere—usually frustrated artistic ambitions that make them unhappy during the day, petulant and irritating. But actually, despite appearances, Thomas Krügel wasn't one of those guys.

After studying law, he had worked in the legal department of his father's pharmaceutical company in Vienna before giving it all up and coming to France, attracted by the country and its language. Here, he had discovered aviation, which had quickly turned into a passion. He spent his free time reading books on the subject and taking classes with the firm intention of becoming a pilot. His past gave him a particular kind of poise and self-assurance. Tom didn't need to tend bar for a living; it was just an easy, pleasant job that allowed him to get out of the house and gave him the comfort of being around people.

I'm sure you're wondering why I went out with Tom. Why I'd more or less let him move in with me. Why I'd even introduced him to my sisters. I can answer all those questions with a single metaphor: to avoid "Sammy Davis Jr. Syndrome."

After THE EVENT and Sara's slow fade-out, I wanted to get back to my life—but I realized that there was no life waiting for me anywhere. My existence was made up of drifting islands, each of which I had managed to stand on for a while, achieving a shaky equilibrium amidst the general chaos. But I didn't have that kind of energy in me anymore.

I spent months roaming the streets of Paris, wandering through a world in which I no longer felt like I belonged. Like Darius, only walking soothed my anxiety. I mechanically drove my body to the point of exhaustion and then collapsed each night on Leïli's sofa, or Mina's, or a hotel-room bed. I'm certain it was the fact of spending so much time with my sisters as they went about their daily lives, watching them cling to their families and their jobs so as not to sink, that awoke the desire for stability in me. And not just my sisters, but my nieces and nephews, too. I found their noisy presence and endless needs, which were a constant push to act, to get up, prepare meals, listen, care for, play, unexpectedly comforting; they gave me a sense of reality, from which I no longer wanted to be cut off. I started telling myself that, whoever I was and whatever my life was, I was no less worthy than any other woman of being a mother.

Don't think for a second that my relationship with Tom was strategic in any way. I was ready to change well before I met him, and his presence obviously filled a void in my soul. Before I go any further, I want to clarify something important for you. (Since I started writing this chapter I've been imagining all the voices wondering, "Wait, so is she a lesbian or not?," a question that disturbs my peace of mind, and which I need to settle before I go on.)

In my life, I've met some homosexuals who were disgusted by the opposite sex, and some heterosexuals for whom the reverse was true. At the other extreme, I've met people who were unabashedly bisexual, claiming a free and variable sexuality. But between those two ends of this spectrum lies a whole range of inclinations and individuals, from the homosexual who falls in love with someone of the opposite sex, to the straight person attracted to a member of the same sex, and from the hetero who experiments with a homosexual relationship to the "occasional gay" who can't seem to make up his or her mind. Basically, if you pay enough attention you'll see that desire is an endlessly shifting thing, and the variations are infinite. I fell somewhere in the middle of the sexual spectrum. Even though I started almost at one extreme, thanks to encounters and reflections and liberties taken during shared experiences, I'd gradually moved toward a more flexible inclination. To sum up: I felt stronger desire for women, but I wasn't totally indifferent to men.

Now that I've gotten that off my chest, I need to talk to you about love. I think the worst damage done to me by the chaos of my life has to do with love. Love, in the sense of *falling in love*, was a feeling I couldn't access. I could never get there; I just wasn't capable of overcoming a barrier that had been put up somewhere inside of me. Something had been destroyed in me, had broken off and fallen away. Something vital had disappeared. When I see children of war or poverty on the TV news, placed in refugee camps or discarded on the side of the road, I can tell right away that they have the same kind of love disability I do. But, strange as it might seem, this affective disorder never bothered me. I mean, *some* part of the machine always has to break down, right? Given the choice, I'd much rather have lost the ability to love than woken up one morning covered with psoriasis, or been in the grip of multiple addictions. That being said, like a deaf man who lip-reads to conceal his handicap, I did end up pretending sometimes, imitating the things I'd seen other girls do, in an attempt to pull the wool over everyone's eyes (the only thing I could never bring myself to do was to slide my hand into the back pocket of the other person's pants. My apologies to anyone who likes that sort of thing, but it's beyond my capabilities). I wasn't proud of acting that way; I knew I was an impostor, but I hoped that one day my awkward play-acting might unlock something and I'd be able to do it for real.

I wasn't in love with Tom. I liked being with him, and that was enough. I don't know if he was in love with me. I never asked myself that question, for fear of having to question my own feelings. In any case, he seemed attached enough to sleep over, cook in my kitchen, and talk about taking trips together. With him I discovered what it was like to share everyday life with someone and, amazingly, the go-with-the-flow Kimiâ liked it a lot. It was new—just as new as moving to a different country—and I'd always liked new things . . .

We'd been together for ten months when, one morning while I was making the coffee, he came into the kitchen and asked me—in a carefully neutral tone, as if he didn't want to attach too much importance to what was obviously an important question—if I maybe wanted to stop taking birth control. I stood dumbstruck, the kettle in my hand. Nothing in his attitude had prepared me for that question. He'd never made me think he wanted children, let alone with me.

Close-up of my stunned, unsettled expression. A smile. My head nodding. Joy. "Of course I want to!" Tom laughing, taking the packet of pills off the counter and throwing it into the wastebasket. "Forget the coffee. Let's go out and get some, with croissants and bread and butter!"

Five days later, everything changed dramatically.

For some reason, when I was rereading this chapter this morning, I was reminded of the famous answer given by Mahmoud Ahmedinejad, then President of the Islamic Republic of Iran, during a debate organized at Columbia University in September 2007. Asked about the treatment of homosexuals in his country, he responded, with a straight face: "In Iran, we don't have homosexuals like in your country. We don't have this phenomenon. I don't know who's told you that we do."

If, once you've stopped laughing, you decide to explore this question further, you'll find that in Iran, homosexuality is considered a supreme violation of God's will, and is a crime punishable by death. Women as well as men, sometimes only teenagers, are blindfolded and hanged from cranes in public. Homosexuality is generally not cited as the main reason for these executions, due to pressure from Western countries and the fear that these acts will damage their complex relationships with Iran. In any case, it's estimated that, since 1979, more than four thousand of these public hangings have taken place. You'll also learn that, because sex changes are legal in Iran, some homosexuals have turned to this means of saving their own necks. Others flee to Turkey, one of the rare countries that doesn't require a visa for Iranians. Gathering in the city of Denizli, where they form an unstable community, they wait for years in the hope of moving on to Canada, the United States, or Australia, one of only three countries that accept gay refugees registered with the Office of the United Nations High Commissioner for Refugees.

As ridiculous and shocking as Ahmadinejad's remarks may be, they nevertheless attest to a mentality as deeply entrenched in Iranian society as the burnt residue on the bottom of a pan. I once heard one of my female cousins say that the only good thing the Islamic regime had done was kill homos. You might think that a person who held views like that must be uneducated or very religious, but she's highly educated and sophisticated, claims to be non-religious, and is part of Iran's upper class. She holds chic parties, loves trendy filmmakers, and travels to Europe and the United States several times a year to go shopping and enjoy a few months of freedom in which she doesn't have to wear a veil and can smoke mentholated cigarettes and drink alcohol on bar terraces.

So, anyway, five days later, the phone rang and everything changed dramatically.

"Hi, it's me. Anna. "

She hadn't needed to specify who it was. I'd recognized her husky voice and Flemish accent immediately. Yet, I hadn't thought about Anna for years. She remained associated in my memory with a carefree time which I sometimes thought hadn't actually been real.

"Oh I remember you . . . "

"I looked you up on the Internet," she said, as if this simple piece of information explained her call. "The Internet is so great!"

"Yeah . . . "

There was a silence. She seemed to be waiting for me to say something. Except that I didn't know what to say, or how to pick up the thread of the conversation. I was trying to puzzle it out when she said:

"We're playing a show at La Maroquinerie tomorrow night. We could see each other beforehand, if you want . . . "

If I'd been better at human relationships, I would have asked her for her phone number and taken some time to think.

"Sure, let's get together. Are you already in Paris?"

"Yes, I love this city!"

We agreed to meet that evening at The Bottle Shop.

After hanging up, I felt a sense of melancholy welling up in me like a Portuguese lament. It didn't have anything to do with Anna, but she had triggered it in me. My relationship with the past had never been simple, but since THE EVENT it had become utterly hostile. I had been driven out of paradise for the second time, and I didn't want to hear anyone talk about it, ever again. Except for Leïli, Mina, and a pair of scissors, nothing around me had any connection to the past. I'd gotten rid of my clothes and my records and my books. I'd thrown it all away and started over again from scratch.

The closer it got to the time of our meeting, the more I regretted it. One minute I felt like I had to back out, the next minute I knew I'd feel miserable and cowardly if I did, which was no good either. The whole time I was walking down the Rue Saint-Antoine, I thought of Darius. Darius, who would have just continued on his own way without having any moral qualms about it, because he knew he was unpredictable and temperamental, and he just accepted that about himself.

The Bottle Shop was jam-packed and muggy, as usual. What little space wasn't occupied by bodies was clogged with a dense grey mass of cigarette smoke. It was so noisy that you couldn't hear the music, which was reduced to pointless background static. Anna was sitting at a table near the bar. Behind the bar, Tom was mixing a pitcher of mojitos while joking around with a customer.

I stayed frozen by the door. Like a photographer focusing his lens, I readjusted my gaze to her presence. Her hair was still platinum blonde but it was now cut very short, very *JeanSebergui*. She wore a crumpled white T-shirt that looked like she'd slept in it, and black jeans tucked into high-heeled lace-up boots. It was really her. Here, under this familiar roof. She hadn't changed. Nothing earth-shattering, no major upheavals had happened in her life, it seemed. Suddenly, I was overcome with a sense of danger. A murmur of panic rose from deep in my gut. I'd made a mistake . . . but what was it? Shaken, I was about to turn and leave, when she called my name.

Maybe because of the Tigra cigarettes she still smoked (and which I'd smoked in Belgium); maybe because of her *bruxellois* turns of phrase and the scent of road dust and rock music that emanated from her body, she represented everything, absolutely everything, that I'd missed. And, through her, the Kimiâ I'd once been. It was as if she'd put us on pause, and now she was picking up where we'd left off. She talked and told stories and rhapsodized and laughed for a long while. Truth be told, despite my interested expression, I was hardly listening. Her presence unsettled me. I'd spent a lot of my life being anyone else, taking on other identities, running away, hiding behind pretense—and now, just when I thought I had left all that nonsense behind with Tom, Anna had shown up and brought with her the troubling idea that I was still getting everything completely wrong. My mistake was meeting here there, in this bar, where I kept catching glimpses of Tom out of the corner of my eye.

An hour later, when two of the musicians in her band came to join her on the start of a bar crawl, she invited me to come with them. I declined.

I stayed there, waiting for Tom to finish his shift. I wanted to tell him we were over, but the bar refused to empty out. The clock on the wall read 1:45 and it was Friday, September 7, 2001. In four days the world would change, abruptly and for ever. In four days, the shock waves rippling out from the Iranian Revolution would make America tremble. Like in the story of Frankenstein, the monster assembled by the West from many separate parts would turn against it. Soon, words made famous by Khomeini in 1979, like "jihad," and "Islamophobia," and "Islamic hijab," words symbolic of his bloody tyranny, would make their appearance on this side of the world. Wars would break out, other monsters would rise up, oil would be sold under the table, and, as always, innocent people would die. Fear would invade and pervade every street, here and elsewhere.

It all took time. Leaving Brussels (Anna), getting out of the lease on the apartment I was subletting (me), looking for a new place to live (both of us). In the meantime, George W. Bush finished crafting his plan of attack against Iraq, the unspoken goal of which was to destroy the Mustachioed One his predecessors and their European allies had so misguidedly supplied with weapons. So we had to mobilize, and demonstrate. It wasn't part of Anna's culture to pound the pavement, but she followed my lead.

While we marched in unison through the streets of Paris as part of a compact and determined crowd, between shouting slogans we talked about having a baby. How? With whom? I quickly nixed her suggestion of going to Brussels or Amsterdam to be artificially inseminated by an anonymous donor (though, as she informed me, in the Netherlands a child is legally permitted to learn its father's identity once he or she reaches the age of sixteen).

I wanted this child to have a father. I couldn't imagine deliberately bequeathing both exile and the impossibility of fully knowing its lineage to a baby. I didn't want to create a being who would suffer from the same "Sammy Davis Jr. Syndrome" I had. I might have considered Anna's solution if I'd had both my parents there, a real family, or one country. If I'd been able to take them back to the neighborhood where I was born, show them Emma's tomb and the Caspian Sea. If I'd been able to give them more than stories gone musty with time. In the language of symbols, it's the mother who's linked to the land. In my case, though, it could only be the father.

Though she didn't openly refuse the possibility, Anna was afraid it would "create too much noise," as she put it, she was afraid she wouldn't fit into the picture. We had different images of family life. My sisters and I had grown up between two apartments, thinking of the Nasrs as our second parents. I thought having two mothers or two fathers might even be considered a lucky thing in an urbanized Western society, where neighbors and friends usually play a minor role in a child's upbringing. I was starting from the theoretical principle that humans are made that way, and that there's never enough of anything. Even parents.

Months passed, and then years. And we were still debating. And yet it felt to me as if it should have been the same as it was when I'd been with Tom. On that day in the kitchen, all I'd had to do was exclaim with joy and nod my head and stop smoking in order to have one foot in the elevator to motherhood. If I'd opened the window and made a public announcement, no one would have wondered if we knew each other well enough to take on a responsibility like that, or if we planned to get married, or buy a flat, or open a joint bank account. But now we had to reflect, conduct incessant tours of our own lives, navigate through forests of questions and mazes of doubt. More than anyone else, any person who might rise up in our path and tell us that what we were trying to do was reprehensible, we were aware of the situation. The best interests of the child, its well-being, its future, were so vividly present at the heart of our concerns that sometimes I felt like it was already there, an acne-ridden teenager slumped on the sofa, demanding that we answer for ourselves.

Anna eventually came around to my way of thinking, undoubtedly because she came to understand, little by little, who I was. I should say that I had begun telling her everything, in small, disordered snippets. My discussions with Marteen had helped me to be steadier about certain parts of it, but the rest was piled up inside me, in heaps as unstable as Agha Mohabati, the greengrocer's merchandise. At first I didn't recognize my own voice, which sounded like a recording as poor in quality as the one on the cassette tape Bart Schumann sent me after THE EVENT. Anna listened attentively and kindly, not moving. I kept expecting her to interrupt and say she didn't understand a thing I was babbling about, but it was always me who interrupted myself, lost and confused. Had I really lived through all these things? Had I really known the people I was describing? Up to that point, my lies had served to shield me from the truth, like when a child closes its eyes and thinks that turns it invisible. Now, I was like an abandoned house in which all the windows are thrown open all at once, letting in a blast of air and light. I felt revived, relieved of a weight I didn't even know I was carrying. Slowly, I was learning to be happy.

Pierre came into our lives on a Tuesday afternoon in October.

We'd come back from Belgium five hours later than planned. Genet had just closed out a week-long tour with a huge concert at the Muziekcentrum Trix in Anvers, playing to a hypnotized crowd. Charged with adrenaline, we hadn't slept that night. Marteen had promised to come, but at the last minute he'd been too lazy to travel from Greece, where he was living now. However, Anna's parents had been there, so I'd met them for the second time, along with her older brother.

Lisbeth and Erik De Grave looked like one another, and both of their children looked just like them. Tall and blond, with blue eyes and short hair. Looking at them, as with other

Flemish families whose genes had been passed from generation to generation without encountering a single obstacle, I felt the same cognitive confusion as I did when I encountered a group of Japanese tourists. Their physical homogeneity harkened back to an old world, without immigration or interbreeding, that I wasn't used to anymore. Looking at them made it easier for me to understand their national identity and the spectacular rise of the far-right Vlaams Blok party. There must have been something reassuring and soothing about evolving in a world where everyone looked alike; as reassuring as walking in a pine forest, or listening to Bach's Goldberg Variations. No need to worry about others or be suspicious of them, or to question your own existence. Sure, it would never give rise to the blues and the samba, but you can't have everything.

I only exchanged a few words with Lisbeth De Grave. She wanted to know how things were going in my country since the war and the fall of Saddam Hussein. I told her I didn't know, because I was from Iran, not Iraq. She grimaced and made a dubious "Ah!" noise before looking down. It was like a painstakingly-constructed piece of scaffolding was falling to pieces in her head.

Anna and I were waiting for a taxi in front of the Gare du Nord. The headline of *Le Parisien* that day was "BLACK TUESDAY" and the whole city was in the throes of a strike.

Despite the cold, the streets were packed with people at the end of their tether. People trying to get home by any means possible. Cars sat for hours in one traffic jam only to get stuck in another one immediately. People honked and yelled and banged on hoods. Taxis came in dribs and drabs, to be greeted with cries of relief or despair.

At some point, someone decided that people going in the same direction should group together and share cabs, which resulted in a surge of movement. In the general confusion we found ourselves next to a man with an unruly shock of hair and a pleasant smile who was also going to the 20th arrondissement.

We introduced ourselves.

Anna, Kimiâ.

Pierre Favre.

Pierre Favre had just come back from Lille. He was a landscape designer working on the development of a park in the city center.

The act of waiting together created an immediate intimacy. We talked about this and that, shared bars of Belgian chocolate and cigarettes. After forty-five minutes of waiting without the slightest hint of a taxi, since the sun was going down and it looked like rain, we decided to go on foot, stopping in a bistro to eat.

Outside, rain poured down on the city with excessive fury. Even before our dinners arrived, Pierre admitted that he'd been single for a year and a half. After seven years of marriage, he and his wife Gabrielle had mutually decided to separate. Since their apartment belonged to him Gabrielle had moved out, taking most of the furniture, which he hadn't yet replaced. He was even thinking of selling the place, which he said was too big for just him. Then, suddenly, he fell silent.

This was one of those moments on American TV when the screenwriters cut to a commercial break, leaving the viewer hanging in anticipation of a revelation to come. What had happened? Why hadn't they given their marriage a second chance (that typically American idea)? In reality, Pierre just drained his glass. He was clearly not ready to confide anything more— but Anna wasn't the kind of person to stop after the first episode. She always binged on the whole season at once, otherwise she felt like she was wasting too much time. She was the same when she performed—she didn't stop until she reached the point of total exhaustion. "Why did you separate?" The question, asked in an impatient tone of voice, broke all the rules of decorum—but Anna didn't care.

I'll pause here to clarify that it wasn't only Anna's individual nature that made her behave like that. Unlike the French, who are often quite laconic in their responses, the Belgians love to elaborate. When you ask a French person "How are you?" they always answer, indifferently and mechanically, "Fine, and you?" A Belgian, on the other hand, will take the question very seriously and launch into a recap of their whole day, from their morning coffee and shower to an argument with their neighbor, the drive to work, the unexpected phone call from their mother, etc. etc. They commit themselves. They take their time. And they open up to you with refreshing spontaneity, without stopping to think about whether you're really interested or not.

Pierre looked at each of us in turn, like a person wondering whether to turn right or left.

"I'm HIV-positive."

In the time it took for this information to reach our brains and release its emotional payload, he explained to us that he'd already been diagnosed when he met Gabrielle. After they got married and started thinking about children, Pierre had spoken to his doctor, who had directed him to Cochin Hospital and CECOS. He'd managed to convince Gabrielle to follow the protocol, and they had followed all the necessary procedures, but the waiting time was horrendously long, and Gabrielle, already filled with anxiety that she or the child might be infected, had become discouraged.

"We were arguing every day. It had become unbearable. In the end we decided to separate. When she'd gone, it hit me that it wasn't only her I was losing—it was the baby too."

"We want to have a child too, actually. Don't we, Kim?"

When her second daughter was born, Mina decided (read:

decreed) that we should go to Montparnasse Cemetery to visit
Darius's grave on All Saints Day. To inform us of her decision,
she sent all of us a mass e-mail that was as long and explana-
tory as one of her lectures. Here's part of it:

"[. . .], because I think the children should know why their
grandfather is buried here. They need a ritual to understand
the magnitude of it; to make our story part of their own.
There's nothing better than a ritual for erasing borders and
going back to our mutual roots, to who we are, and where we
come from. Do you remember that day when Uncle Number
Two took us to Mother's tomb? We left secular time behind and
stepped into a sacred time that connected us to the very
essence of our lives. Remember, Kimiâ? You'd never even
known Mother, and yet I can still see your face, shining with the
love you felt for her. You were part of it all, part of a whole
larger than the chaos that surrounded us at the time. And it
was because that whole existed, because those rituals had
been created around Mother, that we could bear all the rest.
I'm talking to you directly, Kimiâ. Since you don't have children, you might think that what I'm asking you all to do
doesn't concern you. You might even be opposed to it, figuring
(like always) that we should leave the past in the past. But this
does concern you, because without you the circle wouldn't be
complete. So I'm asking you not to take my request as just one
more family obligation, but rather as a gift given to your nieces
and nephews. I know that when they grow up, the children
might never go back to Montparnasse, but at least they'll
remember this day when we all went there together. How many
times has Sara told us about the Fridays when Emma took
them to visit their father's grave? Those memories are rooted
in her as happy ones, as loving times. That's what I'm trying
for, here. So the best thing, I think, is to have this ritual on All
Saints Day, and do what everyone else does [. . .]."

I don't know if "everyone" (by which Mina meant everyone French) actually goes to visit the graves of the dead on

All Saints Day, but for Mina, in her pathological desire for normality, this ritualized trip could only happen on that day. In a way, I understood it. From the children's point of view, this date was significant despite everything, even if only because it corresponded to the school holidays with the same name. But Mina also wanted to give them a reality, one that wouldn't make them feel more French, but might just make them feel more Persian, more connected to a country that didn't represent anything for them, but had represented so much for us.

We always start this day by gathering at Leïli's, which is halfway between Mina's house and my apartment. Most of the time, Leïli's husband Louis, a Breton as laid-back as Leïli is neurotic, goes off to spend the day with Diego, Mina's husband, who was born in France but has Spanish roots. My brothers-in-law eat together and then play tennis at the indoor courts a few streets away from Mina's house. Once or twice Anna has joined them, but she doesn't like tennis enough to make the long trek out to the suburbs.

While Mina's three kids (two girls and a boy) play with Leïli's two girls, we have a coffee in the kitchen. Then Leïli puts rice on to cook in the rice-cooker and starts the *gheimeh* (a meat dish with split peas and a sauce made with several different spices). *Gheimeh* is a specialty of Qazvin—and thus of the Sadr family. On Friday nights, when the Sadrs gathered, *gheimeh* used to take pride of place in the center of the dining table, surrounded by a dozen other second-tier dishes. Year by year, Leïli has perfected her *gheimeh* recipe until it finally has the same texture as true Qazvini *gheimeh* now, if not quite the same flavor.

We spend the two hours that the stew simmers on the stove chatting, there in the kitchen. We could go into the living room, but staying in the kitchen gives our little reunion an Eastern flair to fit the general atmosphere of the day. Of course, we're careful to avoid serious subjects: THE EVENT, Sara, politics.

The night before this particular Tuesday in November, Mina had watched Jean-Pierre Jeunet's *A Very Long Engagement* on DVD. Since neither Leïli nor I had seen the film, we ended up talking about the actors in it, and Mina mentioned that Jodie Foster was part of the cast. Talking about movies was a roundabout way of remembering Darius. He'd instilled in us his love of films, and actors too, whose life stories he'd known in detail. Our dad was part of a generation for whom American actors, most of them of working-class or middle-class origins, symbolized humans' ability to take control of their own destiny, regardless of social or familial predisposition. Cary Grant's mother had been put in a mental institution. Bette Davis's parents were divorced. Susan Hayward was born into a working-class family in Brooklyn, and many others were from Jewish families who had fled the Holocaust. They represented everything Darius admired.

As we were discussing Jodie Foster's filmography, Leïli turned to me and said, in a falsely naïve tone, "They still don't know who the father of her children is . . . " I knew Leïli was alluding to the actress's homosexuality, without really understanding what she was trying to do by bringing it up. But her remark unsettled me.

My sisters never addressed the question of my sexuality, at least in my presence. Leïli had never brought it up again after the Mazandaran episode, and after Emma's letter, neither Sara nor Mina had ever mentioned the company I kept. I don't think they agreed with Emma's imaginative interpretation, but her request to act as if nothing was wrong stood to reason. Leïli and Mina hadn't made any comment when I left Tom for Anna, and they had welcomed Anna without asking how we'd met. Still, I wondered whether their silence meant unconditional acceptance, or if it was just part of the mutual desire to avoid difficult subjects we'd had since THE EVENT. But now, in bringing up the father of Jodie Foster's children, Leïli was reaching out in a way I couldn't ignore.

"She might have used an unknown sperm donor."

"Well, good for her if she did! If God didn't want lesbians to be mothers, He would have made them without uteruses!"

The second the words were out of Leïli's mouth, she froze. And Mina and I did too. All three of us were struck by her tone of voice, and the way she had emphasized the end of her sentence, as if adding an exclamation point. It was almost like Sara had suddenly spoken through her to defend one of the causes dearest to her heart: motherhood—which, let me remind you, she considered the Holy Grail of existence, the most important part of which was married life.

Leïli's emotion at seeing herself superimposed on Sara—the kitchen, the *gheimeh*, and now the voice—was so great that she turned her face away and quickly called out "KIDS! Come and set the table! KIDS!"

"Wait, I'll go get them," volunteered Mina, standing up.

Passing Leïli, she leaned in to kiss her sister's cheek—but the two of them suddenly wrapped their arms around each other and dissolved into tears.

That night, walking home, I chastised myself for having missed the opportunity to talk to them. *Okay, stop crying and come sit down, I have something to tell you.* Leïli had stepped in as a substitute for Sara and encouraged me to have a baby, and I should have told them about meeting Pierre a month previously.

I would have done it for sure, if Pierre hadn't been HIV-positive. Just the word would have sent them into fits. "Do you realize what you're saying, Kimy? What, do you want us to have to bury you too?!" Leïli would have screamed. And Mina: "Millions of guys on this planet and you have to choose one that's HIV-positive? Tell me this is a joke!" The thought of losing me would have put an end to any explanations, any rational conversation. The fact that we got along really well with Pierre, that he was ready to take responsibility for the baby, to be a father and not just a sperm donor, that we wouldn't have to move to the Netherlands or Belgium, that I'd be monitored right here in Cochin Hospital, that the odds of infection were infinitesimal—none of that would have mattered.

Later, I decided not to tell them until I was certain I was pregnant. News like that would soothe their fears, surely. On that day I would remind them of what Emma had said to us so often: "There are always risks in life, my little ones. If you don't take risks, you simply endure, and if you endure, you die— even if it's only boredom that kills you."

OF COURSE YOU'LL HAVE CHILDREN!

I owe you an explanation," says Dr. Gautier, as she puts away the ultrasound probe. "I saw on your pre-insemination sonogram that there was one eighteen-millimeter follicle and one fourteen-millimeter one. I completely forgot to talk to you about it because of all this endless construction work; it's so distracting. I'm sorry. I always tell my students that at fourteen millimeters and up, there's a possibility. It's minimal, but it's real. Patients have to be warned about the risk of multiple pregnancy, and I didn't do that, but that's what has happened. Well, it'll keep you from having to come back in two years when you want another child. Personally, when my patients get pregnant with twins, I always think that, given everything they've been through, it's a real stroke of luck. It's overwhelming at first, but you'll have to try to get over that, and quickly (pulling her chair up to her desk). Anyway, I'm going to make you an appointment to see our psychologist right away so you can talk to her about it. That's what we always do in these cases."

As she dials the psychologist's number, I wipe the jelly off my stomach, incapable of forming any rational thought. Now, don't get me wrong: a small part of me—the part that sat in Uncle Number Two's kitchen, my head full of sepia images of far-flung ancestors, feeling our family's destiny flow in my veins—knew, has always known, while the other part—the one that leans on the counter and orders a coffee, pragmatic, realistic, raised in the shadow of French Cartesianism—had no reason to believe this could happen. What still surprises me is the way the facts have slotted together—the construction work, the distraction, the fourteen-millimeter follicle—to bring Science and Chance face to face, hand in hand, to make old Bibi's prediction into reality. The one that started, remember, with "First, you'll have twins . . . "

Dr. Gautier's voice startles me out of my torpor. "Here," she says, handing me a Post-It with the date and time of the meeting written on it. "It's a good surprise, right?"

I agree, with a dazed smile.

I take my coat from the chair and put the Post-It into a pocket. When I look up again, Dr. Gautier is standing next to the open door, her hand extended.

"Well, there should be no further reason for us to see each other again. Your gynecologist will take it from here for check-ups and monitoring. All that's left is for me to wish you good luck."

As I shake her hand, in a burst of sincerity and gratitude, I feel a rising urge to tell her the truth, to tell her about Anna. I feel as if I'm poised on the edge of a swimming pool, just about to jump into the freezing water. Hesitant, anticipating the moment of impact. Then suddenly we're outside, and she's walking away quickly down the corridor. She stops at the waiting-room door, calls out a name in a loud, hurried voice. As I pass behind her I glance at the couple jumping to their feet, and I get out of there.

Those of you who are familiar with Paris will know that I can't walk from Cochin Hospital to Bastille, where I'm meeting Anna and Pierre at noon, without going through the 13th arrondissement. I've avoided this area since THE EVENT, unable to face the streets Darius and Sara used to walk through, or the café where they sat together every morning, or the stationery shop where Darius bought his Pentel pens with black ink. I'm not sure how, but today, in my efforts to avoid those places, I end up in the inner courtyard of the residential home where Leïli ended up putting Sara. And yet, I had to punch in the access code on the door to get here. And then I had to cross the lobby, and pass the reception desk . . .

I look up at the windows of her third-floor room. The wind rises, blowing hard enough to make my eyes tear up. One of the two windows is open to let some air in, but I know Sara isn't the one who opened it. Sara is sensitive to the cold; she never opens the windows in winter. She must be cold right now, and not daring to say it. Or maybe she doesn't even feel the cold anymore. That thought, added to the idea that her condition has probably gotten worse since the last time I saw her, makes my throat burn.

As I enter her room I murmur "Mom . . . mommy," my voice so low that she doesn't hear me over the sound of the TV.

She's sitting in an armchair, facing the screen. Her body, bent and folded in on itself like an autumn leaf, is lost in a sweater Mina gave her years ago. Her hands rest on her thighs, which are covered by a plaid throw. Her wedding ring is loose on her third finger.

The room is heavily decorated. Everywhere there are photos, familiar objects, books, cushions. A Persian rug covers the floor. We brought all of this to her, in the ridiculous hope of making the place cozy, and to fight the enormous sense of guilt we've felt ever since we put her here. Inside all of us there is a bottomless well of conflict between reason and culture; between the fact that our lives don't allow us to keep her with us, and our Persian honor, which dictates that you never abandon your parents, no matter what condition they're in.

Sara doesn't need any of these objects. She's living in a space-time bubble where memory doesn't exist. If I had to describe her state, I would say that she bears a strange resemblance to a cinematographic process called rear projection, which was widely used in the 1950s and '60s. Remember? A character sits in an unmoving car pretending to drive, while pre-filmed scenery disappears in the distance on a screen behind them. Watching these scenes, we're aware of the trickery taking place behind the scenes, and yet we accept it, because what's happening in the car is more important than the background décor. Sara is that character. No matter what position she's in, sitting in this chair or lying in bed, images of her past are being projected all around her on the walls of the room. She's reliving them permanently, without effort. It makes her think she's moving, even though she's not.

I approach the television and lower the volume. It takes a few seconds before she turns her head. She looks at me. Afraid she's confusing me with someone else, I hurry to say: "It's me, Kimiâ."

"Oh, Kimiâ! Go and wash your hands, please. It's late, and I don't want you to go back out into the courtyard."

"I've washed them already. Aren't you cold?"

Instead of answering me, she casts a worried glance at the door.

"Your father isn't home yet. I don't know where he is. It is Friday, isn't it?"

"Yes, it's Friday. You know he'll be here. He must have run into somebody on the way."

I squat down next to her, putting my hand on her arm to reassure here. I swallow the lump that forms in my throat when I feel how thin her arm has gotten.

"Frankly, I don't even know why he even bothers wearing a watch. I tell him every day, ten times a day, 'Look at your watch, Darius!' And do you think he listens to me? It never occurs to him that I'm here waiting for him."

I shrug my shoulders with a knowing, resigned smile. "You're never going to change him."

"Do you know what Mother used to say when she wasn't happy with one of her sons?"

I do know, but I shake my head.

"She'd heave a long sigh and mutter, in her Qazvini accent, 'Oh, those Sadrs . . . ' Summed up her whole life in those three words, poor thing. You have hair just like hers," she says, stroking my head. "You were born on the day she died. I don't know if that's the reason for the resemblance, but it's pretty incredible when you think about it. Where are your sisters?"

"In their bedroom."

"Well, sit down here, by me. I already told you I don't want you going back outside."

I pull up a chair and sit down across from her, taking advantage of the moment to switch off the television. She watches me and then leans over, taking a cookie from the packet next to her and handing it to me. She continues to watch me as I crunch into it, just to make her happy.

"I need you to promise me something, Kimiâ, okay?"

"Okay."

"I want you to promise me that when you grow up, you'll go to France. Your sisters will go, no question; they can't wait for it. But you—I'm afraid you'll refuse to leave this damned courtyard. But you're going to have problems here, my darling. This place isn't made for people like you. You're too little for me to explain it to you; you wouldn't understand. You never know what might happen to me; I could die tomorrow, and so could your father. Your sisters are bigger, and I know they'll look out for you, but they're going to have their own lives to think about. That's why I want you to promise me that you'll leave. I don't want anything to happen to you; do you understand?"

I feel my heart start to pound.

She had known since the beginning, then. Even before Leïli. Even before Grandma Emma's letter. If we'd had this conversation earlier, when I was a teenager—if she hadn't left me to play hide-and-seek with my real self, and with them, for so many years—there's no question that my life would have been very different. I would never have left Paris to wander the world; I'd never have met Anna, or Pierre. I would never have ventured into the labyrinthine corridors of Cochin Hospital.

"So, my sweetheart, do you promise?"

"Yes. I promise."

"Good. That's very good. And you know we must always keep our promises, right?"

"Yes, I know."

"And whatever kind of life you lead, make sure you have children. You have to have children, you know. It's the only consolation."

"I'll have children."

"Of course you'll have children! Who knows? Maybe you'll even have a little boy with blue eyes," she adds, with an impish smile. "That would make your father so happy!"

I take her hand in mine, biting hard on my lip to keep from crying. She's still smiling, satisfied and comforted by our exchange. Just then my mobile phone rings, and her expression changes suddenly.

"I hope nothing's happened to Darius."

"No, don't worry. He'll be home soon."

If doubt has brought you to this page, you probably need a little genealogical cheat-sheet:

Kimiâ Sadr, the narrator.

Leïli Sadr, Kimiâ's oldest sister.

Mina Sadr, the younger sister.

Sara Sadr (née Tadjamol), Kimiâ's mother.

Darius Sadr, Kimiâ's father. Born in 1925 in Qazvin, he is the fourth son of Mirza-Ali Sadr and Nour.

The Sadr uncles (six official ones, plus one more):
Uncle Number One, the eldest, prosecuting attorney in Tehran.
Uncle Number Two (Saddeq), responsible for managing the family lands in Mazandaran and Qazvin. Keeper of the family history.
Uncle Number Three, notary.
Uncle Number Five, manager of an electrical appliance shop near the Grand Bazar.
Uncle Number Six (Pirouz), professor of literature at the University of Tehran. Owner of one of the largest real estate agencies in the city.

Abbas, Uncle Number Seven (in a way). Illegitimate son of Mirza-Ali and a Qazvin prostitute.

Nour, paternal grandmother of Kimiâ, whom her six sons call Mother. Born a few minutes after her twin sister, she was the thirtieth child of Montazemolmolk, and the only one to inherit her father's blue eyes, the same shade of blue as the Caspian Sea. She died in 1971, the day of Kimiâ's birth.

Mirza-Ali, paternal grandfather. Son and grandson of wealthy Qazvin merchants; he was the only one of the eleven children of Rokhnedin Khan and Monavar Banou to have turquoise eyes the color of the sky over Najaf, the city of his birth. He married Nour in 1911 in order to perpetuate a line of Sadrs with blue eyes.

Emma Aslanian, maternal grandmother of Kimiâ and mother of Sara. Her parents, Anahide and Artavaz Aslanian, fled Turkey shortly before the Armenian genocide in 1915. The custom of reading coffee grounds was passed down to her from her grandmother Sévana.

Montazemolmolk, paternal great-grandfather of Kimiâ and father of Nour. Feudal lord born in Mazandaran.

Parvindokht, one of Montazemolmolk's many daughters; sister of Nour.

Kamran Shiravan, son of one of Mirza-Ali's sisters and Ebrahim Shiravan. Cousin of Darius . . .

ABOUT THE AUTHOR

Négar Djavadi was born in Iran in 1969 to a family of intellectuals opposed to the regimes of both the Shah and Khomeini. She arrived in France at the age of eleven, having crossed the mountains of Kurdistan on horseback with her mother and sister. She is a screenwriter and lives in Paris. *Disoriental* is her first novel.